RUSH

More from Joan Swan in the Phoenix Rising series

Fever

Blaze

RUSH

JOAN SWAN

KENSINGTON PUBLISHING CORP.
www.kensingtonbooks.com

For Rick

Thank God I married a firefighter . . .

BRAVA BOOKS are published by

Kensington Publishing Corp.
119 West 40th Street
New York, NY 10018

All Kensington titles, imprints, and distributed lines are available at special quantity discounts for bulk purchases for sales promotions, premiums, fund-raising, educational, or institutional use.

Special book excerpts or customized printings can also be created to fit specific needs. For details, write or phone the office of the Kensington special sales manager: Kensington Publishing Corp., 119 West 40th Street, New York, NY 10018, attn: Special Sales Department; phone 1-800-221-2647.

BRAVA and the B logo are Reg. U.S. Pat. & TM Off.

ISBN-13: 978-0-7582-8825-7
ISBN-10: 0-7582-8825-5

First Kensington Trade Paperback Printing: September 2013

10 9 8 7 6 5 4 3 2 1

Printed in the United States of America

First Electronic Edition: September 2013

ISBN-13: 978-0-7582-8826-4
ISBN-10: 0-7582-8826-3

ACKNOWLEDGMENTS

"You should marry a firefighter. They cook, they clean and they're only home a few days a week."

This wisdom, imparted to me in my teens, made no sense. Now, after two decades of marriage to a firefighter, I've discovered these special men do far more.

Endless and unspeakable gratitude to my husband, Rick, for cooking, cleaning, and letting me do my own thing once in a while. For taking care of sick kids, running car pools, helping with homework, fixing everything, knowing everyone, and generally keeping the sky from collapse when I'm under a deadline. Which is, like, always. For giving me perspective, helping me cope, and brainstorming over breakfast. I love you.

Deep appreciation to my daughters for understanding that dedication to a goal often requires sacrifice and for supporting me during those times. An extra thumbs-up to my youngest, who has given me the gift of time by running my errands, handling my office tasks, and taking those Jamba Juice runs to keep me infused with energy.

A special thanks to Russ Hanush, math, science, physics expert extraordinaire and longtime tutor to my daughters, for generously sharing his time and knowledge, and taking questions like "Could a natural substance be engineered to detonate inside a person's body remotely?" with enthusiasm.

To Margie Lawson, whose expertise of language and emotion have done more for my writing than any other single source, all while making me laugh until I cried. (I back loaded that just for you, Margie.)

To my editor, Alicia Condon, who had a deeper vision for *Rush*'s villain, and for trusting in me to shape that idea into the novel. To my agent, Paige Wheeler, who helped me fully understand that vision and gave me the confidence to jump in.

To Despina Konstantinopoulou, an editor and reader in Athens, Greece, who generously translated all Mateo's Greek throughout *Blaze*. A shout to my street team, Swan's Sirens, for their support and enthusiasm. Thanks to my sisters, Jane, Clare, and Anne, who are always pushing my latest book into their friends' hands.

And last, but never least, to my amazing critique partner, Elisabeth Naughton, without whom I would be lost. Thanks for propping me up, E.

ONE

Truckee, California
Five years ago

That could not be Jessica Fury's husband. Not the man hanging upside down, fifty feet off the ground over unforgiving asphalt, prepared to perform a midair flip, hoping—*hoping*—to grab that ladder and scale down to safety. Not all in the name of some spontaneous, reckless, madcap training drill. Sure as hell not after he'd just been trying to coax her into making a baby with him hours ago.

Only it was. It so was. Goddamnit.

The catcalls and laughter from the other members of their hazmat team usually filled Jessica with joy. Tonight, the boisterous encouragement egging her husband on in his latest stunt made her teeth grind.

She stood at the base of a ladder, securing the structure for what should have been Quaid's execution of a simple bailout maneuver during one of their standard team training sessions. But what kept flashing in her mind—over and over, like the repeat of a movie clip—was the love of her life, her brand-freaking-new husband, diving out that fifth-story window headfirst, wrapping his leg in the safety rope instead of avoiding it, and pushing off the rungs of the ladder he should have been holding tight, then . . . letting go.

Just *letting go* fifty feet in the air.

Beads of sweat burst across her forehead. The building spun in her vision against the darkening sky. Jessica swayed and tightened her grip on the ladder.

He looked amazing, she couldn't deny that—his strong body filling out the heavy turnouts and silhouetted against the evening, red helmet gleaming in the sunset. That mischievous, full-of-himself grin lit his handsome face. Confidence, courage, and challenge electrified the air around him.

No doubt about it—this was one-hundred percent authentic Quaid Legend in his element.

"Hey, buddy," Teague called from where he stood on the other side of the ladder. "Hope your life insurance is paid up. If you don't die from this stupid stunt, you can bet your ass Jess is gonna kill you when you touch down."

Another round of laughter erupted. Jessica fingers tightened on the ladder until they stung. Quaid's joyous grin dimmed and his beautiful eyes darted to hers.

"Legend!" Battalion Chief Kai Ryder, their team leader, yelled at Quaid from so close beside Jessica, she jumped. "What the *fuck* do you think you're doing?"

"Kai." Jessica's voice scraped out of her throat. One more crack to her heart and it was going to explode. "Scream at him *after* he's on the ground. Please."

Kai's attention jerked from Quaid's precarious sway to Jessica's face and, damn it, pity crept into his eyes.

The sting of tears pressed across the bridge of her nose. She would not cry. She would *not*. Damn Quaid for scaring her so badly she hurt. Damn him for putting her in this position with her team.

Kai approached the building. "Get your ass down here, you sonofabitch. A simple bailout, Legend. What part of that didn't you understand? You've only done it a million fucking times."

"Well, yeah, chief," Quaid said with typical ease. "That's why I wanted to work on this one."

This was classic Quaid—going rogue. Quaid the adventure seeker, the adrenaline junkie. Once upon a time, and not all that long ago, it had been sexy. Exciting. Only occasionally annoying. Now married, with him nudging her toward a family, it was terrifying.

"Goddamnit, Quaid," Jessica whispered.

"It's what happened with Duke," Teague said at Jessica's side, using his smooth mediator tone. "He hasn't been able to shake it."

Her thoughts turned to their friend, another firefighter, who was still in a coma with severe brain damage. Duke had recently found himself right where Quaid hung now after being blown out a window at a structure fire. Only Duke had been trapped as the building collapsed around him.

"I know." Her heart felt too big for her chest. "But if he wants to practice getting out of a bad situation, he has to plan for it. He needs an air pad out here. He needs to start lower and build up. He needs—"

"He's been doing this for weeks, Jess. He's gone higher—"

"*What?*" Her gaze broke from Quaid and cut to Teague. His blue eyes shone bright beneath the brim of his helmet.

Teague shrugged and returned his attention to Quaid.

Jessica followed Teague's gaze and wondered what other risks her husband had been taking without telling her. But she wasn't going to ask and put Teague in the middle. She didn't need to put any more pressure on their friends. As it was, she and Quaid were lucky to still be on the team together.

At the base of the tower, Kai had stopped yelling at Quaid and started coaching him through the steps of this new drill. Quaid's grin was back. Mischief sparkled in his velvet brown eyes again as he prepared to defy gravity like the rebel he was. Rebel to the core. Which was one of the things she loved about him. One of the things that shot heat through her veins and pumped adrenaline straight to her heart. The very damn reason she loved him so much sometimes it hurt to breathe.

But she wasn't breathing now—as Quaid pushed his body backwards for momentum, then swung toward the ladder. Every muscle in Jessica's body tensed. She leaned into the metal and held tight. Quaid twisted, then flipped like a gymnast, and righted himself. His gloves slapped metal. His single free boot found traction on a rung. But momentum tugged at the other leg still wound in the rope and that planted foot slipped.

Jessica sipped another frightened breath. Then Quaid regained his footing. Only when he unwound his other leg from the safety-rope-turned-death-trap did Jessica start breathing again.

"I thought he'd grow out of this kind of shit when you two got married," Teague muttered. "But it's not lookin' good, Jess."

Quaid couldn't even do something as simple as descend a ladder without flash. Instead of climbing down the rungs, he straddled the metal, settled his boots on either side of the vertical supports and started a stealthy slide toward the ground. He released one side of the ladder and turned to look for Jessica. As soon as his gaze found hers, he smiled. A big, warm, intimate smile just for her. A smile of shared excitement. A smile that said everything from, "Hey, babe, I'm back," to "Did you see that?" to "You're not really mad, right?"

And damn it, she didn't want to be mad when he looked at her like that. But she was. Which led to an on-slaught of guilt. Followed by a burst of unrestrained anger.

By the time his boots came within a couple feet of the ground, his smile had vanished, and concern made that cute little V appear between his eyes. The one she loved to kiss away. Before he touched down, Jessica headed toward the station's engine bay.

"Jess?" he called. "Hey, Jessie. Wait."

He jogged up beside her, but didn't touch her, didn't try to slow her down or force her to look at him. He knew better.

"Come on, baby," he crooned in a voice that should have been outlawed. Deep and smooth and so damn sexy. "I know, I shouldn't have surprised you like that, but I did good, right?"

She clenched her teeth.

He bent forward, trying to look into her eyes. He'd taken off his helmet and in her peripheral vision she saw the dirt smudges on his face, his thick black hair mussed. She bit the inside of her cheek to keep a flood of tears from pushing over her lashes. He never looked better than after he'd been working. The light in his eyes, the excitement on his face, the raw life buzzing over his skin, and that smile . . . Never was he more pure Quaid Legend, the man she loved heart, body and soul, than after he'd been working.

"Jessie, stop for a second." They passed through the huge bay doors and in one swift move, he darted in front of her, then blocked her every attempt to get by with a simple shift of his body.

"Quaid, knock it off."

Whatever expression she wore shocked him. He jerked his head back as if dodging a punch, and the playful frustration drained, replaced with something dark and far more serious. Something that made Jessica's chest cinch down tighter.

He dropped his helmet. The *thunk* against concrete

shocked Jessica, and she jumped, frantically searching for the gear as if he'd dropped a child. She'd never seen him drop anything, especially not a piece of equip—

He slipped his hands beneath her turnout jacket and around her waist, pulling her up against him. He was strong and warm and familiar. And they fit so perfectly together. In so many ways. She hated the way he continued to put that at risk.

"Hey." He lifted a hand to her face. "What's this? I've never seen you like this."

"Quaid . . ." She glanced over her shoulder for the rest of the team. "Don't—"

"Screw them. Look at me. You're scaring me, Jess."

Her gaze shot back to his. Her hands fisted in his jacket. "Scaring you? No, Quaid, scaring you would be more like me jumping out a fifth-story window on the spur of the moment while you were watching."

Guilt flooded his eyes. "I'm sorry, Jess. I . . . didn't think—"

She pushed back, breaking his grip, her anger, terror, pain renewed. "You can't just say you're sorry and make it all go away. Do you have any idea, *any* idea, how it felt for me to stand there and watch you? *Watch you* roll out the window and *let go* of that ladder?"

"I know. I—"

"No, you don't know." Tears spilled over her lashes before she could stop them. "I thought I was going to stand there, helpless, and watch you fall to your death."

"Oh, shit. Christ, don't cry, Jess. That's not what I was . . . I was trying to . . . I wanted to . . . with what happened to—"

"Duke." She pulled the hem of her shirt up and wiped her face. She hated how he caved when she cried, how he completely lost focus on the argument at hand. How he'd promise her anything just to get her to stop. "I know, but that doesn't—"

Their pagers went off at the same time and a stereo of beeps echoed in the bay.

"Ah, shit." Quaid glanced at the display hooked to his belt and Jessica silenced her unit. "Just a warehouse."

His turnout jacket fell back into place and he reached for her again.

She stepped back. "This is serious, Quaid. I need you. I depend on you. You're—" Her throat closed. Tears renewed and she took a breath to keep them back. "You're everything to me. *Everything*. If you really want a family you *cannot* be pulling shit like that. Do you understand?"

"Absolutely." He nodded, his eyes serious and intent on hers, and so very clear. She knew he meant what he was saying. "Yes."

The tension inside her shifted from heavy despair to blessed relief. She threw herself into him, knowing he'd catch her. He held tight, pressed his face to her neck and wiped his damp eyes on her skin.

"I'm sorry, baby. I love you so much. I worry all the time, you know? Shit like what happened with Duke . . . I just want to know how to stay safe. How to keep you safe. I want us together . . . forever."

Footfalls sounded on the concrete, and for the first time since she and Quaid had started dating, she didn't care who saw them together at work.

"I told you she wouldn't stay mad at him longer than ten minutes." Keira's voice cut into Jessica's moment of relief, which was just as well. She was ready to melt into her husband and let him take over. Let him do whatever he damn well pleased just to see him smile, which was exactly how they'd gotten here.

"You're one to talk, sweetness," Luke, their teammate

and Keira's new boyfriend, teased with a tousle of her hair. "You can't stay mad at me for two."

"Knock that shit off," Kai grumbled, passing them on the way toward their hazmat rig. Jessica pulled away from Quaid just before Kai slammed Quaid's helmet against his chest with a glare of steel. "Watch your gear, Legend. And one more epic act of stupidity like that, and I'll kick your ass to Iceland. Load up."

Quaid's ass could have already been in Iceland. Despite his close seat alongside Jess in the back of the truck with her fingers curled into his, the look he'd seen on her face earlier still chilled him. It was the same look he saw on Duke's wife's face whenever a doctor entered Duke's room in the ICU. And Quaid didn't want to see that look in Jess's eyes again. Ever. His efforts to master that damn drill had been for exactly that purpose—to keep that look *out* of her eyes.

Fucking-A.

He pulled his hand from hers and sat forward in his seat, leaning elbows on knees. She might think he was everything to her, but she was his goddamned universe. And the road noise and others talking wasn't helping him think. Wasn't helping him figure out where his damn defect was or how to repair—as Kai had so perfectly put it—his act of epic stupidity.

Jess leaned into him and combed her fingers through his hair. Love, rich and warm and sweet, pushed wetness into Quaid's eyes. He closed them, pressed his fingers against the lids to ease the sting and let his mind wind around every possible way he could make this up to her.

They'd been riding twenty minutes, now well into the desolate mountains of the Sierra Nevada, when Kai called attention and started giving information.

"This is a government storage warehouse," he said, reading from his iPhone, where he stored data on all area buildings. "It houses machinery and supplies. We shouldn't run into weapons or biohazard, but we'll have petroleum-based products and cleaning supplies. May have high combustibles burning toxins and no doubt our beloved plastics."

The vehicle slowed and bounced onto a rough road. Quaid grabbed a handlebar above Jessica's head and braced her with his body.

"I'll take the entry team with Teague and Luke," Kai continued. "Keira, Jess, Quaid and Seth take second in. The hazmat team from Carson City will be there as backup."

Quaid saw an opportunity for redemption. The first step toward taking that look out of Jess's eyes forever. And after Luke and Teague popped the vehicle's doors and the team dropped into the cool night, Quaid went in search of Kai.

The scent of pure mountain pine mixed with smoke. One deep breath and excitement rushed his system. Adrenaline fueled his muscles and pumped his energy. His thoughts sharpened, his reactions quickened. He was high and ready to take on the flames.

But he couldn't do that tonight. He couldn't play that reckless cowboy anymore.

Local firefighters already had their ladder truck positioned alongside the building, their hoses pouring water on fiery tongues licking through a hole in the metal ceiling. Three other engines were positioned near the main door. Firefighters hauled hose from the back of the trucks, the thick canvas slithering along the asphalt like tan snakes. Light from flood lamps cascaded over the surrounding terrain, making the aspens' flat leaves sparkle gold among the dark towering pines.

Quaid followed Kai to the opposite side of the vehicle and stopped close. "Chief, I'd like to be on the entry team."

Kai yanked open a compartment. "As if."

"I know I screwed up. Give me a chance to fix it."

"If you can't act like a professional in training—"

"Give it a rest, Kai. We've worked together for eight goddamned years. Do you want me to remind you how many times my unorthodox ways have saved your ass?"

Kai shot him a heavy-lidded look around the metal door, but his silence said he was considering. Quaid held his breath, waiting . . . hoping. After several seconds, Kai finally said, "Fine, you're on the entry team. But Quaid? I want you to think about how ball-shriveling glacial it is in Iceland right now."

"Yes, sir."

"If you make even half a misstep, you're off this team. You got me?"

Quaid exhaled slowly. "Yes, sir."

With purpose and a plan, Quaid headed back toward the truck. He found Jess on the far side, unloading gear while studying the fire. He smiled to himself, a little surprised at the new sense of maturity and pride rising inside him.

"Lucky this didn't spread," she said, her gaze straying to the tree line. "If it had reached the forest, we could have lost thousands of acres. And look at those aspens. They're so pretty. God I *love* this time of year." She set her oxygen tank on the ground at her feet. "Where'd you go?"

"To talk to Kai. I'm on the entry team."

"Quaid, you don't have to do that."

But her little smile and the way her eyes softened reinforced Quaid's decision. She was proud of him for taking this step in leadership, too. Maybe this growing up and flying right thing wouldn't be as vanilla as he'd thought. There were definite perks to seeing that look in her eyes. Like the way his heart was somewhere up in the stars right now.

"I want to do it." He reached for the shoulder strap of

her breathing apparatus and hoisted the tank off the ground. "Turn around."

She turned and slipped her arms through the straps. He settled the tank on her back, then spun her around and snapped her fittings closed, double-testing their security before pulling on his own tank.

He took his time getting the rest of his gear together, knowing Jess would wait. The team drifted toward the warehouse, where flames dimmed and smoke billows grew, signaling a dying fire. As soon as everyone was out of earshot and their backs were turned, Quaid grabbed the collar of Jess's turnout jacket and gently backed her against the rig.

"What?" she asked, looking up at him, eyes worried. "What's wrong?"

Diffused light from the scene made her face glow. With her auburn hair pulled into a ponytail, those big, soft brown eyes looked doelike. He released her jacket and cupped her face with both hands.

"Do you know how much I love you?"

The worry in her eyes eased. "I love you more."

He brushed his thumbs over the smooth skin of her cheeks and those delicate freckles, and stared at her perfect lips before he kissed her, slowly, tenderly. "I know what you need, Jess," he whispered. "You can depend on me."

"I believe you." Her lips curved against his, and her arms locked around his neck. "I have an idea for your birthday next week."

"Yeah?"

"You and me, a weekend away, somewhere isolated where we can spend the entire forty-eight hours doing nothing but"—her grin widened, her eyes sparkled—"making a baby."

A bubble of joy slid up his chest and burst from his throat in laughter. Those words coming from her mouth were sheer heaven to his heart. Yes, he could do this. He could take that next step toward stability—for her, for him, for *them*. He leaned in and kissed her hard. She opened to him, all sweet and hot. Quaid groaned and lost himself, just for one blissful moment.

"Ready for your boys, Chief Ryder." The shout to Kai came from a distance and signaled the beginning of a new chapter in Quaid's career.

Time for their team to get to work. And the sooner they got started, the sooner they could finish and the sooner Quaid could get his bride home and into bed, where they could practice more baby making. If practice made perfect, their kid was going to be utterly flawless.

Quaid stepped up to the entrance of the warehouse with Teague and Luke at his side and waited for the last hose team to pull out. Few flames still snapped inside. Smoke grew thick and pumped out fast, signaling a mostly extinguished blaze. Quaid spotted Gary Hernandez from Truckee Fire dragging hose. His turnouts were soaked and the mask of his breathing apparatus had been tugged aside and hung askew.

"Gary," Quaid called to get his attention. The firefighter looked his way and Quaid lifted his chin in greeting. "What've we got in there?"

Gary grinned and walked over to the group. "Aw, a pallet of something plastic caught." He pushed the brim of his helmet up with his thumb, leaving a soot ring on his forehead. "Probably a load of dildos from China."

Keira stepped forward, making a show of peering into the wall of smoke. "Dildos, huh? You think anything's salvageable?"

"You little . . ." Luke gave the strap of her oxygen tank a playful jerk, sending a ripple of laughter through the group.

"But that's not why we pulled out." Gary's expression

turned serious again as he addressed Quaid. "There's real methel-ethel bad shit in there, dude."

The all-inclusive slang firefighters used to refer to any potentially serious chemicals made Quaid's stomach tighten with a mix of excitement and dread. "Methel-ethel" bad shit was not a simple toxin produced by burning plastics, not a regularly encountered mildly explosive petroleum product. Methel-ethel bad shit was the kind of chemical that ate through skin or blew a body clean apart.

Gary turned, crouched and pointed beneath the smoke roiling across the ceiling. "See that glow?"

Quaid squinted toward a faint yellow-orange radiance. "Yeah."

"Metal canisters of something. They're secured to a concrete wall by metal straps and bolts as big as silver dollars, off all by themselves like they're contagious or something. And whatever's inside them is as hot as molten lava, 'cause look at them, brother, they're fucking *glowing*."

"What do the hazard symbols show?"

"Couldn't get close enough to see before those plastics went up. Fire's almost out. It's safe to go in, but—" Gary pulled off his gloves and slapped them against the arm of Quaid's yellow hazmat suit. "Watch your ass in there, my friend. My gut tells me those fancy threads ain't gonna save you."

Hernandez returned to his company and started cleanup.

"Still want entry team?" Kai's quiet voice sounded right next to Quaid, startling him. "You've got someone else to think about now."

Quaid took a breath to ease the sting of fear in his gut. He needed to demonstrate his commitment—for Jessica and Kai and the others. Hell, for himself. He had to prove, with actions, that when he took responsibility for something, he wouldn't shirk it at the first sign of trouble. He was in this—firefighting and his marriage—for the long haul, 'til death did they part.

Quaid met Kai's eyes. "I *am* thinking about her. *She* is why I still want entry team."

Kai held his gaze for a long moment, then stepped back. "Luke, Teague," he called, "Quaid's your lead. Go."

When Kai huddled with the others, Teague grinned at Quaid. "All right, hotshot. Let's mop up your earlier mess."

The three secured their Plexiglas face shields. When Quaid turned to shoot Jess a wink, Kai tossed him a thermal-imaging camera. He caught it against his chest. Instead of throwing it back at Kai, as he had in the past, Quaid grit his teeth and powered on the unit.

He'd always bitched about TICs as rudimentary devices, but the truth was Quaid wanted to seek out the source of a fire on his own, with eyes and ears and *instinct*. He had built killer instincts over the years, and he got a thrill out of using them. He didn't want a piece of machinery stealing all his fun.

Only Quaid wasn't in this just for the fun anymore. There was a lot more at stake now.

He walked into the muck with his Maglite in one hand and the TIC in the other, smiling. No drastic or dreaded changes had overtaken him when he'd turned on the TIC. Adrenaline still thrilled through his body. Excitement to nail those wicked chems still lightened his head. God, he loved that woman. Jess never failed to lead him in the right direction in life. She was his true north. And he'd follow her to the ends of the earth.

Thick smoke immediately smothered his vision. Even though he knew exactly where the threat lay, he had to force himself to think by the book. The haphazard Quaid would head straight for those glowing tanks, do not pass go, do not collect two hundred dollars. But the responsible Quaid made the requisite methodical sweeps of the area for suspicious contents.

Teague and Luke flanked him ten feet back on either side. The thermal detector was used to identify hot spots within the smoke, but as Quaid suspected, the TIC was useless to him here. Today, the TIC only caused Quaid to waste valuable time.

When they reached the tanks, Quaid almost believed they were alive. Their glow had intensified from yellow-orange to vibrant vermillion. Looking directly at them threatened to sear his retinas. In the extreme heat their metal encasings appeared liquid, rippling like the disturbed surface of a lake. Quaid swore the damn things were breathing, expanding and contracting in a slow, steady rhythm.

"What the hell?" Luke's voice was little more than a husky whisper in Quaid's earpiece.

"This is way beyond us," Teague said. "Let's get the numbers off the hazard symbol and get out."

"I'll get them." Quaid gestured for them to stop. "Stay here."

Excitement escalated to fear. He gave his TIC to Luke and used his hand to shield his face from the glare as he approached the tanks. Their suits were designed to protect them at extreme temperatures, but Quaid could swear his skin was roasting right through the material.

His fear escalated to alarm. A huge part of him wanted to call if off. To back out without the information. But he couldn't take one more failure tonight. Not in Jess's eyes. Not in the team's eyes. Not in his own eyes.

He crouched to the level of the diamond symbol showing a number at each of the four corners, indicating the chemical's characteristics. Once outside, he could compile those numbers with an index of chemicals and figure out what they were dealing with. Then if they needed to call in big guns, they could do it without looking like total screwups.

Inching forward, he thrust the flashlight as close to the sign as he could, peering through the illuminated smoke and against the glare, but still, the numbers shimmered in and out of sight. In his hand, the Maglite's black housing changed shape. At first he thought it was the rippling heat waves altering the atmosphere—until the casing slid over his gloved hand and the flashlight shorted out. Then he realized the damn thing had melted right off the metal frame beneath.

A sharp *crackle* brought Quaid's gaze back to the diamond-shaped sign. To the tank beneath the sign. To a dark, linear crack sliding along the canister from the floor upward.

Oh, fuck!

Terror struck his spine like lightning. He pivoted and launched himself into a sprint. Opened his mouth to yell *run*—

Heat slammed Quaid's back. Pain, ripping and raw, consumed him. His arms, already outstretched to wrap around each of his teammates on the way to the ground, hit them both across the throat. They hit the cement. Bounced. Broke apart. Hit a pallet of boxes. Ricocheted in all directions.

Then it was over. The blast dead. The fire gone.

Quaid knew nothing but pain. Engulfing, snarling, ferocious pain.

His eyes were open. He didn't know how. He should be dead. But he could see Teague and Luke lying nearby. Completely still. Their hazmat suits burned and torn. Bodies black and twisted.

Voices bled through the deafening ring in Quaid's ears. Not the words, but the tone. The terror and anger in shouted orders.

Don't come in here.

His fear flooded back. His mind circled around that second tank and fear turned to terror. He put all his concentration into moving his mouth.

"N . . . No." Shit, pathetic. He focused his thoughts to Jess. To saving Jess. Gathered energy and tried again.

"Don' come in . . . 'nother tank . . ."

Did his headset even work?

He fought to move some part of his body. Got a few fingers to wiggle. Then a few toes. The cement rumbled under his cheek—the clomp of boots nearing.

No.

He forced himself to lift his head, as heavy as an oxygen tank, as dizzy as a tornado. Just as he recognized Jess's silhouette headed straight for him, the rest of the team fanning out toward Luke and Teague, a familiar *crackle-fizz* penetrated Quaid's fuzzy brain.

"No. Get . . . out."

He tried to push himself up, but his arms wouldn't work. Another *crackle-crackle-crackle* sounded. An angrier, heavier *fizzzzz*. Panic rushed his chest. *Jess. Protect Jess.*

He pulled one knee under his body with strength born of sheer horror. The move knifed pain through his leg and hip. Jess crouched before him and time slowed. He watched her beautiful mouth form his name, her tortured expression peer at him through the Plexiglas facemask.

Love you, Jessie. Love you so much.

He pushed with every ounce of power in his damaged legs and thrust himself forward. He knocked her over and covered her body with his. Absorbed the feeling—the very last time he'd touch her, he knew.

She grabbed his arms. Called his name. The blast came a second later. Ripped him away and speared him across the warehouse with the speed of a rocket. But his mind kicked into a time warp, slowing the seconds, drawing everything around him into something from a slow-motion, action-movie sequence.

Including the sound of his voice screaming her name, until he slammed into a concrete wall and felt his body shatter like sheet glass.

TWO

Washington, D.C.
Present day

Jessica Fury paced the length of her office, trying to concentrate on the men's voices coming through her Bluetooth headset. Even though the space was quiet at seven a.m., her mind was frayed at the edges.

She couldn't get over this jet lag, couldn't get any decent sleep, couldn't cope with this agonizing build of endless days toward the fifth anniversary of Quaid's death.

Out her expansive windows, the Capitol building stood strong, regal and righteous against a crisp blue sky. Golden, amber and fiery-red hues of fall lined the streets leading from her office building to the gleaming white dome.

The whole vision was so postcard perfect she thought she might just snap.

God, she *hated* this time of year.

Emotions stirred like acid at cell level. Emotions that would consume her if she let them. She'd made that mistake already. Repeatedly.

"Jessica." Congressman Wyle's senior aide's voice vibrated in her ear, bringing her to attention. "You've been awfully quiet."

She rubbed at the burn in her eyes but pushed her voice into a buoyant tone. "No need to add anything to an already brilliant presentation. Morgan is handling this legislation beautifully. He is beyond capable. I'm only here for support."

"I agree your new associate is sharp as hell, and I'm glad you and Daryl finally pulled some help aboard, but you know I'm going to get my ass handed to me if I take this to Wyle without your opinion."

The truth was, at the moment, she couldn't even scrape the bottom of her soul for a sliver of enthusiasm about this initiative. But then, waking up tomorrow seemed rather pointless right now, too. Out of habit, she glanced at the wall where her calendar normally hung. She'd taken it down the last week of October, unable to face the word *November* for thirty damn days straight.

Focus. Inspiration. Purpose. Damn, she needed help.

She looked around her gorgeous office and mentally catalogued all its material comforts. She envisioned their private lobbying firm's bank account with the National Air Transportation Safety Association's multi-million-dollar retainer snuggled away.

The emptiness inside intensified.

She flipped open the NATSA file on her desk and the heart-crushing image of plane wreckage glared up at her. Real lives had been taken in this crash. In so many crashes like this. Lives as precious as those with whom she'd shared her flight home from Venice two days ago. She still remembered a friendly couple and their baby daughter who'd been sitting in her row.

"My opinion is"— Jessica closed the file and made small circles at her temple to release the tension—"that this proposed hazardous materials addendum to the air cargo security legislation should have been drafted into the original 9/11 security objective. Had our leaders confronted the threat with foresight instead of fear, we wouldn't all still be taking our shoes off at the airport."

Stan chuckled. "Well said. Over a decade later and we're still playing defense instead of offense."

"Exactly," Jessica continued. "They put a bomb in a shoe, we inspect everyone's shoes. They mix chemicals for explosives, we limit the toiletries in carry-on luggage. They use an ink cartridge to build a bomb, we ban all ink cartridges over one pound in cargo. It's all reactive.

"Our research was conducted by specialists from around the world who have projected every possible situation. They've developed a standardized method for properly labeling, packaging and storing all hazardous chemicals for air cargo. This initiative is part of the offensive we've been missing to ensure safe air travel with hazardous chemicals."

"Bravo, Jessica," Stan said with an appreciative lilt in his smooth, deep voice. "Wyle will eat that shit up."

Morgan, based in Sacramento, California, where it was barely four freaking a.m., picked up the ball and started tossing in powerful commentary supporting NATSA's position. Jessica let out her air and turned her mind to standby.

Her gaze followed a row of young aspens, freshly planted throughout Capitol Hill by some restoration society—just another secret plot to torture her, she was sure. The trees swayed together, standing strong in the gust of a mystery breeze, reminding her of the soldierlike camaraderie she'd once shared with her firefighting team. Reminding her of that night she'd lost Quaid.

She turned away from the window only to have her gaze land on the wide dark expanse of the flat panel television mounted in the corner of her office. Usually, she kept it on and muted. But today it was off, turning the massive, silent, black span into a threat, just like every other smooth reflective surface—mirrors, ponds, shiny chrome bumpers, for crying out loud. If she stared at any of them too long, shadows began to dance, take shape and not just show her events in other locations, but open doorways into other realms, beckoning her to take one dangerous step closer.

That damn fire had destroyed everything good in her life—stolen her husband, split her team, annihilated her sense of security and purpose. And it had imposed haunting powers. Powers Jessica didn't want, need or understand.

She reached for the television remote on her desk, hit the power button and soaked in a split second of anticipated relief. Her panel lit up with three news channels, all reporting on some obvious disaster. Angry flames snapped across all three screens and hope for a respite to her agony dissolved.

Damn it, she was so tired of this. She yanked open her top drawer and grabbed the Xanax she left there—just in case. Even though she knew *just in case* meant: weakness. Plain and simple. This drug was no different from the others she'd used. Yes, this one might be legal, but that didn't make it any less of a crutch.

But if she ever needed one . . .

Do you know how much I love you?

. . . it was now.

She closed her eyes on the memory. Picking up the locket lying against her chest, she fisted it in her hand and fought back the pain that could pull her so deep, it took days to recover.

With the Xanax bottle clutched in one hand, her locket in the other, she tuned into the phone conversation again; this time with an ear toward getting off the line. She needed to make a call to her sponsor. Arrange an appointment with her therapist. Check into the local asylum.

Now there was the best idea she'd had in months.

Jessica opened her eyes and released the locket. Outside, the mystery breeze had turned into a full-fledged wind, buffeting the tender aspens until they bent to its will. Her inner disquiet was probably wreaking havoc in the local meteorologist's office. Her mood's bizarre effects on the weather would probably cause miscalculations in the forecast for the next two days.

Just one more thing she could blame on that damn fire.

She shot a quick glance at the television screens, even though she knew she shouldn't.

It's not clear yet what caused the explosion. . . .

The words popped up on the screen in closed captioning. Fire still undulated in various wide-angle video shots. But what riveted her vision and halted her breath was the color of the flames—a shifting kaleidoscope of orange, blue and purple.

Jessica squeezed her eyes shut. Shook her head so hard, the bun she'd thrown her hair into that morning uncoiled. But when she opened her eyes again, the flames on the screen continued to change color and spit cobalt blue sparks. The text on the bottom right of the screen read: *Rachel, Nevada.*

"*. . . the government facility reportedly housed a state-of-the-art laboratory . . .*" Jessica lunged for her desk, trading the Xanax for the remote, and hit the mute button to enable audio.

"*. . . run by the Department of Defense. The building, originally built back in the early 1900s, was a rather majestic structure of concrete resembling a castle you might see in Ireland or Scotland and was referred to by workers and locals alike aptly as 'The Castle.' The fire broke out sometime in the middle of the night. No word yet on the extent of the damage, though sources say this was no accident. Speculation among locals is that a homegrown terrorist cell may be responsible for today's disaster. . . .*"

Discomfort tightened the muscles along Jessica's shoulders. The flames were eerily familiar. Like the ones that had erupted from those chemicals stored in that warehouse five years before. The fire that had taken Quaid's life. The fire that had poisoned the entire team and left them all with bizarre paranormal abilities. Chemicals Teague's research had traced back to the Department of Defense.

How *dare* they blame this bullshit on a fake terrorist cell of traitorous American citizens to cover their own sick screwup.

This was no different from the lies Schaeffer had created about the warehouse fire to cover the true cause of Quaid's death. No different from the way that bastard— the director of DARPA's Biological Sciences division then, a senator now—had declared the warehouse fire classified and then barred her team from ever understanding what had really happened.

And then he had the audacity to follow them all like members of the FBI's top ten most wanted.

Teeth clenched, she tossed the remote down. It clattered against the cherry surface of her desk, tipped over her pencil holder and sent her cell phone and the Xanax skidding across her blotter and onto the floor.

"Jessica?" Morgan's voice floated through her fog. "Everything okay?"

She tore her eyes from the television. Holy shit. She'd forgotten she was still on the phone. Had completely tuned the men out.

"Yes, of course." Her shields came up. Her discipline took over. She hurried to the other side of her desk and crouched to scoop her cell phone from the carpet while still talking into her headset. "What you need to stress to Congressman Wyle is that in a recent poll, eighty percent of his constituents in the beautiful state of California had high concerns over this topic, and a whopping seventy-six percent voiced being in favor of *immediate action* to remedy the problem.

"Listen . . ." She wiped a palm over her damp forehead. Her hand was shaking. Her mouth was dry. A tight sensation tugged at her stomach. God, she hadn't had a craving attack like this in . . . months. "Something's come up. I've got to get going. I'll talk to you both soon."

She barely heard the men's good-byes, already pulling the Bluetooth off her ear and dropping it on her desk.

She picked one news channel and brought it up full screen. A beautiful African-American woman reported from the ravaged area, the scene a significant distance behind her. Still, pillars of smoke spiraled from the decimated remnants of torn concrete buildings and turned the sky an angry iron. "*. . . sixteen confirmed dead with thirty-eight still missing, including a high-ranking official of the Department of Defense. . . .*"

Jessica pulled in a shocked breath and wrapped her arms around herself. "Jesus."

What did this mean? Her mind strayed to Kai, their former team leader, and his ability to sense when the team was in danger. Surely he or someone on the team would have alerted her. She and Kai had their issues, but still . . .

An unfamiliar fear vibrated deep inside her. *Deep breath in. Slow breath out.*

She dialed Keira's number at the FBI field office in Sacramento, where she'd become a special agent after leaving the fire service within a year of the warehouse incident.

After only three rings, Keira's voicemail picked up, and a sickening sensation stabbed at the very pit of Jessica's gut. As an active member of the FBI SWAT team, Keira always forwarded her calls, always carried her cell and *always* answered.

"Shit." Jessica disconnected and dialed Keira's home number. She and Keira had remained close despite much of the discord Jessica's move had caused with both her family and some other members of the team.

Her friend's phone rang five times before an answering machine picked up. Jessica sucked in a pained breath and stabbed END. She refocused on the television as if the news would tell her what to do next.

"*. . . the United States military has taken control of the scene and is receiving much of its investigative and search and rescue support from personnel and resources housed at Area 51, the highly secure military base in the middle of the Nevada desert. Secrecy and speculation have surrounded Area 51 for decades and with the lack of information coming out of its neighbor, the Castle, that reputation won't be changing any time soon.*"

A pained, worried sound bubbled up from Jessica's throat as she dialed Teague's cell. God, she hated to bother him now, with his new wife, Alyssa, nearly eight months pregnant. But aside from Keira, Jessica was closest with Teague and Alyssa, and spoke with them and their daughter Kat weekly over Skype. Teague had suffered the most at DARPA's hands and kept his fingers on the DoD's pulse. If anyone knew what was happening, Teague would.

As the fire raged on television, Jessica listened to the news anchor drone in one ear and Teague's phone ring in the other. He'd recently joined the ATF alongside Luke and had always been as available by phone as Keira. When Teague's voicemail answered, she disconnected, clutched her phone, crossed her arms again and swiveled toward the window.

"Damn it," she whispered, holding tight to the panic

that tried to spill over. Outside, the smooth blue sky was gone, replaced by sleek storm clouds, mirroring her emotions. "What's going *on*?"

Maybe Alyssa had gone into early labor. Maybe everyone had joined her and Teague at the hospital. But if that were the case . . . No. Teague had promised to call the minute Alyssa went into labor so Jessica could make arrangements to be there. Maybe she should check into available flights . . .

She wiped at her forehead again. Her throat felt thick. Her heart beat fast. Her breathing came shallow and quick.

Just because ninety percent of addicts and alcoholics relapse within the first year doesn't mean you have to be one of them. Her sponsor's encouragement whispered in her head. *You will be the one out of ten who makes it. I have no doubt.*

Jessica closed her eyes and focused within. After a year of daily meditation, she centered quickly. Her mind and body aligned. Fused. Settled. Now, she just had to hold herself there.

Trying again, she lifted her phone and tapped into her contacts. But she had to brace her arm against her body to control the shake as she dialed Alyssa's number.

"Great, that lasted all of thirty seconds." She put the phone to her ear, vowing to give the rest of the day over to yoga, meditation, the spa, whatever she needed to get back into complete balance.

A hard knock sounded on her office door. Jessica startled and dropped her phone. Outside the clouds burst and poured.

She turned, a scowl and a scolding ready for her partner, only she found Teague standing in the doorway.

Teague? Jessica's mouth dropped open, but before any sound emerged, Keira pushed past him and into the room carrying a very big, very black, very frightening gun.

"Jessica." Keira's voice was steady and even, but cold. So very cold. "Is anyone else here?"

Jessica shook her head, unable to form even a basic question. "What . . . Why . . . How . . . *Shit.*" She covered her face with both hands, half believing her mind had finally cracked and that when she took her hands away, she'd be alone in the office. "What the hell is happening?"

"Please, Jess." Damn, the Keira replica was still there. Still talking. Still sounding exactly like her friend. "I need to know. Is there anyone else in the office?"

Hands still on her face, Jessica shook her head. This was just too much. Too damn much.

The door to her office clicked shut and the room fell silent. For a surreal moment, Jessica wondered if asylums really had padded cells. If pink was truly a calming color. Whether or not they still made patients wear straitjackets. Surely modern medicine had advanced beyond such barbaric treatment. Hadn't it?

A strong arm circled her shoulders. Teague. His body was tall and steady and warm alongside hers. "Hey, Jess. That glad to see us?"

His touch, his voice—she couldn't deny the reality of it any longer. Terror gripped her lungs, making it hard to breathe. She turned to him and clutched at the soft cotton T-shirt over his hard chest. "Alyssa?"

His fingers tucked a strand of her hair behind one ear. "She's fine."

"The . . . baby?" She almost couldn't get the word out, terrified of the response.

"He's fine, too. Almost here."

Relief softened Jessica's bones and her knees gave. Teague tightened an arm at her waist to keep her upright. When she looked up at him, a soft smile curved his lips and the condition of his handsome face registered for the first time.

"What happened to your—" Another wave of fear crested. "What in the hell? Why are you here?"

"We need your help, Jess." Keira put a warm, firm hand on Jessica's arm. When she glanced at her friend again, she got her first real look at the scrapes and bruises she hadn't been able to absorb in her panicked state. Keira's sweet freckles and striking, sky blue eyes seemed to make the damage to her beautiful face that much more severe. "We need to talk—now and privately. Can we do that here?"

Their expressions were similar to that day five years ago when they'd come into her hospital room and told her Quaid had finally succumbed to his injuries. That he'd passed in the night, alone, because the staff at the military hospital wouldn't allow Jessica to stay in his room.

She stepped away from Teague, suddenly afraid to maintain contact and pressed both hands against her chest as if she could help herself drag in air.

"The others?" Her voice came out tight and feathery. "Luke, Seth, Kai? Are they hurt? Are they . . . ?" Jessica couldn't bring herself to ask if they were dead. "Just tell me."

Keira's stern expression softened and she slid a wry smile at Teague before returning her gaze to Jessica. "They're all a little too fine. Bitching, moaning, complaining and harping on each other as usual. We'll see them soon."

"They're *here*? All of you are here? Together?"

Keira hadn't spoken to Luke since their breakup three years before, and wasn't particularly chummy with Kai, who'd moved to bum-fuck-nowhere, Wyoming, about the same time.

"Shit," Jessica said, "this has to be really bad."

"Shh." Teague slid his arm around her shoulders and squeezed Jessica tight to his side. "Listen to Keira now, honey."

The last time Teague had called her "honey" had been

at Quaid's funeral. Jessica wished she'd downed a triple dose of Xanax.

"It's *that*, isn't it?" She waved at the television. "That DoD lab in Nevada."

"Whoa, whoa." Keira put her hands on Jessica's arms, a gentle touch. "Sweetheart, slow down. I know this is a shock—"

"You could have all been killed." Jessica's veneer of control cracked. Keira's lack of denial was as good as a confession. "My God. What would I have done if that had happened? Did you even *think* about what getting that news would have *done to me*?"

Suddenly cold, Jessica hugged herself again. She was always left out. Always alone. The irrational, childish hurt welled up beneath the fear and tangled with her growing anxiety. She couldn't pull the emotions apart or control them.

"Maybe I'm no federal agent like all of you or a military contractor like Kai or even a damn firefighter anymore like Seth. Maybe I couldn't have helped whatever the hell you were doing—not that I would have even wanted to—but you could have at least *let me know*. Not blindsided me like this."

Keira pulled Jessica into her arms. "Okay," she whispered, compassionate, understanding, but not coddling. Not enabling. "Shhh, now. You can handle this. Hear us out."

"We didn't forget you, Jess," Teague said. "You were in Venice."

"So, you couldn't let me know what was happening?"

"Kai called your hotel. Left you a message."

"Kai?" Of all the team members to call, Kai would have been the last she'd expect to pick up that duty. Kai was the source of her deepest hurt. The one who'd been the

most frustrated with her inability to move on after Quaid's death. The one who'd taken the greatest offense to her move across country. And aside from Jessica, Kai was, ironically, the one with the most guilt over Quaid's death, the least able to accept or deal with the tragedy and the last to admit it.

"I didn't get any message. And something is terribly wrong for Kai to call. He hasn't talked to me for four years." She crossed her arms, squeezing them over her stomach and the new burn there. "Shit, *what* did you do?"

"Long story, Jess," Teague said. "And we don't have a lot of time."

"Jessica," Keira said, "do you remember the coin we all received for our work at the warehouse fire?"

The question came so far out of left field, it could have been a meteor. "What could that possibly matter—?"

"Humor me." It wasn't a request.

Jessica clenched her teeth, rolled her fingers into fists. This was a bitter, bitter subject. In a bitter, bitter month. "The meaningless scrap of metal they gave us for ruining our lives? For *killing* Quaid?"

Keira took both of Jessica's arms, her expression imploring. "Do you still have yours?"

"No. I had it melted down and donated the gold to the Joseph Still Burn Center. How could you even think I'd keep something symbolic of the worst day, the worst pain of my life?" She didn't wait for an answer. "They said a high-ranking official of DoD is missing. Who is it?"

Teague shared a look with Keira before he said, "Dargan. Pretty sure it's Jocelyn Dargan."

Jessica pulled in a surprised breath, her mind spinning so fast she could have levitated. The deputy director of DARPA had worked under Schaeffer while he'd been employed there. Even after Schaeffer had become a senator,

Dargan continued to run his black ops for him and had been dogging their team for years. "What does this mean? Will they finally leave us alone?"

"Doubtful," Keira said. "What about Quaid's coin, Jess? It was buried with him, right?"

Out the window, the storm clouds had descended upon the streets of the Hill, obscuring the Capitol building. Rain fell in sheets now, flooding the gutters, and her mind felt just as congested. She could barely think around the confusion, the loss, the memories.

Keira's eyes narrowed as she looked out the window at the foul weather. "You're doing that, aren't you?"

"I'm not *doing* anything."

"This is important, honey," Teague said. "Where is Quaid's coin?"

"They buried it with him, yes. I didn't want them to. I told them no. But those bastards did it anyway, just like they did everything else."

"Look at me, Jessica. Listen to me, now." Keira took hold of her arms again, her fingers so tight they stung. Outside the wind grew stronger, slamming the rain against the windows. "The fire in Nevada was in a military laboratory and I'll tell you everything that led up to that later. Right now what you need to know is that we went into the facility to rescue a prisoner. But when we got in, we discovered he wasn't the only one. They were holding another man, too."

A million questions circled in Jessica's mind. Before she could form even one, Keira said, "That's where we found Quaid's coin."

Jessica's mouth fell open. Her brain froze in midthought. "*What?* No. No you didn't."

"His is the only coin unaccounted for. We found it in a cell used by the other inmate."

Fear. Panic. Terror. It toiled and coiled and rose toward her throat. Couldn't breathe. She couldn't breathe.

A sensation of complete chaos, of her world crumbling around her, had her seeking logic. "They didn't bury it with him? Someone stole it?"

She pushed past Keira without hearing her answer. At the windows, she turned and sought reassurance from Teague. But she got just the opposite. The look on his face—tortured, filled with anguish and guilt, burned through Jessica's heart like a live wire.

"Teague?"

When he didn't answer, she pressed her fingers to her temples.

Logic. Logic or she'd crumble.

"Okay." She looked up, stared straight at the wall across the room. "It obviously can't be the same coin. They must have given out similar coins for other incidents." She turned her gaze on Keira, then Teague. "I don't understand—"

Teague pulled his hand from the front pocket of his jeans and opened his palm. The sight of the coin that symbolized so much pain, such unfathomable loss stopped her mid-sentence. Her stress level spiked when she was already too close to the edge for safety.

"What . . . why do you have that?" Her gaze clung to the gold piece centered in Teague's palm, glinting in the light. Her hand floated to her neck, and she slid the chain there through her fingers until her locket rested in her hand again. It always gave her strength. But today, she needed so much more than the small talisman could provide.

"We have it," Keira said, "because we were hoping you could scry with it to help us find the other prisoner, the one who had this coin."

Jessica's brow pulled and she looked from Keira to

Teague and back. There was more. Far more. But the churn of her belly warned against asking. Against voicing her deeper fear—if the coin was indeed Quaid's and she scryed with it—she risked seeing things she couldn't bear. Things that would drag her under.

"You know my powers are worthless." She worried the locket's engraved platinum surface between her fingers. "I've long since killed whatever abilities I might have had with the drugs."

"If you've killed your powers, Jess"—Keira lifted a hand toward the window— "I'd say they're rising from the dead."

Jessica glared out at the sheeting rain and slashing trees. "That's just . . . a response to my bad mood."

"Only because you've never tried to control it."

"There's no point." Jessica didn't want to argue. But she didn't want to relapse either. She didn't want to go back to that life. And she'd never been so close to the cliff edge. "They're chaotic and erratic and unreliable. I may as well try to calm the sea. *Just drop it.*"

Keira clenched her teeth and pressed her lips together. Pain joined the frustration in her eyes and she cast a look at Teague before turning away.

Guilt flooded in, but Jessica shored up the dam. She had to take care of herself. She had to set limits. On a heavy breath, she looked at Teague. "I'm sorry, I just—"

"There's more, Jess," Teague said.

Fear flared again. Anger raced in to stand guard. She let her hands fall and slap her thighs. "It doesn't matter—"

"We believe the other prisoner is Quaid."

Jessica's mouth hung open for a long moment. White-hot pain overran her like wildfire in dry grass, leaving behind a swath of charred emotions. She snapped her jaw shut and her teeth clicked hard. Her heart iced over in protection. "Enough."

Keira spun around, her eyes crystalline and sharp. "They call him 'Q.' He's been there at least four years that we know of, probably more. They're testing him, experimenting on him in a program *Dargan* was managing for *Schaeffer*." She took two meaningful steps forward. "We *believe* this man is *Quaid,* Jessica."

No. No, no, *no.* She wanted to put her fingers in her ears and sing *la, la, la, la, la.* She couldn't do this. Couldn't let herself hope. Hope always led to despair.

In her world, despair led straight to alcohol, cocaine and heroin.

And just one more time down that road would lead her straight to the grave.

No one will take care of you if you don't take care of yourself first.

This was possibly the hardest thing she'd ever done short of rehab. To give herself the strength she needed, she envisioned a steel pole replacing her spine.

"We're done here." She crossed her arms, squeezed herself tightly against the slicing pain of her next demand. "Get out . . . of my office."

Jessica met Keira's stare with her own expression of rock solid conviction.

Teague took Keira's arm and guided her toward the door. Keira's gaze turned worried, even a little panicked.

Teague simply nudged her out the door with, "I'll be right there."

It took everything Jessica had left to hold onto that steadfast commitment to her own needs, her own safety when Teague turned back to her.

"I'm so sorry, Jess." He came toward her, head down with that pitiful, sorry-I-brought-a-frog-in-the-house remorse and the coin turning over and over between his fingers. "We didn't mean to hurt you. Really, we . . ."

He lifted his head and met her gaze. The anguish and

hopelessness there twisted the knife already stabbing her heart.

"No." She reached out and grabbed hold of his forearms. Tears she'd been holding back flooded her eyes and spilled over. "*I'm* sorry. I'm sorry for a million things. But I can't do this to myself. It would break me."

"I understand."

He took her face between his hands and kissed her forehead. Then he laid his palm over her heart. The thermo-kinetic abilities he'd acquired at that terrible fire infused heat and healing. The pain dimmed, but didn't disappear. It would never disappear.

"Take this." He pressed the coin into her hand. "It's rightfully yours." Teague kissed her head one more time before he turned to leave.

The coin pulsed with heat and energy. Powerful, vibrant sensations shimmied up her arm and spread through her body. Sensations of love. Of hope. Both so long forgotten they stole her breath. She turned toward the windows, moved around her desk and slumped into her chair. Blue lightning crackled across the sky, making the charcoal clouds glow.

A roll of ground-rocking thunder passed through the streets. A millisecond later, one quick strike of lightning split the sky. The jagged bolt speared the glass and smashed against the coin, refracting directly into Jessica's eyes.

She yelped and shaded her face, but the luminosity intensified, showering her with heat, engulfing her in a cone of golden light. Sizzling tingles traveled across her body, matching the effervescent sound rising in her ears. A sense of weightlessness made her dizzy. Then she was moving, a rush of air and pressure and prickles over her entire body. She grabbed for the arms on her chair, but found nothing. Panic seized her chest. She gasped for air, but her lungs clamped down tight. And just when she thought she'd lose her mind to the hovering terror, she slowed. The pressure eased. The light's intensity faded at the edges. The fizzing in her skin calmed.

Her heart thudded hard. Air scraped in and out of her throat. She squinted past the light still shining off the coin and the foreign sight of pine trees drifted through.

"Oh, no," she whispered. *Shit no.* Another doorway. Only this time, she'd gone through the damn thing. *Hell, no.* She hadn't signed up for this.

THREE

Beneath the tires, the ground turned from cracked asphalt to gravel. The car's front right tire took a deep divot at forty-two miles per hour. Q could calculate their speed by feel. His body jerked side to side, his shoulders knocking the men flanking him in the backseat of what he guessed was a Ford Taurus by the construction of the bench beneath him.

That jolt had pulled him right out of his memories of *her*. And that really pissed him off, because memories were all he had anymore. Q had stopped dreaming about her almost a year ago now. Every time he closed his eyes, he hoped and prayed the fiery redhead whose mere presence had a way of holding him together, would be there. But every time, he was disappointed. And he was beginning to lose hope. Considering his situation, that said a lot.

"What the hell, Davis?" Moist heat from his breath filled the black cloth bag covering his head, making it even harder to breathe. "Are you taking this piece of shit off-roading?"

His question went unanswered. They rarely spoke to him, and Q normally preferred it that way. But this was no ordinary transport to just another testing center. Those he took in the back of a windowless van, cuffed to a bench, alone. Now, he was stuffed into a sedan with their four best men—Davis, Samuels, Pike and Green. And the Castle he had called prison for as long as his memory stretched lay in rubble behind them. That caused a bizarre illogical mix of emotions within him. Emotions he didn't have time to analyze. Emotions he couldn't risk feeling in this situation or in this company. So he shut them off. And they disappeared instantly.

"How long have we been driving? Three, four hours?" He knew exactly how long—five hours, forty-two minutes. He shifted his numb ass on the bench seat. "Can't you take this hood off now? I'm having a hard time breathing. Wouldn't want me to keel over, would you?"

Nothing. Not even a grunt.

Fuck this. He'd had enough. He lifted his cuffed hands toward the mask's edge and dragged it up. Before he cleared his eyes, Samuels, on the left, knocked Q's hands down. "Leave it."

Q shoved the asshole's hand back. "Or what? You'll kill me?"

Samuel's backhand connected with Q's cheekbone. His head snapped sideways. Pain launched through his face. "You couldn't get that lucky."

Q shook his head to dispel the burn. "Not my fault you got dragged out of bed. Beat up on Dargan for a change."

Complete silence swelled inside the car for a heavy second, followed by a simultaneous *shhhhh*—the brush of skin against dress shirt collars as the men turned their heads and looked at each other.

"I wish you'd just left me in that dungeon to burn with the others." He paused and listened closely. More looks among them. Tension within the car thickened. "The lab is dust, isn't it? How many died in there?"

Samuels and Davis ground their teeth. In the remaining silence, Q worked past the knot in his gut and built enough nerve to ask the dreaded question.

"How about that other guy? The one in the cell next to me? I heard someone in the sally port saying he escaped."

Q held his breath. *Please let him be alive. Please make all this hell worth something.*

A furious heat wafted off Green in the front passenger's seat, making a new layer of sweat break out over Q's covered face. The other three men tensed, their muscles emitting a low-pitched moan that only Q's heightened senses could perceive as the fibers contracted and slid against tendon and bone. He had his answer.

Q relaxed. Then laughed, a low chuckle he hadn't known was coming. But as reality and deeper relief poured in, the chuckle grew into a full, hearty laugh. Getting one over on these pricks was the most satisfying thing he'd done since he'd messed up that psycho Gorin's latest experiment with a food strike. The best part was that he knew Cash was somewhere laughing, too. Somewhere free. A rare and delicious joy flashed in Q's veins.

Samuels's elbow landed square in Q's side. Pain ripped through his abdomen. A faint click hinted that Samuels had just broken one of Q's ribs. His laughter died. His momentary joy faded. But not his bubbling sense of success or his hope for Cash.

"Jesus, Samuels." This from Pike on Q's right. "Lay off."

Q liked Pike. He was young, raw, which was why he still had a soul.

Pike yanked the mask above Q's mouth and nose. "Stay quiet, it stays off."

Q took a deep breath of uninhibited air, sat back and shut up.

"Pussy," Samuels shot across Q toward Pike.

"Scab," Pike shot back.

"Shut up," Davis snarled from the driver's seat. "All of you."

Green said nothing.

In the volatile silence that followed, Q thought of Cash out there, headed toward a reunion with his son and sister. He couldn't be happier for his friend. His one and only friend. And at the same time, something unsettling nagged inside him. Questions about his own past—one missing from his memory banks—crept out of the shadows. He didn't allow himself to think about this often, but now he wondered what, exactly, these bloodsuckers had taken from him.

The gravel road gave way to dirt. Q tuned into the sounds around him. More smells. Sensations. All their fucking with his brain had given him advantages even their best scientists didn't know about. His hearing had grown as accurate as an owl's. His sense of smell as keen as a bear's. His eyesight as sharp as a raptor's.

They had developed other abilities within him. Paranormal abilities. But those were a mystery to Q. He only knew about them because he'd overheard them talking.

He often wondered if the woman in his dreams came to him because of those powers. He'd never interacted with her, never been ordered or asked to interact. And if one of his powers was to bring her to him, he sucked at it. His dreams of her always began in watery distortion, like viewing a scene through a rainy window, only becoming progressively clearer as the dream went on until he was left watching her sleep in clear, crisp Technicolor.

Technicolor. Q made a quick search of his mind, but found no reference for the word, and tucked it away in the mystery file.

Just the thought of watching his gorgeous redhead fast asleep warmed him. Relaxed him. Filled in all those empty spaces inside him with contentment. Which was the main reason he didn't think those dreams were one of the sick fucks' imposed abilities—because seeing her made him happy. But also because he remembered every dream.

Every moment with her. And when Gorin tested him, whatever he used to put Q under wiped out his memory upon waking.

And he desperately wanted to find a way to bring his beauty back.

If he focused and took advantage of this rare opportunity with his captors, maybe he could learn something that would help. Plus, minimal security equaled maximum possibility for escape. The stars had aligned, giving karma the perfect chance to kick some ass.

The car slowed and Q tightened every muscle in preparation. Of what, he had no idea. He was working completely on the fly here. But with no past to remember and no freedom in his future, he had nothing to live for. And with nothing to live for, he had absolutely nothing to lose.

He picked up the scent of salt through the air vents and grew restless to feel the direction of the wind, to listen for animals, vehicles, planes, voices. Anything to give him a better feel for their new location. Nearing Salt Lake—definitely. But how close to the city?

"I have to take a piss," he said.

"Keep your dick on," Ice Man Green growled from the front seat.

"He speaks," Q said. "Thought you'd had a coronary."

"You wish."

"Hell, yes."

The engine cut out and all four doors clicked open. Q sucked in the air—dry, hot, salt-laden. And thin. They were in the mountains of Utah above Salt Lake.

"What's this place? Not one of your rat labs. I've been to them all."

Facts about the Salt Lake area clicked through his mind. There was no government testing facility that he knew of in this area, so unless they were going to use some private laboratory they'd cooked up like Colombian drug runners . . .

His mind took one of those bizarre hairpin turns, the ones it made whenever he stumbled upon information he had no way of knowing, but did. And the endless questions followed: Was he from Colombia? Had he worked in Colombia? Did he have relatives in Colombia? How did he know Colombia had a drug problem? Why did the phrase "Colombian drug runners" roll off his tongue?

And the questions were inevitably followed by doubt. What kind of man would know such people? Who was he to be so well acquainted with such behavior? Had he harmed others in his involvement with or knowledge of these people?

Ultimately, all the questions boiled down to one: Was this information leaking into his conscious from his stolen past or his hidden present?

That uncomfortable ripple up the back of his neck continued over his skull. The scars there caused the skin to stretch unevenly and pain burned across each thin, raised line.

Q pushed the useless musings away. He'd save those for the long hours he spent alone, caged—or, if he succeeded in the next few moments, running. To make that happen, he forced his mind to the present.

Pike hooked a hand around Q's bicep and pulled him across the bench seat. The other three started toward a building several yards away. He knew the structure was there by the way sound traveled around it, by the way the atmosphere felt denser in that direction. Sure enough, their feet pounded up wooden steps, then strolled along a deck and inside over wooden floors. He detected no other presence—no other voices, no other movement, no other body heat. They were alone. As for technology, he sensed no fences, no all-terrain vehicles, no helicopters, not even a garage on site. He heard no buzz of high-tech security systems, no electrified boundary, no listening devices, no satellite dishes, not even a damn two-way radio system.

No props—aside from the weapons, of course.

Now, Q let a smile tip his mouth.

It was one against four.

His best odds ever.

"I really have to piss." Q kept his voice low so the others wouldn't hear. "Come on, Pike, just show me a tree."

"Can't you wait?"

"They're going to take forever to case the house." And every moment lessened Q's chances.

The nearly inaudible swoosh of Pike's skin against his shirt meant he was contemplating the request as he turned his attention toward the house. Pike let out a frustrated breath just before his feet crunched mulch. He pushed Q toward a thick copse of trees—pines by the density, size and scent.

"Make it quick," Pike said. "I don't need Green chomping on my ass."

Q pulled the bag off his face, let it rest on his forehead. He didn't want to toss it to the ground and snap the filament of Pike's good will. He squinted, allowing his eyes to make the adjustment. He'd been right—pines. But they were interspersed with aspens. The round gold leaves of the thinner, white-trunked deciduous trees shimmered in the hot fall air. The sight of them pulled at something inside him. He walked toward the copse, wondering if the natural beauty he so rarely experienced at the concrete prison and industrial testing sites caused this longing in his chest or if it was something else.

Reaching out, he fingered one of the beautiful leaves and found it surprisingly soft and supple. Nothing sparked in his mind. But nothing ever did. The only way he'd ever learn anything about himself was to get away from these people.

Without moving his head, Q surveyed the area, gaze keen, hearing perked. One small cabin-style structure sat on the secluded property, covered in trees as far as Q could see—which was damn far. A hawk screeched overhead. Something small rooted nearby. By the distance they'd traveled on dirt and gravel roads, Q guessed he was two hundred miles from any type of civilization.

Didn't matter. He didn't need civilization. He'd been jailed in a ten-by-ten concrete box forever, exposed only to Gorin, the psycho scientists' assistants, Castle guards and Cash—his lifeline for the last three of Q's unknown number of years at the Castle.

Please get Cash to his family.

Q let the prayer float out to the universe as he unbuttoned his jeans with his left hand, leaving his weaker arm in the sling he always wore. He hadn't needed the aid for months, but the guards didn't know that. Gorin still thought he'd permanently disabled Q's entire right side. It was weak, yes, but not completely worthless.

In his peripheral vision, Q saw Pike look back at the cabin, hands on hips, sport coat pushed back, revealing the standard-issue Glock nine in his belt holster.

The sight of the weapon made something click in Q's mind. As quick as he shut down his emotions, something else clicked off, too. Something he couldn't explain or describe or even understand, but internally, he went cool, hard and sharp.

Now or never.

Before the thought had dissipated, Q was moving. He pivoted, raised his good elbow and whacked Pike in the cheekbone.

Q shifted within time and space until he had a strange sense of being slightly removed from his body . . . yet, not. Pike's head jerked sideways, eyes closed, spittle flying, arms flailing. Q felt himself reach out. Felt the butt of the weapon in his hand. Felt his bicep tense and jerk the weapon from Pike's holster.

For an extended instant, Q stood over the unconscious Pike, gun in hand. The steel-cast stranger inside Q tensed his finger on the trigger. If the man lying at his feet had been any of the other three, Q would have let whatever this instinct was take over. He would have emptied the gun into the bastard's brain. Since it was Pike, Q turned toward the trees and ran.

He stripped the sling from his weaker arm and let the canvas trail behind him. He pushed a swing into his gait to aid his bad leg forward, but it remained as stiff as the tree trunks he dodged. Somewhere beyond this obstacle course of pines, aspens and shrubs a creek trickled. Q ran scenarios through his mind as he moved. Get to the bottom. Follow the creek. Find a hiding spot. Hold out 'til nightfall. Head out again before they brought in dogs. Choppers. Crews.

"Q!" Davis bellowed, still near the structure. "Get your ass back here or you're a dead man."

He was already a dead man. A walking dead man. No past. No future. A present that amounted to existing in a cage, tormented, abused. Used. Escape was his only chance at life.

The mountain air exhilarated his lungs with every breath. The earth underfoot infused him with life. Had he loved the outdoors in his past? Had he hiked, fished, camped as a kid like the stories Cash had told of his childhood? If Q got out, he'd sure as hell give them all a try.

Voices echoed at Q's back as the men dispersed into the forest—Davis in the lead. Pike somewhere behind and to Davis's right. Samuels three hundred yards to Davis's left.

But Green . . . Q heard nothing from Green. No threats. No footsteps. No breathing.

Q's bad knee buckled and he hit a tree with his lousy shoulder. Pain stabbed his arm. He gritted his teeth against the need to cry out. Chest heaving, determination renewed, Q lunged forward.

The crunch of a boot on the forest floor behind him sounded a split-second before a crack landed on his skull and a jolt of heat seared his brain.

He hit the ground on his injured shoulder. Rolled to his stomach. Pulled a knee under him. Before he could push off again, that boot smashed his spine. He hit the dirt face first, took a mouthful of mulch and turned his head to spit. That's when he saw the gun centimeters from his cheekbone.

"Do it," Q rasped through harsh pants. "*Do it,* you sorry sonofabitch. Fucking shoot me already. *Shoot me!*"

"I'll shoot you, asshole."

Green put something between his teeth. Pulled it out with a soft *pop.* A geyser of panic erupted in Q's chest. *No, no, no.* He pushed and twisted against Green's boot, a rock in Q's back.

Green's arm swung down. The needle stabbed into the muscle of Q's bicep. And the sedative—that fucking sedative signaling his torture was about to begin all over again—burned through every tissue.

The idea of reaching his fiery redheaded beauty again faded along with his consciousness.

FOUR

Jessica stepped back and something crackled. She looked down and found dirt, twigs and pine needles carpeting a forest floor beneath her bare feet.

"No," she whispered. "This isn't real."

She'd worn sandals to the office and kicked them off as soon as she'd walked in the door. Plush carpet had snuggled against her feet just seconds ago. But the prickly stab of those pine needles wasn't her imagination.

The blinding light faded and other objects in the distance came into focus—a small house straight ahead. A car parked to the right. More trees in every direction. And above her, towering mountains.

"What the . . . How . . . ?" Her mind scrambled to understand. The coin tingled against her skin and she looked down, remembering Teague pressing it into her hand.

Anger nudged her fear aside. "That bastard." He'd known if this coin had been Quaid's, she would feel something. See something. "Bet he didn't expect this."

Hell, she hadn't even expected this. Whatever *this* was.

She scanned the area for an escape. Trees. Nothing but trees. She needed a way out, but the shimmering light that had accompanied her here was gone, and instinct told her the door leading back to her office had closed.

"I can't believe you let him take your gun, Pike." A disgusted voice cut through the silence. Fire launched through Jessica's stomach, and she jerked that direction. "If I don't find it, I'm gonna let Q stuff mine in your mouth."

They call him Q. Keira's words filtered through her memory and confirmed Jessica's worst fear—she'd gone and somehow freaking transported to Q's location. She ground her teeth as some small part of her psyche laughed at her and whispered, *I told you not to get near those doorways.*

A man stepped out onto the porch. Dressed in black slacks, a white button-down and a crimson tie pulled loose at his neck, he looked fortyish and fit. He unbuttoned one cuff and rolled it up his forearm, then the other. The handle of a gun rose from the holster at his waist.

Jessica sucked in a breath and froze while her mind spun for some excuse for her sudden appearance in the middle of nowhere. He put his hands on his hips and frowned down at her where she stood.

"I . . . Hi. I . . . I was . . . camping nearby." Words spilled from her mouth before she thought them through. "And . . . and . . . I must have gotten lost. . . ." *Right, wearing no shoes. Brilliant.* "But I'm sure my family is right nearby . . . if I could just . . . um, use your phone . . . ?"

The man looked up, scanned the tree line and muttered, "Such an idiot."

He jogged down the cabin's narrow front steps, heading directly toward Jessica with a brisk, purposeful stride. She cringed, tried to sidestep, but his left side collided with hers. Yet . . . didn't. And he continued past. The entire left side of her body sizzled like a shaken bottle of soda, as if he'd *passed through her.*

Holy shit . . .

"I hope that dipshit gets canned for this," he muttered, stalking away as if he hadn't seen her. Or felt her. "I'm so fucking sick of that asshole."

Disoriented, Jessica swayed and reached for the stairway railing. The rotted wood snapped, and the crack echoed in the dense silence. She jumped back just as two other men came out on the porch, weapons drawn and aimed in her direction.

"I just . . . was lost and . . ." *can't breathe* ". . . wanted to . . . to use your phone . . ."

"Piece of shit," one of them said. "I'll check Q and the back. You look around out here."

Body bunched with tension, Jessica held her breath, waiting for them to *see* her. The first man headed back inside. The other jogged down the steps.

Jessica gasped, tensed. But he strode right freaking past her, too.

Her heart rate shot up. Her adrenaline surged. *Oooo-kay.* She'd experienced some weird stuff in her life, but this topped it all.

She was *so* killing Teague when . . . if . . . she ever made it back there.

She stuffed the coin in her jeans pocket, eyed the man's retreating back, then the stairs. Indecision warred. Q was here. Great, she'd found him. Only she hadn't. Not really. Because she didn't know where in the hell she was. And she didn't know how the hell to get back home.

Maybe Q did. But did she want to see who this mysterious Q really was? He had some connection with Quaid, or he wouldn't have had her husband's coin. What she'd told Teague was true—she couldn't allow herself to slide back into that gritty, dark place where she'd hidden from the pain. But nor could she ignore the suffering of another human being. And if there was a man being held prisoner here, that meant some other family was suffering without him, the way Jessica was suffering without Quaid.

No one deserved that kind of pain. Well, except Schaeffer. Schaeffer deserved much worse.

Jessica took a focused breath and studied the stairs again. Lifting her foot, she tested the wood to see if she'd slide through like a ghost, or if it would snap like the railing had. When neither happened, she hurried into the house and quickly checked rooms as she passed.

The space was small and dark and dank. Musty as if it had been closed up for years. A flimsy table set up with cards and poker chips sat in the middle of the living room. She passed a tiny kitchen, an ancient bath. At the end of a short hall, she paused to glance into a small, empty bedroom.

Dim light filtered through the trees, barely illuminating the gray space. A dirty, tattered mattress lay on the floor in a corner—

Jessica's breath stuttered to a stop. The room was *not* empty. A man lay on the mattress. He was turned toward the wall, one arm cuffed to a metal ring bolted into the wall above his head, the other thrown over his eyes.

An icy chill washed Jessica's body, freezing her in place for a moment. Her gaze darted down an adjacent hall. It was empty, but men's voices sounded just beyond.

"Hey," she whispered to the prisoner from the doorway, keeping an eye on the hall. "Can you hear me?"

When he didn't move, she slipped inside the room and dropped to her knees beside the mattress, taking him in with a panicked glance. His dark hair was cut military close. A bizarre techno pattern of short, linear scars covered his scalp. Bruises and scrapes in various stages of healing marred the arm covering his face. His jeans and plain gray T-shirt hung loose over a malnourished frame.

They're testing him, experimenting on him in a program Dargan is managing for Schaeffer.

"Those damn animals," she whispered, then leaned over him and caught a confusing whiff of mixed scents—both stale and crisp. "Hey, wake up."

He didn't respond. Didn't move.

Shit. She stared at a blotchy bruise on his muscled bicep. The other men had passed through her. She probably couldn't touch him to wake him, but . . .

She brought her index finger down on the purple edge of his bruise—and met solid flesh. *Yes!* She gripped his arm and shook him lightly. "Hey, Q, you gotta wake up."

Still no response. She shook harder. Tried to lift his arm, but it was dead weight, so she checked his pulse instead. Slow. Weak.

Footsteps sounded and Jessica turned. A man filled the doorway. She fell back on her butt and scooted away, but he seemed oblivious to her presence. He was older than the others, his face stern, eyes cold and completely emotionless.

He stalked into the room, kicked the unconscious man's foot hard enough to shake his whole body. Jessica watched for a reaction, but the man didn't wake.

"He's still out," the older man called as he turned from the room. "I gave him a shitload of that tranquilizer. He'll be out for hours."

Jessica's shoulders sagged. "Shit."

Now what? She squeezed her eyes shut and rubbed them with her palms, letting her head rest there a moment while considering her options. It didn't take long—there weren't many. She had to find a doorway and go back. Maybe . . . maybe she could somehow take him back with her.

As if I know how this whole freaky doorway thing works.

Jessica lifted her head and stared at the man's shoulder blades stretching his cotton tee. It was worth a try. Not a lot to lose at this point.

She drew up close beside him and pulled the coin from her pocket. Rising up on her knees, she leaned in to speak near his ear. The very warm scent of a man's skin rose through a thin veil of soap. He was the crispy half of the smell she'd caught earlier. Lemon . . . Spice . . . For his condition and surroundings, she hadn't expected him to smell so . . . well, good. It had been a long time since she'd enjoyed the scent of a man's skin. Jessica closed her eyes and breathed him in. Oh, yes, he had one of those scents that made a woman want to burrow her face in his neck, snuggle naked under the covers, wear his clothes. . . .

We believe this man is Quaid, Jessica.

No. Her eyes popped open and she leaned away, her stomach fluttering. So he smelled clean. So what? She could look at this man's size, his build, and know this wasn't Quaid. Her husband had been heavily muscular, thick in his chest, arms and thighs. He'd lifted weights and easily retained mass. This man's smaller frame couldn't begin to hold that amount of muscle.

A futile and far-too-familiar brew of anger and loss tightened her chest. She didn't understand how her closest friends could have even *voiced* such a wicked possibility as Quaid still being alive.

She curled her fingers around Q's wrist and held tight. With the other hand, she tilted the coin toward the small window, trying to catch a sliver of daylight to open a doorway.

"Come on, baby," she murmured to the coin. "Bring us home."

The man shifted on the mattress. The movement pulled at the cuff on his wrist and muscles flexed through his arm, rolling beneath the cotton. She reassessed the sinew in his forearms and biceps. Maybe she'd mistaken extreme fitness for malnutrition.

Her gaze traveled from his bicep to his face, and the sight of his jawline, now exposed, shot a tingle of awareness across her chest. Before her mind had time to wander to places it didn't belong, he yanked at the cuff again.

"Shhhh." She leaned close, her mouth just inches from his ear, her gaze darting toward the door. "They'll hear you."

A noise rumbled from his throat, and he turned his head in a languid, sleepy way that swept familiar currents through Jessica's belly. His eyelids fluttered and his head turned toward her voice. When his dark eyes found hers through that thick screen of lashes, Jessica's whole world slid sideways.

Velvet brown eyes. Sexy. Molten.

We believe this man is Quaid.

Self-protection raised a barrier on her thoughts to keep out the *what ifs*. Hope pounded against that barrier, searching for a miracle. While all Jessica could do was stare.

His lashes lifted a little more, and Jessica's stomach caught in her throat. "Oh . . . oh, my God."

She sat back to get a full view of his face. Took his head in both hands and turned it toward her, so she could see his features all at once. One side of his face was scraped and raw, the cuts still harboring dirt.

No, this isn't Quaid.

Wait . . .

No.

But . . .

She scoured his face, forehead to chin, over and over, trying to convince herself, one way or the other. He didn't have Quaid's nose. And there was something different about his mouth. The set of his jaw was wrong. But, damn, those eyes just sucker punched her.

His face was just as handsome, rugged, sexy and well-proportioned as Quaid's had once been, but also . . . a little too off to be Quaid.

They say everyone has a twin somewhere. But what were the chances Quaid's twin would be here?

Nil.

She refocused on his eyes, and the breath left her lungs in a quiet swoosh. How many times had she dreamed of looking into his eyes again? Millions. It had to have been millions.

This isn't reality. You're not really here. This man's eyes look like Quaid's because you want them to look like Quaid's.

And she did. God help her, she did. She so badly wanted these eyes to be Quaid's she would have sold her soul to the Devil. Which was exactly why she'd told Teague and Keira she couldn't do this.

"Shit . . ." Her voice shook as her logical mind tried to make sense of what she saw even if her heart was ready to leap at the one-in-a-billion chance.

Then he smiled. Or tried to around the cuts. His lips curved and his deep brown eyes glinted beneath those heavy lashes . . . and . . . Jesus, Mary and Joseph . . . that was *her* Quaid in those grinning eyes.

"Haven't . . ." He licked dry lips. "Seen you in so long." His voice was rusty, not altogether different, but not familiar either.

He rolled toward her, and the chain above his head clanked. She lunged to grab the metal and keep it quiet. The move pressed her body against his and an instant, deep hit of tingling awareness penetrated everywhere they touched. His free arm curved around her hips and his sultry hum lit off fireworks throughout her body. He turned and pulled her into him until her breasts were snug against his chest. He kept his head tilted back, his eyes on her face with an expression of awe and pleasure and affection. But he was obviously a little gone, because he showed no fear, as if her presence didn't pose a threat to them both.

"You have to be quiet." Her breaths came quickly—

because of the fear, she told herself, not the way her body heated being pressed against him.

"I miss seeing you." His lazy gaze slid down her throat, lower to her chest and rested on her breasts. She knew that look. The hungry one. The one that made her skin tighten and her nipples harden. Like now. "Why were you gone so long?"

Confusion. Desperation. Suggestion. That's what this was about. Because if this was truly Quaid, those comments didn't make sense.

"Look at me." She lifted his chin. When those brown eyes were on hers again, she just pushed out the words before she couldn't. "Who am I?"

His smile grew wider. His lids grew heavier. The man was half drugged out of his mind. This was a ridiculous effort. Then his arm tightened around her, drawing her closer. "Woman of my dreams."

She frowned. This was crazy. She was starting to believe *she'd* gone crazy. Or she was about to. Those eyes had to be a fantasy. A trick of the mind. Something she saw because she so desperately wanted Quaid. Or because she so desperately didn't want this to be just another dream where she would wake up to the stone-cold reality that her husband was in the grave and she'd never touch him again.

"Who's with you?"

His whisper brought her gaze up from full lips surrounded by several days of dark stubble to find his eyes filled with a liquid heat that made her body ache in ways she'd forgotten.

"No one." Which reminded her of what a mess she was in. "It's just me."

"Then . . ." His smile faded. His gaze darted past her, scanned the room, and came back. "Why are you here?"

What kind of question was that? And why the hell *was*

she here? And where the hell was *here*? Her mind wobbled on a razor-thin tightrope wire.

"To find you," she only half-lied. "I came for you."

"You came . . . for me?"

The astonishment in his voice, the surprise in his eyes, made guilt resurface for having refused Keira and Teague. "Yes."

"I've waited so long to hear you say that."

The sexy timbre of his voice was still caressing her when he lifted his head and pressed his lips to hers. Jessica pulled back, an instinctive move made out of confusion. But his hand slid up her spine and cupped her head. And his lips moved over hers, firm and warm and oh, just . . . so . . . right.

His lids fell closed, and those long lashes lay just millimeters from her own. Her brain clouded. Her body softened. A fresh undercurrent of power flowed between them, sending adrenaline to her heart and energy to every cell in her body.

His kisses lengthened, deepened, until his lips caressed and suckled hers as if he were exploring them for the first time. And like waking from a deep, refreshing sleep, everything inside Jessica lifted, stretched and filled. Each press, pull or slide of his mouth erased a shadow from her past.

A sound floated from her throat, one of pain and loss, disbelief and hope. She tried to remember if Quaid had ever kissed her so perfectly when the slow sweep of his tongue along her lips stole her breath. Then he tilted his head, opened his mouth on a groan and fully tasted her.

And she knew.

This was her husband. This was Quaid.

Jessica whimpered, tightened her arms around his neck and kissed him hard and deep while a tidal wave of emotion flooded her chest. She couldn't stop, couldn't let go, couldn't open her eyes for fear he'd evaporate into the mist of a fading dream. Nor was she able to conceive what she'd done to him by believing he'd been dead all these years. Guilt and pain and fear prowled like starved beasts waiting to attack, but she had to do whatever it took to remain strong long enough to get Quaid out of here. Then she could feel all she had to feel. Deal with all she had to deal with. Then she could spend the rest of her life making it up to him.

When she broke for air, Quaid's dark eyes burned with lust beneath heavy lids. His lips were wet, his mouth open and ready for more. He breathed hard, his muscles straining as he pulled against the restraint to bring her closer. "I knew you'd taste amazing."

"Don't talk." She pressed her fingers against his lips. His words were messing with her head, and she needed to stay focused. "You're not making sense right now. It's the drugs. I just want to get you out of here and then we can talk, straighten everything out. Oh, *my God.*" All those emotions crashed in another heavy wave. She took his face in both hands and pressed her forehead to his. "Then we can be together forever. I won't ever leave you again."

He grinned—all straight, white teeth and uneven crescents curving deep on either side of his mouth. *Her* Quaid. She'd never forget his grin as long as she lived. Her heart blossomed, so big, so beautiful, she was sure her ribs would crack.

"I knew it would be like this with us," he whispered before taking her mouth again with vital, life-affirming passion.

She was completely lost in Quaid when he turned his head sharply, breaking the kiss.

"What the fuck are you doing awake?" Another man's voice came from the direction of the door.

The man lifted his foot and kicked out. A tingling rush zipped through Jessica's whole body as his boot passed through her. She gripped Quaid tighter, trying to protect him, but the boot hit his chest, dead center, as if she weren't even there. He jerked hard and flew back against the wall.

"Quaid!" She reached for him. The coin flew from her hand, hit the wall and rolled across the floor.

The man stood over Quaid, where he'd slumped onto the mattress, coughing and wheezing.

"No!" She froze, torn between going after the man and saving the coin. Deciding she couldn't harm the man, she scrambled for the coin. On hands and knees she crawled and lunged just as the thin metal dropped into a gap between warped floorboards. She pulled at it with her fingers, but it had wedged itself into the tiny space.

"Shit." She pried at the metal, dug at the wood, grasped the coin's edge. It wiggled but didn't come free.

Quaid coughed, then groaned. She glanced over her shoulder in time to see him roll to his side and fall still.

"I'm here, Quaid. I'm right here. Hang on, baby. I'm going to get us—"

The big man kicked Quaid again. Jessica screamed. Dropping back on her heels, she covered her mouth with both hands, unable to breathe.

Quaid groaned again. Jessica let out the air she'd been holding. Relief eased the sting of terror, but rage grew in its wake. She was going to kill that man—she didn't care who he was. She was going to find him, hunt him down and kill him when this was over. But she had to get Quaid out first. She went back to work on the coin.

The man rolled Quaid onto his back and pressed his boot to his sternum. "You know what I think, Q? I think you're just more goddamned trouble than you're worth."

Pain chewed at Jessica's fingers and still she couldn't get the coin loose. The scene flickered. Chaotic horizontal static patterns blocked her vision.

"No, no, no!" she screamed and pulled harder at the coin. Complete static overtook the scene just as her body went weightless. "No!"

FIVE

"No, no, no . . ." Jessica choked out the words and rubbed the coin like a genie lamp, even though she knew that's not how it worked.

Her throat burned from screaming. Her mind turned inside out. The gapped wooden floor of the cabin had transformed back into the dove-gray commercial carpet of her office. The water-stained sheetrock walls back into sleek floor-to-ceiling windows facing the Capitol building.

"Jess, what's wrong?" The voice startled Jessica and she jerked her head in that direction. Keira crouched next to her on the floor. "What happened?"

Jessica stared at Keira, her mind chugging to a stop. She looked up. Around. Her office. She was in her office. Kneeling on the floor. With the coin in her fingers.

Her gaze blurred as her mind struggled to draw a line between fantasy and reality. Tremors overtook her arms, crawled down her back. Pain beat at her temples to the rhythm of her heart.

"Jess?" Teague's big hand pressed against her shoulder from behind. "Honey, are you okay?"

What in the hell . . . ? That couldn't have been merely a vision. Could it? It had all been too vivid. Too *real*. She couldn't have glimpsed Quaid only to have him taken again. That couldn't happen. It just *couldn't*.

"I have to get back," she murmured. "I have to . . ." She pushed to her knees, lifted the coin toward the window and screamed, *"Take me back!"*

"Back where?" Keira's hand squeezed her arm. "Where are you trying to go?"

Jessica didn't answer. She didn't know. God, she didn't know anything anymore.

The coin was dull and the dismal weather outside didn't provide any reflective light. Even the furious desperation whipping up inside her was answered by nothing more than a distant roll of thunder.

"We can't stay here," Teague said to Keira over Jessica's head. "I didn't think it would take this long."

Sweat broke out on Jessica's chest, her face. Her heart thudded against her ribs. She couldn't get enough air. She didn't know what was happening. Her brain wasn't working and it hurt. Her stomach hurt. Everything hurt.

A cramp tore at her stomach, and Jessica doubled over, clutching her belly. She could only stare at the carpet until the twisting pain passed. Her gaze caught on a pill bottle at the foot of her desk. Her mind turned, searching for its identity, and it hit her just as the cramp released and the shakes kicked in. Her Xanax.

And that's when she knew what this was—withdrawal. This was one of those rare, bizarre, phantom withdrawal episodes. She'd had two others since rehab, and even her doctors didn't understand them. But it was as if the mere consideration of taking drugs had corrupted her system into believing she'd actually taken them, then she had to go dry all over again.

"This isn't fair," she moaned, closing her eyes and sinking into a ball. Still, her mind struggled with questions from every angle. Pain built inside her head until she couldn't think. Expanded in her chest until she could barely breathe.

"It's okay, sweetheart," Teague murmured. "I've got you." He dragged her up from the floor and lifted her into his arms. "Easy now, sweetheart."

The movement brought on a wave of nausea. Jessica moaned, squeezed her eyes tight and pressed her mouth against Teague's shoulder.

"One minute," Teague said, "and I'll get you to the car."

Car? She pried her eyes open, but couldn't focus on anything, which made her head swim again.

"Fuck." She clamped her head between her palms and squeezed her eyes tight again. "My head."

"Hold on, sweetheart." He jostled her down stairs. "Just hold on."

"Teague." The splitting sensation grew worse by the second. She'd never experienced this kind of sharp, biting, all-consuming pain. "*Stop,* damn it!"

They passed from dry warmth into freezing rain. Jessica gasped and curled into Teague. The movement sent the pain in her head stabbing down her neck. "I hate you."

"I know," he said. "I'm a prick. Ask anyone."

"He is," Keira said.

"Is your name anyone?" Teague asked. "I think not."

He stepped inside a darkened space and the rain stopped pelting Jessica. Teague eased her into a seat and she forced her eyes open to slits, but everything spun. They were in the back of a vehicle; that much she knew.

"What's happening to me?" She couldn't clearly remember why Keira and Teague were there.

"We'll talk in a second." Teague leaned over and pulled a seatbelt across her body. "Let me get your head settled first."

The engine rumbled and they started moving.

"Teague," Keira said from the front, "brace her. I've got two shadows I need to lose."

Groaning, Jessica fisted her wet hair and planted her elbows on her knees. There was no way she could handle a swerving car right now.

"Come here." Teague gripped her shoulders and turned her toward him.

He sandwiched her knees between his, then pried her hands away from her head. An instant later, his big palms and long fingers covered her skull. Warmth instantly penetrated her head. And like an eraser, Teague's touch wiped out the torment, calmed overzealous nerves and relaxed bunched muscles. Blood rushed into her head, opening constricted vessels and feeding her brain.

The jostle of the vehicle as Keira braked, turned, gunned it, swerved and then did it all over and over again didn't cause even a ripple of discomfort. Without Teague, Jessica would have been curled on the floor, puking.

She didn't understand how Teague was able to heal with his hands, but she'd heard about the positive thermo-kinetic effects from nearly every member of the team, his own wife and daughter included. Now, she appreciated them firsthand.

Chancing a glance through her fingers, she saw Keira in the driver's seat and Teague next to her in the back of an SUV. The relief Teague had brought left her with a migraine-type hangover, but allowed brain cells to connect.

"What just happened?" She stood on the cliff edge of sanity. "Someone might want to start explaining before I go postal."

"Tell us what you saw, Jess," Teague said, his voice soothing, but insistent. "Let's start there."

"Let's start with that sleazy stunt, Teague," Jessica said, her head too heavy to lift from the seat.

He shrugged, but sincere regret showed in his eyes. "It was a last resort, honey. I was desperate."

Desperate people did desperate things. Jessica knew that fact all too well.

"It was still wrong." But she couldn't stay mad about it. She hurt too much—physically, mentally and emotionally. Jessica leaned forward in her seat and rested her head in her hands. "Where are we going?"

"Speaking of sleazy," Teague said with a smirk, "Mitch has a place for us to use as a base camp for the moment."

"Mitch?" She lifted her eyes to Teague's. "As in your brother-in-law Mitch?"

"Is there another Mitch?"

"Not like him, that's for sure," Jessica muttered and returned her stare to the carpeted floor, trying to sort out and prioritize all the main events with a low thud rolling behind her eyes and fragmented memories of the . . . hallucination . . . vision . . . whatever thrumming through her heart. "Why is Mitch here?"

"Because he has abandonment issues," Keira said, "and can't be left out of anything."

Teague laughed. "Save the good ones for when he's around." Then to Jessica, he said, "Mitch is here because he's in this up to his eyeballs, and he's a worrywart about Alyssa's pregnancy, and he"—Teague shrugged and grinned—"can't be left out of anything."

"Thank you," Keira said.

Their banter carried on in one ear, but Jessica's mind drifted. *I knew you'd taste amazing.* The memory of that kiss created an ache down the center of her body. She pressed her fingers to her lips, unsure if they were tingling because of the freezing rain or—

She stopped herself. Looked out the window where droplets darted diagonally along the glass. *This* was reality— the rain-soaked streets of Washington. Teague. Keira. This trouble. Her lips had to be tingling from the rain. Or maybe lack of blood supply to her head, because if she believed she'd actually kissed a real man, let alone her dead husband, she really *did* need that asylum she'd been considering in jest earlier.

Leaning on the armrest, head braced in her hands, she said, "Who are you running from?"

"That's not entirely clear yet," Teague said. "What happened with the coin, Jess?"

She lifted her gaze to his. Held it. Road noise filled the silence for long seconds as Jessica tried to form an answer. She finally exhaled a heavy breath, slid her hands over her face and groaned, "I have no idea."

"Then just tell us what you saw," Keira said.

Jessica sat back and closed her eyes. The weight of hopelessness that always came when she thought of Quaid's loss slowly filled her chest even as she battled it back. This was why she did everything she did—the move, the job change, the drugs, avoiding her abilities—because after coming so far in both life and rehabilitation, she was convinced there was only one thing that could break her: having to face that kind of loss a second time.

But she wouldn't have to face that—because the man she'd seen . . . imagined . . . envisioned . . . had not been Quaid. She could recognize that now in hindsight. And she could even understand why she'd thought—for that blissful moment—it had been.

"One car," she said, closing her eyes to aid the memories. "A few men . . . three, no four . . . wearing dress pants, shirts and ties. They were working together, but arguing like they didn't get along. I saw another man, and he was a prisoner. But before you ask, I can't even believe I'm having to answer this question seriously." She straightened and held up a hand in warning. "No, it wasn't Quaid."

Keira and Teague remained silent. They shared a look in the rearview mirror.

Keira opened her mouth and Jessica cut off her next question with the answer, "Yes, I'm sure."

Jessica glanced out the windshield as Keira turned toward an upscale neighborhood. Teague leaned in and took her hands. "How do you know?"

She pulled away, pushed her hands between her knees, and held tight to her last strand of sanity. "I know because Quaid is dead. I know because I've been living alone for *five years*." She paused, and banked her temper. "The man I saw had a shaved head covered in scars. And he was small. Even if Quaid had lost fifty pounds, he'd still be a big guy.

"His nose was too straight, his chin and cheeks too square—" She shook her head, the prisoner's image flitting out of her memory when she tried too hard to recall. "His face . . . it just . . . was all wrong. Damn it, I would have recognized my own husband."

"He's been gone a long time, Jess," Teague said. "I know my memories of Suzannah started to fade as early as six months. By the time she'd been gone a year, I had to look at a photograph to remember the details, the unique things that made her Suzannah."

Jessica couldn't remember the last time Teague had spoken of his former wife. Suzannah's depression-induced suicide would always be a deep wound for him, which made his mention of her now especially unsettling.

Keira glanced in the review mirror, meeting Jessica's gaze before saying, "You told me you hadn't looked at a photo of Quaid—"

"In four years. No, I haven't. It's too painful." She wouldn't be able to hold her temper much longer. Or the pain already tearing at her heart. "And what about *him* not recognizing *me*? Do you have an excuse for that, too? Because he didn't know who the hell I was. Why do I feel like I should be tied to a chair under a spotlight? I'm not the one acting crazy here."

Keira and Teague fell silent, and Jessica's mind drifted right back to that cabin.

I miss seeing you. Why were you gone so long?

The more Jessica thought about it, the more surreal the memories became. She had scryed a time or two early on, when she'd been developing her abilities, but whatever she'd done today had not been scrying. And she'd never interacted with others when she'd scryed. But that man had seen her, engaged with her.

Or she'd been hallucinating.

Judging by the dryness of her mouth, the uncontrollable trembling that came and went and the deep craving for a hit, Jessica leaned toward the explanation of withdrawal-induced hallucination. This felt a lot like withdrawal to her and that wasn't something a person forgot.

The car slowed, then stopped.

"Did you leave your body, Jess?"

The seriousness of Keira's voice even more than the crazy question pulled Jessica's head up. Keira stared over her shoulder at Jess from the driver's seat. A red traffic light shone through the rain-splashed windshield behind her.

"Did I . . . *what*?" Quick bursts of sensation, like sparkles, flashed through her body, making her feel light and dizzy, like she'd suddenly experienced a head rush.

"You looked like you . . ." Teague started. "It's hard to explain, but it was like you were gone and your body was a place holder. There's a power called astral projection—"

"Holy shit, Teague." Jessica leaned away like he might be contagious. "Like I don't have enough to deal with?"

"Okay, you're right," Teague said in his ever-patient voice. "Listen, Jess, there is a lot we need to tell you, but you're going to have to keep an open and clear mind to hear it, and it's important stuff."

"Fine." Jessica sat back in her seat and crossed her arms, her gaze intent on Teague even though she was exhausted and wanted nothing more than to close her eyes and fade into oblivion. "I'm ready."

"Incoming!"

The Marine's yell brought Owen Young's gaze up from his path of charred concrete chunks and twisted rebar. An Army Black Hawk floated overhead with another bundle of supplies wrapped like a cocoon and swaying at the end of a rope.

Owen squinted and held his hard hat down as the chopper's rotors whipped the air. The supplies hit the ground with an earthshaking thud, the rope snapped free and the Black Hawk angled back into the blue Nevada sky, just starting to peek through the spiraling pillars of smoke.

His eyes burned and watered, but he'd stopped paying attention long ago. He was numb. At least for now. As soon as night fell without word of Jocelyn or they had to suspend the search because of the site's instability or . . . God, forbid, they found her body . . . then he would be in deep-ass shit. Which was why he couldn't think of that now. He had to continue to hope. And search.

Military personnel crawled over the new supplies like ants on a sugar cube, and Owen continued his slow trek over the rubble, looking for signs of life. Or death. He would find Joce. Until he did, he held onto the words she'd spoken to him on the phone just hours ago. *"I want to talk to you when this is all over. About what you said the other night. About wanting you. I do."*

He'd been waiting a long time to hear those words from her. Now, after finally hearing them, she'd gone and gotten blown to hell? Could fate be that cruel?

He knew damn well it could. He knew damn well it was, more often than not.

But he hoped like hell this time fate had taken pity on him.

The dismal thought brought his gaze up and over the vast devastation again. The one-hundred-thousand-square-foot, four-story, state-of-the-art military laboratory was now a fifty-foot crater in the desert floor. Military firefighters poured water on still-burning sections and dug through debris for hot spots. Military investigators pored over every inch of rubble and ash. Military personnel provided aid in every fathomable facet at the site from medical care to administration. All military. *Only* military.

Something big was going on here, but nobody would talk. He still didn't know why in hell Jocelyn would have been here, but he'd been told half a dozen different times from half a dozen different sources she was here immediately before the disaster.

Owen didn't know of any business she'd have to warrant a site visit to a place like this—one of the darkest government testing facilities in the country, complete with experiments utilizing human subjects.

Decades-old images from a village halfway across the globe floated from a dark corner of Owen's mind. Men, women, children, even babies with their open wounds oozing puss and exposing bone. Their cries of agony tore through his head. All that pain, suffering and loss of life to shortcut the strict drug trial laws within the U.S.

"Colonel Young!"

Owen startled at his name. His vision sharpened as if he'd just woken and he wondered for a dizzy second if he'd fallen asleep on his feet.

"Colonel!" the man called again. He waved from fifty yards away where he stood beside a crane dragging cement pilings off a mountain of rubble. "We've got a survivor here."

"Yes," he murmured. "Yes, yes, yes . . ."

He picked his way over cement blocks, broken glass and rebar prongs until he was at the rescuer's side, peering into the newly discovered darkness. Holding his breath, Owen crouched at the mouth of the cavernous space, and shone a flashlight inside.

Come on, Joce. Be here, baby. Be here.

His beam joined the others shining into the hole from rescue workers rimming the opening, waiting for the okay to go in. Down in the rubble, something moved.

"There." Owen pointed directly below him, and the light beams followed, illuminating a dust-covered hand. To the right, he spotted the top of a head, the hair caked with ash. "Right there!"

Owen pocketed the flashlight, yanked off one glove, dropped to his stomach and stretched out over the edge of the hole.

"You can't go in there," someone above yelled. "It's not stabilized. The whole thing could cave in if you—"

"Screw stabilized, someone's alive in there. Grab my legs."

Two strong pairs of hands gripped his calves. He dropped the top half of his body into the hole and stretched for the victim's hand. But it had stopped moving and Owen couldn't reach it on his own.

"We're here," he yelled. "My hand is right above you. Reach for me and I'll pull you out."

Movement. Just the fingers at first.

"Come on. I'm right here. Just a little more."

The victim—*please let it be Joce*—finally seemed to get the idea. The arm pushed through the rubble and the hand gripped Owen's.

In that second, he knew it wasn't Joce. The hand was too big. Too rough. Too strong.

A sob of disappointment choked him, but he put all his energy and focus into the survivor and dragged him upward. As the rock fell away, the head and torso of an older man appeared. He blinked, squinted, and choked on ash and debris. Several men ran off in search of stabilizing equipment and first aid.

"Take it easy," Owen said, his voice too shaky for reassurance. "Nice easy breaths. We're going to get you out. Just stay still."

The man sputtered, took in the chaos surrounding him and panicked. He gulped air as if he were drowning, clawed at the rock still surrounding two-thirds of his body and tried to scream, but the sounds came out as guttural scrapes. His movement shifted the already-unstable rock walls.

"Stop!" Owen yelled, his command voice automatically emerging for the situation and the man froze. Owen forced his voice down. "You're making it worse. Hold still and talk to me while the crews bring equipment."

The man's eyes flicked toward Owen. "O—Okay."

"What's your name?"

"D—Dawes. Com—mander Kenneth Dawes."

"Commander, are you hurt?"

"I . . . I can't feel my legs."

"Do you remember what happened?"

Dawes's eyes had taken on that glassy look of shock. He didn't answer.

Owen squeezed the man's hand to hold his attention. "There was a very important member of the Department of Defense here. A woman. Tall, blond, beautiful. You couldn't have missed her." He swallowed, his throat dry in anticipation. "Deputy Director—"

"Jocelyn Dargan," Dawes said before Owen could. "She was here."

Fuck.

"Where? *Where* did you see her? *Where* is Dargan? Was she here? Near you?"

"She was, but . . . then . . ." Dawes's eyes closed, his head fell sideways. Owen yanked on his arm again and the man perked up. "Then she went back to the cells . . . the prisoners' cells. Wanted to take another look for something. Missing . . . a key . . . Needed it . . . Thought O'Shay . . . thought O'Shay . . ."

"Thought O'Shay *what?*"

". . . had it."

"Why was she here?" Owen asked.

Dawes coughed. Wheezed. "Wants his formula. The one he's been working on for the last year."

The man's ash-covered eyelids slid closed. This time when Owen tried to rouse him, Dawes didn't respond.

Owen dropped the man's hand and let the other rescue workers take over. He pushed to his feet, this new information rolling around in his brain—key, formula, cells, O'Shay—but none of it made sense.

He glanced around the site, spotted a man with a yellow helmet and floor plans rolled out on the bed of a truck and ran toward him.

He hit the side of the truck full force. "We found Commander Dawes. He said Director Dargan was headed back to the cells to look for something. I want you to get rescue crews to that area immediately, start a full-scale search—"

"Colonel." The man's expression suddenly registered with Owen. He'd seen it before—on the battlefield. He reflexively tightened his gut for the hit. The man turned and gestured toward the lowest part of the crater, where everything had been pounded deep into the earth and incinerated. "That's where the cells were located."

Owen's stomach dropped. His knees went out, and he had to hold onto the truck to remain standing.

When Owen didn't respond, the man said, "We've got rescue teams in every area of the site, sir. The deputy director is our top priority."

Owen nodded, got his legs under him and wandered away. His mind circled and circled for his next plan of action, but couldn't land. He'd seen this type of controlled chaos so many times—but that had always been during war. After senseless slaughters, misaimed bombs, a rebel insurgent attack. He'd always been prepared. And Jocelyn had always been by his side. Never under the rubble.

The thought of her slim, fragile body beneath all that jagged, harsh material pushed a sound of anguish into his throat. He forced the idea from his mind. She was strong. More than that, she was tough. If Dawes could survive, Joce could survive.

Another Black Hawk set down at the edge of the main carnage. A young Air Force sergeant climbed out and spoke with a member of the ground crew, who pointed in Owen's direction.

Goddamnit. He knew they'd come for him, but it was too soon. He wasn't ready to take over Jocelyn's work. To give up searching. To give up hope.

His pain brought up anger. Which quickly rallied rage. Fury toward the fuckers who'd done this. Who'd stolen his golden opportunity to be with Jocelyn. And by the time the sergeant had jogged the distance and stood in front of him, saluting, Owen was ready to hunt the bastards down.

"Colonel, sir," the sergeant said. "I've been assigned to escort you to the airstrip at Area 51. A C10 is waiting to take you to the Pentagon."

Q could do this. If he'd brought her to him once, he could do it again. He sure as hell had never needed her as much as he did right now.

His face throbbed. His chest ached. His belly screamed. Green had beaten him just short of killing him. The animal would never give Q the reward of death.

In this case, Q hoped the pain would be a gift, because it pulled him from the void of unconsciousness just enough to use his mind. Or at least try.

Remembering her was easy. He swore he could still feel her mouth on his. That kiss had been amazing. Absolutely amazing. Whatever he'd experienced with her had definitely been different from seeing her in his dreams. In his dreams, he never touched her, never smelled her. In his dreams, visions of her dissipated over time. But today, he'd had all of her, and she'd been crystal clear . . . right up to the moment Green had nailed him in the chest.

Fiery hatred bubbled up from deep inside him. Q didn't waste energy on anger; it never served him. But this was an involuntary rage that coiled hot in his belly when he remembered her panic. If he'd been able to speak, he would have told her he'd be fine. Not to worry. But Green had stolen his air on the first kick, and then she'd vanished.

Q could still see her, on her knees, searching for something on the floor. Could hear her screaming . . .

The sound tore at him. His thoughts hazed. Images faded. He fought the pull of darkness and dragged his mind backwards in time, to the moment he'd first opened his eyes and seen her. She'd been holding . . . Something shiny. Gold.

A coin.

He envisioned her there, sitting beside him, tilting the coin toward the window. God, she was more beautiful every time he saw her. Her deep red hair long and shiny over her shoulders. The skin of her face so creamy and perfect with that little spray of barely-there freckles across her nose. Her lips . . . His mind transitioned from the sight of them to the feel of them as she'd kissed him. Pleasure and relief replaced the tension in his body and he drifted. . . .

No. No, he wanted to remember. To bring her back.

"Bring us home."

Her soft, sweet voice filled his head. He focused in on the coin again until the gold disk filled his mind. The surface blurred. Then shimmered like a reflection on the water.

Control over the direction of his thoughts slipped away. When the shimmering reflection stilled, Q stared at many coins, not one. And he wasn't envisioning anymore, he was seeing. A box of *real* coins in shades of silver and gold and bronze sat on the ground in front of him where he knelt on sandy earth beneath harsh sunlight.

Q tensed. His mind scavenged for traction. He was fully conscious. Fully in control of his mind again. If he could call this *in control,* because he didn't know what the hell was happening.

He did know he was no longer at the safe house. No longer restrained. And he knew this was not an illusion or a dream. He didn't know *how* he knew, but he had no doubt that this new . . . situation . . . was reality.

External sensations hit him—hot, dry air and sweltering sun on his skin, the scent of oil, gasoline, gunpowder and sweat, the sound of angry voices.

"It's about fucking time." One of those angry voices shot toward Q from behind. "What the hell is going on with you? You can't go disappearing anytime you fucking feel like it."

Everything inside Q clicked on. He pulled his gaze from the coins and looked over his shoulder toward the voice. A man stood twenty feet away. He held an M90 assault rifle on a group of six young men, dark hair, dark eyes, dark skin. They stood with their backs to a crude canvas structure, hands up.

Q took a quick survey of the camp. Small, temporary, apparently deserted but for the men standing at gunpoint.

"Q?" The man holding the weapon called to him. "Come on, man. What's going on?"

Q stood and turned, squinting from the strength of the sun. His ribs groaned. His head swam. Sweat broke out across his body. "I . . . don't know."

But he recognized the new weight on his shoulders as his burden of responsibility to this man. He was Q's partner. They were in the desert. Judging by the desolation, the sandy soil, the bare mountains, and the dark look of the men, it was a Middle Eastern desert.

"Those fucking sons of bitches." His partner wiped a hand over his wet face. He wore a tan T-shirt turned brown with sweat, desert fatigue pants and boots. "What are they doing? They know I need you. Do they want these weapons or not?"

Q started toward his partner . . . he knew his name, but couldn't remember. Nearing, Q studied his face—strong features, gray eyes, short brown hair, but not as short as Q's. No scars on his head like Q. "Where . . . are we?"

His partner stared, his eyes like stone. Then a slow smile turned up one side of his mouth, but there was no humor in the expression, only irony. He shook his head and looked at the six hostages again. "Fucking beautiful. The first time I get within choking distance of Gorin, I'm gonna—"

"Gorin?" Q took another quick look in every direction. "This is another test? I've never been tested with anyone else before."

When he refocused on his partner, the man was looking at Q with more pity than anger. His partner's shoulders sagged. He glanced down at the ground, shook his head. Wiped his forehead again. "This is not a damn test, Q."

One of the men, the one on the end of the line closest to Q, moved. Barely. Just a shift of weight. But the sound of the sandy ground moving beneath his foot raked across Q's brain. When the man broke from the line, darting toward the darkness of the nearest tent, Q was already on the balls of his feet, and took off after him.

Q had the back of the man's shirt gripped in his fist before he ever reached the shade of the tent. Q was already anticipating attack when the man twisted and kicked out. Threw punches, elbows. Q reacted without forethought. Without afterthought. Dodged the blows and hit back. One fist to the nose. One to the gut. One to the jaw.

The guy went down, sending up a puff of sand.

Q stood over him, shaking out his punching hand, holding his aching ribs with the other arm. Breathing hard. "Shit, that hurt."

"At least you're still good for something." His partner, Q still couldn't remember his name, or what they were partners in, sounded defeated. "Gorin didn't send you, did he?"

Q didn't know what that meant. "What makes you say that?"

"You're still in civvies."

Q recognized the term for civilian clothes and glanced down at himself. Gray tee, worn jeans, bare feet. Bare feet on hot earth. The burn suddenly registered and Q moved into the shade of a tent.

"How are you getting here if he's not—?" His partner squinted, his gaze suddenly intense. He seemed to forget the prisoners for a moment, lowering his weapon to take two steps toward Q. But raised it again when one of the men shifted. "Wait. Do you . . . have control over that now, man?" He spoke like he was sharing a secret. "'Cause you gotta tell me how to do it."

"I don't know what I'm doing. I don't know where I am." He glanced around. "I know . . . I should be here with you, but . . . I can't remember who you are."

That tiny flicker of hope Q had seen in his partner's eyes drained and his hard, gray expression returned. He darted a look at the prisoner, still unconscious on the ground, then refocused on Q. "Well, you may as well be of use for as long as you're here."

His partner pulled the strap of a second M90 over his shoulder and tossed the rifle to Q. He caught it in one hand, positioning the trigger beneath his finger without ever looking directly at the weapon. It felt good in his hand. It felt right. Even when Q knew this whole setup was very wrong.

"Take his shoes," his partner said. "And help me move all the weapons and food into one tent. If I'm lucky, we can finish this mission before you disappear again."

Six

Jessica glanced out the SUV's window toward the top of the luxury condos, some twenty stories high while Keira punched the security code into the gate for the underground parking structure. Above the modern building, the sky remained broody and gray, spitting rain flurries, but the lightning, thunder and wind had mostly disappeared.

"This is a pricey building," Jessica said. "Condos start at a million dollars. But you always told me Mitch runs with a unique crowd."

"Heh." Teague smirked toward the rearview mirror where Keira met his gaze. "That's a creative way to put it."

"I don't recall ever using the word *unique*." Keira paused just inside the gate and both she and Teague took keen interest in watching the gate close all the way to the cement.

Keira's intensity remained on high as they continued through the lot of mostly luxury vehicles. She lifted the lid on the center console, pulled out a semiautomatic and laid it on her thigh. And the way her gaze swept every shadow of the subterranean lot made Jessica's shoulders tighten and hunch.

"What are you expecting to happen in a secure parking structure?" Jessica found herself whispering and felt stupid. This whole situation seemed so melodramatic.

"You know enclosed spaces make me jumpy," she murmured as she backed into a parking spot with cement walls on two sides.

She turned off the vehicle, rolled down her window and leaned toward it, listening. When only silence filled the space, Keira released her seat belt and turned sideways so she had a good view of Jessica.

"We can talk here for a few minutes. Then we'll head up."

"Why not just go up?" Jessica asked.

"It's busy up there," Teague said. "We can't talk about some of this in front of the kids."

"Kids? What k—?" Her confusion turned to shock. "*Kat's* here? Why is . . . Is *Alyssa* here, too?" She didn't even need an answer. Wherever Teague and Kat went, his wife, Alyssa, went. Alarm crept in. "She should be home, near the hospital where she's going to deliver."

"That's not possible." The stress of that fact showed in the tight lines of Teague's face. "She's fine and she'll tell us if she needs anything. As for Kat, she thinks we're on vacation."

Jessica's rain-soaked clothes suddenly registered cold against her skin and she shivered. Gooseflesh rose in painful sheets across her arms and legs. "I feel like I'm on a roller coaster. You know I hate roller coasters."

"Teague," Keira said, "grab her a jacket from the back."

Teague pulled a navy blue parka from the cargo space, clicked Jessica's seatbelt loose and dragged the jacket around her shoulders. But nothing would warm her now. Alyssa and Kat and this new baby meant everything to Teague. For him to put them at risk meant none of this was at all haphazard on his part. Which meant this was all very real because no one on the team would support Teague putting Alyssa, Kat or the baby at risk.

"Okay—" She stuffed her arms into the jacket and pulled it tight around her. "I'm officially, completely, totally *freaked out*."

Keira let out a heavy breath and leaned forward, resting her elbows on the seat's armrest. "We'll condense this for you, Jess. You don't need to know all the gritty details right now, just what will keep you grounded, informed and safe. The rest will come in time."

Jessica fisted her hands in the arms of her jacket and nodded.

"I have a brother," Keira said. "That's who we went into the lab to rescue. My brother."

"A *what*?" Jessica searched her memory for this information, but it was absent. "You never told me about a brother."

"I thought he'd died in a house fire when I was five. Turns out, he'd run away to escape our abusive mother. How we found each other is a story for later. What I want you to know is that he's the one who told us about the other prisoner, the man he's known all these years as Q. We tried to get Q out of the lab, too, but his cell was empty. When we went through his things, we found the coin."

Jessica's barriers went up and she sat back. "I thought this was about you and the team. I've already told you—"

"Let me finish," Keira said, firm, but compassionate. "There's a lot to get through."

Jessica pulled her lips between her teeth and forced herself to keep quiet.

"A week ago, I went to retrieve a child in what I'd been told was abduction by the non-custodial parent. In the end, it was another twisted attempt by Dargan's team to manipulate our powers. They wanted access to this boy who turned out to be my nephew, which was how I discovered my brother was alive."

Keira paused and all Jessica could do was shake her head. She heard Keira, trusted Keira, yet found it difficult to assimilate all this bizarre information. "Why did they want the boy?"

"He's gifted, like us."

Jessica's mouth dropped open. "But how? Our powers came by chemical exposure not heredity."

"That's a little more complicated," Teague said.

"I just wanted to explain that much," Keira said, "because my brother and nephew are upstairs, too, so you'll meet them."

Jessica blew out a breath, already uncomfortable with the idea of reuniting with her entire team. But just as Jessica loved Alyssa and Mitch because they were Teague's family, she would love Keira's brother and nephew.

"There's something I want you to consider, Jessica." By the serious tone of Keira's voice, Jessica could already tell she wasn't interested in considering. "When you think back to the man at the cabin, and compare him to what you remember of Quaid, take into consideration that Quaid was thrown against a cement wall at hundreds of miles per hour. Nearly every bone in his body was shattered."

Jessica sucked in a sharp breath. Her words brought back a vivid and horrific memory and pain burst at the center of her body.

"We all have some ability to heal ourselves," Keira said, "so Quaid would have, too. But his injuries were so extensive he might not have been able to heal himself perfectly. It's important for you to rethink whether or not that man could have been Quaid."

Keira climbed out and shut the door. Heavy silence followed.

"She's just trying to—" Teague started.

"What? What *exactly*, Teague? Convince me that my husband *hasn't* been dead for five years?" Jessica clenched her teeth around the need to lash out. "I know how much you all loved Quaid. I know how badly his death hurt all of you. I can even understand, considering all the bizarre things that have happened to us, entertaining this crazy notion. Hope springs eternal, right?"

She reached for his hand, then met his eyes again. "You just have to be able to understand why I can't join in, Teague. To do that, I'd have to believe it was possible. To believe something so *im*possible would be setting myself up for relapse. I can barely face the calendar as it is. I wouldn't survive reviving a hope that would only bring back that loss." She searched his eyes. "Do you understand what I'm telling you?"

"I do." His clear blue gaze never left hers. "So, think of it this way: There is a man being held prisoner and tortured by these sick fucks. He's a human being, he's important to Keira's brother and he deserves his freedom just like we deserve ours. If we could find him and get him back but didn't at least try, we wouldn't be able to live with ourselves."

Jessica squeezed Teague's hand and nodded. They understood each other. That was something.

When she opened the door, she found Keira waiting, gaze scanning the parking lot, weapon held tight to her thigh.

Silence filled the cherrywood-and-mirror-lined elevator for the ascent of the first several floors and Jessica tried to remember the man from the cabin. But her mind was so full, his image had faded and she gave up.

"Everyone is here," Teague said, "except Seth. He's doing some research and will catch up with us when he can."

Jessica lifted a brow at Keira. "How's your reunion with the—and I quote—'pissant-asshole-arrogant-sonofabitch Luke,' going?"

To Jessica's surprise, Keira's mouth kicked up at one corner. She shared a look with Teague before saying, "Better than expected."

A burst of hope, an emotion Jessica hadn't felt in a long time, tingled in her chest. "What does that mean?"

The elevator doors slid open on floor sixteen and before Keira answered, Mitch stepped in front of the elevator.

He wore a black button-down open over a white wife-beater and faded jeans. His feet were bare. He would have looked urbanely stylish and handsome if he hadn't been carrying a semiautomatic, with every knuckle on that hand scraped and raw.

"Looks like you have matching cuts," Jessica said, taking in the slash on his temple, the few scrapes coloring his opposite cheekbone.

"Told you," Keira said, passing Mitch with a light jab to his stomach, "he can't be left out of anything."

"I'd love to be left out," Mitch called after her as she followed Teague down the hallway of plush fawn carpet, cherry walls and alcove lighting. "But some people who *can't count* keep calling me with urgent requests like, 'Can you trace Keira's phone? And, yeah, one more thing, I need a plane *and* a pilot.' "

"*Pffffft.*" Keira dismissed him with an absent wave of her hand. "Whatever you gotta tell yourself, Foster."

When Mitch's gaze returned to Jessica, he was grinning that perfect my-parents-spent-a-fortune-on-braces-as-a-kid smile. "Finally, we meet in person. I should have known you'd be just as much trouble as the rest of them."

She didn't like the implication that this trouble had anything to do with her, but smiled anyway. "Good to know I still fit in."

"Oh," Mitch sighed and swung an arm around her shoulders in a friendly gesture. He walked her toward the open door where Teague and Keira had disappeared. "I'm not so sure that's such a *good* thing."

As they neared, the sound of laughter drifted out. A child's laughter—sweet, light, filled with innocence. Jessica stopped.

Mitch's arm tugged against her shoulders until he realized she'd paused. He eased back and looked down at her. "You just lost two shades of color, Jess."

She pulled in a sharp breath, blew it out. The tightness in her chest remained. "Just . . . need a minute."

"Alone? Or . . . ?"

She darted a look at him, then the door. "I might not make it inside if you leave me alone."

He nodded, leaned against the doorjamb and slid his fingers halfway into his front pockets. His phone rang three different times, but he didn't answer. Just waited. Silently. Patiently. Only this wasn't helping. The more time that passed, the harder it became for Jessica to move her feet forward.

"Kai isn't here," he finally said, his voice low and mellow, "if that's what's making you—"

"No. I mean it is, but not really."

Another peal of laughter hit her and she flinched, then laughed, the nervous sound making her unease even more obvious. "Guess it's been a while since I've been around kids," she murmured. "Didn't realize . . ."

"That's Mateo," Mitch said. "He's quite a kid. One of those you can't help but love, you know?"

That's what she was afraid of. Which made no sense. She nodded. Took a deep breath and looked at the carpet as she blew it out.

"What's this I hear about you having two shadows following you?" Mitch asked.

"What about it?"

"Everyone else only has one DoD tag-a-long," he said.

A slight smile turned her mouth. "I learned how to lose them early on. I think they had a problem with that."

"Nice to see our tax dollars going to such conscientious employees."

"I thought so."

"Why were you dodging them?" Mitch's amusement shone in his hazel eyes. "Needed an excuse to miss one of those scintillating senate hearings?"

Jessica chuckled. "Hardly. I ditch them when I want to hunt for dirt on Schaeffer. Some people knit, some people geocache, I stalk Schaeffer."

"Yeah?" His dark brows rose. "Get anything good?"

Her amusement faded. "Depends on what you mean by good. I haven't got enough on a man of his standing in Washington to have him investigated or thrown out of office yet. But it is my goal in life."

"It's always good to have a goal. Where do you have your dirt stored?"

"On my laptop."

Mitch's face fell. "Don't tell me your laptop—"

"Is at the office. Yes, it is." Jessica waited, let Mitch grimace and squirm for a moment, then said, "Luckily, I have all my information stored on three different servers with full mirror backup."

Mitch's face registered shock, then slid into a sly grin. "You're clever. I'll bet you've got some dirty dirt in that library."

"Dirty is my favorite kind of dirt. Not worth getting if it's not dirty."

"Agreed." He took her hand and tugged her gently toward the door, then stepped aside so she could go in first. "I knew I'd like you."

She glanced over her shoulder. "You just said you knew I'd be trouble."

"That, too. Let's work on downloading that Schaeffer

stash ASAP. The sooner I get him off our backs, the sooner we can all relax. And I'd really like to have that happen before my nephew decides to pop into the world."

"Agreed."

Mitch put a hand on her shoulder, keeping her from stepping forward. "Do you have any cash with you?"

She shot another look over her shoulder. "Uh . . . no. I don't have anything with me. We left the office kind of fast. Why?"

"Because Alyssa has the swearing jar out." Mitch pointed to a small, nondescript jar stuffed with bills sitting on the bar between the kitchen and the dining room. "Just a heads up. And"—he grinned—"it's always good to know where I can go to borrow some cash."

Jessica patted Mitch's hand with a smile. "Thanks for the warning."

Her chat with Mitch had distracted her from her anxiety and she walked into the white marble foyer, feeling stronger.

The vastness of the apartment struck her first. But after a second glance, she realized the space was quite small, and the white furniture, carpet and walls along with floor-to-ceiling windows looking out over the rainy city gave the living space its airy feel.

"Wow," she said, glancing over her shoulder at Mitch. "Your friend must not have kids."

Mitch grinned and shook his head, closing and locking the door behind her.

"Jessica," Alyssa's voice called from somewhere around a corner and Jessica's nerves eased a little. "Don't make me pry this huge belly off the sofa."

Mitch put a hand on her shoulder and guided her a few more steps into the apartment. "Make yourself at home."

Then he started for the kitchen, where she could see Keira. Jessica turned the other way toward Alyssa, who had no trouble getting up and giving her a long, tight hug despite her big belly. A web of emotions spun inside Jessica and tears filled her eyes.

When she leaned back and looked down at Alyssa's belly, Jessica had to wipe her eyes, and a fresh wave of concern hit her. "You're so big. You really shouldn't be here, Lys."

"Two strikes right out of the gate," she said and wiped at more of Jessica's escaped tears. "Watch your step, Jess."

When Alyssa moved aside, Jessica's gaze fell on a man who could only have been Keira's brother. He had the same black hair and striking blue eyes. Tall and fit, he was an attractive man, and he held an adorable little boy in his arms. His son hadn't taken after the O'Shay side of the family. Olive skinned, with a headful of endless golden-tipped brown curls, he had brown eyes and a little toothy smile that made Jessica's heart feel uncomfortably gooey.

"Jess," Alyssa said, "this is Cash, Keira's brother, and his son, Mateo."

Cash smiled, but he seemed preoccupied and Jessica had the uncomfortable sensation of being studied. She was probably guilty of the same curiosity. This was a man who'd been rescued from a lab where they experimented on people. He had apparently been this mysterious Q's friend for years. Q, who'd somehow gotten hold of a coin that should have been buried with her husband. And now Cash stood before her, one hundred percent real, which seemed to take the entire situation from an elaborate, twisted tale into the unbelievable-but-possible range. All the holes in her information lit up like floodlights, spurring a million questions. And even more fears.

She stepped forward and offered her hand to Cash. He took it, his grip firm, dry, steady and warm.

"Hi." She released his hand and crossed her arms. "We're not meeting under the best circumstances, but after what you've been through, maybe this doesn't seem so bad." She shrugged. "Welcome to our . . . highly dysfunctional little family."

He gave her an easy, "Thanks."

Her gaze shifted to Mateo. His big brown eyes seemed to absorb everything. "He's five?"

"Yes." Cash didn't take those invasive blue eyes off her. "Six soon."

"Cute." So cute it hurt to look at him. "Is he always this happy?"

"So far."

"Aunt Jessica!" Kat's exuberance made Jessica gasp and jump.

She returned the girl's hugs with her heart beating twice as fast as it should. The next few minutes passed in a blur of Kat's excited chatter about Mateo, her almost-here baby brother and first grade.

Finally, Mitch shepherded both kids toward a corner of the living room stacked with Legos and Jessica settled on the loveseat beside Alyssa. While Teague and Mitch found places among the other sofas and overstuffed chairs, Cash and Keira held a private meeting near the windows. Jessica didn't like the confirming nods from Cash or the way they both looked directly at her when they finished and started toward the group.

Jessica grabbed hold of her paranoia and her emotions and shoved them into a very dark corner. Logic—she needed logic now. Reasoning, decision making and risk assessment skills.

She curled her feet underneath her. "Where are Kai and Luke?"

"They're picking up some supplies," Keira said as she and Cash took chairs across from Jessica. "Okay, stay with me, Jess. This is going to get . . . convoluted to say the least."

"I work with politicians. I can do convoluted."

Keira flashed a grin before growing serious again. She settled back in her chair and met Jessica's gaze. "Like I told you in the car, Mateo is the reason Cash and I found each other again. A member of DARPA, a Russian scientist who'd come to America to advance the DoD's paranormal warfare program, was involved in our team's case after the warehouse explosion. His name was Rostov. He was trying to recreate our abilities with test subjects, but having little success.

"He had a theory about how genetics could add to the success rate, but the DoD wanted a direct approach and Rostov wanted to go off on tangents. They came to an impasse and Rostov left the department to start up his own in-vivo testing site. He bought cheap land in the Nevada desert and covered his activities with the façade of a religious group."

"This is the compound near Las Vegas that caught fire last week?" Jessica asked.

Keira nodded. "Because Rostov had worked on our team's case, he had all our personal information. At that time, Teague and I were the only members of the group who had young relatives carrying our genes. For Teague it was Kat. For me it was Mateo, who I didn't know about, of course. He lived with Cash and his wife, Zoya, in Greece, and Kat lived with Teague and Suzannah in Truckee."

Alyssa, a physician, picked up the medical thread. "Suzannah's suicide was depression induced. Depression has been known to run in families. We think Rostov chose not to take Kat because he wouldn't have wanted the possibility of a genetic disadvantage tainting his experiments."

"Which left Mateo," Keira said. "And to get to him, Rostov . . ." She stopped, swallowed and darted a look toward Cash.

"Rostov," Cash followed through where Keira stumbled, "killed my wife, Zoya, and kidnapped Mateo."

Jessica gasped. "Oh, my God." Horrified by the images popping up in her mind, she couldn't find anything appropriate to say to Cash for his loss. "When?"

"Three years ago," Cash said. "Either Rostov or someone from DARPA would have killed me, too, to keep me from searching for Mateo and uncovering Rostov's history, but Dargan saw my background as a military chemist, and she and Schaeffer decided I was worth more alive. That's how I ended up at the Castle."

She closed her eyes and covered her face with both hands. "Can someone stop this ride? I want to get off."

"I agree, this is getting boring. Let's jump on another." Mitch pushed himself from his chair and sauntered toward the kids. He dropped into a crouch next to Mateo, ruffling the boy's curls. "Hey, little man. Let's play find the hostage."

"Mitch," Alyssa reprimanded. "Sometimes you are so blatantly inappropriate, I don't think you belong in mainstream society."

"That's a matter of opinion." He picked up a few Legos and added a bridge over the moat in Kat's castle. She grinned up at him. "My clients, my lady friends" —he tapped Kat on the nose— "and my niece like me fine."

"Your niece is six, your lady friends want your—" Alyssa stopped abruptly and everyone looked at her.

Mitch grinned, both brows raised.

"Favors," she improvised, making her brother laugh. "And your clients are desperate."

"Your point?" Mitch took Mateo's hand and led him toward the dining room table, an expanse of glass and chrome. Outside, the storm had settled into a gloomy sky and light mist.

"Her point is you need a real life," Keira said.

"You mean one where I actually work for a living instead of covering all your asses? Novel idea." Mitch stopped at the table, where a pile of maps sat in the center, a laptop off to the side with Google Earth already pulled up on the screen. "Then let's find this Q character. The longer that takes, the less chance it will ever happen. And damn it, I've got a pathetic life to live and violent criminals to free. Ain't that right, Creek?"

"Do you ever wonder why we don't invite you up for dinner, Foster?" Teague asked.

Mitch just laughed.

But Jessica wasn't feeling lighthearted. "What are you doing?"

Holding Mateo by the hands, Mitch swung him over the back of the chair and the boy squealed with glee. Once on his feet again, Mateo turned around, every little tooth showing, arms stretched up to Mitch. "'Gain! 'Gain!"

"*A*gain," Mitch said, stressing the "a." Then he turned to Jessica. "Can we have the coin?"

Her chest tightened. *No,* rang in her head. She reached up to find the chain to her locket and slid it through her fingers. It was stupid to feel so possessive of something that had meant nothing to Quaid. Still . . .

"*What* are you *doing*?" she asked again, pointedly pinning Mitch with her gaze.

His eyes, a mysterious but bright mix of amber and moss, darted toward Keira.

Frustration broke through her thinning patience and she dropped her arms and whirled toward Keira.

"Mateo . . ." Keira said, looking at the boy with soft eyes and a reassuring smile, then grew serious and addressed Jessica, "is a remote viewer—someone who can use their mind to see things happening in other places in real time. We just got him back, so we're still learning the full scope of his abilities, but he has a talent for connecting with a location or person through a map. If he can gather enough . . ." she waved her hands as she tried to find the right word "personal energy from someone, he can find them.

"He located Cash at the Castle for us right down to his cell in the basement of the massive structure."

Jessica's breathing had picked up again. Her blood throbbed in her temples. She rubbed her face with both hands. "I feel like I fell down the rabbit hole."

Alyssa grimaced and sucked air between her teeth. "How I hated the movie."

"Wizard of Oz was worse," Keira muttered, arms crossed over her chest. "Damn flying monkeys will haunt me 'til I die."

Mitch heaved a frustrated breath and braced a hand against the chair Mateo stood in. "Shall we stop to take a poll of the most damaging children's movie in history— *Alice in Wonderland* or *Wizard of Oz*? Or did you two want me to get a *real* life?"

"Don't waste your time," Cash said. "*Willy Wonka and the Chocolate Factory* wins hands down. Drowning in chocolate can't be much better than getting sucked under by quicksand."

"Second that," Teague offered.

"Guys." Jessica closed her eyes and pressed at the beat in her temples. "I'm going to snap soon." She pulled the coin from her pocket but didn't hand it over. "If he can use an item to find a person, why didn't you just have him use the coin to find Q earlier and leave me out of it?"

"We did," Keira said. "When he tried to read off the coin alone, he got nothing, like it was empty."

Which was the same sensation Jessica had received when she'd searched for Quaid's essence after his death. A thought that made gooseflesh slide over her arms.

"Then *what* are we doing?" She was growing unable to control her agitation.

"We've learned that we can combine our powers," Keira said, "and we think by combining yours and Mateo's, we could have a shot at finding Q."

Jessica turned the gold metal over and over in her palm. "I don't know what that episode was earlier. It could have been nothing but a hallucination."

"And it could have been a clue to Q's location," Keira said. "We won't know until we work on it some more."

She didn't want to work on anything and closed her hand tighter around the coin. But Teague's concerns over the fate of a tortured man kept Jessica trapped in an impossible situation. "I can't do that again. I can't go back—"

Keira put a hand on her arm. "Mateo will view the location. All you have to do is hold his hand. We're hoping that your previous vision of the property will guide him."

"I've waited so long to hear you say that."

Jessica remembered the joy and affection in Q's eyes. Those beautiful eyes. If he was real, she wouldn't be surprised to discover his eyes weren't even brown. That she'd just superimposed her memory of Quaid's eyes onto Q's out of sheer desire.

She held the coin out to Mitch and he took it, giving her hand a reassuring squeeze. But it didn't help. She was scared. Scared of what they'd find. Scared of what they wouldn't find.

And that's when she realized, what she'd been fighting to avoid had already happened. By the team simply being who they were and believing what they believed, some part of Jessica had jumped on board, too.

The rain picked up outside and lightning sparked within the charcoal clouds. Jessica crossed her arms and pressed her lips together in determination. It was simply a game of the mind. She'd just have to find a way to adjust her mind to deal with that tiny sliver of herself that would always wish things could have turned out differently.

"That is really cool," Mitch murmured, looking out at the flashing sky, "but in a really creepy sort of way."

Mateo bounced on the chair, his dark eyes sparkling, his face alight with energy. Jessica's polar opposite. He grabbed the coin from Mitch's hand, held his other hand out to Jessica, grinning with the kind of enthusiasm only a child's innocence could produce, and said, "Find Q!"

"I think this kid was born ready." Mitch pried one of Jessica's hands from the crook of her elbow and guided it to Mateo's. "Just visualize the house, Jess. That's all you need to do."

Jessica took the boy's tiny hand in hers. The fingers of her free hand curled into a fist and her lungs shrank, making it difficult to pull in a full breath. She closed her eyes— not because she needed to, but because she couldn't stand seeing everyone stare at her. They all went silent, except for Mateo. He murmured something in Greek and held Jessica's hand so tightly, sweat formed where their palms met.

After about two minutes, he let go of her hand. "No work."

Jessica blew out a relieved breath and opened her eyes, only to find Mateo reaching for her again. With a determined frown pulling his brows and puckering his cupid lips, he pushed the coin into Jessica's hand. Then he covered it with his, sandwiching the metal between their palms.

As soon as he turned his attention back to the map, heat flowed up Jessica's arm. Mateo bounced on his toes and pointed to the United States. "There."

Mitch pulled a bigger map of the U.S. from the pile and set it on top. The current grew stronger and heated Jessica's whole body. The boy pointed to Utah. *Utah?* And Mitch changed the maps again. The room grew warm. Stifling.

"Doing good, little man," Mitch said.

Jessica's heart thumped against her ribs, as annoying as someone popping gum in her ear.

Haven't seen you in so long. Who's with you? Why are you here?

She would say he'd mistaken her for someone else, but that would be admitting that she'd really seen and heard and felt everything she swore had been a vision. For him to have seen her, she had to have been there. To have been there . . . something really freaking crazy had to have happened with her powers.

"Q is here!" Mateo's excited cry brought Jessica's attention to the map—and to the way a cold film of sweat had developed over her face, neck and chest.

His palm lay flat over Salt Lake. Cash was already at the laptop, pulling up the area on Google Earth.

"Good job, buddy." Mitch patted the boy's head and looked over at Jessica. "I really need you to focus here. This is where it counts."

She came out of a trancelike fog she hadn't realized she'd fallen into. An enlarged map of Utah lay on the table now, all the elevations marked in thin lines. Her head felt dizzy enough to spin off her body. And the ripping fear she'd suffered when she thought she was leaving that cabin without Quaid grabbed her by the ribs.

"I . . . I . . . don't . . ." She put a hand to her chest. Panic crawled up her throat. Lightning flashed beyond the window, full, thick bolts piercing the sky, followed by the thrum of thunder. "I . . . can't . . . breathe."

Teague appeared in front of her. He put his open hands on either side of her head. His touch melted the anxiety like warm honey over ice. Her muscles relaxed. Her lungs expanded. The nausea slowly dissipated.

"You're okay," he whispered. "I know this is hard, but we're right here. Better?"

She took a few deep breaths, then nodded. Teague stepped aside. Jessica didn't close her eyes this time, fearing the darkness would bring back the vertigo. Instead, she tried for that hundred yard stare where everything blurred into a monotone waterscape.

She visualized the forest surrounding the cabin, the break in the trees where the building stood, the porch. She didn't let her mind go inside the house, but remembered the part of the floor plan she knew—the living room, hallway, kitchen, bathroom, bedroom. . . .

You came for me? I've waited so long to hear you say that.

"Q!" Mateo yelled, jerking Jessica from the confusing memory. "Q is here."

Mateo's little finger traced a ridgeline along Salt Lake. Cash roamed the area with Google Earth, a barren wilderness where nothing but acre after acre of forest filled the screen.

"There," Mitch said. "Go back."

Cash manipulated the computer to Mitch's instructions until a little structure filled the center of the screen. The same silver metal roofing. The same blue sedan sitting out front. Jessica squinted. Even the same porch railing.

"That's it," she said, voice shaky. "That's the house."

She hadn't imagined it. She hadn't imagined the man inside.

"Oh, my God," Jessica whispered, pressing the fingers of her hands together, then to her lips. If she hadn't imagined the house, she hadn't imagined the man. "Oh, my God."

No. That didn't mean anything. Okay, the man was there, but he was *not* Quaid. *He was not.* She'd buried her husband. She'd lived without him for five excruciating years.

And even as she continued to deny the whitewashed memories from the cabin, Jessica also recognized that sliver of hope hiding in the shadows. And she had no idea how she'd protect that fragile part of herself from the disappointment of finding another man, and not Quaid, in that house.

"Good work, my man!" Mitch touched buttons on his phone and raised it to his ear while he swung his other arm around Mateo, pulling the boy up and out of the chair.

Mateo squealed and laughed. Mitch carried him into the open living room and turned in circles, swinging the boy as he spoke into the phone. "It's a go. Get the guys to the airstrip. I'll call the pilot."

Fear, pure and hot, smashed Jessica's sternum. "What?" She searched the room of faces. "What do you mean? What guys? What pilot? What are you doing?"

"We're going to get your man, Jess."

The new voice hit her from behind like an unexpected smack on the back, and she gripped the chair in front of her before turning. Kai and Luke stood behind them. Jessica noted Kai's overly excited expression and her whole body tightened with tension. Her gaze skipped to Luke. If Kai looked strung out, Luke looked almost zenlike, the two men a study in opposites.

"Hey, Jess," Luke said with that easy, sexy grin—not at all the demeanor he'd had in the years following his and Keira's breakup. "Lookin' good."

"Luke." Jessica's eyes narrowed. She turned her head and caught Keira grinning at him like a love-struck idiot.

Keira met her eyes, tried to stifle her smile and raised her eyebrows and her shoulders at the same time. "What?"

"You know what." Jessica couldn't hold back a smile even with all the turmoil circling. Keira and Luke were perfect for each other. Jessica was thrilled they'd finally overcome their demons and figured it out. "When did that happen?"

Keira pulled her lower lip between her teeth, darted a look at Luke, then returned her attention to Jessica, unable to keep the smile off her face any longer. "Last week, during, you know . . . this mess."

"I guess meeting up again *did* go better than expected," Jessica said. "Much better."

Jessica looked at Luke, put two fingers to her eyes and pointed at him.

He laughed. Saluted. "I'm on my best behavior."

Bracing internally, Jessica met Kai's eyes. "Kai."

Kai's intense gaze made Jessica feel trapped. His beautiful green irises were so bright, his grin so sharp, he reminded her of a junkie on a high. But she knew Kai wasn't high on drugs. He was high on this insane idea of Quaid being alive.

He advanced on Jessica and took her into a sweeping hug that pulled her off her feet. "He's alive, Jess," Kai said against her hair. "He's *alive*."

Emotions of love, loss, confusion, grief, too many more to name, twisted through her, and she pushed away from him. He put her down and leaned back, his smile so extreme he looked a little crazed. A little like the Batman's Joker.

"Kai, God." She pulled out of his arms, anxiety growing. "This is insane. This is *insane*. Yes, there is a man being held prisoner in this house. Yes, in some ways, he looks like Quaid. But there are more differences than similarities. One coin, a few coincidences and you're all ready to believe Quaid has come back from the dead." An eerie sensation swept over her, and she sought out Cash, then Keira. "Unless you know something I don't. What aren't you telling me?"

"It's not what we're not telling you, Jess," Keira said. "It's what you're allowing yourself to consider. You have all the same pieces we do." She brought up a hand and started ticking off fingers. "The classified chemicals at the fire, our paranormal abilities, Teague's false conviction of murder, DARPA's attempt to duplicate our powers, Mateo's abduction, Mateo's testing, Zoya's murder, Cash's imprisonment."

Keira dropped her hands, but the plea in her eyes implored Jessica to walk off that cliff edge, just as if a dealer were holding out a dime of coke. "I think the real question is: Why *couldn't* Quaid be alive? And if he is, what are we going to do about it?"

SEVEN

The pilot announced their imminent landing at Bolling Air Force Base. Owen straightened and looked out the window, but he didn't see the familiar sights marking his many flights in and out of the base. His mind wrapped around questions. And suspicions. And doubts.

He'd showered the filth off him on the jet and changed into his uniform, but inside his mind and heart the grit created by the carnage he'd witnessed earlier in the day remained. And the flight had given him too much time to worry and wonder about Jocelyn. Too much time to replay her last words to him in his head. And too much time to create theories as to why she'd been at the Castle.

The plane's landing gear rumbled into place and Owen did what he'd done for the last two decades when he needed to focus—he closed off his emotions and operated on logic. At least, it was the best he could do under the circumstances.

A car waited to take him to the Pentagon, and on the drive, Owen thought of the Castle's destruction, the three downed Apaches, the dozens of deaths, the lost years of experimental data, the millions of taxpayer dollars in ruined equipment.

Then, like a ghost, Dawes's words floated into Owen's mind. *"Thought O'Shay stole it."*

Stole the key. The only key Owen could think of was the one in the envelope that had come just last week from Jason Vasser's attorney. Since Jason had left his assets to Jocelyn in his will, Owen could make a fair guess the key probably fit either a building or a safe-deposit box. Stephanie, his secretary, was looking into both possibilities. How O'Shay could have gotten possession of the key . . .

Owen rubbed a hand over his mouth. *Don't go there.*

Of course, he couldn't *not* go there. The idea of Jocelyn having been close enough to O'Shay for him to gain access to something that personal . . .

He didn't even know if it *was* the key from that envelope. That thought helped him put a stop to those torturous thoughts.

But then there was the other little bomb Dawes had dropped. *"Wants O'Shay's formula."*

Owen knew Cash O'Shay was serving out a sentence for treason at the Castle utilizing his genius chemist's brain to benefit the military. How Jocelyn could have possibly had a reason to interact with O'Shay was completely beyond him.

Owen definitely wasn't being told the whole story. Jocelyn had been harboring secrets. Which left him in complete limbo as to what she'd meant by telling Owen she'd wanted him just before the explosion.

"Doesn't matter," he told himself. But it did. How she'd felt about him mattered in ways he couldn't name at the moment. Mattered beyond their romantic relationship.

He wanted answers. He wanted justice. And by the time he walked the long, cold halls of the Pentagon toward the office Schaeffer inhabited as a member of the Armed Forces Committee, Owen was itching to lead a team of Special Forces soldiers toward an assassination of whoever had committed this act of terrorism. And after mulling over the possible culprits for hours on the flight, he'd pretty much narrowed it down to one group.

He entered the outer office and greeted Schaeffer's secretary, a pleasant, middle-aged Asian woman named Cherry.

"Yes, sir." Cherry stood with a friendly smile, smoothed her straight navy skirt and opened the office door for him. "The senator is expecting you."

But Owen wasn't expecting the senator . . . at least not *this* version of the senator.

Gil Schaeffer paced the room. The man never paced. His never-touched, two-hundred-dollar cut was mussed and standing on end. His expensive suit jacket lay crumpled in a heap on a couch and his shirtsleeves were rolled up to the elbows.

Owen slowed his step, donned mental body armor and stood at ease in front of Schaeffer's desk. It took every ounce of patience he still possessed not to open with an attitude-laden, "You rang?" Instead, he waited.

As soon as the secretary closed the door, the older man turned his way. "Any sign of her yet?"

Damn. All Owen's fears surrounding Jocelyn's status slammed against his shields. They held, but only barely. "Not yet, sir."

"All right, then." Schaeffer picked up a stack of files and dropped them on the other side of his desk. "Sit. We have a lot to go over."

Schaeffer squeezed his overfed, under-exercised frame into his desk chair and pulled out a tablet.

Owen eased himself to the edge of the chair across from Schaeffer's desk, already uneasy. "What, exactly, are we going over, sir? I can't stay for an extended amount of time. I have to get back to the site and rejoin the search. And I'm in the middle of a project at DARPA—"

"I've already cleared your current duties with Cox. He's

delegating. As for Jocelyn, if they haven't found her by now, they aren't going to." He waved Owen off with the flick of one hand. "We've got serious damage control to deal with."

Schaeffer's comment about clearing Owen's duties with the director of DARPA, Carter Cox, went right over his head. It was the allusion to Jocelyn's death that hit him in the chest with the force of a sledgehammer. For a moment, Owen couldn't breathe.

"We?" he finally asked.

"Yes, Owen, *we*. You're directly under Jocelyn in the DoD org chart."

Jesus, she hadn't even been confirmed dead, hadn't even been missing more than a few hours, and life was already moving on as if she'd never existed. An eerie chill settled over Owen. What kind of life was that? To be forgotten before your body was even cold?

The kind you lead, dipshit. Who would care if you died?

Not his soon-to-be ex-wife. Hardly his kids. And certainly not the man across the desk. Schaeffer cared about one person—and one person only.

"What do you know about this op?" Schaeffer asked, looking up from beneath manicured salt-and-pepper brows. "And don't bullshit me, Owen. We need to go at this straight up. What has Jocelyn told you about the work at the Castle?"

That chill turned into foreboding and had him positioning his feet to stand, pivot and run. As always, he braced himself for battle instead.

"I'm realizing I had very little knowledge of what Jocelyn was working on. I know nothing about the Castle or the projects there. I only know Cash O'Shay was incarcerated there, working off a sentence of treason. Now, why don't you bypass the bullshit on your end and tell me exactly what the fuck was going on at the Castle that made someone—and not a phantom homegrown terrorist cell—angry enough to want the facility blown into Arizona."

Schaeffer's lips parted in surprise. His gray-brown eyes glazed over. Owen basked in the satisfaction of getting under the asshole's skin until Schaeffer pulled himself together.

He sat back in his chair and regarded Owen with eyes positioned too close together. "You're a smart man, Owen. I expected you to have that figured out by now."

"With what? No one on scene will talk to me. I have no history of the activities at the Castle. Jocelyn obviously wasn't sharing information."

"Make an educated guess."

Okay, so Schaeffer was going to play power games. Owen had come on strong, so Schaeffer needed to take control back. Owen was a pro at these games. He'd mastered them a long time ago. And mastery included knowing when to lose a battle for a better shot at winning the war.

"Considering Jocelyn told the phoenix team about Cash's existence in a power play for his son, I assume the team stormed the Castle to break him out."

"Phoenix team?" Schaeffer asked.

Owen shrugged a shoulder. "Their scars resemble the shape of a phoenix. Jocelyn coined the name."

Schaeffer only nodded.

"What I don't understand," Owen said, "is if they caused this catastrophe, why no one has come out and identified them as the ones responsible for the attack. Or why this homegrown terrorist rumor is floating."

"That's not all you don't know or understand." Schaeffer's arrogant tone grated on him, but Owen let it pass. "This is one time I wish Jocelyn hadn't been so goddamned good at keeping secrets. Now, tell me what you know about the team."

Owen's anger built like steam in a kettle. "They were exposed to classified chemicals in a fire that altered their DNA, resulting in paranormal abilities. One man died. The others recovered from their injuries and all but one left the fire service. All are intelligent and skilled and formidable. I know they have agents assigned to shadow them, to monitor them and their powers as they develop. And I know O'Shay's and Ransom's powers are enhanced when they're together." His gaze dropped to the files. "Sure as hell not enough information to fill all those."

Schaeffer pushed himself from his chair with enough effort to make the spectacle an uncomfortable one to watch, and then paced in front of the windows. "I'll give you the highlights. You take those folders back to your office and get yourself up to speed on the details *tonight*. This is a matter of national security."

Owen's brow fell. National security? Like hell. Who the fuck did this guy think he was talking to? Before Owen let his temper loop a noose around his own neck, Schaeffer said, "The firefighter that supposedly died—"

"Quaid Legend. Jessica Fury's husband."

"—didn't die," Schaeffer finished. "He was the first on scene. The one who got hit with a double dose of the chemicals. Which made him the best research candidate."

Owen stiffened. "The best . . . *what*?"

"He's been housed at the Castle since the incident, his abilities developed and utilized to gather military intel from all over the world—Afghanistan, Iraq, Iran, Syria, North Korea, Hong Kong, China, Egypt. His intel comes in at ninety-eight percent accuracy.

"The recent arrests of eleven al-Qaida-linked terrorists with bombs ready to blow up the Western Diplomats'

Conference? Legend. The Hezbollah cell arrested in Mexico with truckloads of C-4 meant for the Golden Gate Bridge and smuggled into the States through undiscovered tunnels? Legend. Rescue of eight Marines in Afghanistan scheduled for beheading? Legend. Rescue of the Atomic Energy Coalition's CEO from terrorists with plans for a dirty bomb? Every single one of those happened because Legend gave us the intel we needed."

"Holy. Fuck."

Schaeffer glanced over his shoulder at Owen's stunned face. His mouth barely turned, but a condescending smile played at the corners of his eyes. "And those are only a sample of the ops he's been involved in. He's saved an untold number of American lives, both here at home and overseas, civilian and military."

Owen didn't know what to make of this. The information was probably true. The incidents were too high profile for Schaeffer to pull them randomly. He'd know Owen had the clearance to find out if he was telling the truth.

But Schaeffer was painting a rosy picture. Owen had been around too long to forget the flip side of every op. Things no one liked to talk about. Things like how many people died for the information Legend pulled in. Like what Legend did or said to gain access to such sensitive information. Like what else Legend was doing that didn't necessarily benefit the American people, only Schaeffer specifically.

"How?" Owen asked. "How is he performing these miracles from a cell in Nevada?"

Schaeffer turned toward the window and clasped his hands behind this back. "That's classified as need-to-know, colonel."

Owen clenched his teeth. Fine. He'd find out on his own. "So what about him? If he was at the Castle, isn't he dead?"

"He was getting ready for transport to another facility for testing when the chopper hit the lab. We got him out, detoured him to a safe house in the mountains of Utah with a transport team until we get this mess settled."

Owen narrowed his eyes, a hot stream of alert sliding down his chest. "Transport team?"

"Four of our best agents are on him."

Owen waited for more security details, but got nothing. He wasn't sure why he had the inclination to laugh. There was a prisoner out there—a powerful, skilled prisoner—inadequately guarded, and yes, that did make Owen's skin tighten with the urgency to act. But he just sat there with the irony blooming in his chest until he couldn't stem a smile and the shake of his head.

"That's it?" Owen asked.

"What do you mean, 'that's it'?"

"I mean, that's the extent of your security on a high value prisoner?"

Schaeffer thrust his shoulders back. His mouth tightened. "That's why I've called you in, Owen. You're the expert, not me. Take whatever measures you feel necessary to secure him."

"And what budget am I using, sir?"

"The black budget," Schaeffer said.

This was a black op. Fine. Owen had done his share of black ops. But there was something very wrong about this one.

"Does Cox know—"

"No one is in on this unless I say they're in on this." Schaeffer turned on Owen with a gaze so fierce, Owen almost flinched. That would have been a very poorly timed submissive move. "This is a need-to-know operation. Do you understand, colonel?"

This was why Schaeffer had everyone scared shitless of him—he had a frightening ice-cold streak that gained teeth whenever something he wanted was at risk. And a man like Schaeffer didn't waste his time with anger unless he had something important to lose.

"Seems like there's a lot of that going around," Owen said. "You still haven't explained what any of this has to do with the media spreading disinforma—"

He didn't need to finish the leading comment before he saw below the surface of Schaeffer's fury. Owen stood, grateful for the desk between himself and the other man or he'd already have his hands around the bastard's neck. "What do they have on you?"

"It's not just me." Schaeffer's indignant tone only intensified Owen's anger. "There are a lot of important people whose reputations and careers will be damaged if Mitch Foster leaks the information he's got. But the American public will go ape shit if they discover some of the projects going on at DARPA."

He knew about Foster's sketchy documents and photos. "Jocelyn didn't say anything about DARPA's projects being exposed."

"As I said, Jocelyn was an experienced operative. She kept secrets well. Don't think you're an exception to this exposure, Owen. A breach of this magnitude would irreparably damage the DoD's current ability to work in the dark. And your projects are as deep in the devil's lair as the ones taking place at the Castle."

The rumble of vehicle engines cut out. Large, well-tuned engines. Some type of heavy-duty truck, but not industrial. Doors clicked open, whispered closed on another faint click. Boots touched down. Careful. Quiet.

The distant sounds drifted into Q's head as he struggled through layers of consciousness to reach that perfect balance—where he could reach *her,* but not get trapped in that bizarre world where he'd been earlier. But he was fighting a shit-load of drugs and his brain felt like a ping-pong ball in a bucket of water.

Hadn't Gorin used that as a test of some kind once? The thought slipped as his brain sloshed back and forth in his skull. When he managed to part his eyelids, he couldn't see straight or sharp. Couldn't hold a thought more than a few seconds. Couldn't control his mouth to speak. And the ribs Green had broken were mending slower than usual, their creak and moan a distraction all their own.

Whispers met his ears. Disjointed murmurs from a distance. Not the guys. Davis and Daniels played cards in another room. Pike paced out front. Green sat on the back steps, whittling wood with a pocket knife. Those sounds came in as clear as if Q were inside their bodies.

He must be hallucinating. They were too far from civilization for even his hearing to pick up voices.

Q's mind slipped off the thought. Descended into the dark.

". . . *two in the living room, one at the front, one at the back . . .*"

". . . *putting two on each, three on the bad-ass guy at the back . . .*"

". . . *stay low, move fast . . .*"

". . . *grab and go . . .*"

The fragments brushed through his thoughts like a bird's wings, tugging him from the void.

Green must have given him a triple dose of the sedative after *she'd* been here. Q wanted to laugh. He must have been revved. Must have scared Green. Q saw it sometimes, a quick dark flash in the man's eyes—that fear. Curious.

He'd had reason to be plenty revved—she'd *kissed* him. She'd fucking *kissed* him. His mouth wouldn't move, but he felt the smile at the center of his body. The joy. The excitement. And while their first kiss hadn't been anything he'd expected, it had been everything he'd secretly hoped for. Filled with passion, free of gratuitous lust. Because that's how she kissed the others—with a careless, thoughtless, meaningless slide of her mouth.

No. She'd kissed him with purpose. Desire. Emotion. She'd kissed him like she *cared*. He'd tasted it all. And, yeah, he was seriously high and it was possible she hadn't been here at all, but he still thrilled with the realization that he might have found a way to bring her to him instead of having to hang in the shadows and watch her with another man.

Boots shuffled in the mulch. Soft, swift, careful.

"Jess, stay close to me."

A different voice, closer. Familiar? Alarm sizzled along Q's skin. His muscles tightened. At least they would have if he could control them. The fact that he didn't have control over his body, couldn't see, couldn't think, made the apprehension ratchet higher. Which brought him closer to the surface.

He didn't want that. He wanted to relax. Sink deep. Find her again. The thought of being able to bring her to him whenever he needed her was a blissful fantasy. He might even be able to endure the cages he lived in if she was haunting them with him.

No. No, that wasn't right. He couldn't want this for her. But he needed her.

". . . on three . . ."

". . . two, three . . ."

A burst of activity sounded outside. Just outside. Q broke the film of consciousness and his body reacted instinctively. His arm jerked against the restraint. He rolled to his side, but couldn't sit up. Peered through barely open eyes, but saw only darkness.

Think, damn it. Why couldn't he think?

From the front of the house, a grunt was followed by

the quick, hard *smack, smack, smack* of flesh—knuckles to cheek. Then quiet. From the back, far more struggle. The crack of bone. A muffled expression of pain. More struggle. More grunts.

Q smiled. Even with the clear threat looming, he smiled. Whoever was out there had cracked Green's skull. Q knew the distinctive sound because he'd had his own skull cracked. He just hoped the bastard didn't pass out. Hoped he was in a world of hurt. Wished he'd been the one to cause Green's agony.

Q's mind started to fade again. He struggled to hold onto consciousness. He needed to know what was happening. Who knew where they were? Who would risk attacking these guys? Why? How much more danger was Q in now?

The answers hovered like shadows just outside his reach. He grabbed for them, but missed, and kept sinking into the dark quicksand sucking him under.

Q slid back toward consciousness to the sound of splintering wood and shouts. The guys must have gotten into another fight over their card game. They argued a lot. About everything. Maybe Samuels was just bitching at Pike again for letting Q get his gun.

That's all the work his mind could do before his semiconsciousness slid slowly back toward that abyss. Q let himself drop into the coldness, keeping warm inside with thoughts of *her*—the fiery, red-haired beauty. He replayed her words like music: *I came for you.*

Outside the lacy black veil shielding Q's mind, doors slammed, furniture toppled, footsteps echoed on the wood floors. Alarm resurfaced, but Q couldn't sustain it more than three seconds. Behind his closed lids, tiny streams of light bounced around the room. *Flashlight* flickered through his mind.

"That's him." The voice. There. Right there next to

him. One he recognized instantly, a blend of sweet and strong and, tonight, scared.

She was back. *She was back.* He'd done it. Excitement tingled through his body. He pooled all his strength to hold himself there, in that state where she could reach him.

Light hit his face. He wanted to wince, to put his hand up and shield his eyes, but his limbs wouldn't obey his mind. He didn't blame them. His mind was seriously fucked up.

"My God," she said, her voice wavering and rising. "What did they do to him? He didn't look like that when I left. The blood, the cuts, that bruising . . . none of that was there."

Her voice grew closer until she had to be kneeling beside him. And, oh, yeah, he could smell her now. Why hadn't he noticed her scent before? So . . . delicious. He didn't have words to describe it, only thoughts like beautiful, safe, peace, warm, happy. Everything. Her scent was his *everything*.

Q used all his strength, but couldn't pull his eyes open. Tried to form words with his mouth. Had to speak. Had to keep her close.

"I'm . . . here," he managed to whisper. "Don't . . . go."

"We're not going anywhere without you, buddy."

The male voice hit Q like a hammer. Fear pounded through his heart. His body reacted as if it was a separate entity, as if it had a mind and soul of its own. His free arm swung up. The man ducked, but Q's body anticipated and twisted. He caught the side of the man's neck in the crook of his elbow, wrapped his forearm around his throat and yanked upward.

The fucker turned his head and escaped a broken neck. This would take longer than he expected. He didn't want her here. Didn't want her to see. Didn't want her in danger.

"Get . . . out, girl," he rasped. "Run. Hide. I'll . . . find . . . you."

But she wasn't listening. "No, stop. Let him go. You have to let him go. We're here to help you."

The man bent Q's wrist back and loosened the hold enough to speak. "Q, it's me—Cash. It's Cash."

Q froze. Something happened inside him, a strange fusing of mind and body. The strength that had come out of nowhere slowly drained. His hold on the man slipped.

"That's it," the man said. "I told you I'd come back for you, buddy. It's okay now. The four guards are down. It's just us."

Cash.

"Cash?"

Q's chest surged with excitement and relief, but also fear. If it was Cash, Q could be rescued. But if it was Cash, Q would fall out of this place where she could reach him. But it didn't seem he had any choice, because he'd returned to that place where his body was worthless and his mind slushy. He slumped back to the mattress, boneless.

"Q?" Big hands grabbed Q's face. "Come on, man. I'm here. Look at me, buddy, it's Cash."

Another, harder slap on his face brought a sting. A flash of anger gave Q enough strength to open his eyes. A man filled his wavering vision. Camouflage paint. At first, that's all Q could see—a face covered in green and brown patterns surrounding bright blue eyes.

"Blue . . . eyes?" he slurred. "Not . . . what I . . . expected."

Cash laughed. Q knew that laugh and the sound washed him with a combination of warmth and disappointment. He wasn't alone anymore, but he'd lost her.

"That's it." Cash jostled him. "Come on, Q. We gotta get you out of here."

"She's . . . here, Cash." He pushed the words through his throat. His cement lids closed. If he left here, would she be able to find him? "Saw . . . her . . . The woman . . . in my dreams . . . Want to . . . stay with her."

"She's still here," Cash said. "Jessica, come here. Her name is Jessica, isn't that pretty? Do you remember the name, Q? Jessica. Does it feel familiar?"

Q smiled. He wasn't sure if his mouth turned, but inside he was smiling. Jessica. Yes, that was beautiful. It fit her perfectly. "Jessica." It felt good in his mouth, on his lips and tongue. And he wanted to kiss her again. So badly. "Jessica."

"I'm right here," she said from somewhere behind Cash, her voice unsteady, as filled with emotion as her kiss.

He loved that voice. He wanted to tell her how sweet it sounded. Wanted to tell her to keep talking. Never stop talking. The other men never let her talk. Never wanted to listen. They only wanted her body. Q wanted *her*. All of her. He didn't know why. Only knew it was right. Perfect.

"Jess-ca." His words slurred again. He was going under. "Don' go."

Cash moved from Q's side and messed with the metal around his wrist. Swore. Then Jessica's hand pressed against Q's chest, the heat of her body by his side.

"I'm right here." She put her cheek against his and whispered in his ear, "Right here. We're taking you home."

Joy and relief and about ten other emotions he couldn't name swelled up inside him. His eyes grew wet behind his closed lids.

"Do you remember me?" she asked, emotion choking her voice. "Do you know who I am?"

"Woman . . . of my . . . dreams . . ."

A loud clank sounded overhead and his arm dropped. Her hands left him.

"All right, buddy," Cash said. "I hope you haven't been packing on the pounds at this resort because I'm going to be lugging you out of here. Can you put your arm around my shoulders?"

"Drugged," Q slurred.

"Yeah, I figured that out."

Q tried to laugh. "Genius."

Cash pulled him into a quick, fierce hug. Gratitude flooded Q. What he'd done to earn a friend like Cash he didn't know. "Thank . . . you."

Cash smacked one hard thud on Q's back with a murmured, "Love you, man." Then he hefted Q over his shoulder.

EIGHT

Jessica worried her locket between her fingers as she left the dingy, musky cabin behind for fresh mountain air. But she didn't feel any relief. In fact, as unbelievable as it seemed, her heart and mind were even more twisted than when she'd entered.

Her heart had skipped two full beats when she'd heard him utter the words, *"Want to stay with her."* Yet, he still didn't know her. On the flight here, Cash had explained all about the loss of his memory prior to his time at the Castle. She shouldn't have been surprised that he didn't recognize her as anyone other than just what Cash had described—a woman he'd dreamt about.

What she hadn't realized until now, watching Q hang like a limp doll from Cash's shoulder as they descended the back steps, was just how deeply she'd been hoping something about this visit to the cabin would be different.

"Choppers inbound," Teague called from the forest line. "Get your asses in gear."

Cash stopped at the base of the stairs, waited until she was beside him and turned to her, his arm tight around Q's legs. "Well? What do you think?"

Her mind zinged in ten directions. Her heart broke in a dozen different ways. The night seemed so much darker than it had going in. So much colder. The black hollow beneath the trees seemed more like a wormhole and less like a path to safety.

"About what?"

He gestured to Q with a *what the hell do you mean what?* look on his face shining in the flashlight's side beams. "Him. Q. Does he look any more like Quaid to you this time around?"

She opened her mouth, but the tightness in her chest choked her answer. She was already crushed; she didn't want to smash everyone else's hopes right now, especially not with so much turmoil still ahead of them. That could wait, couldn't it?

"I don't . . . can't . . . It's dark. He's covered in cuts and bruises and blood. . . ."

And, no, he still didn't look any more like Quaid or sound any more like Quaid than he had the first time. Yet, there was still something about him that pulled at her heart. The smell of his skin, those damn eyes, the sentiment behind his words . . . Or maybe it was just his situation.

She didn't know anything anymore.

"Is there a problem?" Keira stood three yards away, shining her flashlight at their feet. She looked like one of those anime warriors, her features harsh in the flashlight's reflection. Dressed in fatigues, decorated in camo paint like the rest of them, Keira carried three weapons, one over her shoulder, one strapped to her thigh and one in her hand.

"Come on, Cash. I'm starting to think you were lying about Special Forces. Grab and go means *grab and go*. Sort out all the other shit later. Don't you hear those choppers?"

Jessica cleared enough crap from her head to tune into

the sounds around her. In the distance the metallic whap of blades set off the burn of panic.

"Looks like you're in for a run tonight," Cash said, already headed for the trees. "Move, Jess."

She dropped her locket and pushed her legs forward. The run to their waiting trucks was a blur, her mind occupied with incredibly random thoughts inappropriate for the moment and the situation. How could she simply return to her work like nothing had ever happened? Where would this Q go? What would the team do now? What had Q been through? How had he gotten Quaid's coin? What would this do to her rehab? She was already showing about eight of the ten warning signs of relapse. She already craved the taste of coke in the back of her throat. She would claw someone's eyes out for a soothing shot of heroin.

"I'm so screwed." Her whisper vanished in the swoosh of passing air.

Voices, then shouts came from the direction of the house and echoed through the trees.

Fear exploded at the center of her body and burned into her limbs. She increased her speed. Keira stayed close to her and Cash. Teague and Luke flanked them several yards out. Mitch, Kai and the four soldiers Mitch had rummaged up from God only knew where were ahead and behind them. Jessica was damn sure she'd never run this fast. Hoped she'd never have to again.

"Took them . . . long enough . . ."—Mitch said between pants for air—"to figure it out. I have . . . serious concerns about . . . national black ops security."

Mitch and his four guy-pals bantered over something completely inane—lack of leadership, guys in the trenches winning battles and wars—or some such shit.

Until Keira said, "If you don't shut the hell up, your

asses are going to end up in a trench and I won't be pulling them out."

After a mutter or two, they all went silent for the rest of the run.

God, she loved Keira. Wanted to be just like her when she grew up. All kick-ass and taking names. Just maybe in a different life. Because Jessica couldn't even consider how many men were in those choppers. Or how many of them were hunting them down right now. Or what her partner, Daryl, would be told when she was found shot in the back in the mountains of Utah when she'd told him she was home with the flu.

No. She couldn't go there. She was not Keira.

Her mind, heart and body were numb by the time they finally reached the trucks. But she must have been feeling something underneath because the sky, which had been clear when they'd set out on this mission was now thrashing the treetops with wind and rain.

"They're gaining," Keira said in a hushed but urgent voice. "Load up! Go, go, go."

Mitch's men got behind the wheels of both trucks and started the engines. The guys threw open the camper shell doors, let the tailgates fall and everyone scrambled in— Mitch and his men in one, everyone else in the other.

Cash went in with Q first. Kai gripped Jessica's waist and hoisted her to the edge of the truck bed before jumping in after her. The rest of the guys were onboard, Keira still on the ground poised to throw the tailgate into place. But the truck took off too soon.

"Fucking morons," was all Keira said as she sprinted after them and grabbed for the open tailgate, as if this was just one more irritation in her regular day.

"Damn it, Keira." Luke sounded more concerned than his words implied. He held onto the truck with one hand

and lunged for her with the other. He grabbed a strap of her backpack and held her steady as she climbed on, secured the tailgate and closed the camper shell.

Then he pulled her into his lap with an incredulous, "Seriously? The way you're going, sugar, I've only got about five years left to live."

"But you're gonna be *so* happy for those five years," she cooed, smiling up at him, hand against his face.

"Gag me," Kai said while rummaging through canvas bags.

"Love to," Keira said without looking at him. "But let me make Ransom happy first."

And she kissed him. Or, he kissed her. Or . . . whatever, they were, *whoa,* really kissing. The sight shot a burn of awareness straight through Jessica's chest and into her belly where it sizzled. Had she looked like that earlier kissing Quai—?

Her stomach quenched the fire. No, not Quaid. Q. She turned and looked at the man lying on the truck bed.

She didn't know what to think. Or how to feel. Or how to act. She didn't even know who the hell she was anymore, running around the hills of Utah, risking her life to rescue unknowns from the captivity of the Department of Defense.

"What the hell happened to my life?" she muttered.

"Does he have a chip?" Kai asked. "We've got to get it out or cover it up, quick."

"A what?" Jessica crawled to Q's side, where Teague was running his hands over the man's arms.

"A GPS tracking—" Teague started, then, "Yep. Left triceps."

"All right." This seemed to make Kai happy, and he pulled something metallic out of the canvas bag. "That's an easy fix. Make sure he doesn't have more than one."

Kai unrolled something that looked suspiciously like . . .

"Is that *Reynolds Wrap?*" Jessica asked, disbelieving her eyes.

"Yep." Kai's smile widened as he wound the foil around Q's upper arm, then secured it tight with duct tape. "You know how I love low-tech solutions."

"If you like low-tech solutions," Teague said, "I'm Florence Nightingale. I can't find any more."

A chill shimmied over Jessica's arms and she hugged herself. "A tracker? They . . . they *track* him . . . them? Like *property?*"

Teague lifted those crystalline blue eyes to hers with an unspoken *you don't want to know what all they do* and returned his focus to Q.

Still unconscious, Q's head tipped to the side, his body rocking with the truck's motion as they moved fast over rough road. The sight of Q's face in the shadows, the angle of his jaw, something, made her lean over him. Made her reach out and take his face in both hands and turn it toward her. Her stomach floated to her throat.

"Where's the light?" Keira asked from behind her.

Someone hit the overhead and dim light filled the interior.

"God damn them," Jessica whispered when she got a better look at what they'd done to him after she'd disappeared. The guilt of having been the cause made her eyes well with tears. "He was chained to a wall. Drugged half out of his mind. He couldn't fight back. He wasn't giving them any trouble. They did this for the hell of it."

Kai threw a duffle to Cash, who drew a penlight from a pocket and lifted Q's lids, shining it into his eyes. The light illuminated rich, warm coffee-colored irises. Jessica held her breath and leaned closer, looking for what she'd seen before that had made her trip over the line from suspicion to belief. It had been something in his eyes. But now they were fixed and blank, and once again, she found no hint of Quaid.

She sank back on her heels and reached for the bag of first aid supplies. When she looked up again, she found everyone gathered around, staring down at Q. Only Cash continued to work, cutting his T-shirt up the middle with a pair of emergency shears.

Then Jessica stared, too.

She'd been very wrong. Q was not skinny. Nor was his frame small. His body was an incredibly honed mass of sculpted muscle. Lean, tapered, sleek, powerful.

"Hey, buddy," Cash said to Q as he peeled off the shirt, revealing more cuts and bruising. "Looks like you've gone a little OCD on that workout we set up. Think you're good. You can back off some. Can you hear me, Q? Lot of people here who want to say hi. Wake up for us. I've told them all about how smart you are, so don't make me look bad by acting stupid."

Q didn't stir.

"Jessica." Keira's voice was soft beside her. Filled with awe and emotion. She knelt close, inspecting Q's face, then smiled up at Jessica with tears in her eyes. "Oh, my God."

Alarm and confusion melded. "What?" She leaned in, frowning, searching for something she'd missed. "What is it?"

Keira gripped her arm. "What is it?" Her voice rose with disbelief. "It's Quaid." She shook Jessica's arm. "It's *Quaid*, sweetheart. Look at him, Jess. That's *Quaid's* handsome face."

Fear and excitement stung her ribs. Her heart kicked up and hammered her breastbone. Jessica looked at him again. Searching. But she still saw the same man. "I . . . I . . ." She shook her head and shrugged, helpless to make her eyes see the husband that lived in her memory. "I don't . . . I mean, yeah, I can see how he might . . ."

"What the hell is wrong with you?" Kai's anger vibrated through the space and took Jessica by surprise. "It's obviously Quaid. One look at his face and I can see it's him."

Keira jabbed Kai's arm with a fist. "Don't be a jerk."

"Both of you, shut up," Teague said, his voice low but fierce. "Neither of you have lived through the death of a spouse. Neither of you know what's involved in that grieving process. Give her some time."

Jessica's eyes shot to Teague and she saw the lingering pain of Suzannah's death so long ago. Even deliriously happy with his new wife, daughter and soon-to-be son, he was still haunted by his former wife's death. Jessica knew without any doubt, she couldn't do what he'd done. She was not as strong as Teague. Just as she wasn't as strong as Keira. She could not continue on without Quaid, no matter how much time she was given. She'd tried her best, but this event brought the reality home. And maybe that was the purpose of it all.

She ignored the heavy silence weighting down the rocking vehicle in the wake of Teague's order, and pulled gauze and hydrogen peroxide from the bag and started wiping the blood from Q's face.

Cash took the shears to the sleeve of his shirt, cut it and peeled it away. "Here's his mark."

Jessica looked down at Q's arm. The purplish-blue hue of a design curved over the round of his shoulder. Jessica's breath caught at the sight of what would be the wing of a phoenix brushing the top of his shoulder before disappearing behind him.

"God," Keira whispered, "it's beautiful."

Jessica's heart stuttered with hope. How many people could have that matching mark? But they'd said Mateo had one because he'd been exposed to those chemicals. And they also said Q had been used in experiments. . . .

She put a hand to her stomach where the burn from the stress of this want versus need, reality versus fantasy ate at her.

Luke straightened from where he'd been leaning over to see the mark and repositioned himself behind Jessica and Keira again. He kissed Keira's cheek and whispered, "Yours is prettier."

Jessica looked over her shoulder at Luke and his smiling blue eyes sobered. But something there offered security and pushed Jessica to ask, "Luke, does he look like Quaid to you?"

Luke rubbed her shoulders and nodded. "He looks like Quaid to me, sweetheart. Even if he was a little off, which I'm not seeing, but then again I didn't kiss the guy"—that brought a round of chuckles through the truck—"he looks a hell of a lot more like Quaid than Quaid himself would have looked after that explosion."

Jessica had known if Quaid had survived his trauma at the warehouse, he would have faced a life of painful surgeries and skin grafts. But that was before they each had developed some level of self-healing. They should all have scarring from the fire, but the only mark left on their physical bodies was their phoenix scars. But even back then, she hadn't cared if his appearance had changed. Nor did she care now—she loved her husband heart and soul. She just needed to know for sure that this *was* her husband.

She pressed a hand to her forehead. It was damp and hot. "What's wrong with me? Why can't I see it?"

Teague sat back on his heels beside Q. He'd been quietly concentrating on Q's body, searching for injuries. Now he met Jessica's eyes with compassion and strength. "The mind plays strange games during trauma. You know

that. For months after Suzannah died, I'd find myself starting a conversation with her, only to realize she wasn't
there."

A fine tremor started in her arms. She swallowed. Her
throat burned. "You think it's Quaid, too?"

Complex emotion stormed in his blue eyes. Finally, he
nodded.

"Well?" Kai's irritable bite raised the hair on Jessica's
neck.

"Would you shove the attitude already, dude?" Luke
said to Kai. "This isn't easy on any of us and you're making it a whole lot worse."

Cash looked at Teague, worry clear in his expression.
"Is he okay? Or going to be okay?"

"I've never . . . felt anything like this before." Teague's
gaze swept the group. "He has . . . dozens and dozens of
old injuries. I can feel the previous breaks in his bones
even though they're healed. It's like running your fingers
over a crack in the sidewalk." Teague looked back down
at Q with anguish in his expression. "He has them . . .
everywhere. All over his body."

"I told you," Kai started to stand up, realized the space
was too confined and sat back on his butt instead. "I told
you it was Quaid. Those are from the explosion. Remember, at the hospital, they said he had breaks in almost every
bone in his body? That he'd shattered—"

"Kai!" Jessica hadn't realized the yell was coming until
it was too late. Her stomach squeezed, but she looked Kai
in the eye. "You can be the biggest asshole on the planet
and it still won't alleviate your guilt. So just *shut up.*"

The truck went quiet.

I did not just say that.

But, oh, God, she had.

And she'd meant it.

And hated herself for meaning it.

Loathed herself for causing that ripple of grief and pain crossing Kai's handsome face.

But it was too late. She'd just have to add that outburst to the list of things she shouldn't have done in her life, the list that gave her those million and one reasons to hate herself.

Kai dropped his head against his arms where they rested on upturned knees. The sight pushed the wetness in her eyes over her lashes and she grabbed hold of herself before the dam broke.

She refocused on Teague. "What else?"

Teague looked at Cash when he spoke this time. "His head . . . his brain . . . is, I don't know how to describe it other than, a mess."

"Try," Jessica said through clenched teeth.

"It's like . . ." He lifted his hands, and made small circles as if nudging the words free, "I don't know . . . like scrambled eggs."

Jessica stopped breathing. Dropped her gaze to the man at her knees, to the road map of scars on his scalp, and released her air on a hissed, "Those goddamned *animals*."

She wiped at another streak of blood on his temple, uncovering a scar. An inch-long scar. It puckered gently, the skin lighter than the surrounding tissue. Jessica's stomach caught on fire. She scooted close, cleaned the area again and ran shaking fingers over the scar.

"Oh, God."

"What?" Cash moved first, leaning over Q, looking for the problem. "What's wrong?"

Keira peered over her shoulder. "What is it?"

"The scar." But Jessica wasn't looking at the scar anymore. She was looking for signs of Quaid in this man's face again. "Quaid had one just like it—"

"That snowboard stunt," Keira said. "I remember."

"You mean the one when he was bored during a slow winter shift," Luke said, "and got the grand idea to snowboard off the roof of the station, down the stairs and through the parking lot? Damn lunatic."

There was a smile in Luke's voice and the sheer absurdity of Quaid's renegade madness made a laugh jump from Jessica's throat, only it sounded like a sob. And, honestly, she couldn't tell the difference.

Teague chuckled, too. "And rammed that snowboard right into his forehead. Dumb shit."

"Thirty stitches." Kai's voice had leveled. "I had to cancel the hottest date of my life to sit in the ER with him. Pissant."

Another sob caught in Jessica's throat. This one more pain than laughter.

"Didn't he . . ." Keira reached around Jessica and tugged at the right side of Q's waistband. His jeans were loose and lowered easily to reveal a diagonal scar near his hipbone. "Have his appendix out?"

Jessica's lungs tightened and she struggled to pull in air. She thought back, fighting to remember Quaid's other scars.

"Remember when we were at the Painted Cave fire?" Luke said. "And he went all soft for those horses—"

"Penned up at that ranch." Keira took over the tale from Luke, reaching for Q's arm. "We told him to wait for Animal Control, but they were in the path of the fire and he couldn't stand the thought of leaving them, so he opened the gate—"

She lifted his right arm, exposing another long, thin scar down the inside of his forearm. Everyone went silent.

Jessica's fingers traced the line. "One huge black mare spooked," she finished the story, "and slammed him against the gate."

"He got blood all over the front seat of my vehicle," Kai said, his voice melancholy now. "Another damn trip to the ER and a reaming by my battalion chief. He and the ER docs were on a—"

"First name basis," Jessica finished.

Silence again. Thicker. Heavier.

The pressure of an impending emotional tsunami crushed Jessica's chest, and she didn't know what to do.

Keira's hand rested on her shoulder and she murmured, "Remember that thing with his hand, Jess? His left hand?"

Jessica's gaze tore from Q's right arm and held on his left hand, laid out by his side. Her fingers found the locket beneath her cotton turtleneck. More tears spilled down her cheeks. Her throat closed. Her chest constricted. The most bizarre blend of fear and hope twisted her inside out.

"What happened to his hand?" Cash asked.

"We were at a vehicle accident," Keira said. "A car had been hit and crushed by a gasoline truck and we'd gone as a team. It was just a few months before the warehouse fire. We'd used the JAWS to open the roof of the car to get the driver out. Quaid was keeping track of her vitals and they started to dip. The tool caught up on something, I can't remember what, but Quaid, in his typical zeal to get the woman out before she died, used his hand to free up the metal jamming the JAWS. The cut edge of the metal sliced into his glove and caught on his wedding ring—"

"He shouldn't have been wearing it at work," Jessica said, her voice rough with emotion. "But we were out to dinner, celebrating our six month anniversary. Got called in. And . . ." She laughed through the tears. "When I reminded him about it, he got all pissy. Hated taking it off anyway and said he wasn't taking it off on our annivers—"

She choked and couldn't continue.

"He's lucky he didn't lose his finger," Keira said. "He never argued again."

There wasn't much time after that for him to argue again.

She was suddenly terrified the scar wouldn't be there. It was so specific. So unique. And if it wasn't there . . . God, if it wasn't there . . .

"We're here, Jess." Keira wrapped an arm around her shoulders. Pressed her forehead to Jess's temple. "We won't lock you out this time. We won't leave you alone. That was wrong of all of us. It won't happen again."

A hand closed around the back of her neck, sturdy and reassuring. Kai. She knew that gesture. Knew that touch. "That goes for me, too, Jess."

She shivered. The support she'd needed, craved, ached for surrounded her. The man that made her whole was possibly lying before her. And she was frozen with fear.

Cash reached across Q and covered her hand where it lay on his arm. "It will be there."

The surety in his voice gave Jessica the strength to reach for Q's hand. She held her breath, turned it over, pulled open his ring finger and middle finger.

The air left her lungs as she squinted and rubbed her thumb at the grime. Blood and dirt and . . . "Keira, give me your water."

Keira uncapped a bottle and poured water over Q's hand. Jessica scrubbed with both thumbs. Her heart pounded. Her lungs throbbed. Her eyes scoured his finger for that telltale scraggly white line against his tanned—

And it appeared. As if she'd rubbed it into existence, the irregular line created by Quaid's dedication to their marriage, his all-consuming love for her, glowed up at Jessica.

Her head went light. A sob escaped her throat. She sat there frozen, for how long she didn't know—three heartbeats, ten, a hundred—while the emotions swept in and overwhelmed her.

Joy, relief, gratitude, love, excitement . . . they rushed in, slamming against her heart.

She couldn't think. Couldn't talk. She could only touch him, and kiss him and sob against his chest, welcoming every last detail—shaved head, scars, unfamiliar face, changed body.

This *was* her husband.

NINE

Owen had to take a piss, but he didn't have the energy to unsink himself from the corner of his office sofa where he'd planted his ass—he looked at his watch and grimaced—ten hours ago?

He pulled his aching legs from the coffee table and sat forward, tossing down the file he'd been reading. His eyes had long since blurred over the type anyway and ached for sleep. But he knew that even if he allowed himself to lie down, his mind would never stop spinning.

He glanced over the piles again—spread out on the sofa, the coffee table, the floor. The deeper he'd delved into the information, the more careless he'd become, scattering files everywhere. The depth of deception astounded him, which took a lot. Owen was no stranger to the dark ways of the government. He was also a firm believer that fighting wasn't prevented, suffering didn't end, and lives weren't saved by following a shitload of rules. Weapons weren't seized, murderers weren't eliminated, dictators weren't overthrown by coloring inside the lines.

Maybe that's why Schaeffer hadn't been afraid to give him all this information. Owen wasn't sure yet if Schaeffer believed everyone would immediately bend to his corrupt will or if the fucker knew Owen would be smart enough to see the house of cards constructed over his own damn head, ready to tumble and bury him with one wrong breath.

He stared blankly at the paper, still dazed by the realization of just how thoroughly Jocelyn had set him up. And his own screwups left him with no one to confide in. No one to seek out for help. Or even guidance. At least not without putting himself at risk.

If it was just him, it would be an easier decision. But it wasn't. If Owen lost his job, if this went wrong and he was court-martialed—he'd seen it happen far too often to better men—he'd lose his income. His pension. And his kids would lose their financial support.

He and Libby had always had big hopes and dreams for them. That was one goal they still shared, despite the divorce. A goal they'd instilled in the kids. He'd already done a bang-up job of fucking up their emotional support system with the divorce. He hoped someday, maybe when they were older, they could understand, forgive. If he screwed them over financially, too? Not only would he not be able to live with himself, but he'd be dead to his kids. They'd loathe him.

His gaze drifted to the painting framed on a wall to his left. One Jenny had given him maybe five years ago now. One of those typical sunshine and rainbow watercolors with stick figures dancing on a bed of green grass. All innocence and joy.

To put his problems into perspective, he opened Cash O'Shay's file. O'Shay had lost three years of his life. Three years of his son's life. O'Shay had lost his wife.

And Quaid Legend. Turned into a warrior of the future and used against his will to further the American military's political agendas through warfare. The ops also hinted toward technical developments Owen would bet his precious pension coincided with Schaeffer's manufacturing corporation, Millineum's discoveries and their accompanying military contracts. Legend had also lost his wife. And his freedom. And his memories.

Then there was Teague Creek, who'd been framed for the murder of his girlfriend, then an assistant district attorney. Framed and sent to prison for the rest of his natural life so all his questions into the cause of the warehouse fire and the chemicals involved would go into the hole with him.

Owen's building anger exploded and he pushed up from the sofa and dug both hands into his hair. He'd believed Creek guilty of the murder, just as he'd believed O'Shay guilty of treason. Jocelyn had made sure of that. She'd known he would never have stayed quiet while men rotted their lives away unjustly. He'd kept information secret that could have freed both men. He'd done favors for Jocelyn that had drawn complete innocents into this vortex—Alyssa Foster for one. Kat Creek for another.

And Mitch Foster . . .

Owen dragged his hands over his face. Fucking Foster. When that man discovered just what part he'd ultimately played in this cluster fuck . . .

"Christ. What is the furthest point across the world from here?" he wondered aloud. Might be a good time to consider retirement there.

He dropped his hands, slid them into his pants pockets and wandered to his window, where he let his gaze blur over the lights of Arlington.

Foster was too damned smart for his own good, just like Creek. Asked too many questions. Dug too deep. Only Foster was savvy as well as smart. He'd fashioned himself a sweet little safety net out of blackmail, and it had kept his ass on the right side of the grass. At least so far.

Owen didn't need paranormal abilities to see he was headed down the same path. He could only hope he was as smart, if not smarter, than Foster. He certainly wasn't too proud or too arrogant to take a strategy from the man's playbook. He'd need some heavy counter-ammunition if Schaeffer came gunning for him. Which Owen could predict approaching with ninety-nine-point-nine percent accuracy.

Because, no, he would not play by Schaeffer's rules.

But, nor would he risk his children's future.

"Joce," he murmured, staring out at the night, "if you're not already dead, you're going to wish you were when I get ahold of you."

He picked up his cell from his desk, hit speed dial and waited as the phone rang at the crash site.

"Sir." The sergeant in charge who'd been keeping Owen informed had obviously memorized Owen's number and now answered with all the latest data. "Another three tons of rubble have been removed from the main building."

Owen gritted his teeth, holding back the complex emotions only time could settle.

"We've cleared the floor underneath, checked every cell, all the hallways. We've recovered sixteen additional bodies. But not Deputy Dargan yet. I'm sorry, sir."

"Thank you, sergeant."

He pulled the phone away from his ear, heard a faint, "Sir?" and brought it back. "Yes, sergeant?"

"I thought you'd want to know that the lab manager, a Mario Abrute, was off-site during the explosion. He's in detainment at Area 51 now."

"Isn't the investigation team handling staff interviews?"

"Yes, sir. But the security logs show—"

"I thought the security system and all its files had been obliterated." Owen rounded his desk, sat and picked up a pen just to have something to stab at his blotter.

"Everything within the Castle," he said. "These logs

were from the gate. They only show official entries and exits."

Damn. Still not a sliver of evidence of who had gone into that site and broken O'Shay out. Sure, everyone who knew about the operation and the relationships also knew who'd done it, but Owen couldn't officially, legally or morally go after their asses without some shred of evidence . . . which they'd incinerated.

Or rather, the Air Force Apaches had incinerated trying to catch them.

While they'd been helping someone escape who'd been wrongly imprisoned.

Alongside their teammate who'd been claimed dead, had his memory erased, and turned into a human military weapon.

He rubbed his temple. "What's worse than a cluster fuck?"

"What was that, sir?" The sergeant raised his voice over the roar of a Black Hawk's engine in the background.

"Abrute, sergeant," Owen said. "The logs. What did they show?"

"They show a Sergeant Decker entering the premises approximately an hour prior to the explosion, then exiting again just twenty minutes before. When he heard the explosion, he held onto Abrute and secured him to the base. But with all the commotion, that information wasn't relayed until just now."

"Which is important because . . ." Owen hurried the sergeant along.

"Because, sir, Decker was dispatched to bring Abrute back to the site for questioning related to O'Shay's project."

Owen straightened. His mind sharpened.

"He said," the sergeant went on, "Deputy Dargan directed him to take Abrute back to his residence to retrieve some notes. These notes were reportedly in a secure briefcase of some kind. He reported that Deputy Dargan told Abrute that if she received the briefcase that night with the notes intact, and I'm using Decker's words here, sir, he would 'suffer no harm.' "

Owen looked at his watch. Another flight to and from that godforsaken desert? No way.

"Sergeant." Owen firmed his voice. "I'm giving you a direct order. Get Abrute's ass on a C10 and get him to my doorstep. *Yesterday.*"

"Uh . . . I mean, yes, sir. I just, there are forms—"

"I am well aware of every goddamned fucking form this military creates, sergeant. And I'm an expert at completing every goddamned fucking one." Owen paused to breathe. To control his temper. This information should have been relayed to him while he'd still been there this morning. This was completely unacceptable and someone's ass was going to burn for the oversight. "And make damn sure that briefcase with every page of notes is on that plane with him, sergeant, or your career will look like your current environment."

He disconnected. Slammed his phone on his desk, closed his eyes and pinched the bridge of his nose. Deep breath in. Deep breath out.

Damn Jocelyn.

Damn Schaeffer.

Owen had to force himself not to call the sergeant back and apologize. But he did redial the man.

"Yes, sir," the man answered in a brusque, guarded tone.

"Well done, sergeant."

A moment of shocked silence. "Thank you . . . sir."

"Abrute and his information are need-to-know."

"Absolutely, sir."

"Senator Schaeffer is *not* in the need-to-know category."

Another second of silence. "I understand, sir."

"If you get any static, send it my way."

"My pleasure, sir." A hint of humor played in his voice and relieved Owen's guilt.

"Thank you, sergeant."

He set the phone down again and stared at it for a long time. The pieces were starting to click together now, the puzzle's image beginning to take shape.

He'd spoken to Jocelyn only half an hour before the explosion. Which had been after she'd discovered Abrute had O'Shay's formula. Why she hadn't been able to get it from O'Shay himself, he didn't know. Yet. But when she'd spoken to Owen, when she'd told him she wanted him, she'd been planning a celebration. She'd been planning on rewarding herself for a job well done.

Owen slumped in his chair. How was it that he fixated on women who saw him as a prize instead of a person?

Jessica had been drifting in and out of sleep for the last hour, lying curled beside Quaid on the floor of another truck, her head on his shoulder. She secured his body against the hard bump and rock over rough Vermont roads leading into the Appalachian mountains with an arm tight across his abdomen.

Thank God they were approaching their final destination. At least for a day or two. No one really knew what life held in store for any of them from day to day at this point. After they'd evaded whoever had been sent to keep them from rescuing Quaid, they'd picked up Alyssa and the kids and driven back to the plane. From there they'd flown sans-flight-plan to the border of New Hampshire and to yet another private airstrip in the middle of nowhere. Two trucks had been waiting, loaded with supplies, not a human in sight. They'd parked the plane beneath a shelter built under a heavy covering of forest that looked as if it would crumble in the next high wind, and headed toward the Vermont border.

After the second flight and this second long drive, all while helping to carry Quaid, nursing him with liquid, stressing over his physical and mental well-being, his future, *their* future . . . she was exhausted. As was the team surrounding her. Everyone dozed in the darkness.

The entire landscape of her life had changed. And she had no idea what skills or knowledge she would need to navigate this new terrain. Considering that Quaid might truly not remember her, Jessica wondered if she'd be making all these changes alone. And whether the end result would earn her what she needed most—the love of her husband.

Finally, *finally,* the truck slowed.

"We're here." Kai put his hand on Jessica's arm. "Wait. I'll be back to help you with him."

Everyone piled out and as she waited, she pressed kisses to Quaid's face and ran her hand over his soft bristle of hair. The scars rasped against her palm and stirred anger and sadness. "We're here, baby. Can you wake up for me?"

She didn't get any more response this time than any of the other eight hundred times she'd tried.

When Kai returned, Jessica helped move Quaid toward the end of the truck bed and hoist him over Kai's shoulder. She walked beside them toward a building—an old barn shining in the trucks' headlights. Other than a covered carport, nothing but thick forest shone in the side beams. They were on thirty acres of uninhabited land owned by a "friend" of Mitch's.

The air was crisp and clean. The night as silent as the dead. And as dark. Until Mitch slid open a panel beside one of the doors, revealing a power grid hidden beneath something that had looked like just another piece of weathered siding, and flipped a switch.

Three different floods swamped the area with warm light. Jessica winced, shielding her eyes. The rest of the group groaned in unison.

"Damn it, Foster." Teague worked three padlocks on the doors. "Would you warn us before you do that?"

"Bitch, moan, complain . . ." Mitch put both hands against the edge of one of the doors and leaned his weight into it. "Ransom, get your lazy ass over here and help."

Luke sauntered to Mitch's side. "Bitch, moan, complain . . ."

Keira laughed.

Cash put his sleeping son into his sister's arms. "I'd better get over there, too. God forbid I catch that wrath."

Jessica had her hand wrapped around Quaid's dangling wrist, her fingers on his pulse. The feel of his blood beating steadily through his veins was the only thing that kept her calm. She searched for Alyssa and found her standing off to the side, one hand around Kat's shoulders, holding the exhausted girl to her side, the other pressed to her big belly.

"Alyssa?"

Her friend's response was slower than usual, the turn of her head too languid, the look in her eyes too glassy. Jessica stepped in that direction and her hand tugged against Quaid's wrist. She glanced between them, torn.

"Go," Kai said. "I've got him."

Jessica took in the sight of Quaid limp over Kai's shoulder and swallowed the knot in her throat. She rubbed her hand over his prickly hair again before going to Alyssa. Jessica crouched in front of Kat. Finding the girl asleep on her feet, Jessica lifted Kat into her arms.

"Lys, you need to sit down. Let's go over to that boulder, get you off your feet."

Alyssa shook her head and propped her shoulder against a tree. "If I sit down now, I'll never get up. I'm okay for a few more minutes."

At the barn, Teague and Cash pushed aside one door, Mitch and Luke the other.

The sight of them made her remember the four military men who'd been with them since the rescue. "Where are those other guys?"

"Forming a secure perimeter," Alyssa said, rubbing her belly with a wince.

Jessica repositioned Kat's slumping weight in her arms. "Alyssa, tell me you're not having labor pains. Please."

She let out a tired laugh. "No. He's kicking me in the ribs. Little shit."

Jessica laughed. "It's so funny to hear you swear."

"If you can't beat 'em . . ." Alyssa grinned. "I'll add money to the jar in the morning. Word of advice, Jess. Don't make a baby in a wine closet. They're a little . . . wild."

Jessica's smile widened. Her brows rose. "Wine closet, huh? I want that story." Jessica turned to check on Quaid. He still lay as limply over Kai's shoulder as Kat in Jessica's arms. "And honestly, Lys, if I ever get the chance to make a baby with Quaid, I'll make one however, whenever and where ever I can. Waiting to get pregnant is one of my greatest regrets."

Jessica looked toward the barn. Only the barn wasn't a barn. Not really. The guys had pushed the doors back to reveal the concrete brick walls of a massive building with another set of heavy metal doors beneath.

"What the hell?" Jessica asked.

"It's a bunker," Alyssa said. "I haven't had time to sit down and grill Mitch on what this is all about, but his work has given him not only endlessly grateful and generous contacts who have amazing resources and skills, but these contacts also seem . . . " She paused to consider. "At one time I would have called them paranoid. Extremists. But with everything that's happened to us and as often as these paranoid extremists have saved someone's ass on this team or come to Mitch's aid . . . Honestly, the larger ramifications are starting to scare the hell out of me."

Jessica tightened her arms around Kat. "Is your house going to be okay?"

Alyssa nodded, watching the guys work on the locks along the metal doors. "Teague, Luke and Mitch set up an elaborate security system complete with booby traps. We've got neighbors watching it, a few friends in the police department doing drive-bys. A few of Teague and Luke's ATF coworkers are keeping an eye on it. We've got insurance. I'm not worried about the house."

She turned her gaze on Jessica, those gorgeous amber eyes serious. "I *am* worried about Quaid. And I'm worried about you."

Alyssa's directness was nothing new, but it had never been so completely focused on Jessica. And never on such a painful subject at such a vulnerable time.

Jessica forced a smile. "You're not the only one."

"Has Keira talked to you about Mateo? About the chips in his brain?"

Shock unhinged Jessica's jaw.

"Obviously not," Alyssa said. "We can talk about this in depth tomorrow, after you've had some sleep. For now, I just want you to consider hypnotherapy for Quaid."

"Okay, but what does that have to do with Mateo and brain chips . . . ?"

"When we got Mateo back, we discovered he had a tracking chip in his neck, which was why they looked for one—and found it—in Quaid."

Jessica nodded, her stomach turning a little when she remembered Alyssa removing the chip from Quaid's arm earlier in the night.

"Mateo's chip was different. It was also a type of computer interface, a control chip, if you will, that connected many other chips, which are still imbedded in his brain tissue. That's where Seth is, tracking down information on these chips. Teague searched for those in Quaid when he did the exam and didn't find any. But the scars on Quaid's head and the fact that Teague senses a mismatch or scrambling of sorts in Quaid's brain makes me think they may have attempted to use them. Maybe they didn't work and they were removed. I don't know.

"Because of what's happened with Mateo, I've done a lot of advanced research on the brain. I've also been consulting with a psychiatrist who specializes in hypnotherapy. When we learned of Q, I proposed a hypothetical situation to this doctor to gain some insight into how we might best help him once we had him."

Jessica waited. Found herself leaning forward in anticipation. But Alyssa's expression had grown increasingly tight, and now she glanced away, toward the bunker, lips pressed tight.

"And?"

She took a deep breath of the cold night air, winced and rubbed at her belly near her ribs again. "Trauma victims are unpredictable. Those with more severe trauma and longer exposure have, understandably, the lowest success of recovery. Now—" Alyssa held a hand out, silently asking Jessica not to panic, but her heart rate was already rising. "Mitch said almost these exact same things to me about Teague's chance of recovering from his time in prison. And Teague's a perfect example of how resilient human beings can be. So I don't want you to lose hope, but I do want us to approach Quaid's recovery carefully."

"Okay." Jessica tried to slow her breath. "Fine."

"It probably won't feel fine. Because the best form of recovery is slow. The best form of recovery is one Quaid brings on himself. In fact, telling him of his past before his mind is capable of adjusting has the potential of shocking his brain into shutdown, and can actually do more harm than good."

Jessica's mind was spinning fast, processing the information, imagining scenarios and what-ifs. When Alyssa didn't go on, she said, "So, what does that mean? For when he wakes up, I mean. If Cash is right, and Quaid has no memory from before his time at the Castle, he's going to want to know who the hell we all are. He's going to want to know how this all happened. How do we handle that?"

"Slowly, with a lot of finesse."

A new tightness squeezed Jessica's chest. "Are you saying . . . ?" No, she couldn't be saying . . . "That if he doesn't remember me, I can't tell him I'm his wife?"

"I'm saying it would be best to wait and see how he handles the smaller pieces of information he needs before we give him the bigger, more emotionally charged ones.

"You need to remember, the loss of memory isn't the only major issue he's going to be facing, Jess. He's used to living alone, being treated badly, ignored, pushed around, abused. We'll have to see how he adjusts to being here with all of us. How he adjusts to sounds, schedules, food. How much stimulation he can handle before it's too much. What physical issues come about—headaches, pain. . . . He has a lot of adjustment in his future. For him, it would be best to limit the information we share until he's ready to receive it."

"You know I can't lie, Alyssa." Truth was the foundation of Jessica's rehab—of all addicts' and alcoholics' rehab. And at this point, it felt as if the truth was the only rule of rehab she hadn't broken. "I especially can't lie to him. I've already broken every good habit I've spent the last year establishing. I just . . . I don't know what will happen. . . . I can't start lying again, too."

"I understand, Jess. Let's just take it one step at a time." Alyssa gave her shoulder a squeeze. "Go on back to him. I'm fine."

She carried Kat back to Kai and managed to position herself to hold both the girl and Quaid's hand. And as soon as his blood pulsed beneath her fingers, relief gushed through her body. She had to maintain hope. She had to believe in Quaid the way Alyssa had believed in Teague. Yet again, she knew she wasn't as strong as Alyssa, either.

Tears stung her eyes. She pressed them against the back of Kai's shoulder and felt him turn to look at her.

"I'm sorry about earlier, Kai," she whispered. "I didn't mean—"

He turned, wrapped an arm around her shoulders, and hugged her, careful not to squish Kat, and pressed a kiss to her hair. "No. I'm sorry. I've been an ass, Jess. Worse than an ass. I'm going to make it up to you. Both of you."

She wanted to say more, but everything was jumbled in her head, in her heart, and all she could get out was, "I love you."

"Love you, too." He pressed his cheek to her head, and squeezed her tight. "Love you so much."

"Come on," Mitch called. "Everyone inside. Alyssa, sit your ass on a couch and don't even think about getting up. Jailbird," he called to Teague, "help me move the trucks under the carport."

The inside of the building was as simple as the outside, but with flair. Unfinished block concrete made up the walls; stained, polished slab concrete the floors and some type of slanted metal roofing created a cathedral ceiling. One large living space held several leather sofas and lounge chairs, coffee tables, side tables and lamps. It looked like the small lobby of an upscale urban hotel.

A long island separated the living and kitchen spaces, where an industrial-looking kitchen took up one corner, two wooden dining sets another. The kitchen included restaurant-sized, stainless-steel appliances and granite counters. In an alcove opposite the kitchen, a dozen flat screen monitors lined a portion of one concrete wall. Beneath those, a workstation sat covered in electronics.

"This *bunker* is nicer than my house," Kai muttered on his way to a sofa, where he and Jessica laid Quaid on his back.

Jessica lifted Quaid's head onto her lap and settled into the comfort of the soft sofa. Mitch and Teague returned and Mitch took the floor like a seasoned speaker, with supreme confidence and utter control. Jessica could definitely see how he would grab hold of a jury and never let go.

"Okay," he started as everyone found seats and sprawled their tired bodies out across the furniture and each other. "The property is thirty-two acres surrounded by other multi-acre parcels, the smallest of which is eighteen acres. We have no neighbors. So if you hear or see something or someone, that's a problem. The property is surrounded with electric fencing. My guys are out patrolling the perimeter now. One of those guys, Brody, is the owner of said property, so if we have problems, we've got the expert on site.

"That," he pointed to the corner with the monitors and electronics, "is the brain of the security system. That brain will keep us *alive*. If you're better with people than you are with electronics . . ." He drew out the last word, staring pointedly at his sister. "Leave. It. Alone."

"Ha, ha," Alyssa said, from where she sat with her head on Teague's shoulder.

"It's okay, babe," Teague said, kissing her forehead. "I'm glad you're better with people."

"The roofs of all the buildings are covered in a material that hinders infrared detection. There are several scramblers distributed throughout the property centered near the bunker to interfere with cell phone and Internet tracking. That *does not* mean we can use these electronics casually."

"Meaning," Kai said, "your three-hundred-and-two girlfriends will have to suffer without hearing your voice for a few days."

Mitch gave him a heavy-lidded, long-suffering look. "There are thirty-six video cameras set up around the property and the house. They have a rotating image display on those monitors—"

"Waaaaait a minute," Luke said. "Exactly *where* are these cameras? None in the bedrooms, right?"

Mitch let his hands fall and slap against his jean-covered thighs. "Can't you guys think about anything other than sex?" He put his hands out wide as if eliciting a response. "*Anything?*"

A grin lifted Luke's mouth and he looked down at Keira. "Someone sounds jealous."

"The day I'm jealous of your sex life, Ransom—no offense, Keira, you know I think you're totally smokin'—just put me in the ground."

"No offense taken," Keira said, grinning back at Luke. "I happen to be damn impressed with Ransom's sex life."

"And can we get on with this," Alyssa said, "so some of us can *have* a sex life?"

The room filled with a shocked silence and everyone turned and looked at her.

Her head came off Teague's shoulder. "What? I'm pregnant, not dead." She gestured toward Teague with both hands. "Do you not see this fine specimen of man sitting here?"

Everyone laughed. Teague tipped her head back and kissed her on the mouth.

Mitch, the drama queen, slapped a hand over his face and stumbled back a few steps. "It burns. It burns!"

Everyone laughed harder, and the kids slept through it all.

Jessica's spirits rebounded. She looked down at Quaid and ran her thumb over his lips. He looked so obviously like her Quaid now, she couldn't imagine how she'd denied it before.

"The refrigerator is stocked and there are linens in the closets," Mitch said. "The bedrooms are down that hall. Save the two at the end near the other door for Brody's guys. Now go, you heathens, get out of here. We'll unload the trucks and try this again in the morning when we can all think straight." He pointed at Kai. "Not you, sucker. You don't have a girl or a kid. You and I are setting up and testing this electronic masterpiece."

TEN

Gil Schaeffer pulled a fresh roll of antacids from the outer pocket of his briefcase. The morning's infinitely boring senate hearing topic—the increasing lack of equal access to higher education in America—drowned out the rip of the wrapper. He popped three of the chalky tablets into his mouth, congratulating himself on having avoided producing a spawn of his own.

His phone vibrated at the same time a staff member approached his row of seats. He glanced at the caller ID first. Gorin. Only the eighth call this morning. Taking on that crazy scientist as a business partner trumped the stupidity of the millions of Americans who'd had children.

He pressed IGNORE and took the note from the staff member waiting patiently at Gil's side.

Colonel Young to see you. He's waiting in the foyer. Urgent.

Gil's blood pressure climbed. He gave the attendant a terse nod, crunched another trio of antacids and picked up his briefcase.

In the grand, domed foyer of the Russell Senate Office Building, Owen Young paced between two pillars, hands clasped behind his back, head down. He glanced up just as Gil crossed the seal inlaid on the lobby floor, and the expression on his face told Gil he would need both a refill on antacids and his blood pressure meds.

He glanced at those close by, making sure no one important stood within hearing distance, then stopped two feet from Owen, leaned in and asked, "What's wrong?"

"They got Legend."

The words bounced off Gil as if he were made of rubber; still, the shockwave vibrated through his body. "That's not possible. Where did you hear that? Your intel is wrong."

"I heard it directly from one of your four *best agents*—Davis." The edge in Owen's voice matched that glint of superiority in his eyes. "They were ambushed by at least nine others, knocked out and restrained. Legend is gone."

The beat of Gil's heart tripped and stumbled before recovering at a far quicker pace. Legend couldn't be *gone*. He had enough information on the Pakistanis' smart weapons to keep Millennium Manufacturing in military contracts for the next ten years. Contracts that would easily net six hundred-*billion* dollars.

A veil of black darkened Gil's vision and his head grew heavy.

"Senator." Owen's voice sounded very far away. Muffled. A hand gripped Gil's arm. *"Senator."*

The compression on Gil's brain released. He shook off Owen's hand. To keep his voice under control, he scraped words through clenched teeth. "You were supposed to handle that. How could you screw up such a simple job?"

"You pulled me in too late." Owen's voice took a tone of controlled condescension. "By the time I sent reinforcements, your team had already been overpowered and Legend was gone."

Gil had known Owen would be a problem—in many ways. That thought had been among his first when he'd heard of Jocelyn's probable demise. Gil could have chosen to use someone else to lead this op, but of the available choices, Owen was by far the most experienced, the most focused, and held the best track record. But the characteristics that made Owen so successful also made him difficult to handle—his intelligence, his confidence, his need to be in control.

"Where. Are. They?"

Owen hesitated and stared at Gil as if he were as dumb as a dirt clod. No, this man would not be as easily controlled, swayed or bribed as Jocelyn.

"Are you aware, sir, of Mitch Foster's resources?"

"Of course, I'm aware—"

"Then you know they could be anywhere in the country by now. And they'll be guarded by the highest technological devices and the best trained forces, all of whom owe Foster their freedom, their lives, their first-fucking-born, or all of the above."

"And it's your job to find them. So *do it*."

Owen straightened. His hands dropped to his sides and something cold and sharp glinted in his eyes. Gil's hands fisted in an unconscious effort to grasp hold of his slipping control. He needed to keep Owen on his side, and he preferred not to threaten unless every other avenue had been exhausted. He'd play the patriot card, always a winner with a vet.

"Q has been making headway in uncovering a stash of smart weapons in Pakistan," Gil said. "Weapons that have the potential to annihilate our troops. We have to get him back to Punjab in two days or all the intelligence, the weapons themselves, and the men who designed the weapons will be history. That's months and months of work down the toilet and increased risk to our troops overseas. This is totally unacceptable. You're a decorated colonel, Owen. You've pulled off shit far more difficult than finding two men. You've got a multimillion-dollar budget at your disposal for Christ's sake." Gil's vision split horizontally, a haze coloring the bottom portion like a red tide rising. "Get. Them. Back."

He pulled a piece of paper from the outside pocket of his briefcase. "This is the name of an asset I've used in the past. He's good. And discreet. I dispatched him yesterday to locate O'Shay. But since we suspect O'Shay and Legend are together now, update him on the situation."

One side of Owen's face scrunched in distaste as he read the information. "Asset? You just said—"

"The others on their team will never let them go. If they're taken and the others are left, they'll never stop searching. The asset will capture O'Shay and Legend and eliminate the others without a trace."

"Now hold on, senator. You're taking this awfully far, awfully fast. It's a little soon to be setting up assassination orders. Give me a couple days to—"

"No. We don't have a couple of days." His face felt like it was too close to the sun. Sweat leaked from his hairline. "As I said"—Gil shook out his shoulders and pulled at the hem of his blazer—"in a couple of days, Legend needs to be back in Punjab. The asset has already been activated. Just tell him about Legend and let the man do his job. That's an order, Owen."

Q hit another shallow pocket of consciousness and clawed closer to the surface, desperate to hear her, see her, feel her. He'd bubbled up from that abyss several times, though he didn't know in what span of time. It didn't matter, because Jessica was always right there. Always touching him. Or kissing him. Or lying against him.

The last time he'd surfaced, she'd been wiping his body with a warm, wet cloth and some kind of clean, spicy soap that made him feel refreshed. She'd dawdled over every inch of his chest, arms, neck, face, dipping and wringing the rag dozens of times, inspecting every surface, every hill and valley. At some point, she'd even shaved his face. She often trailed kisses over his skin after she'd cleaned him, sending him into wild fits of pleasure he couldn't act on because he was still trapped in semi-consciousness.

Now, he brushed the surface and found her right where she always was—by his side. Her warm hand lay against the center of his chest, her hip against his side. Whispers touched his ears, but she wasn't talking to him. She was talking to another woman. The other voice was also familiar. From the vehicle that had brought them here.

Wherever the hell here was.

"You need to rest, Jess," the other woman said. "You're going to get sick. Then you won't be doing either of you any good."

"I'm not going to be gone when he wakes up."

He was close. Almost there. At the surface and ready to break through.

"Will you eat something?" the other woman asked. "It's after lunch and you didn't touch your breakfast. Kai has been making these crazy custom power smoothies for everyone—"

"Not right now."

The other woman sighed. "Need anything?"

Her fingers closed, scraping gently against Q's chest. Sensation skipped across his skin. Caused his hands to flex.

"Just for him to wake up," she said softly. "And remember."

"Give him time, honey."

The room fell silent again. He felt Jessica's stare on his face. Fought to open his eyes, but only got a flutter of lashes.

He pushed his mouth and tongue around. "Jess . . ." Came out in a rasp. He cracked his lids as she pushed up on her knees.

"Right here." She reached for something beside him. Slid one hand behind his head and lifted, bringing a straw to his lips. "Take a sip. It's orange juice, your favorite. We need to get some sugar into your blood."

Q sucked at the straw. The tangy, sugary liquid hit his tongue and lit off an immediate unquenchable thirst. As if he'd been fueled with instant energy, Q opened his eyes.

"Hey, there." Her voice was so soft, so sweet, it made his chest ache. "Are you really awake? Or is this just another temporary visit?"

The straw dried up and a slurping sound came from the glass. She set the empty drink on the ground, laid his head back carefully on a pillow and remained leaning over him, her hands caressing his face.

"Feel like heaven," he managed, finding it easier to talk with a moist throat, though his voice didn't sound any smoother. "So beautiful."

A slow smile turned her lips. Her eyes grew wet.

He managed to get one of his hands up and over hers. The orange juice seemed to be hitting his bloodstream. "Missed you so much. Don't leave."

"Never." Her whisper sounded rough as she shook her head. Tears dropped from her eyes and hit his cheeks. "I'll never leave you again."

Relief and excitement surged like a tidal wave and rocked him. No words could ever bring him this much joy. She lowered her head and kissed him. Just a touch of her lips, but Q needed more. He strained toward her, waiting for her lips to come back, but they didn't.

Need gave him the strength to slide the hand covering hers around the back of her head. Gravity did the rest. When her mouth met his, he took as much as he could, unsure of how long he'd have her. She gave with generous lips that caressed and sucked his in ways that made his mind twist and his body want. The sounds she made, emotional, heart-wrenching sounds, shivered through his mouth and ignited need throughout his body.

She tasted sweet, so sweet. Or maybe that was just the orange juice he'd been drinking. But she was fresh, warm, succulent. She was a drug. But nothing like the drugs those bastards used on him. She didn't suppress him, she lifted him. She was ecstasy. He was completely high. His entire body buzzed with excitement. Bright white light pulsed in his chest.

He felt alive.

Finally felt *alive.*

He rolled toward her and tried to wrap his free arm at her waist, but it was his bad arm and he didn't have the strength. He managed to fist the fabric and drag her with him as he rolled back. She moved easily, sliding on top of him and aligning their bodies. And, oh, she was so much more than he'd dreamed. Soft and strong. Lush and lean. Alive and pliant and warm. She was heaven. Absolute heaven.

His hunger intensified to starvation and he tasted her with a stroke of his tongue. She immediately responded, and the sensation of tongue against tongue diverted blood from Q's brain straight to his cock. The pressure was so intense he lifted his hips and rubbed against Jessica for relief.

She groaned, long and deep, before lifting her head and breaking their kiss. Tears shimmered in her eyes. They were so big. Such a soft, warm brown. Her rich, tawny hair spilled around her face, silky against his bare shoulders.

She gazed down at him, her lips turning in a tentative smile. "Am I hurting you?"

"Only if you stop." His voice sounded so hideously rough compared to hers. "I can't tell you . . . how long I've dreamt of this."

He raked his hand through her hair gently, absorbing

the feel of it between his fingers. She closed her eyes, those long lashes, which were the same gorgeous color as her hair, curved gently against her cheeks. A soft spray of freckles lay beneath, barely visible.

His chest had grown so incredibly tight, ribs squeezing his lungs until every intake of breath burned. Emotion welled inside until it overwhelmed him. Thoughts swirled in his mind without consent. Words pushed at his lips.

I love you.

The realization floated close as he held her face in one cupped hand. Fear encircled the warmth and excitement. How could he love her? How could he feel so over-whelmingly attached to her? And if Gorin found out how he felt . . .

Gorin.

Years of self-preservation and logic battled with the new and powerful emotions. His mind drifted to the man in the desert with the weapons and the hostages. Q still didn't know what that had been. A test? And this, was this a test?

Or now that he'd escaped, was this a *trap*?

The word vibrated in his head. Internally, a thin, cold veneer slipped into place, pushing his emotions into the background, bringing instinct and intellect to the fore-ground. The orange juice? Had it been drugged? Was this some new experiment? Something they'd been prepping him for? Something they'd implanted in his subconscious for years in case they ever needed to pull it out and use it as a weapon against him?

"What's wrong?" Her voice brought his eyes up to hers. They were worried. No . . . frightened. They were defi-nitely frightened. "Quaid, honey? Are you o—"

Muscle memory took over. Q had no idea where he found the strength or the coordination, but he flipped her and closed his hand over her throat.

"Stop," she rasped, clawing at his fingers. "Quaid, please. Stop. You're hurting—"

"Why are you calling me Quaid?" And why did holding her down like this make him want to put a gun to his own head? "Who are you? Who do you work for?"

"Quaid!" She turned her head and dragged in air, squirming beneath him. "I can't breathe!"

"What the fuck is going on?"

The deep voice sounded in the doorway. Q's body reacted again, thought only a hum in the background. He jerked Jessica off the floor and pulled her in front of him with an arm around her neck. The man at the door was big. With an authoritative presence. But he wasn't holding any weapons.

"Teague, take it easy." A woman appeared beside him. Mixed race, part Asian with long black hair, light eyes, very pregnant. Unless that was fake, too.

More people rushed through the door. He didn't know anyone. Didn't know where he was. Didn't know what the hell was going on. His body hardened. His mind sharpened. Fear pumped in his veins, preparing him for action.

Finally, a weapon appeared—pointed at his head. Yeah, now he knew where he stood. Only it was held by another woman. That was new.

Always kill the female terrorist first. They're the most unpredictable, the most unstable.

Q's gaze locked on the barrel of the Heckler & Koch Mark 23, his mind struggling to find the source of that terrorist trivia—until he realized he'd recognized the type of weapon pointed at him. Then he chalked it all up to a crazy-ass medicated hallucination.

But the woman holding the weapon ruined that idea when she spoke. "Let her go, Quaid."

This was shaping up to be a perfect training scenario.

Training for what? another part of his brain asked, which was when he considered this might not even be a hallucination. Maybe Gorin had finally spilt one too many brain cells and Q had gone schizophrenic.

"Should have known." One of the men spoke and Q's gaze darted toward him. He was leaning against a wall with one shoulder, arms crossed. Q narrowed his eyes, then cut a glance toward the Asian woman. They were family. Definitely. "This kind of shit is par for the course with you people."

"Mitch," the woman snapped with more force than her appearance suggested she commanded.

This Mitch put both hands on his hips. "Out of all the people here, Quaid, she is the last one you want to hurt."

Q sidestepped the other men to better see the woman holding the weapon. Something about her . . . Black hair, blue eyes, pretty. Something seemed familiar. He repositioned his grip on Jessica.

"Don't you dare." The brown-haired man next to the woman with the weapon obviously recognized the dangerous hold Q had on Jessica's neck. He put a hand up and stepped forward with fear and fury in his eyes. "If you hurt her, you're going to wish you were back in that fucking hell hole, Quaid."

"Stop calling me Quaid." His chest felt like a time bomb.

"Kai," Jessica rasped from beneath Q's arm. "Shut up."

A crawling sensation started low in his belly. One he definitely didn't understand. He only knew he had to escape. Get away from these people. This situation. "Get out of my way."

"Q." Another man pushed through the crowd. Where were they all coming from? "What are you doing, man?"

Cash's voice. Finally, something that resonated with Q. He froze and focused on his friend. Black hair, blue eyes . . . Q's gaze flicked back to the woman holding the gun—his sister, Keira. Cash had shown him a picture of her while they'd been in prison together. He'd slipped it through the vent between their cells just days before the explosion.

Q didn't know whether to feel relieved or not. "Cash, what's this? What's happening?"

"Cash," Keira said from behind her brother, her voice raised and worried. "Make him drop that damned neck-breaking hold on her. Damn it, Quaid, don't make me shoot you, you asshole."

"Listen to her, dude." This came from the blond next to Keira. "She won't kill you, but she'll make you wish you were dead."

"Keira," Cash said, "put the gun down, you're making this worse."

"Not until he releases that hold on Jess."

Cash glanced back at Q. Evaluated his grip. "Where the hell did you learn that? Come on, Q, you're not going to hurt her. You're scaring everyone. Just take her out of that hold."

Q didn't move. Didn't like his odds or his options.

"Quaid," Keira said. "I love you, and I'm thrilled you're alive, but if you don't release Jessica's head, I'm going to *take off your fucking ear.*"

The blond next to Keira lifted his brows and said, "Listen to her, Quaid. She's a sniper in her day job."

"This might go better if you called him Q," Cash said.

But Q was still stuck on the *I love you* and the *I'm thrilled you're alive* statement.

"Qua—Q." Jessica faltered on his name. The fact that she'd deliberately called him Q, even though they all clearly thought of him as Quaid, softened something inside him. "Please."

That damn voice did it. He took his hand off her head and wrapped it around her waist, then loosened the arm at her throat.

Keira lowered her weapon, turned toward the blond—Luke, they'd called him—and dropped her forehead against his shoulder. "Asshole is so going to pay for that as soon as he remembers enough to make it worth my effort."

Luke put his arm around Keira and turned her toward the door. "You can beat up on me until that happens."

Q backed away from the group, pulling Jessica up against him. The perfect curve of her lower spine cradled his erection, which was incredibly distracting. As distracting as her scent. Her hair smelled like flowers and sunshine, though how he knew that was a mystery. He'd never seen real flowers, let alone smelled them. A spicy scent rose with the heat of her body and another layer of something earthy, musky and deliciously seductive lurked beneath.

Cash turned to the others. "Can we have a few minutes?"

The quiet dark-haired woman, whose name still hadn't been mentioned, took the guy named Teague's arm. Teague glanced at the one they called Kai, who was still glaring at Q.

"Come on, Kai," Teague said on his way out the door.

Kai was the last man out. He paused in the doorframe, turned halfway back and set fierce green eyes on Q. "I'll still kick your ass to Iceland, Quaid. I don't give a shit what you do or don't remember."

Once they were gone, Q muttered, "What the hell did I do to him?"

A second of heavy silence broke with Jessica's raspy, "You died."

He hadn't realized he was still holding her. She was small and warm and fit him so perfectly, like she belonged right here. She swallowed, her delicate neck rolling against his forearm, making him realize his arm was still across her neck.

"On his watch," she finished.

He abruptly let her go and backed across the room, scanning his peripheral vision for escape, for weapons, for . . . something that said *safety*.

"Q, relax," Cash said. "Let's sit down and talk. We'll straighten everything out."

Q's gaze came around and he found Cash. Then Jessica. She stood at the door, one hand on her throat, one wrapped around the end of a necklace, tears wetting her face. She wore shorts and a fitted top with thin straps over her shoulders. Her arms and legs bare. Her sweet little feet bare. And that hair, that glorious hair he'd dreamt of touching for years falling everywhere.

His gut squeezed with guilt and confusion. He still wanted to touch her. To kiss her. To hold her. Yet he didn't trust her. Different parts of his brain warred and pressure built in his head.

He lifted a hand toward her, but spoke to Cash. "How'd she get here, man? Out of my dreams?" He lowered his voice. "I think she's Gorin's. You know how he gets me addicted to things and then takes them away to mess with me."

"No," Cash said, his tone firm. "Stop right there, Q." Then he turned to Jessica. "Let me straighten him out, Jess."

She pressed her lips together and lowered the hand at her throat, but continued stroking whatever lay on the end of the chain around her neck. Dropping her gaze to the floor, she turned for the door. But before she closed it behind her, she glanced back and met Q's eyes.

"No one can take me away from you." Her voice was soft but serious. "I make that decision, and I made you a promise. I'm not going anywhere."

The door clicked closed behind her.

ELEVEN

The only thing Q knew about promises was that there were no such things.

He moved to the window of the small room, stood to the side and peered out around the flat concrete edge. His heart thudded beneath his breastbone. His mind and body pulled toward Jessica even though instincts pushed him to escape.

"Where are we? How far to the nearest road? Is there a car close we can hot-wire? I have no idea how I know, but I could rig almost any kind—"

"What the hell are you talking about?"

"I'm talking about getting us the hell out of here."

Q scanned the terrain. In the distance, two men in fatigues carrying Colt M4A1's passed. They spoke for a moment and then moved on. For a reason he couldn't begin to comprehend, the sight settled him. Men with high-grade weapons, he understood. That, he could deal with. But women who battled with the insanity of emotion? It was no wonder his mind told him to kill female terrorists first.

"How many guards do they have?" he asked. "And who the hell armed these guys? They've got better weapons than the Castle guards. Doesn't matter. We can take them out. We just need a plan."

"Q."

"What?" A wash of exhaustion weakened his muscles and he used the wall to hold himself up. The drug's after-effect was right on schedule. "Stop jabbering and start using that genius brain of yours, Sci-fi. I'm fading. If we're going to get out of here, we've got to break now—"

A hand gripped his arm and spun him around. Q looked into Cash's still unfamiliar face. Even features, strong jaw, straight nose. His blue eyes were striking against his black hair and lashes.

"We're not going anywhere." Cash spoke deliberately, his eyes sparking with frustration. "Slow *your* genius brain the hell down so I can talk to you."

"No time. Can't you see this is another trap? Gorin must have planted Jessica in my subconscious, pushed her into my dreams, so when they needed leverage, they could send her in person to manipulate me. If I let her in, I'll walk right back into their hands. We both will."

Q flipped the lock on the window and hauled it open. Hands on the sill, he ducked and leaned out, scanning the field and the trees beyond with the intent of listening and staring into the distance. But the sweet taste of the air hit him. Crisp and alive, it filled his senses like the first bite of that rare, real apple Gorin gave him once a month. But only if he'd been cooperative.

Q sucked in a big beautiful lungful of the stuff, wondering if they grew apples here. Imagined sitting at the base of a tree, eating apples right off the branch.

Cash gripped the waistband of his jeans and hauled him back. Q smacked his skull on the window frame. Pain cracked through his head.

"Shit." He ducked into the house, rubbed the back of his head and turned, glaring at Cash. "What the hell, man?"

Jaw tight, Cash pointed to the bed. "Sit."

Fine. Q couldn't hold it together anymore anyway. That smack on the head brought all his exhaustion and pain into acute focus and his whole body sagged. His bad limbs, which had pulled their weight in the heat of things, were now weak and aching.

Q slumped to a seat on the bed. He wanted to close his eyes and fall into this fatigue, but knew he couldn't. Cash took the only chair, sitting on the edge. Elbows planted on his knees, his friend looked at him with a gravity he'd often imagined during their conversations at the Castle.

"Relax," Cash said. "Just long enough to listen for a few minutes. You won't get anywhere by passing out."

Q fought to sit still, even though instinct urged him to act. "You're not what I expected. Not like I had pictured in my mind."

Some of the distress left Cash's face and one side of his mouth lifted. "You either."

"I thought you'd be . . . I don't know, smaller for some reason. Less bulk."

Cash narrowed his eyes, but the stare completely lacked menace. "You calling me fat?"

Q huffed a laugh. Let the smile come. Let the tension ebb. "Hardly."

"And you." Cash lowered a brow, and scanned Q's chest. "What's up with all the muscle? That didn't come from my workout plan. And there's no difference between your right and left sides, like there should be from the injury you described."

Q glanced down at himself, but didn't see anything unusual.

"Listen, I know you're freaked. I know this is all foreign to you." Cash adjusted his seat, pressed his hands together and aligned his palms and fingers. "But you're among friends here, Q. There is no reason to run. Nothing to escape."

Q glanced at the closed door, remembering the anger, the bottled emotions and shook his head.

"Q, look at me."

He did.

"Do you trust me?"

Q's stomach tensed. He stared hard at Cash. Opened his mouth, but couldn't answer. His intellect told him, yes, he trusted Cash above all others. His instincts told him, no, he trusted no one.

"You know no one understands what you're going through more than I do," Cash said.

Q nodded.

"You need to get your head straight on a few basic things before you go out there."

Q stiffened.

Cash put up his hand. "You *are* going out there, Q. That's the first thing you may as well just accept right now. These people risked their lives to get you out of that safe house. *I* risked my life to get you out of there. You will damn well not throw that back in our faces by running away."

"That's not . . ." He slid toward the end of the bed and leaned against the footboard for support. "I'm not trying to hurt anyone. I just . . . don't belong here."

"Q, after what you've been through, you wouldn't feel as if you belonged anywhere. And this is *exactly* where you belong," he said, voice low but imploring. "There is nowhere on earth you belong more than *right here,* with *these people*. This is what you've always wanted. You have it all right here, within reach. A family. A place to belong. People who *love you.*"

"Love me? They're all pissed off at me. Your sister was going to *shoot* me. I may not understand much about real life, Cash, but I know that's not love."

"You put her in an impossible position. You forced her to choose between two of her best friends. They all love Jessica, too, Q. And there's also something called tough love. When loving someone means giving them hard limits, making them live up to certain standards, forcing them to be the best that can be, even if that means being hard on them. Kind of like me telling you to stop acting like an asshole. And if you don't pull your head out pretty quick, I'll be using that tough love a lot more."

Best friends. The sentiment tugged deep in his chest, yet nothing moved in his memory.

"Besides," Cash said, voice downgrading from anger to annoyance, "she wouldn't have killed you. She would have just maimed you—enough to get you to let go of Jessica. She's an FBI sniper."

"*FBI?* Does she realize the people who sign her paychecks are in the same family tree as the people who had me locked up?"

"As a matter of fact she does. And yet she's here." Cash spread his hands wide. "What does that tell you?"

"That she didn't get your IQ."

Cash laughed, a tired sound, reminding Q of his friend's long hours in the lab. "I wouldn't suggest saying that to her, unless you're willing to give up that ear."

Q stood and paced across the room, trying to find some safe place to ground himself before he started with all the questions waiting to explode in his brain. But he just kept seeing all their faces, yet not getting one flicker of recognition. They were all completely blank canvases. Absolute strangers. All except Jessica.

"I don't understand *anything.*" His gut felt heavy, as if he'd swallowed a truckload of cement. "I don't remember them, Cash. I don't know any of them except Jessica. And how do you explain her?"

"You know I can't answer that any more than you can. All I can tell you is that these people are the kind of friends who become family over time. Each person in the other

room has made a conscious sacrifice to be here—*for you.*
They dropped everything in their lives when they found
that coin in your cell. They spent every waking moment
searching for you. Pulled in favors. Set up a rescue operation. Executed it. Saved your sorry ass. Brought you here,
where you're safe . . . where Gorin can't get you. And
what are you doing?" Cash's voice turned sour and disappointed. "Trying to escape."

The disapproval stung. Then something else registered,
and Q swung toward Cash. "What did you say? About my
coin?"

"I didn't get out of the Castle on my own, like you and
I had worked out," Cash said. "Keira and her friends had
a plan to rescue us and surprised me halfway. They went
to your cell, but the guards already had you in the sally
port for transport. That's when they found your coin. And
they knew there was a real possibility that you were alive.
Their dedication to finding you from that moment on
never wavered. They were two hundred percent on board
to get you back."

"They risked their lives *twice* for the *possibility* . . . ?" Q
trailed off as a staggering realization hit him. One even
deeper than the astounding insight he'd just made. "For
the possibility they'd found *Quaid.*"

Q's stomach dropped. His mind spiraled. He thought of
the planning and coordination and resources this type of
operation must have required. He remembered the love in
Jessica's eyes, the emotion in her kiss. *I made you a promise.*

At the window, Q braced himself on the concrete sill.
All the fight drained out of him. Who must this Quaid
have been to win that kind of loyalty, that depth of feeling?

Someone Q was not. Someone Q could never be.

The weight of that realization made him heavier than

his muscles could bear. He turned his back to the wall and slid down until his butt hit the floor. Then he laid his forehead against his knees. "My God."

"Look, this is going to take time. We're safe. We have everything we need: food, clothes, computers, weapons. We can stay here for a while. Figure out our next move."

Q wasn't listening, his mind still searching, questioning. He lifted his head and met Cash's eyes. "Who are they to me?"

Cash hesitated. "The doctors think it's best for you to remember things on your own—"

"Fuck the doctors. Psycho doctors are the reason I'm so screwed up."

"Q, don't yell. There's enough tension here already. And watch what you say about doctors. Alyssa is a doctor. A very good one who cares about you."

"Which one is Alyssa?"

"Teague's wife. Long dark hair, pregnant."

"The quiet one."

Cash's mouth lifted in a wry smile. "She's not all that quiet. She's plenty good at getting her point across when she needs to."

Q scraped his fingers over his scalp, feeling his scars. "Who are they to me, Cash?"

"Some are members of a firefighting team you were on. Alyssa and Mitch are Teague's family."

The words fell into a black void and faded until they disappeared. Nothing pinged to life—no memories. No sensation.

"I was a . . . firefighter?"

"Yes, on a hazmat team—a special hazardous materials team."

Q waited. Searched his mind, his body. Shook his head. "I get nothing from that."

Cash nodded. "Okay. That's okay."

"What about names?" Maybe that would spark something. "What are their names?"

Cash took a breath and watched Q as he said, "There's
Teague Creek."

Q shook his head and made a keep-going motion with
his hands.

"Kai Ryder was the chief of the team." He paused.
"Luke Ransom." Now he paused between each name.
"Keira O'Shay. Seth Masters."

"Was he in the room? I didn't hear that name."

"He's not here. He's tracking down leads related to
those microchips they use for tracking . . . and other
things." When Q just shrugged, Cash said, "And just one
more, Jessica Fury."

His entire body tingled, twisted, throbbed. Hell, yeah.
That name did all kinds of shit to him. "Jessica Fury. Fury.
Fury." He repeated the name, closed his eyes, reached and
searched. And came up empty. He pounded his palms
against his eyes. "*Shit*. I remember *nothing*. I swear to
God"—he lifted his head and met Cash's eyes—"Gorin
better hope I never find him."

"Let's hope Gorin never finds you." Cash sat back, and
then stood. "And let's get you something to eat or you're
going to start losing all that muscle. Do a meet and greet
while we're at it, because, hell, we're so good in social settings. And you may as well get used to them calling you
Quaid, because that's your name, buddy—Quaid Legend."

Gil patted his mouth with the three-hundred-count
white linen napkin and refolded it on his lap, still laughing
appropriately at Senator Perino's fishing tale.

"I kid you not," Perino said, his balding head red from
laughing at his own story. "I smelled like fish for a week."

Gil's phone vibrated just as his fork plunged into another bite of quite possibly the best macadamia nut en-

crusted salmon he'd ever eaten. He kept his smile in place, but ground his teeth and pretended to listen to Perino and two other senators from the Armed Forces Committee debate the pros and cons of various fly-fishing reels.

Since Gil didn't fish—what a damn waste of time—he glanced at his phone and read the name he'd expected to find—Abernathy. Gil tapped the IGNORE button on Major Abernathy's third call of the day.

He glanced up with the thought to call Owen after lunch to see what strides he'd made in tracking down Legend and O'Shay, and realized the men at the table had gone silent. The hair on Gil's neck rose. He cast a quick glance at each of their faces, then followed their gazes to the man standing beside their table.

Gorin stared back at him, looking like the classic mad scientist with his long white tattered lab jacket, mussed hair, thick-lensed glasses and crazed eyes pinned on Gil.

He set his fork down, put his napkin on the table and offered a controlled, polite, "I'll be right back, gentlemen."

Pushing his chair back, he took Gorin's arm and walked him toward the exit, meeting every gaze that turned his way with a smile and an apologies-for-the-circus-sideshow nod.

"You told me you'd find him." Gorin spoke quickly as they moved. "You don't understand how difficult it will be for him to cope in the real world. I don't have him programmed for that. You promised me there was no way for him to escape. You said I didn't need to worry. You didn't want me to take the time to code him to go out there, do his job and come back under *normal conscious conditions*. Now he's out there alone—"

"Wait until we're outside," Gil said through a smile of clenched teeth.

"But, but, anything could happen. He could snap and

go insane. He could turn into a mass murderer. He could come searching for us. He could remember everything we've trained him to do. All he's already done on missions. *Everything*, Gil."

Gil pushed the outer door to the restaurant open and then Gorin through it. Finally, fresh air and privacy. After one quick glance around uncovered no immediate witnesses, Gil fisted the front of Gorin's button-down shirt and slammed him against the nearest wall. "Shut. Up. Max."

The shocked look on Gorin's pale face and the blessed silence gave Gil a moment to collect his temper. "There," he said on a deep breath. "Better."

Gorin jerked out of Gil's grasp and leaned in. "I need him back. He was in the middle of two important missions. Major Abernathy and General Cochrane are calling me every hour because you're not answering your phone."

Great, it was only a matter of time until Cochrane was jumping down Gil's throat, too.

"Don't you think I know that? I'm doing all I can. I've got Owen Young running things and an asset on Q's tail. What more do you want, Max? Magic tricks? My future depends on him, too. And I want that fucking formula from O'Shay. I notice you haven't mentioned that. All you care about is your little protégé." He pushed Gorin back again, more to get the man out of his face than to intimidate. "You'd better remember that it's O'Shay's formula that's going to finance all the games you like to play with Q, especially if his escape costs Millennium those weapons contracts.

"In fact, this is a good time for you to refocus on Millennium, Max. You know, the company that lets you play with your science, something no other company would allow." Schaeffer put a rigid finger against Max's bony chest and poked hard. "The company that's been backing you on your badass plan of cloning the invincible soldier."

"And I will, Gil. I will. Q was coming along so nicely. You know he will be the prototype for a whole new army of the future—"

"Not if we don't *get him back*. And I can't strategize plans with the people searching for Q if I'm getting calls from you every hour of the damn day." Gil sucked air into his lungs. "I'll handle my end of the business, Max. You stay out of it."

Q fisted his hands as he followed Cash down the cement block hallway with a cement slab floor. While those were the only similarities to the Castle, they were enough to give Q that sick feeling of walking the Castle's yard toward Gorin's lab.

He tried to focus on the amazing scent of food. His stomach was doing a great job there, rolling and growling like a monster. There were so many new smells, they overlapped and mixed. Strawberry was the scent that dominated, but he detected other fruits, too—pineapple, orange, melon, kiwi, mango. Though he had no idea how he knew how to identify those smells. And beyond fruit, other foods delivered olfactory messages, too. Bread, spices, meat . . .

While his salivary glands were operating on high, his mind cataloging foods he craved, it was also untangling the multiple voices carrying on several different conversations. Voices of people who'd apparently risked their lives to rescue him. Voices of people who thought they knew him. Voices of people he had absolutely no recollection of and wasn't sure he wanted to get to know now.

Cash turned a corner and disappeared into another room. Q's feet came to a stop. The scents and sounds faded into the background and fear jumped forward. His hands tensed and flexed. His teeth gnashed. Sweat broke out across his forehead. Across his shoulders. A buzz grew in his ears.

"Q?"

Q looked at Cash, who'd returned to stand in the middle of the hallway, waiting for him, but couldn't speak. What was he going to say? *I'm having a panic attack because I'm free and I don't know how to be free? There are people that exist who love me and I don't know how to be loved?*

The simple change in Cash's expression from confusion to compassion told Q he understood . . . which was bizarre in itself, because he'd just seen Cash for the first time twenty minutes ago and now he could read the other man's expressions.

Q dropped his face into his hands and rubbed hard.

"Hey." Cash's voice was low, gentle. He put a hand on Q's shoulder and squeezed.

There had been a guard who'd done that once in a while. One who used to sneak Q extra food and bring him old Clive Cussler novels. Q pictured the guard's dark face, his broad smile.

"Q?"

He lifted his head. "Did Dooley die in the explosion? Chet Dooley, the guard? He had a family. A wife and three daughters."

"I . . . don't know. But I'll do what I can to find out, okay?"

Q took a deep breath and let it out. Nodded. Glanced toward the end of the hall. Looked at Cash.

"I know," Cash said. "Take your time. Just know these are the good people. They would go to the ends of the earth to keep you safe."

Q just couldn't grasp the existence of that kind of loyalty, especially toward him. And the noise from the next room was already rubbing his nerves raw. Talking, laughing, things banging, doors opening and closing.

Eventually, his curiosity over these mysterious people from his past surpassed his fears and he followed Cash.

The size of the room registered first. Enormous with high ceilings. Then Q catalogued the doors. Windows. Layout. Furnishings. Then the fact that Jessica wasn't there. *No one can take me away.*

"Where is she?" he whispered to Cash.

"Don't know. Outside maybe."

Outside? He glanced at the glass doors again, restless. Could he go outside?

"Later," Cash said. "Focus."

No one had noticed him yet and Q took the opportunity to observe and take a quick head count. Four men and two women, not including him and Cash. Teague and Alyssa sat on one sofa, Luke and Keira on another, the two couples talking. Kai and Mitch stood in a room off to the left where every horizontal surface was covered with food.

Q forced his gaze away from the sight of Kai cutting some type of fruit and onto the middle of the living room floor, where bins of colorful things surrounded two . . .

"Are those . . . ?" Q realized what a ridiculous question he was about to ask. "I mean, I know they're kids. They're just so . . . small."

"Kids generally are." Cash grinned. "Mateo, come here and meet Quaid."

Q tensed and stepped back. Everyone in the room turned or looked up and Q felt the pressure of eight new pairs of eyes.

The boy popped to his feet and sprinted across the space, rounded a couch and ran right into Cash's legs. *"Baba!"*

From where she still sat on the floor, Kat said, "Hi, Uncle Quaid. Do you like Barbies?" And without waiting for an answer, returned her attention to whatever gadget she held in her hand.

Uncle Quaid?

Q's throat thickened until it became uncomfortable to swallow. The boy bounced at Cash's feet, reaching up, babbling about winning a video game—whatever the hell that was—distracting Q from the sudden and unfamiliar emotions.

"Mateo," Cash said, his voice smooth and patient. "English, son, English. My Greek isn't—"

"He beat the cat at a video game?" Q said, questioning his translation, wondering how a cat could play a game. "They bet . . ." Q tilted his head. "Nail polish? And what are 'Barbies'?"

Cash started laughing. A deep, rolling, rich laugh, but the rest of the room had gone completely quiet.

"He beat *Kat* at a video game," Cash said, grinning. "I didn't know you spoke Greek."

"I . . ." Another surge of fear pulsed through him. Translating the words had been automatic, as if he thought in multiple languages. ". . . didn't either."

Cash's smile didn't just fade, it dropped and concern etched lines between his eyes. Then he lifted the boy into his arms and his expression changed again. He looked at his son with so much love, Q experienced a sense of yearning as deep as the longing he'd felt to remember his past. Which made as much sense to Q as the fact that those with knowledge of his past filled the room and all he wanted to do was run.

He looked at the big glass doors, then beyond, as far as the trees allowed. But he couldn't even catch a glimpse of Jessica.

Cash smiled at Q. "This is my son, Mateo. Mateo this is—"

"Q!" He drew out the sound as if in celebration, throwing his arms overhead. Then he fell forward, would have fallen right out of his father's arms, but stopped himself with his hands on Q's shoulders.

The touch launched a fierce sensation of turbulence through Q's system, and it took a moment for him to realize it was a good feeling. One of energy and happiness and hope.

Mateo lifted his head and smiled up at Q with big, warm brown eyes filled with joy and innocence. "Thank you for my daddy, Q."

He turned his head, planted a kiss on Q's shoulder and squirmed out of Cash's arms and to the ground. "Love you, *baba*."

He shot off toward the back of the house again, leaving the room silent and Quaid trembling with a sense of blissful possibilities and tormented loss. His time at the Castle was starting to look positively serene in comparison to his first few hours free.

"Bet you're hungry." The voice came from the kitchen behind Q. He turned just as Kai set down a knife and picked up a bowl of strawberries piled beyond the rim.

He came around a counter toward Q and the scent that came with him was so strong, so absolutely, deliriously amazing, Q's head went light. Fresh, ripe, pure strawberry. Saliva filled Q's mouth. His stomach rolled with hunger. Craving tugged deep inside him.

Kai plucked one huge, perfect strawberry from the bowl and popped it in his mouth. The damn thing was so big it barely fit, filling one cheek as he chewed, and he was already dipping into the bowl for another. "These are amazing, even out of season." He held the bowl out to Q. "They used to be your favorite."

Q tore his gaze from the bowl. "They were?"

"We used to have to hide them from you if we wanted

any." Kai pushed another into his mouth. "You'd eat an entire half-flat in one sitting. Try 'em."

Q took the bowl and found himself frozen. The scent was overpowering. As was the fear.

Trap.

He glanced at Cash, who nodded. So he pushed the fear aside and met Kai's gaze. "I know why you wanted to kick my ass, but why to Iceland?"

Surprise flashed in Kai's eyes before he grinned. "It was the furthest, coldest place I could think of."

"Actually, Antarctica is the coldest place on earth and Turkmenistan is the furthest place from—"

"Shut up, man." Kai laughed and shook his head. "You always had a smart mouth. Hell, I know I shouldn't, I know you're totally freaked out, but . . . I'm so happy to see you . . . what the hell, I don't even care if you try to choke me. . . ."

And before Q could think to react, Kai pulled him into a tight hug. A sudden, sharp sense of claustrophobia closed in. He was about to break away from Kai when Cash patted his back and took the bowl of strawberries from his flailing hand.

You're among friends.

"Shit, man," Kai rasped, still holding Q bound, which somehow felt . . . both frightening and awkward. "I've never been so glad to see anyone in my whole life."

Q didn't know if it was the words or the emotion behind the words, but something reached into his gut and yanked hard. Then something else swept in. Overwhelming affection. Crushing gratitude. An awesome sense of brotherhood.

He didn't even know what the hell *brotherhood* was. And he wasn't sure if the emotions were coming from Kai or from inside himself. But it didn't matter. They were short-circuiting Q's overtaxed psyche.

He pushed at Kai's chest.

"Sorry, dude." Kai immediately stepped back, rubbing at his eyes with the back of his hand, the other hand on Q's shoulder, his expression both relieved and pained. "Welcome back."

Q's chest ached. Part of him wanted to hug the man back, which was just . . . too weird. Part of him was crawling out of his skin to dive through the nearest plate-glass window in escape.

Kai turned and walked back to the sink, where he started working with the fruit again, sniffling and wiping at his face.

Cash held the strawberries out to Q, a warm smile on his face. "You okay?"

"I don't know what I am."

He took the strawberries back, and stared down at the plump, ruby-red fruit. He wanted to do a face plant into the bowl and devour the fragrant jewels, but still couldn't bring himself to take even one. He'd conditioned himself not to show any level of desire for anything. Especially not anything he really wanted. As soon as Gorin identified something Q desired, he used it as a reward, a punishment, a bribe, a threat . . . anything to get Q to perform to the scientist's standards.

Cash took a strawberry, murmuring, "Eat them. No one will take them away. I promise."

Only the sight of Cash putting one of the berries into his mouth, two others cradled in his hand, pried Q's self-control loose.

Q picked up a strawberry and bit it in half. Sweetness burst into his mouth, cool and fragrant. He chewed, slowly. Juice pulsed from the fruit and coated his tongue. "My God."

"We've got three more flats of those." Kai waved a dismissive hand. "We'll all be sick of them by tomorrow. Eat as many as you want."

Q wrapped a possessive arm around the bowl and found a wall to lean against while he savored every precious berry.

"Q has questions," Cash said to the room in general. "Wants some answers."

"Who doesn't?" Mitch said. He stood at another counter shaking spices onto slabs of beef and rubbing them in. "We're all here for the same thing."

"How can that be possible?" Q asked around two full strawberries.

"Freedom. Justice. Security," Mitch said. "They're inherent human desires."

Q shoved another berry in his mouth, gauged the risk of asking the question hovering at the forefront of his mind, then gave up. "Did I . . . know you?"

"Nope, not me. You and me, we're starting with a clean slate. I didn't come on scene until after Alyssa hooked up with jailbird over there."

"Watch yourself, Foster," Teague said, "or you're gonna find some of those strawberries where you least expect them."

Keira snorted a laugh. In the living area, all four people on the sofas watched him. All four grinning with a peculiar look in their eyes that made Q decidedly uncomfortable. At least, Keira didn't have a weapon in her hand. The fact that both Teague and Mitch appeared amused eased Q's tension. They must have been joking, the way the guards used to.

"Quaid," Teague said, "you might want to slow down."

Even though Teague was all the way across the room and the strawberries were almost gone, Q tensed. He glanced at Teague and found his brow creased with worry.

"You probably want to go light and bland for the first couple weeks," he said. "Those are pretty acidic. They might be hard on your stomach, buddy."

Teague's concern layered on top of all the rest was too much, and Q found it hard to swallow the berry he was chewing. He nodded, dropped the one held between his fingers and sucked at the red stains as he tried to get his thoughts and emotions back in line. But he was starting to feel swollen with them all. Like a balloon ready to burst.

Even though he wanted to down the berries left in the bowl, he set them back on the counter.

"Where's Jessica?" he asked, yearning for the sight of her.

"She went for a walk." The pregnant woman's voice flowed over Q like cool water. She'd risen from the sofa and now set two drinking glasses on the counter in the kitchen, then walked toward Q with one hand on her big belly.

"I'm Alyssa," she said. "Teague's wife. You and I didn't know each other from before either, so we're starting fresh, too."

She put her hand out. It was small, but looked strong.

"We're both a little rusty on the manners," Cash said, then elbowed Q's ribs.

Q braced himself in preparation for . . . whatever came . . . and reluctantly took Alyssa's hand. The same sensation her voice brought, one of calm waters, spread through his body at her touch and eased his tension.

She was smiling. A real smile. Warm, sincere. And she was beautiful. Perfectly balanced face, wide, unusual eyes, full mouth and a little nose. Her black hair seemed to stand out against the creamy paleness of her perfect skin. Yet he felt no interest. No attraction. No arousal.

Nothing like what he felt when he touched Jessica.

"How's your pain?" she asked.

He withdrew his hand and checked in with his body. It only ached for one thing. "Fine. Which way did Jessica go?"

"Out the back, through the sliders. But it's a huge property—"

"I need air." He sounded like he needed air—breathless. Strangled. He started toward the big glass doors.

On the porch, Cash stopped him with a hand on his arm.

Q turned. "I can't do this. I'm ready to crawl out of my skin."

"I understand," Cash said, his eyes serious, devoid of pity. Q realized that was one of the emotions he saw in everyone else's eyes and it was grating on him. "I want you to get some space. I'll buffer you. Run interference. But you have to promise me, Q, give me your word, friend to friend, that you won't leave without telling me."

His jaw pulsed. He didn't want to give that promise. He wanted to be free to cut ties if he needed. But this man had kept him going for years.

He started for the stairs leading to the open land and forest beyond.

"Quaid?"

Q clenched his teeth, but stopped and turned. Keira and Luke stood on the porch, their expressions serious. He tensed.

"We, um . . . " Keira glanced over her shoulder at the blond standing close, hands in the front pockets of his jeans, his easy-going smile replaced by a tight set to his mouth. "We have to leave."

Q turned fully toward them, a new sense of alarm burning along his spine. "Why?"

"Remember that key I pulled from the necklace around Dargan's neck?" Cash asked at Q's side.

Q thought back to the night Jocelyn Dargan had surprised Cash at the Castle in the middle of the night. She'd come to incentivize Cash to finish his formula by showing him a photo of Keira and Mateo and alluding to the threat of killing them if Cash didn't finish the project fast.

Cash had lunged at her, gripped her jacket collar and broken her necklace, which he'd then hidden until she'd gone. By the time she'd realized it was missing, Cash had tied dental floss to the key that had been hanging on the end of the necklace and swallowed it. He'd retrieved it by pulling the key back up his esophagus by the floss.

"Yeah," Q said. "I remember."

"It fits a safe-deposit box," Cash said. "We've narrowed down the banks it could belong to and Keira and Luke are going to try to find the box it matches and see if there's anything in it that can help us."

Q searched his memory, but came up empty. "What's a safe-deposit box?"

Keira's mouth opened as if to say something, but nothing came out. Keira, Luke and Cash shared a look. Obviously, a safe-deposit box was something Quaid would have known.

"Never mind," Q said, suddenly irritated. Wanting Jessica that much more. "How long will you be gone? You're coming back?"

"We'll be back as soon as we can," Keira said, both of them smiling as if he'd said something amusing. "You didn't think you were getting rid of us that easy, did you?"

She stepped toward him at the same time he moved toward her and they walked into a hug that felt natural and comfortable. A completely different sensation than he had with Jessica. Holding Jessica made Q restless in a very sexual way. Made Q's heart tighten and twist and turn.

With her arms wrapped tightly around his neck, Keira whispered, "So good to have you back."

That damned annoying wetness pushed at his eyes again. He gave her a squeeze and said, "Watch your six."

Keira released his neck and pulled back. Tears wet her lashes and made her eyes shine a brilliant blue. "Wh-what?"

"Be careful."

He let her go and turned to Luke, who maintained a lazy stance. His easy grin had returned. Q didn't know how or why, but his gut told him Luke could be one of the most intense in the group. But he was obviously content and deeply happy right now. And Q had no doubt that had everything to do with the blue-eyed sniper. The same way Alyssa made Teague smile. And maybe, Q was growing to realize, why he kept seeking out Jessica.

Q took a few steps toward Luke, not sure what to do. Luke held out his hand, so Q took it. And they fell into a comfortable handshake followed by a tight hug, as if he and Luke had done this all their lives.

Q wondered if they had.

"Good to have you home, buddy," Luke said, his voice thick with emotion. Then he slapped his back and released him.

"Be careful," Q repeated to Luke, then turned and headed down the stairs in search of the one person he needed most.

TWELVE

Jessica stared out over the small ravine that bordered two sides of the property from her seat on the flat, rough surface of a sun-warmed boulder. Charcoal-colored rock lined the ravine walls. Down in the shallow valley a creek flowed through a meadow dotted by multicolored trees. The same trees painted the hillsides as far as Jessica could see with a kaleidoscope of fall colors from mellow yellows to fiery reds. The heavenly landscape all pressed up against a pristine robin's-egg blue sky with distant, cotton-ball clouds.

She couldn't help but smile, even though it sliced her insides. The sheer beauty of it, the perfection seemed so . . . wrong . . . under the circumstances. And if she didn't adjust her emotions, those clouds in the distance would be overhead and pouring rain before she had time to get back to the bunker.

Jessica shook her thoughts away. Closed her eyes and took a deep cleansing breath—in through her nose, out through her mouth. In with clean, crisp perfection, out with ugly, chronic pain. She purposely relaxed each muscle, starting with her face and working her way down her body.

She centered her mind. Then her core. Visualized herself grounded to the rich earth through roots that grew out of her crossed legs and stretched over the boulder, sinking deep into the ground. There they tunneled to the white-hot core of the earth, drew its energy up through the roots like water and pulled that soul-mending source straight into her body. Directly to her heart. Where the organ then pumped that magic back through her system.

And for a moment she felt it—a euphoric sense of total well-being, as if she were floating. Her body light, her soul bright, her future open. A mist drifted over her mind, wiping out all her problems. Bringing love and generosity and hope.

She soaked it in, tucked it away, and stored it in every muscle, fiber, tissue and cell.

"Jessie?"

A hole pricked the bubble of her serenity. Her peaceful inner world pulled away from the walls of her mind like ripping wallpaper.

She opened her eyes, her chest burning with the sting of fear, and twisted toward the voice. Quaid stood ten feet away, hands on hips, still bare chested, jeans still unbuttoned, breathing hard as if he'd been running.

Had he just called her . . . *Jessie*?

"What's wrong?" She darted a glance behind him while scrambling off the boulder. When she realized no other frantic members of the team waited, a burst of hope exploded, searing her lungs until her breath caught. *Jessie.* Could he have remembered? She turned her gaze back to Quaid, searching his face for a clue. *Please, please, please.* "Are you . . . okay?"

He dropped his head. "I'm . . ." He raked his fingers over his scalp. "I'm confused. I'm really confused."

The torment in his voice pulled her a step closer, but also kept her out of his reach. She was confused, too, not sure whether to go to him or keep her distance and give him room to work things through first.

Clasping her hands, she squeezed them tight, wringing out the tension and took another step closer. "What . . . can I do for you?"

He laughed, the sound dry and bitter. "Why would you want to do anything for me?" He shook his head, "I don't know how to apologize. And I can't even say I didn't mean to hurt you or that I wouldn't have, because . . ." He lifted his hand, then let it fall, the gesture and his lost expression so helpless. "Honestly, I don't know what I would or wouldn't have done."

He didn't have to say the words for Jessica to know he regretted what had happened. Cash had explained enough about his time at the Castle for Jessica to understand his response had been an instinctive reaction to fear. She'd seen it on his face the moment he'd let her go.

He turned his back to her as Jessica opened her mouth to tell him not to go, took another step toward him, but stopped. She had to let him walk away if that's what he needed. Give him room to adjust at his own pace. But he didn't go, he just stared out across the ravine in silence and Jessica studied the beauty of his phoenix.

Covering the right two-thirds of his back, the fierce bird's tail tapered at his waist. One wing crested over Quaid's shoulder and decorated the back of his right arm. The other stretched across the opposite third of his bare back.

His body was so different from before. Her gaze slid over the curves of muscle and sinew. The bulk she'd known was gone. In its place sleek, tapered muscle contoured beneath tight, tan skin. He was truly sculpted, and her hands were restless to touch and explore this new man even while a big part of her heart and mind feared him.

"Your mark," she said, "is . . . the most beautiful thing I've ever seen."

A deep sigh lifted and lowered his shoulders. "Jessica . . ."

She waited, smiling at the sound of her name in his voice, something she never believed she'd hear again. But when he didn't go on, she said, "Yes?"

"Who am I to you?"

Her smile dropped. She pulled her bottom lip between her teeth while her mind and heart bellowed *I'm the person who loves you most in the entire world. I'm the woman you chose over all others. I'm your wife.*

"You don't remember anything . . . yet?"

"Not in my head." He turned and faced her and she almost wished he hadn't. His expression was so tortured he seemed almost . . . angry. "But I have all these emotions, all these *feelings* I don't understand. I have no memories, no basis for them."

She nodded, unsure of what to say.

In two steps, he stood in front of her. His scent surrounded her, soap and heat and Quaid. He took her chin in his hand. A thrill teased her heart in anticipation of him tilting her face up and kissing her. But he turned her head to the side, and swept her hair off her neck with the other hand.

She pulled in a breath of shock and fear, and tried to push his hand away, but he was too strong. "Quaid . . ."

He took her face in both hands, this time tilting it up until she looked directly into his eyes. She grabbed one of his wrists, but he wasn't hurting her, so she didn't pull it away. And, God help her, she just wanted his mouth back on hers.

"Why is this tattoo on your neck?"

Her gut tensed. She raised her gaze from his lips to his eyes. Those deep brown, demanding eyes. And hated the way she immediately wanted to lie. "It's a Chinese sym—"

His hands tightened on her face. This time the pressure did sting and she teetered on that line between anger and patience.

"It's the name you're all calling me. Quaid—*my name*—in a Chinese symbol."

She opened her mouth to ask how he knew. No one knew. She'd gotten the ink after his death and never told anyone, not even Keira, what it meant. But his gaze dropped to her lips and the words died in her throat.

"Were you mine?" he asked, his voice softer, his gaze slowly rising from her mouth with a look so heated, so hungry, her control nearly slipped right through her fingers. "Were you mine, Jessie?"

She swallowed. "Y-yes."

His gaze held hers a long moment, filled with shock. She held her breath, fearing and anticipating his reaction at the same time. Shock shifted to confusion. Confusion into disbelief. He let go, dropped his arms and stepped back.

Jessica swallowed, watching his eyes. Those eyes she'd once been able to read so well, now seemed like rich pools of mystery.

"Are you . . . ? How . . . ?" He shook his head, shifted from foot to foot, staring at some unknown spot on the ground. He mumbled something Jessica didn't catch. Rubbed his head.

She feared she'd said too much, pushed him over some cognitive line. When he finally lifted his gaze from the ground and met her eyes again, more questions floated there than doubt. "We . . . were together."

She wrung her hands, trying to smile through all the distress. "Yes."

He chewed on the inside of his lower lip, something he used to do when he was thinking or right before he'd admitted to a change of heart about something. The sight made the threat of tears sting across the bridge of her nose.

His eyes glistened with wetness and he cleared his throat. "Were we . . . happy?"

Oh, God. She tightened the muscles in her abdomen to hold back the sob that wanted to come. If she could just touch him . . . But she stayed where she was and slid the chain of her necklace through her fingers, letting the locket settle in her palm. "Yes. We were *very* happy."

He closed his eyes and wetness clumped his long, dark lashes. He looked away, nodded. Sighed. Shifted on his feet, one step back, one step forward. One step back . . . A torturous tease to Jessica, who had to fight not to beg him to come to her.

When he searched out her eyes again, his gaze had grown sad. So painfully sad. "And who do you belong to now?"

For a moment, she didn't understand the question. Then she realized what he was asking and the look in his eyes clicked. She couldn't take it, that broken, defeated expression. She couldn't stand knowing he suffered the belief he'd lost someone he'd loved. Whether he remembered her or not, that pain floating in his eyes was real.

She closed the distance between them. Quaid's shifting halted as soon as she took her first step, his entire demeanor flipping to defense mode. She didn't let that stop her from getting within an inch of his body. Reaching up, she slid both hands over his head, letting them rest at the base of his neck. When his eyes closed and a look of relief eased his face, her stomach did little somersaults.

"Quaid." She smiled through the volatile mix of pain and hope. "My heart will always be yours. That's why I'm here."

He opened his eyes slowly, cautiously, and gave her that long I'm-not-sure-what-to-believe stare.

When she couldn't take the silence any longer, Jessica laughed, shortly and softly, and threaded her fingers at the back of his neck. She eased forward and pressed her body against his. He felt so good, a wall of warm muscle. "I haven't changed my mind in five years, Quaid. I'm not changing it now."

Still, he hesitated, as if calculating risk factors. His gaze flicked away. He shook his head. Then, without warning, he covered her mouth with his, wrapped an arm at her waist, sank the fingers of the other into her hair. He kissed her fast and hard. Crushing. His fingers tightened in her hair, sending a burn across her scalp. She made a noise of surprise in her throat, but Quaid drank it.

The sudden roughness, the blatantly erotic thrust of his tongue, the raw hunger flowing from every part of him, they all shocked her as much as they excited her. Her world narrowed to the man holding her. Her attention limited to his taste, his scent, the feel of his lips, the heat of his body.

He pulled his mouth from hers, but his lips slipped right to her jaw, his breath fast and hot against her neck. Both arms tightened around her, bringing her into full contact with his body and the long, hard erection pressing into her pelvis. A delicious sensation burst at the center of her body and washed outward. She couldn't remember when a man had felt so good to her. Probably over five years ago.

"Quaid . . ." She hadn't realized she'd said his name until he responded. He raised his head and gazed down at her with so much need, so much desire, she choked on her emotions. "God, I've missed you."

Those rich eyes she loved so much filled with gratitude, love, humility, relief and so damn much desire she would have hit her knees if he hadn't been holding her close enough to be a second skin.

She fisted the waistband of his jeans and held on. Let his

passion overpower her. His mouth was hot, his body forceful, his hands demanding. He was rough, graceless and primal. Jessica had never been so damn turned on so damn fast.

Just as fast as Quaid had started kissing her, he stopped. Without warning, he broke the kiss. His head jerked up and he glanced left. Then he went still. Amazingly, stone still.

Jessica took the moment to gather air. Her body sizzled. Her lungs burned. Her head spun. "What—?"

"Shh." He pressed gentle fingers to her lips, a startling contrast to his unleashed desire.

The sting of fear cooled her passion. She struggled to control her breathing, strained to listen. But all she heard were the same sounds of the wind in the trees, birds, creek. The deep, soothing silence.

"Go inside." Quaid lowered his hand from her lips and gripped her upper arms, bending to look directly into her eyes. The fierceness of his gaze sent a chill across her shoulders. "Do you understand? Inside. Lock the doors. *Everyone. Inside. Now.*"

He pushed her toward the bunker, and she stumbled several steps. "Quaid."

He was already jogging in the other direction. He stopped to shoot her another sharp look. "Inside, Jessie. I mean it."

Before she could ask why, he'd sprinted into the trees. Fast. Agile. Powerful. Without any hint of a limp.

She covered her heart where it beat fast and hard in her chest. Turned toward the bunker. Kai and Cash came crashing through the trees, weapons up and aimed. Jessica jumped, sure her heart would triple time itself right into a heart attack.

"What's wrong?" Kai asked, his compact automatic rifle already panning the area.

"Where's Quaid?" Cash took Jessica's shoulder and pinned her with those piercing blue eyes, so much like Keira's. And, oh, shit, Keira and Luke were already gone.

"He—he—" Jessica couldn't make her brain work. Her mouth work. She pointed in the direction Quaid had run. "How did you know?"

"I felt it," Kai said. "He sent out a spike of fear and anger so strong, I knew it had to be something bad."

She'd forgotten Kai's empathic abilities. But from so far away? And what else had he felt? Jessica pressed her hands to the new burn in her cheeks.

Cash followed Kai into the forest yelling, "Send the others this way."

THIRTEEN

Q paused on the edge of a copse and cocked his ear to the right, where he'd last heard the footsteps. He had to filter out the sound of his breathing and that took several long seconds. Sounds always flowed in and out of his consciousness, just like they had before his hearing had become ultrasensitive. Now there were just more sounds, from more varied distances, creating more depth and more chaos to tune out.

But the same way Q knew that the sound of a certain car door closing in the Castle parking lot meant his week had just gone to shit, the footsteps scraping along dirt and cracking over limbs and leaves signaled someone wearing boots—lightweight, thin-soled, military-grade canvas boots. Something he had about as much random chance of knowing as how to read the Chinese symbols on Jessica's neck.

An unease coming from somewhere or something he couldn't name created a cold track down his spine.

Whoever wore those boots was nowhere near the bunker, but still on the property. From the various *clicks* sounding when he walked, he carried at least three weapons that tapped against each other with his movement.

Q turned east and started running again. He made a wide circle around the intruder to come up behind him.

The trees' colorful leaves blurred in Q's vision. The man's footsteps and the *clicks* from his gear directed Q through the forest, down hills, through the ravine.

Q's mind shifted into some cool, serious, determined mode that felt both surreal and familiar. His body worked better than it had since his limbs had stopped obeying his mind. He weaved through the trees easily and maintained even, regulated breathing. Only a slightly elevated heart rate thumped in his ears. After the first few stabs of pain in his feet from rocks or limbs, they'd gone numb.

Behind him, near the bunker but very distant now, Jessica's voice touched the edge of his mind's filter, then the voices of others—Cash, maybe Kai. A sense of urgency pushed even more adrenaline into his veins.

Have to get to him before he gets to them.

Have to.

He didn't know why he thought these things. Didn't know what he was feeling or why. On the outside he was numb, while deep inside a desperate need drove him forward. He couldn't stop. He knew without having to try that no matter how hard he focused his brain to stop his body, it wouldn't work. His body would continue on whatever the hell mission this was, passion fueling his muscles and organs with more strength and stamina than he could have ever imagined.

The realization would have terrorized him if it weren't for some small sparkle of rightness. A sureness that whatever his brain had planned would benefit his team. Though he didn't know when he'd made the switch from thinking of them as possible enemies to either *his* or a *team*.

After a few more miles of that consistent, driving run, his vision wobbled, turning everything in his line of sight watery. Q recognized an aftereffect of the drugs and checked in with the rest of his body.

His mouth had run dry and his ribs burned. But the

bodily exhaustion from lack of food and water didn't register with this disconnected inner drive. And if he didn't stop now, he'd collapse when he needed his strength most.

He put both arms out in front of him and steered himself toward a tree. He braced for the impact, but his arms still failed and he hit with his chest. His lungs compressed. He bounced off the tree and landed in the mulch ass-first.

He froze, grimacing. Finally, the pain eased enough for him to suck in air. Still he didn't move, unsure if the target had heard him, if he was already moving in.

Target?

Q reached for his weapon. When his hand hit nothing but a jean-covered hip, he looked down at himself. His mind seemed to split in two, one side confused to be reaching for a weapon he'd never even touched before, the other frustrated not to find that same weapon where it should be. Where he always carried it. *Always.*

He turned his hand over and stared at the palm as if he expected the Ruger he'd been reaching for to appear.

Ruger?

He looked up at the kaleidoscope of treetops. Then he glanced around at the isolated forest. What in the fuck was he doing? Who in the fuck was he?

"Schizophrenia?" he whispered the possibility, his rational mind struggling for a logical answer. But he sure as hell felt as if he had two different people working inside him. "Psychotic break?"

Programmed?

For a millisecond, Q stared into the trees and wondered if this was another hallucination. Or a dream, like his dreams of Jessica. Only . . . Jessica was real. Wasn't she? Or maybe an alternate reality, like that little side trip to the Middle Eastern desert. If that's what it had been.

Shuffle. Click . . . click-click.

Whether dream, alternate universe or reality, he wasn't

in it alone. And his gut told him he wasn't safe. His team wasn't safe. Jessica wasn't safe.

Very slowly and silently, Q rolled to his stomach, did a quick push-up and jumped his feet beneath him. He used a tree for cover and peered around the trunk, just enough to look into a distant clearing.

The man stepped into view and Q's vision brought him in with sharp clarity. Military rogue. Late twenties, shaved head, drab olive T-shirt darkened by sweat, matching cargo pants with a Sig Saur strapped to his thigh and—Q zeroed in on his boots—military issue.

The guy held up a small electronic device with a map on the screen and panned it around the area. As he twisted away from Q, a rifle came into view—an HK416 strapped over his back. German engineering, 5.5-millimeter round, twenty-thousand rounds-per-minute, non-jamming gas system; the weapon that had nailed Osama bin Laden.

Whoever the hell that was.

Q wished he could claw his brain out of his skull and stomp on it. Since he couldn't . . . the HK-lover looked like a good substitute.

Moving slower now, Q headed toward the man even as the man headed toward Q. He edged out from the forest's cover and skirted the border of the ravine, moving in quick sprints between rocks and brush. Part of him wondered what the hell he was going to do when he caught up with the stranger. Another part knew he'd take care of that when it happened.

He angled around behind the intruder, who continued hiking toward the bunker. Q's body felt light and strong, his brain alert and sharp. Maybe he could find a way to hold onto this feeling after . . .

After what?

"Stop thinking," he whispered and crouched behind a

boulder, assessing the other man's position as he approached a particularly steep area of the ravine ahead.

Q darted from boulder to brush. From brush to rock cluster. He eased closer to the intruder. The intruder moved closer to the ravine wall—right where Q wanted him. Why, he had no idea.

He eyed the last boulder he planned to use for cover before he attacked. Coiled the muscles in his thighs. A sound pulled his attention left. He scanned the ravine, the brush beyond. Saw nothing, not even a rodent. Then he peered farther, to the outskirts of the forest, then into the forest—and his stomach dropped.

Kai and one of the guards Q had seen patrolling the grounds earlier crept through the trees, crouched, holding semiautomatics. *Shit.* Q looked right, across the ravine and found Teague and another guard skirting boulder clusters. And Q would bet a trip back to the Castle that Cash, Mitch and the remaining two guards were on his ass. He didn't even need to look.

Sonofabitch. He was surrounded.

The intruder found finger and toe holds along the ravine wall and hoisted himself onto the rock. Q skipped the cover boulder and sprinted for the guy.

This time, the man heard Q's movement. Not a huge surprise. The intruder dropped from the wall, maintained his crouch in a twist, aimed and fired, all in fluid, split-second movements.

Q dropped, rolled, scrambled. More gunfire, another maneuver, but this time when Q found his feet he was close enough to lunge. Another shot rang out. This one from a different direction. From a different weapon. From a distance. One of the others trying to take this guy out before he took Q out.

The intruder was still standing, but distracted. Q went

in at an angle, grabbed the wrist of the hand holding the gun, shoved it sideways and jabbed the inner elbow. The man grunted and the gun dropped, but he struck out. Q blocked, caught the guy's jaw with a cross. Ducked a jab, blocked a body shot. Came back with a double punch to his gut. The intruder bent toward the pain and Q kneed him in the chin.

The intruder flailed, stumbling backwards. Q advanced. He grabbed the man's throat with one hand, his shirt with the other and slammed him up against the rock wall. The man reached for Q's face, but came up short. Q body-slammed him again. The man's spine popped and ground against the rock. He clawed at Q's arms. Q hauled him back and drove him against the rock again. And again and again and again, punctuating a very clear message: "I'll . . . never . . . go . . . back."

With the man's spine wedged against the rock, Q squeezed the intruder's throat. He wheezed, gagged, brought up bloody hands to pry at Q's fingers. That's when Q saw the bullet hole through the man's palm, and all the blood spilling from it. He remembered the shot that hadn't hit him. Thought of Keira. Then of Luke. Then of each member of the team. Of Jessica. All they'd sacrificed. And something deep inside him glowed white-hot-pissed-off.

He leaned close, tightened his fingers until the spy's eyes bulged, and vowed, "You'll never get them, either."

Jessica came to an abrupt stop on the border of the ravine. Keira and Luke had disappeared over the edge. Keira must have heard Quaid's thoughts, or maybe Kai's or maybe her own, because she and Luke had come back. Jessica had almost reached the ravine when she'd heard the squeal of tires. Then Keira had raced past her, a weapon in both hands, Luke right behind her. She'd skidded to a stop at the ravine's lip, taken what seemed like less than a second to aim and almost as soon as Jessica realized Keira had fired, a man's screams echoed up from the ravine.

Now, Keira and Luke skidded over the rocky embankment below toward the valley. Jessica peered past them, into the ravine and stepped toward the ledge. But the sight below killed her plans to descend.

Quaid held a man by the throat, smashing him up against the ravine wall. Over and over again, he pulled the other man back and slammed his body against the rock. The man jerked, then clawed and kicked, but Quaid had complete control.

Jessica's mind refused to absorb the scene. It seemed flat and unreal.

Quaid. Violent.

Those two words just did not link up. Yet she couldn't mistake all that blood. It coated Quaid's chest and arms. It was smeared across the other man's T-shirt and pants. His hands, arms and face. She thought of Keira's shot. Feared it had hit Quaid. But, if it had, it hadn't deterred him.

Kai and Teague scrambled down opposite sides of the steep embankment. Two of the military men guarding the property immediately followed. Cash and Mitch came at Quaid from behind. They were closest, and Cash led the way in a dead run.

Jessica dropped to her knees on the rocky soil, hands clenched. Fear sliced through her body in icy cuts as her stomach tightened and rolled with sickness.

"Oh, my God." She barely breathed the words, hardly able to speak through the horror. "Stop. *Stop.*"

She wanted everyone, everything to just *stop.* Reality had exploded completely out of control.

But nothing stopped. Cash jumped on Quaid from one

side, grabbing his arm and prying it from the man's throat. Mitch attacked from the other side, yanking Quaid back by the waist of his jeans.

Kai reached the man on the ground, and Teague helped Cash and Mitch restrain Quaid.

Within thirty seconds, everyone was smeared with blood and yelling.

Jessica dropped her face into her shaking hands. "Oh, my God."

What had possessed him? What would they do if he'd killed that man? Even if he hadn't, how would they hide his attack? And why did she immediately consider lying and evasion as a remedy? How quickly her year of commitment to truth had succumbed to fear.

Maybe Quaid had gone insane in that place. Maybe he hadn't just lost his memory, but his *mind*. And maybe she was going to follow right behind him.

She peered down into the ravine again. Kai had lifted the victim, now apparently unconscious, over his shoulder in a familiar fireman's carry. Cash led Quaid toward the long path up the ravine by the arm. Mitch followed, carrying what looked like the man's pack and Keira wandered behind, her attention focused on a . . . *rifle?*

Jessica scanned Keira's body and found a rifle strapped over her back. A semiautomatic handle stuck out of the holster on her thigh. Her gaze moved to Luke, found his rifle strapped over his back and his semiautomatic in his hand. She quickly took inventory of Brody's two guys, who held their own rifles.

"Oh, shit." The victim was looking less like a victim.

She ran to meet the others in the forest at the top of the ravine. Teague hiked at the end of the group as they headed back to the bunker, and Jessica grabbed his arm. "What in the hell is going on?"

His eyes were sharp, his expression intense. Blood smeared one side of his chin. "We're not sure."

"Is he . . ." She glanced at the pack moving ahead, the limp man bumping against Kai's back as he walked. "Is he . . . alive?"

"Yeah. He's alive." Teague tossed his arm over Jessica's shoulders and pulled her into step beside him. "Look, Jess, I know that may have looked rough, but if that fucker is part of this bullshit, Quaid was far more restrained than I would have been."

Rough? Maybe brutal. Maybe horrifying. But Teague's perspective gave Jessica something to think about on the walk back.

She trailed the team, dividing her attention between the colorful leaf-strewn ground and Quaid's muscled back. Her brain scattered—from the past to the present back to the past. She tried to remember any circumstance, any incident, in which Quaid had shown some hint of violence—even if only the capacity. Had he ever thrown a chair? Had he ever started a physical fight? Had he even engaged in a fight when provoked? The answer to every question she could think to ask was no. Hell, the man had rarely ever raised his voice unless he'd been laughing.

A sharp, clear vision of Quaid—*her* Quaid—laughing, as he often did, filled her mind. The joy that followed was so clean and crisp and pure, it struck her like the stab of a knife. Her breath caught on a sudden and vivid slice of loss. She stumbled and caught herself with a hand against a tree.

"Hey." Teague's voice brought her head up. "You okay?"

Beyond him, several other members of the team had paused and looked back at her, including Quaid. His eyes were unusually dark in the shade of the overhead trees, his hooded brow menacing with that serious, dark expression.

The blood splattering his face and chest made her stomach squeeze.

"Just need to catch my breath," she said. "Go ahead, I'll catch up in a second."

But Teague wouldn't leave her alone with the unknown awaiting them in this multicolored forest, and Jessica gave up the hope of getting a minute to pull herself together. She pushed on against the painful realization that the heart of the man she'd married might not still live within the body of the man that had survived.

Owen sat back in his leather desk chair, one ankle crossed over the other knee, his gaze unwavering on Abrute's face. He rested his elbows on the arms of the chair, steepled his fingers and pressed his index fingers against his lips.

"So, that's all that's missing," Owen said, enjoying Abrute's jittery, restless movements, his darting eyes, his sweat-beaded forehead.

He'd only been questioning Abrute for twenty minutes and the man was ready to split at the seams. All the questions had been asked and answered. Owen had the bigger picture in his mind. Now, he just had to confirm the information by asking a few key questions again and making sure he got the same answers the second time around. Then he had to figure out how to move forward.

"Yes, sir," Abrute said, his dark head bobbing in affirmation. "Just the Method pages."

A soft knock on his office door sounded before it opened and Stephanie, Owen's very young, very pretty secretary, came in with two bottles of water. She set one on Owen's desk and handed the other to Abrute. The man was appropriately polite and grateful, but his gaze lingered a little too long, and when Stephanie turned to leave, Abrute's gaze slid down her backside.

"If you won't be needing me, sir?" Stephanie said when she paused on her way out.

"No, Stephanie, thank you." Christ, where had the day gone? "You can go home."

"Thank you, sir. Also, I put that information you requested in your top drawer. Good night."

Through the open door, he saw the two military guards still flanking the entrance to his office. Owen returned his gaze to Abrute and remained silent until the door clicked closed.

"And you have copies of all the previous Methods pages O'Shay had developed up to the point that the experiment was successful, correct?"

"Yes, colonel." Abrute leaned forward and put a shaking hand on the papers in front of him. "They're all right here, sir. As I told Deputy Director Dargan, I knew how important this project was to our military, and I felt compelled to secure a second set of documents. I know it is against procedure, sir, and I understand why. I take full responsibility and I—"

"Explain again, what this formula is for, Mr. Abrute."

"We call it a second skin in that it is flexible, breathable and impenetrable. Safer than body armor, but weighs almost nothing. Imagine Gore-Tex meets neoprene with a thousand times the security of Kevlar."

Amazing. "Deputy Dargan doesn't run any research branches of DARPA, Mr. Abrute. Who is this project for?"

Abrute's eyes widened. "I . . . can't say, sir."

Owen stood, pushed his shoulders back and stared down at the man. He knew how to use his size to intimidate, and it was easy with Abrute's meager never-drag-myself-from-the-lab body.

Abrute followed Owen's movement with even wider eyes, sitting back in his chair and clenching his hands.

Owen pressed his fingertips to the desktop and leaned toward Abrute. He didn't need to try to look frustrated or angry or impatient or at the end of his rope: He was already there.

"Mr. Abrute," he said, his voice low, "you don't have the luxury of choosing whether or not to answer me. You *will* answer me. And you will answer me *now* because this is about national security. Or are you a traitor as O'Shay was?"

The insinuation that Abrute could end up imprisoned as O'Shay had been made the man sit forward in earnest. "I am no traitor, sir. I've spent my career in service to this country."

Owen slapped the desk with both hands. Abrute jumped. "Then you'd better continue," he said through clenched teeth. *"Now."*

Abrute's gaze flicked away. He licked his lips. "I've only heard . . . rumors." He looked up at Owen with sincerity in his eyes. "Normally, when I'm working on a project, I have direct access to a member of the group I'm developing for, you know, to better meet their needs, to touch base along the way to check if we're on target. But this wasn't my project. I only oversaw O'Shay and reported back to Deputy Dargan. She never told me who this skin was being developed for other than the military—"

"You're testing my patience."

Abrute licked his lips again. Glanced around the room as if he thought he'd see someone materialize. "I could be in danger if I say—"

"You're in danger *now,*" Owen said. "And you'll be in more danger if you *don't* say."

Abute's gaze lowered to Owen's desktop and he thought for a second before plucking a pen from the holder. Then he pulled a blank pad of notepaper toward him and wrote while still talking. "It was only rumor, Colonel Young.

There is no validity in rumor and I could be damaging someone else's career if I spread the rumor, not to mention my own. It was mentioned that the formula was for a company, not the military, and you know we only do work for the government, so it couldn't have been true."

He put the pen down, pushed the notepad across the desk, and looked Owen in the eye, steadier now. "I'm sorry, Colonel Young, do to me what you will, but I don't know anything for sure."

When Abrute didn't go on, Owen cast his narrowed eyes from the man's face to the notepad and read.

A moment of shock burned in his gut, but was quickly replaced with anger.

FOURTEEN

Q entered the supply room and passed the prisoner without glancing at him. The need to choke off the fucker's air still thrummed through Q's fingers, and the only reason he wasn't fighting every other person here to get to the guy was because of the way Jessica had looked at him back in the forest.

Like he was an animal.

An animal that terrified her.

He stalked to the farthest end of the room, then paced along the wall, unable to hold still. Exhaustion dragged at his mind. Starvation gnawed at his stomach. But those were nothing compared to the self-disgust beating through his veins.

"What's wrong with me?" he muttered, trying to understand why his mind splintered. What it meant. How he could make it stop.

He glanced toward the front of the room, where the others had cuffed the spy to a chair. The guy was bleeding from his head, face, arms, hand . . . everywhere. Q didn't remember beating him to that extreme. But he had to claim everything except the bullet Keira had put through his palm.

Keira and Luke had left—for the second time—for their

trip to Washington, but Keira had spent some time with their prisoner and then talking with Kai before she'd gone.

Teague held the intruder still as Alyssa checked his wounds. Kai scavenged through the man's pack and Cash inspected his weapons, now laid out on the floor: three guns and four knives. Jessica stood near the door, arms crossed tightly over her middle, eyes glazed over with shock.

Q turned his back to the sight. He wiped his face and glanced around, trying to clear the confusion from his head. The interior of this small space was the same unfinished concrete as the main bunker. A spare cot sat in one corner, a small table and chairs in another. In the ceiling, instead of recessed canned lighting, bare bulbs screwed directly into ceiling outlets.

As Q stared at one of the bulbs, moths appeared, one by one, and fluttered around the light. Something shifted inside his mind. In his peripheral vision, the moth's shadows danced as black dots along the gray walls. He darted a look that way, tension tightening his shoulders, then back to the bulb on the ceiling, where the moths had multiplied fifty times and fanned out along the ceiling.

"About fucking time you showed up."

Q jerked his head toward the voice. The same man from his previous vision stood with the same rifle strapped over his shoulder, but now his fatigues were caked with dirt, his face scratched.

"What the fuck?" Q stumbled backwards. He shot looks right and left.

He wasn't in the supply room anymore, though he was in some type of building. This one had similar concrete block walls, but it was larger, the floor made up of packed dirt.

And these walls were stacked floor to ceiling with

weapons. Sleek, hi-tech rifles Q didn't recognize were neatly stored in racks. Crates labeled ox6 with the words STABILIZED OCTANITROCUBANE were piled alongside the rifles. A new explosive, Q could only guess by the name, and he damn well hoped that substance *was stabilized* or one poorly placed boot and he and Trent—*that* was his name, Trent—would blend right in with all the grainy dirt on the floor.

Another entire wall was obscured by wooden boxes of ammo, two deep. Magazine casings spilled out of one and bullet bandoliers draped over another, loaded with a size and shape of ammunition Q had never seen before.

He looked down at his hands, his body. Still wearing bloody jeans and nothing else. But the smells were completely different. The air was dry and dusty and gritty. The rank scent of body odor and urine filled Q's head, wiping out the scent of blood on his skin.

Panic grew. He had to go back. He wanted the mountains. He wanted his team.

He wanted Jessica.

How did he get back?

" 'What the fuck?' is right, dude. Where the hell you been this time, a gladiator ring?" Trent swung the rifle off his shoulder and set it on the floor, leaning it against the wall. "You okay, man? You hurt?"

"No." He met Trent's eyes again. Steel gray. Flat. Serious. Then Trent grinned and those eyes sparked. Q knew this man. He *liked* this man. And that's when Q knew, he should be here with Trent. Every time Q left, he was abandoning his partner.

He suddenly found himself trapped between two places he belonged after a lifetime of belonging nowhere.

"Good," Trent said. " 'Cause now I can kick your ass for leaving me in this hell hole with those fucks."

He gestured behind Q.

Oh, God. He didn't want to look. Shit, he didn't want to look.

"Almost makes me mad enough to tell you to stop insisting that Gorin pair us on these missions," Trent went on. "But then I'd never get out of my fucking cell. And since I don't have a *snuggle buddy* like Cash," he ribbed, "I'd have to talk to the walls. You're so much more fun to annoy."

"Trent." Q tried to fill his lungs, but it felt like a rock crushed his chest. "I'm . . . not right."

"Man, you scared the shit out of me." Trent ignored Q's distress and turned toward a box in the corner, crouched and rummaged. "I was starting to think you weren't coming back. Damn, I'm starving. Now we can set up the meeting, dump these guys and get out of this place. I'm not looking forward to seeing Abernathy, though. We're behind schedule and, shit, man, he's going to rip us both new assholes.

"Hey"—Trent grinned up at him—"maybe you could throw some of your new mind control his way. You know, that shit you used to make me give you the last of my beef jerky?" He snorted and shook his head, turning his attention back to the box. "You still suck at it, but it couldn't hurt, right?" He pulled something out of the box and broke it in half, holding out one side toward Q. "I'm still pissed about my beef jerky, but I'll share my last power bar with you anyway. You're looking a little scrawny. When's the last time you ate?"

"Trent . . . man, shut up a second . . ." Panic crawled through Q's chest. He reached out for the other man, not sure why or what it would accomplish. "Something's . . . wrong. God . . . I don't know what's happening to me. . . ."

"Shit." Fear flashed in Trent's eyes. He dropped the power bar and rushed at Q. Grasped both his arms and shook him. "Stay with me, Q."

"I can't control it." He turned his hand over and grabbed Trent's arm. "Can I . . . can I take you? Can you come with me?"

"You can't go."

"I'm sorry . . ."

"No! Damn it. Don't give me that sorry shit. I need you. I can't set up the rendezvous on my own, and I'm running out of food and water." Trent's grip tightened. The *clink, clink, clink* of the moths hitting the bare bulb grew loud. "Come on. You're fine. Everything's fine. Just sit down. . . ."

Trent's voice was drowned in the moths' wild fluttering. Q looked over his shoulder, his last sight as the scene faded that of six young males, gagged and bound and lined up along the wall, their dark eyes fixed on Q and filled with the terror of having just seen a ghost.

When he looked back at the light, the moths were gone. The clinking sound had been replaced by a loud buzz still filling his head. Trent's hands were still on his arms. Shaking him.

"Quaid. Quaid, look at me."

Quaid.

Couldn't be Trent. A female voice. Small hands.

He looked down and into deep brown eyes. Beautiful eyes. Filled with fear and confusion.

"Talk to me," Jessica said. "Are you okay? What's going on?"

He was going insane, that's what was going on. "I'm so fucked up." He put his hands to her shoulders and pushed. "I'm sorry."

He moved back to the corner and paced in the shadows, trying to differentiate between reality and mind games.

There could be a man out there who needed him to get food and water. A man who needed him to gain his freedom. Q couldn't just leave Trent there. How long could the guy survive without water?

He scraped his hands over the itch in his scalp, dropped his arms as he reached the wall and pivoted one-hundred-and-eighty degrees. A hand grabbed his. He swiveled, grabbed the person's forearm with his free hand and met Jessica's gaze.

"Let me get some of this blood off you," she said.

He didn't understand until she held up rags in her other hand. Water dripped down her arm. He released her and stepped back, casting a glance around the room again. The others had gone back to their tasks—Alyssa doctoring, Teague guarding, Kai and Cash inspecting.

"No, don't touch me. I don't know what the hell is happening to my head. I think I'm going crazy and I don't want to hurt you. Just stay away from me, Jess."

"What do you mean?" She came closer despite his warning. "Talk to me. Maybe I can help."

"You can't." He started pacing again, but kept his voice low. "For five years all they've done is fuck with my mind day and night. I don't understand my actions or my feelings. I don't know who I am or who I'm not. I don't trust myself, and I can't have you near me when I can't control this . . . whatever this is inside me."

She caught his arm again, met his gaze with steadfast warmth that settled him deep down. "I'm not leaving you alone, no matter what you say. You may as well just accept that."

Q shook his head, wondering if she had a screw or two loose. "Have you always been this stubborn?"

"No. It's developed over the last few years. I've changed, too, Quaid."

Q let her lead him to a chair in the corner away from

the others. When she lowered to her knees at his feet, an uncomfortable tightness wrapped around his chest. He sat forward, pressing his hands to the arms of the chair to rise, but she put a firm hand on his knee and looked up at him with those damned eyes. They begged for everything he couldn't give and offered everything he'd ever wanted.

"Please, Quaid. I can't stand seeing you like this another minute."

With him leaning forward and her looking up, their faces were only a few inches apart. Her gaze lowered to his mouth. His throat tightened. Her breath touched his lips and she licked her own.

He reached for her at the same time she leaned back. Instead of catching her head, so he could pull her in to taste her again, his hand was grasped by both of hers. She didn't meet his eyes, just started scrubbing at his fingers, his nails, his palm with the rag. And the sight of the blood coming off his hands took his mind off kissing her.

There was something incredibly . . . humbling . . . about the way she willingly sat at his feet, like a servant, caring for him.

"How did this happen?" he asked. "How did I end up at the Castle?"

Her gaze darted up and her hands stilled. "I thought Cash told you. . . ."

"Cash told me we were all firefighters together on some special team. That's all."

Jessica pressed her lips together, rose up on her knees and scooted forward, forcing him to open his thighs to her. She smelled amazing, a pretty sweetness and an edgy spice wrapped around her own sensual scent. He wanted to press his face to her neck and inhale.

She rubbed the cloth along his collarbone and worked

her way across and down his chest. "That's because it's better for you to remember—"

"On my own. I know. How long are we going to wait for that to happen? I want to know now. After all I've been through, I would have shut down a long time ago if it was going to happen."

Her gaze flicked to his, then over her shoulder toward Alyssa. Q put his hand under her chin and guided her gaze back to him. "Jessica, I need to know. If it's too much, I'll tell you."

She held his gaze for a moment, then resumed work. "Do you remember anything about the warehouse fire?"

"No. What fire?"

Pain flashed in her eyes. "Our team was called to a warehouse fire. The building was owned by the government and there were chemicals in the warehouse, chemicals that shouldn't have been stored there."

She glanced up, searching his face. When he shook his head, she said, "The chemicals exploded in the heat and everyone was critically injured and exposed. We were taken to a military hospital nearby, the only location with quarantine facilities large enough to house us all—or so we were told."

She paused to refold the rag. Her hands shook. Q found himself leaning forward. "And then what?"

She pulled in a breath, wet her lips. But couldn't seem to form words. After she started on his other arm, tears slid down her cheek and she rubbed them away with her shoulder.

"And then . . ." she said with a helpless little shrug. "You . . . died."

"You mean I coded? My heart stopped? And they brought me back?"

"No." She looked up at him with a sudden and unexpected rage tightening her expression. "I mean someone decided that you would be a perfect science experiment and told the team that you didn't make it. That you'd died. They *took you*—"

She choked on her emotions. Struggled for air. Q gathered her in his arms, held her close.

"They took you from us," she finished against his shoulder, fingers digging into the skin of his back.

Her pain brought tears to his own eyes, but as the view of his life widened, all the happiness, all the possibilities that had been stolen from him surfaced and his fury boiled. He could see how close this team had been. How important he'd been to these people. How drastically and painfully their lives had been changed by his death. He was humbled to have meant so much to such good people and enraged that those bastards had taken such a rich, meaningful, rewarding life away from him.

Jessica pulled out of his arms and sat back on her heels. She wiped at her wet face with her forearm.

"Why me?" he asked. "If we were all in the explosion, if we were all hurt, why did they take me and not anyone else?"

Her hand paused mid-stroke along the top of one foot. She didn't look up, but her lashes lay against her cheek for a long moment as she closed her eyes. "That's my fault."

"What? How?"

"You were trying to protect me." She lifted her head and met his eyes with so much regret, so much guilt, it made his gut ache. "There were two containers of chemicals. One exploded and hit you. When we came in to help, you knew the second would explode, too, so you knocked me down and covered me."

Q imagined the scenario. A truly heroic act, though Q couldn't see it as something he'd done. He saw it as something Quaid had done. Something Quaid had done out of a deep love for Jessica.

Were we happy?

Very. We were very happy.

Damn it, there had to be some of Quaid inside him if he still had these strong emotions. And he *wanted* to *remember.*

"How did that make me worth taking above the others?" he asked.

"You had double the chemical exposure. It would stand to reason your abilities would be stronger."

Q sat back. "Abilities?"

"Your powers." She raised a cautious gaze to his. "Cash told you—"

Q shook his head.

Jessica's gorgeous mouth rounded into a perfect O. Her eyes widened.

"Well, you'd better tell me now." A new sense of anger lodged between his ribs. "And you'd better be honest with me, Jessica. I've spent all of the life I can remember being lied to, having secrets kept from me. I won't live like that again."

Jessica swallowed. "The first thing we all noticed was how fast we were healing from the burns and breaks. Then how little scarring we had. But later, after we were released, we each noticed different abilities we didn't have before."

"Like?"

"Like Keira is clairaudient, which means under the right conditions, she can hear people's thoughts as if they are speaking. That's how she knew to come back today to help with this guy." She tilted her head toward the prisoner. "She heard a combination of Kai's and Cash's thoughts. And Teague has thermo-kinetic abilities, so he can heal with the heat in his body."

Q's jaw loosened and his mouth dropped open. He'd suspected he had paranormal powers, even though he hadn't known what kind, but he'd been thinking more along the lines of super strength or superfast thinking or heightened intelligence.

"I know this sounds crazy," she said, "but you wanted to know."

"What can you do?" he asked.

She shrugged. "I'm not really sure. I thought I could scry, but then this thing happened with your coin and instead of just seeing another location, I *traveled* to that location. Only I wasn't really there. You were the only person who could see me. So I don't know what my power is exactly."

He lowered his face into his hands and rubbed his forehead. The fact that she hadn't been a dream at the cabin actually made more sense now. She'd never interacted with him in his dreams. What he couldn't get his mind to take hold of yet was whether those other times he'd seen her had been dreams or . . . something else. Something more like whatever was happening with Trent.

He lifted his head. "And the others?"

"Seth, who you haven't met yet, has telekinetic abilities. He can move objects with the power of his mind. And Kai is an empath, which means he senses other people's feelings and can also sense emotion in the universe related to our team. Again, when you went after that guy, Kai knew because he felt the spike of emotion you gave off, not because I told him."

"And Alyssa, Mitch, Cash?"

"They don't have powers. Only those exposed to the chemical have them, which is why Mateo has abilities. Mateo was tested much the way you were. He has the phoenix marking and is a remote viewer, which is kind of like my scrying in that he can see things in real time in other locations. The difference is *how* a person accesses the visions. With scrying, visions arise from a shiny surface or crystal ball or mirror. With remote viewing, there are many more possibilities—touching something related to a person or place, extreme focus, meditation, training. . . ."

Q braced his elbows on his knees and rested his head in his fingers. "Okay, that might be enough."

Her cool hands slid over his head, caressing. Then she kissed the top and rested her head against his. "Things that might seem crazy to you could simply be your powers at work."

"Or it might be insanity."

She hesitated, then with a smile in her voice, said, "There is that."

He laughed.

"What's happening that seems so crazy?" she asked.

"I'm seeing things. Or . . . I don't know what it is. I think I'm seeing things, but then it feels like I'm really there, then the next minute I'm not. Like just now, I was here, then I was in some desert somewhere, then I was back here. Like my dreams of you when I was at the Castle. I have no control over where I go or when I come and go."

She went quiet. Her hands stilled.

"Hold his head straight, Teague," Kai said from behind Jessica. He stood in front of the prisoner and snapped a picture with his phone.

Q was restless with this new information, unsure of how to add it into the puzzle. Uneasy with this growing closeness to Jessica, even though part of him knew it was what he wanted, he stood, pulling Jessica to her feet at the same time. Then he wandered toward the group.

"What are you doing?" he asked.

Kai glanced up and grinned. "Well, look who decided to join the conversation. I'm sending the pic to my boss, see if he can get anything more on this guy than Keira was able to pull from his brain."

"Who is this boss anyway?" Jessica asked. "A private jet. Weapons. Now this?"

"What about a private jet and weapons?" Q scanned Kai again. He was military— Q had noticed that right away. The way he stood. The way he talked. The way he looked at someone or something, or didn't look. His choice of simple, plain T-shirt and cargo pants.

Kai didn't take his eyes off his phone. "He's retired Air Force Intelligence, working contract for the government."

The prisoner's eyelids flicked open.

Kai's mouth kicked up in a lopsided smile. "Sleeping Beauty awakes. Did you want to start talking now, *amigo*? Better for us to hear it from you than from someone else. Either way, we'll find out who you are and why you're here."

The man said nothing.

"Come on," Kai cajoled as if ribbing an old friend. "Not even your name, rank and serial number?"

Nothing.

"Crap, not even a sense of humor." Kai shrugged one shoulder and turned his attention back to the phone. "Keira said his name is Reggie Alsadani, ex-Marine, reporting to Colonel Owen Young. He's on a seek, find and destroy mission."

"She got all that from hearing his thoughts?" Q asked, still finding the idea unbelievable.

"She probably got more and left the colorful stuff out," Kai said. "My boss has face recognition software and I've already scanned in the guy's fingerprints and sent those." He finished what he was doing and looked up while sliding the phone into his pocket. "Within eight to twelve hours, we'll be able to confirm Keira's information plus know when this guy eats, sleeps and shits."

A strange sensation nudged the back of Q's mind. "Is your boss's name . . ." Kai looked up, expectant. "Abernathy?"

"No, it's Waterbury." Kai waited. "Why?"

Relief loosened Q's shoulders. He shook his head. "How are you sending his fingerprints?"

"On the glass. Look here, Boy Wonder." Kai pulled out the phone, tapped the front glass and the face lit up bright blue. Little boxes dotted the display.

"What's 'boy wonder'?" Q asked, watching the colors and information change as Kai touched the glass.

Kai laughed, the sound soft and not particularly joyful. "That's one of the things I used to call you. When I was in a good mood."

"Why?" He looked at Kai now.

"Because you could do anything you set that stubborn mind of yours to. Look," Kai said, pressing his thumb against the face of his phone and drawing it away. A crisp fingerprint remained, the ridges glowing red. Two buttons beneath the image read SCAN and CLEAR.

"If I hit SCAN, the program will record the image and send it wherever I ask it to. If I hit CLEAR, we can start over with your fingerprint."

Even though Q didn't know how to use any high-tech equipment, what Kai claimed this little box was capable of didn't surprise him. "And in the meantime?"

"We research and strategize so we're ready to move when we find out who this guy is."

Damn. Q turned and wandered toward the door. He'd hoped Kai or Mitch or Teague had another trick to show him. He'd spent his entire life—or what he knew of it— waiting. He didn't want to wait another second.

Alyssa snipped the thread. "Done. Brody and his guys

are going to have to monitor his blood pressure and heart rate throughout the night to make sure there's no internal bleeding."

Q's stomach twisted and he grimaced as his gaze skimmed over the black stitches in the man's face. "Was I like this before? Violent? Did I . . . hurt people like I did him?" His gaze pulled from the prisoner and searched out Jessica, fearing the answer to the question. "Did I . . . hurt you?"

"What . . . ? No, never."

"So," he started, casting a look at the others in the room, "I wasn't like this before."

Kai's laugh bounced off the walls. "You couldn't even kill a damn spider, dude. You had to get a container, coax it inside"—he accentuated the statements as if each task was a big ordeal—"then set it free like some freaking pansy. It was goddamned episodic."

"All through school," Teague said, "you were always one of the biggest kids in our class, but I had to step in and save your ass on the schoolyard when someone picked a fight. You could have whipped anyone who challenged you, but you refused to fight."

Teague saved *his* ass? Nobody else saved his ass. Q carried his own weight. Q sometimes carried other people's weight, too.

Trent's face filled his mind. Guilt flowed in its wake. Q wasn't carrying his weight now.

Things that might seem crazy to you could simply be your powers at work.

God, he suddenly wanted, needed to know everything, yet wanted to run in the other direction as fast as he could.

He clenched his hands, drew a deep breath and said, "I want to know who I am. I mean, who I was. I want to know what I was like. What did I love? What did I hate?

Did I have hobbies? Did I make a difference? Was I good at my job? Did I have family?"

He pulled in a breath, checked in with his mind, heart and body after that sudden demand. Found it felt right. Found it was what he needed. "I want to know everything."

FIFTEEN

Jessica stared out the sliding glass doors, her fingers fisting and releasing as she waited for Cash to finish the book he was reading to Mateo so they could talk.

Quaid was in the shower, Kai in the kitchen washing and cutting fruit for his famed power smoothies, Mitch watching the security video screens in the nook across from the dining room. Alyssa, Teague and Cash were in the living room reading to the kids.

The house buzzed with activity and burst with the aromas of fresh fruit and spices.

"Anything out there?" Kai asked Mitch, slicing the flesh of a mango from its skin.

"Not that they can find." Mitch turned from the screens and sat down at the dining room table, where he had three different laptops set up, each searching different information databases via the web. "But there are three dogs working the property now, so if we missed anyone on the surveillance tapes, we'll get them with the dogs."

"I don't think we'll find anyone else."

Mitch slipped on wire-rimmed reading glasses and asked, "Why's that?"

Kai popped a piece of mango in his mouth. "I'd bet my boss's plane he's an asset."

"Asset?" Jessica said. "What's an asset?"

"Black ops assassin," Kai said bluntly.

Shock stung her stomach. *"What?"*

Kai's gaze slid toward the living room and the kids, then back to Jessica. Her gaze followed and she pursed her lips, realizing that even if they didn't look like they were paying attention, kids picked up on adults' stress. She forced an ease into her voice she didn't feel, asking, "And who would be sending an asset after us?"

"Schaeffer or someone higher at DoD. Castle scientists," Mitch said. "Who the hell knows?"

"Which is why we need to figure things out and make a plan," Kai added. "If he doesn't report in soon, they'll send another."

"But why would they send someone to . . . do that?" Jessica asked. "I thought they wanted Quaid and Cash for research. It makes no sense to try to kill them."

"Sometimes," Mitch said, his tone unusually solemn, "people who can't have what they want don't want anyone else to have it either."

She crossed her arms and shook her head. Even after everything they'd been through, the depth of twisted greed she encountered in Washington shocked her. What scared her even more was that she knew the darkness wasn't limited to Washington.

When Cash and Mateo finished their story, Cash stood from the sofa and his son crawled into Teague's lap to listen to Kat read to Alyssa.

Jessica refocused out the sliders, letting her gaze soak in the beauty of the fall foliage as she tried to tune out the various conversations. She searched for a place of peace inside herself, but she only found stress. And fear. Her hands ached with it. She rubbed them together. Massaged her fingers. Still, they hurt.

She took hold of her locket, sliding it up and down the chain as Cash came up beside her. Now, even though she'd asked him to talk with her about Quaid, she found herself lost, unsure of how to put her insecurities into words.

"Do you think that guy is an asset?" she asked quietly.

Cash nodded.

"Can't you make a deal with them? Trade the formula they want for your freedom?"

"I might be able to do that if I had the formula. Unfortunately, I destroyed the Method pages so they wouldn't find them on me. It was part of my escape plan. I thought it would be easier to recall the formulas and recreate them after I was free, and do exactly what you're suggesting.

"What I didn't count on was the way the explosions during the escape from the Castle kinda shook up my head. I'd need access to a lab to recreate those few final steps again and make sure they were right. If I tried to exchange a bogus formula, I'd be dead. If we weren't on the run, I could do it in just about any high school or college chemistry lab, but I'm SOL at the moment."

She sighed and shifted gears. "How do you think Quaid's doing? He seems awfully stressed to me."

Cash turned his gaze out the window and shrugged, the movement tight. "He almost beat someone to death. That's a little stressful."

"Maybe we shouldn't try to reintroduce him to his past right now." She turned toward Cash, but he remained focused out the glass, his hands in the pockets of his jeans. "I don't want it to put too much pressure on him."

"I think not telling him what he wants to know will put even more pressure on him."

The way Cash didn't meet her eyes made her uneasy. She might have only known him a short time, but from the very beginning he'd always been so straightforward.

"Cash, I need to know more about Quaid's dreams. The ones of me."

Cash's head jerked toward her, blue eyes sharp. "Why?"

Cold fingers of dread touched her stomach. "Because I think he has powers similar to mine. He told me he's struggling with what he thought were hallucinations, what he describes as visitations, where he's somewhere one minute, somewhere else the next. He thinks he's going a little crazy, but I think he's traveling and doesn't understand. And if he was traveling to me, not dreaming about me . . . I . . . need to know."

With his jaw muscle flinching, Cash returned his gaze to the forest beyond the glass and pushed his hands deeper into his pockets. "We knew he had some type of powers, but didn't know what. They put him under when they . . . did whatever they did to him—tested him, trained him, whatever. I think they did that so, one, he wouldn't resist them, and two, he wouldn't learn how to use the powers they brought out in him. Easier to control him if he didn't know what he could do, you know?

"But if you think he's traveling," Cash went on, "then they might also have put him under so he could reach a state of consciousness where that type of travel could take place. Because what you're describing is linked to the theory of quantum physics, which takes a certain state of mind, or state of being, to accomplish."

"You're talking way over my head," she said. "Can you just tell me what his dreams of me were about?"

He was avoiding her gaze again. "You know dreams, Jess. They never make any sense."

"You said he's dreamed about me ever since you've known him."

"Yeah"— he shrugged one shoulder—"up until about a year ago."

A year ago? He'd left that part out. "Yet, none ever made sense?"

"I wouldn't put too much emphasis on the dreams. Who knows what any of that means?"

She was growing more fearful that Cash knew exactly what they'd meant. "Cash." She waited until he looked at her. "I'm going to find out, either from you or from Quaid. Which do you think would be better?"

He searched her eyes for a long moment, his unreadable expression darkening. Then he glanced over his shoulder at the others, who were all occupied in their own activities.

He leaned in but kept his gaze averted. "His dreams of you were . . . sexual . . . in nature."

A zing of surprise and awareness traveled through her torso and lodged in her belly. But Cash's demeanor set Jessica on guard.

"As in he and I having sex?" she asked cautiously.

Cash scratched his temple. "Uh, not . . . exactly." He stuffed his hand back into his pocket. "As in you having sex with other men."

Jessica sucked in a shocked breath. Blood rushed into her neck and face, the shame of her past coming back to humiliate her as she'd always feared it would. She took a step back.

He turned and put a hand out to her as if to keep her from escaping. "He just thinks they were dreams, Jess. He was crazy about you. *Is* crazy about you. The other men never seemed to bother him. But that was before he discovered you were real and that you and he have a history. I don't think there's anything wrong with letting him believe they were dreams."

"What?"

"I don't think one-hundred-percent truth is the best answer to every situation. If telling him sets him back instead of moving him forward, then I think it would be better to let him believe what he already believes."

Jessica wrapped one arm tightly around herself and rubbed at the growing ache in her temple. She couldn't lie to Quaid. As tempting as it was, she knew how one lie led to another. The same way lying about her drug habit created the need to lie about where she'd gone, which then created the need to lie about what she'd been doing, which then created the need to lie about whom she'd been with . . . And so it went.

She'd carved out a life of truth over the last year and it kept her honest. It kept her accountable. She would hate herself if she lied to Quaid and risked having him hate her, too. Of course, he could very well hate her when he found out those other men had been real.

"Shit," she whispered, squeezing her forehead between her fingers.

A grinding noise made Jessica jump and turn toward the kitchen. Kai blended something peach colored and she blew out a startled breath.

"Do you even know what's in those powders you're throwing in there?" Mitch's voice rose over the loud whir. "You could be poisoning yourself and not even know it."

"This one's for you, shark." Kai flashed Mitch a devious grin. "Super B complex, selenium, phospha-tidylserine, Tyrosine, Phenylalanine . . . they're all natural mood-enhancing supplements."

Mitch pulled off his glasses and rubbed his eyes. He shot a you're-so-not-funny look and an obscene hand gesture toward Kai.

"God," she muttered, turning back to Cash. "I can't take this anymore."

"Jess?" Concern filled Cash's voice as she moved past him.

She hesitated but didn't turn. It wasn't his fault—none of this was his fault—but she couldn't stand to see the pity on his face a second longer. "Don't worry. I just need to think."

She wandered down the hallway housing the bedrooms

as she chewed her thumbnail and tried to figure out how to minimize the damage her past mistakes could cause to her and Quaid's future. Lying was not an option. But simply telling Quaid how unimportant those other men were to her as lovers . . . Shit. That didn't sound much better. She knew how she would feel if the situation was reversed. Trying to explain how they'd been her attempt at diversion, a human Band-Aid for her broken heart . . . to a man who'd been imprisoned and tortured hardly made a sympathetic picture either.

At the bathroom door, Jessica stopped and leaned her back against the opposite wall. The sound of the shower created white noise, aiding her thoughts. Unfortunately, it didn't help bring forth any solutions.

If she could show Quaid how deeply she loved him, show him how differently she felt about him than she had the others, maybe that would help melt the other memories when they came to full realization. And, maybe, that could even bring back some of *their* memories.

Then again, her attempts to reconnect with him could rekindle his memories of her with other men. And, boy, could that backfire big time. If he asked her about the other men, she could be setting herself up for a situation where she'd have to choose between lying and saving his feelings. Or even saving their marriage.

The shower shut off. She pulled her nail from her punishing teeth and clenched her hands. Her stomach fluttered with indecision. The muffled click of the shower door opening met her ear and she envisioned Quaid naked—all that lean, sculpted muscle, tight, tanned skin. And those hands. She loved his hands. Loved the way they'd possessed her when he'd kissed her.

The memory of his mouth on hers, hot, hungry, demanding, shot liquid fire to the center of her body and propelled her toward the door, where she stared at the flat gray metal. She couldn't think about what would happen if this failed. She needed to connect with him. Needed to reach him on that intimate level only they shared. She needed to help him find his way back from the dark place he'd been for the last five years. And she was running out of options.

Her nerves coiled tighter and tighter in her belly, but she raised her hand to knock anyway, determined to set at least one part of this mess right.

Before her knuckles met metal, Quaid's voice echoed through the door. "It's open."

Her stomach jumped. Then her mind darted back to Cash's explanation of Quaid's heightened senses and she blew out a breath.

Swallowing her doubts, Jessica turned the knob and cracked the door enough to put her head through and glance around. Steam filled the small room and fogged the mirror. Quaid stood in front of the sink, hands braced on either side, staring down at the white porcelain, a white towel hooked around his waist. The sight of his phoenix and all that gorgeous muscle added a heady, tingly sensation to her tension.

"Hey," she said softly. "Are you okay?"

He glanced over his shoulder. Those deep, rich brown eyes stared a moment, and then he looked back at the sink without responding. Her anxiety nudged out the thrill.

She slipped into the bathroom and closed the door. "Pretty rough day for you."

"Equally rough for you." His voice curled around her, as soft and warm as the room.

"I highly doubt it."

She stepped up behind him. He tensed, his head turned just enough to track her out of the corner of his eye. Heat and the fresh scent of soap and skin lifted off his body. She settled her hands at his hips and pressed a kiss to his back.

His muscles contracted beneath her lips and a sound rolled in his chest and vibrated through her lips. Her body hummed with need.

She slid her tongue along the indention of his spine, paused and kissed him again. "Is there anything I can do for you?"

A heavy breath rocked his shoulders. "You can never stop doing that."

A smile turned her lips and some apprehension melted. "That can be arranged."

She kissed her way up his spine, pressing her body to his and slid her hands over his hard, warm abdomen. The ribbed sinew beneath her fingers flinched.

"Oh . . . God . . ." He breathed the words, long and slowly as if he'd never felt anything so good.

Her smile grew, her heart filled. She ached to reacquaint him with a million heavenly pleasures. She felt her way up his abdomen, brushed her fingers across his nipples. He gasped and tensed again.

She laid her cheek against the hard wall of muscle along his back. "I've missed you so much," she whispered, the fear of his rejection restricting her throat. "Will you . . . make love to me?"

"Jessie . . ." he rasped, as if he were in pain. "I . . . don't remember. . . ."

The fear in her stomach hardened into a rock. A surge of sadness washed in, but her determination held its ground. She lowered her hands to his abdomen and her lips to his shoulder blade.

"But you feel it. I can tell by the way you kiss me. You want me even if you don't remember me."

"Not that. I've wanted you . . . forever." His voice shook. "I just don't remember . . . how to . . ."

She waited and when he didn't finish, she realized he

meant he didn't remember sex. He didn't remember how to make love. Which made questions ping quickly through her mind—about what he'd really dreamt about—or seen—when she'd been with other men, about his contact with others at the Castle. All topics she knew would ruin the moment. All topics which were in the past and didn't change the present.

Still, her breath caught in her throat, emotions choking her. Sadness for all he'd gone without over the years, gratitude for having the opportunity to give it all back to him. And loss. A deep, wrenching loss for the sweet, comforting, secure intimacy they'd shared.

She closed her eyes and wiped the wetness there on his skin, lowering her hands to the knot in his towel. "Let me show you?" she asked, her voice shaking. "Can I show you all the things you loved?"

He lowered his head, following the movement of her hands, his muscles so taut his entire body quivered with a fine tremble. He scraped in a shallow breath, scraped out a barely audible, "Yes."

Anticipation flared like hot coals in her belly. Jessica held her breath, pulled the knot and released the towel. She laid her hands low on his pelvis, her fingertips brushing the fine hair leading lower. Still, Quaid didn't move, but his breathing quickened.

She pushed up on her toes, sliding her body along his, and whispered in his ear, "Turn around."

He straightened, released his grip on the sink and turned. Jessica wasn't prepared for the fierce want in his taut expression or the lusty, stormy emotions in his eyes. His restraint . . . or rather what lurked behind the restraint, sent a thrill buzzing down her spine and spreading over her skin.

She moved close, pressed her hips to his, her hands to

his stomach and he gripped the sink behind him again. Her heart squeezed painfully, terrified that every move he made signaled imminent rejection.

"Quaid," she said, her gaze on the mouth she wanted to attack. "What's wrong? You're not acting like you want this. Not the way you wanted it before."

"You're . . . scared. Confused," he said. "You didn't feel that way before."

A trickle of fear chilled her gut. "How do you know how I feel?"

"I . . . don't know. I just . . . when I touch you, I feel it." Those rich brown eyes lowered to her mouth, yearning. "I don't want to hurt you. I don't want you to be afraid of me. But, I understand why you are."

"You can feel my emotions?" The thought first terrified her, then intrigued her.

"Not precisely, not intensely, but yes."

"And others?"

"When I touch them, yes." He hesitated, uncertainty passing through his eyes. "And . . . I can feel how I feel about them, too."

Hope surged in Jessica's heart. She held her breath, waiting for the next logical step in the conversation—him telling her how he felt about her. Instead, he broke their gaze, his eyes sliding to her chest.

An idea formed in her mind, one that caused both excitement and fear. She already had the man naked, and she didn't want to waste this beautiful opportunity.

"Let me just quell any doubts you have about my feelings for you right now."

Jessica closed her eyes, took a breath and relaxed her muscles. She dug deep inside herself, beneath all the shields and layers. While she visualized her heart opening, she slid her hands up his belly, over his chest, wrapped her arms around his neck and pulled her body against his.

There, she relaxed into his strength, his heat. Let all her love for him, her gratefulness at having him back swell and then spill over.

Quaid moaned, sounding pained and needy, yet relieved and happy at the same time. Her emotions flowed, crisp and fresh and pure, like a swift mountain stream. They eddied and tumbled and multiplied. She let them well into her eyes. Let them overflow onto her cheeks.

Quaid growled, a very needy sexual sound, and Jessica's body immediately responded, need throbbing low in her pelvis. Quaid leaned forward, closed his arms around her and turned his face into her neck. Then his mouth opened and his lips pressed against her skin. His arms brought their bodies into full, tight contact and his erection pressed long and hard against her lower abdomen. He moaned again and bit her neck. The sting of pain shot lust straight between her legs.

"Yes," she whispered, holding his head to her neck, gripping his shoulder to get even closer. Her need exploded. She pushed up on her toes, rubbing her hips against his erection. This felt so rich and real and right. "Quaid, God . . ."

She grabbed his head with both hands and pulled it back, found his mouth and kissed him. He opened to her immediately, hesitation replaced by frantic need. Walking her backwards, he circled her tongue with his until she hit the wall, where he tilted his head and kissed her harder, deeper, then tilted it back, licking and sucking and kissing. She skimmed her hands down his chest, his belly and pushed him back far enough to slide her hands between their bodies and palm his erection.

Quaid's body jerked. He swore and then a full body shiver rocked him, shoulders to toes. His intense reactions, his raspy breaths thrilled Jessica, increasing her own desire.

"Jesus Christ, Jessie . . ."

"If you like that," she whispered, "you'll really love this."

She slid down his body. Quaid released her and planted his hands flat against the wall as if he needed it to hold himself up. On her knees, she darted one quick smile up at him before taking the wide head of his cock between her lips. The confusion on his face turned to instant ecstasy. His body stiffened and his eyes closed as his head fell back.

"Holy. Fuck." The words came from deep in his throat.

His taste flooded Jessica's memory, filling her with joy. She took him deeply with greedy strokes of her lips and tongue. Before long, he had one hand fisted in her hair. The force of it stung her scalp and she laid her hand over his. His fingers instantly released. "Sorry, Jess, sorry," he rasped. "That is just *so* good."

The rock of his hips, the sounds from his throat, the shivers across his body made her own sex heavy and wet.

Quaid's hand moved to her chin and tilted her face up to his. "I need . . . more." His breathing came in shaky pants, his eyes barely open. "I need *you*."

He leaned down, gripped her waist and pulled her to her feet. He panted as he pushed at the waistband of her shorts, his urgency renewed.

"Buttons, baby," she said, reaching to unfasten them. "Hold on."

"Fucking buttons," he muttered, sliding his hands under her shirt and across her belly, making her quiver. His mouth found hers, hard and wet, distracting her fingers.

As soon as her zipper rasped down, his hands dove back to her shorts and shoved them over her hips. Everything after that happened in frantic flashes.

He grabbed her ass, pulled her against his erection and groaned, the sound animalistic and impatient. Jessica wrapped her arms around him and pressed her body close, holding tight. He covered her mouth again, his tongue plunging with a force that made her catch her breath. Then his hands tightened painfully and he lifted her. She broke the kiss, to breathe, to get her bearings. This was suddenly moving so fast.

"Quaid—"

She barely got his name out before her back hit the wall. Then his mouth covered hers again. She turned her head to break the kiss and draw air. Quaid's mouth went straight to her neck.

"Quaid, baby . . ." she rasped, breathing hard, growing a little nervous.

He pushed his hand between their bodies and rubbed the head of his cock against her. Oh, God that felt good. But, she wanted to slow down. So they could both enjoy it. . . .

"Quaid, can we—"

He pushed into her. Not fully, but her body stretched. Burned. She gasped and tensed.

Quaid's teeth closed on her shoulder and he growled low in his throat, a very male sound of extreme pleasure that shot lust into her blood. But her body was still adjusting. Only Quaid didn't give it time. He moved his hand back to her ass and used those powerful arms to pull her into him. Too fast. Too deep.

Pain sliced through her pelvis. Burned along her walls. She squeezed her eyes closed as her nails dug into Quaid's shoulders and she tightened her legs around his hips. A sound of pain slid up her throat.

His shaft pulled back and apprehension coiled in Jessica's chest. "Quaid . . . baby, wait a second. . . ."

But it was too late. He'd felt sex for the first time—at least in his memory—and he was gone. He didn't even pause before thrusting deeply into her. Jessica gritted her teeth, circled her arms at his neck and held on. He simultaneously pushed into her body while pulling her hips toward his, the result driving him deep on every plunge and slamming her upper back against the concrete wall.

"God, Jessie . . ."

He didn't choke out any more, but she didn't need any more. He knew he was with her. He knew she was giving him this pleasure. These memories would stay with him.

His thrusts came faster, harder. Jessica turned her face into his neck to smother the sounds she couldn't hold back. Slid one hand up and over his head to hold tight. She tried to stay focused—this was her husband, he wanted her, it was a start. But the leak of tears from her eyes gave away all those underlying emotions she didn't want to acknowledge.

His climax rocked him hard, and he continued to shiver for long moments after while he stayed there, inside her, holding her, his mouth pressing kisses to her shoulder.

She tried every trick she knew to stop the tears. He wouldn't understand. She didn't even fully understand. But even though she didn't clearly remember any of her sexual encounters after Quaid had died, this held far too much familiarity for comfort.

"Jess?" His voice pulled her from the uneasy memories. She turned her head on his shoulder, which he took as indication she was listening and went on. "I'm . . . um . . ."

He rocked his hips, moving inside her and making her catch her breath. He was still hard . . . or hard again . . . she didn't know which. But she was sure he was going to ask for round two, which she wouldn't deny him, but nor did she want right at the moment.

"If you tell me how to move or touch you, I can still do something for you." He turned his head and kissed that sensitive spot beneath her ear. "I want to make you feel as good as you make me feel."

She smiled at the sweetness of the offer, even while experiencing the pinch of disappointment. "Thank you, babe." She kissed his jaw. "But, no. I'm . . . a little sore."

His breath hissed out through his teeth. "I'm sorry."

The regret in his voice made her lift her head and look into his eyes. They were sated, the fire banked to a glowing ember now, and guilt had taken up space in the foreground. She spread her hands on either side of his head and kissed him. "Don't be. I'll be eating up all that passion and power soon. It's just been a while. My body's adjusting."

It took about two full seconds for Jessica to realize what she'd said, *"It's just been a while."* And what doors it might have opened in Quaid's mind, because he continued to stare at her as if he was thinking very hard.

So she kissed him again, relieved to find that just like every other red-blooded man, his mind could be sidetracked with a slow, tongue-sliding kiss.

They dressed in silence. Not as much awkward silence as distracted silence. While her mind acted like the cheerleader, tossing out positive, optimistic messages, her body was the leather-clad rebel still looking for relief, her heart the wallflower still aching for connection.

When she turned for the door, she didn't understand how the emptiness inside her could have expanded. Or how she could be even more confused. Or how her hope could have taken on an even heavier tarnish.

She pulled the door open, but Quaid put his hand flat above her head and closed it again. His other arm slipped around her waist and he pulled her back against him gently. He nudged her hair out of the way with his chin and pressed his mouth to her neck.

Jessica closed her eyes. Tears burned and leaked over her lashes.

"I love you," he whispered against her skin. "I don't know how. I don't understand what it means. I don't even know if I can live up to what it involves or give you what you need or if I'm what you want anymore. . . ."

He paused, kissing her again. Jessica waited, sensing he wasn't done, tears now flowing down her cheeks. Her heart seemed to be mending in some ways and breaking in others. None of which she understood.

"But I feel it, Jess." The tip of his nose traced a path from her neck to her shoulder, where he planted another gentle kiss. "And I know I've loved you a long time."

Chest swelling with emotion, she turned and wrapped her arms around him. She pressed her face to his neck. "I love you more."

When she pulled away, he lifted her face with one hand and used his T-shirt to wipe her tears with the other. "Kai will probably take a hammer to my knuckles if he thinks I made you cry."

She burst out laughing and pressed her forehead to his chest.

"I'm serious," Quaid said. "I'm just glad Keira's not here. Cash is going to have to get moving on that protective skin he was creating at the Castle. I might need it."

Jessica's mind made a hairpin turn as she was recalled to their dangerous situation. When she lifted her head and looked into his eyes again, this brief—very brief—interlude seemed so minor in the grand scheme of all they still had to accomplish to be free to pursue a relationship.

She laid her hands against the soft cotton over his chest. "I know it might be hard to see right now with all the stress they're under, but Kai and Keira would both die before they'd let anything happen to you again. They're just—"

"Protective. I know. I've already gotten that lecture from Cash." He brushed his thumb over her cheek, his dark gaze following the motion. "I love your freckles.

Sometimes they look like they're shimmering when you dream."

Surprise parted her lips.

Quaid kissed her softly. "Ready to face them?"

Confused again, but not willing to delve into the whole dreaming scenario after having so successfully dodged it, she said, "That's my line."

Quaid opened the door and Jessica stepped out into the hallway, her body tingling, her heart yearning, her mind twisting.

Mitch and Kai's argument met Jessica's ears halfway down the hall.

"What now?" Quaid asked.

"Who knows?"

They rounded the corner into the living room and Jessica glanced toward the kitchen, where Kai had been before Jessica had wandered and ended up in the bathroom up against the wall having sex with her husband.

How had that happened, exactly?

"You would *ruin* chili with Heinz 57?" Kai asked.

"Hardly ruining it, Ryder." Mitch still sat at the dining room table, shirtsleeves rolled up on his forearms. He was leaning sideways in a tired slump, one hand holding a pencil over a legal pad, the other propping his head up with his hand deep in his hair. His gaze ran over the screen in front of him, its blue-white light reflecting softly off his glasses. "It's an award-winning recipe."

"Award winning where? The Internet?"

Mitch turned, hooked one arm over the back of his chair and looked into the kitchen. He acknowledged Jessica and Quaid headed that way with a lift of his chin, but kept a scowl for Kai. "The woman who made that recipe for me studied at the Cordon Bleu."

Kai leaned into the counter, arms stretched out and

gripping the edges, his expression confident and superior, like he owned the kitchen. "And did you eat the chili before or after you had sex?"

Mitch opened his mouth, poised his pencil for retort and froze. Then he deflated. He turned back to the table, tossed his pencil on the paper and scrolled through the webpage on screen with a muttered, "You prick."

Kai laughed, the sound deep and rich and familiar, bringing back all the fun memories from Jessica's days as a firefighter.

"I don't care what you say," Mitch said, "that recipe I gave Brody is good shit. Have one of the guys make yours and one make mine and we'll let Quaid decide."

"Decide what?" Quaid asked.

But Jessica already knew. "Which one you like better."

"What difference does eating before or after sex make?" Quaid asked, his frown creating that positively adorable little V between his eyes.

Jessica shook her head, prepared to tell Quaid that Kai and Mitch were full of shit, but Kai spoke first. "Everything tastes good after great sex, brother."

"Good, because I'm starving." Quaid's hungry eyes scanned the counter in front of them, which was covered in freshly cut fruit, and stopped on the mixture Kai had sitting in the blender. "Can I have some of whatever that is?"

Oh, hell. Jessica's stomach squeezed in mortification. She prayed the comment would go right over Kai and Mitch's heads. Oh, but no, she couldn't be that lucky. They both went silent. In fact, everyone went silent, including Teague, Alyssa and Cash on the sofa. The only voices filling the space were Kat's and Mateo's.

Kai's gaze snapped to Jessica's. Mitch twisted toward the kitchen and hooked his arm over the back of the chair again, this time pulling off his glasses. Quaid, totally oblivious, picked up a piece of mango from the cutting board in front of Kai, studied it a moment, then popped it in his mouth.

And even before he said it, Jessica knew what was coming.

"Mmm, that *is* amazing. I never had it before, but it's great now." He picked up another piece and held it out to Jessica. "Jessie, try it. Tell me if it's better after."

Kai snorted a laugh he'd been trying to hold. And Jessica caved.

"Jesus Christ." Jessica covered her eyes and dropped her head.

Kai and Mitch burst out laughing and Jessica's face burned red hot.

Kai picked up a half-cut mango and threw it at Mitch, who caught it at the last second. "You idiot. I didn't even feel it because you were pissing me off."

"You're sick, dude." Mitch pitched the mango back at Kai, narrowly missing his head. It bounced off the stainless-steel refrigerator and hit the floor. "You need to stay out of their business. You need to get laid, dude."

She dropped her hand and found Quaid frowning in confusion, his gaze alternating between the two men, who were laughing so hard they were crying. Quaid stuffed mango into his mouth three slices at a time.

Jessica pushed the cutting board out of reach, laughing. She couldn't help it. The combination of Quaid's pure innocence and Mitch and Kai's antics was hilarious. She just wished it hadn't been over her sex life. Especially now. When her and Quaid's relationship was far from settled.

"No more, Quaid, you're going to make yourself sick."

He eyed the mango longingly and licked his fingers. Then he sent a cautious glance at Jessica. "What did I do?"

"You put us back in the firehouse fishbowl." She sighed, knowing he didn't understand. "Nothing. It's fine."

She pounded Kai's arm with a fist before wandering over to the sofa and sinking into one end sideways, curling her feet under her. She had to hold her breath to keep from groaning. Her body hurt in a few very strategic locations. Which brought back a flash of erotic memories. And that nagging sense of discontent.

When she looked up, everyone was staring at her, part curiosity, part amusement. "I didn't plan it. . . ." She shrugged. "Just kinda . . . happened."

Quaid came in sucking a giant smoothie through a straw and handed a drink to her.

"Made one for you, too, Jess," Kai said, subdued laughter in his voice. "Both have energy boosts."

She shot a look over her shoulder toward Kai cleaning up in the kitchen, then looked at Quaid, sucking down the smoothie like water. "Slow down on that, babe, or you're going to be sick tonight."

He pulled the straw from his mouth and smiled. Jessica's stomach went light, like she'd swallowed air. That was his first real smile.

And, oh, he was so handsome, so purely Quaid, her heart ached.

When she looked at him like that, Q's chest filled until it felt like it would crack open. Only, it wasn't a happy look. She was sad. She looked at him like she *wanted* to love him, if only . . .

If only he could be Quaid. The Quaid she remembered. The Quaid he'd once been.

And he wanted her to love him badly enough to do what he could to find that man inside.

Q sat on the sofa next to Jessica and turned to Teague. He wasn't sure why, Teague just seemed like the go-to guy. "So how do we do this?"

"We've been talking," Teague said. "And we were thinking pictures instead of just, you know, stories."

"I made a Facebook page for our team," Kai said, "a long time ago, before the warehouse fire. Training, goofing around, incidents."

"Facebook?" Q asked.

Kai waved that topic away. "They're pictures."

"Pictures," Q echoed. That felt . . . comfortable? Hell, no. "Yeah. Pictures will work."

"Q or Quaid . . . ?" Alyssa said from her position beneath Teague's arm.

Neither really felt right anymore, like he didn't fit into either mold. "Either."

"You really do need to speak up if you feel overwhelmed or you experience any pain in your head."

He nodded. "Fine."

"And if you have any flash of memory," Alyssa said, "we should also stop and explore that before moving on. Otherwise, it could get lost in more images."

"Okay."

Teague looked at his wife, who nodded, and he picked up his closed laptop from the side table. When he opened it and tapped buttons, apprehension crawled beneath Q's skin and he reached for Jessica. When his hand found empty sofa, he turned. She was gone.

Kai came up behind the sofa and took Q's empty glass. "Showtime?"

"Yeah, where's Jessica?"

"I'm right here," she said from behind Kai.

He reached for her and she came to the back of the sofa and took his hand, her other hand holding a glass of water. Kai rounded the sofa and sat on the floor, and Teague set the computer on the coffee table in front of everyone.

"Come sit," he said to Jessica.

She shook her head, her expression tight, guarded. "I'm going to stand."

"Okay, here we are." Teague drew Q's attention. "Do we want to start with recent and move backward or oldest and move forward?"

When Jessica pulled her hand from his, Q leaned forward, elbows on knees, hands clasped. A beehive had been planted in his stomach. Among a turbulent, rushing river. With moss-covered rocks wedged beneath his ribs. And mosquitoes sucking his blood. He glanced at Jessica again.

Her glassy stare cleared long enough for her to say, "Oldest to newest makes most sense."

Teague shrugged. "Oldest to newest it is."

He clicked into something called a "photo album" and there were several separate albums labeled by year. Teague clicked onto the earliest year and pulled up the first image—a group picture, taken in front of the grill of a fire engine. Seven people posed there, three crouching low, four standing behind.

Q recognized the faces—the faces of some of those in this room, only younger. And happier. So much happier. A sudden, dark weight made his chest very heavy.

"Seth is the one you haven't met," Kai said. "The blond, top right."

Q glanced over Seth's face without any hint of recognition. Then his eyes focused in on the face right next to Seth's—*his* face. Quaid's face. No mistake, Q was staring at *his own* face. His throat dried up as he looked closer.

His head was tipped back and to the side, his mouth open and wide in a smile, as if someone had just made a joke he'd found very funny. Arms crossed over his chest, butt leaning against the fire engine's shiny chrome grill, legs relaxed and crossed at the ankles, he looked completely at ease and carefree.

A chill settled inside Q. And something layered alongside. Something ugly. And dark. Something beyond anger. Beyond fury.

Rage.

The first hints of the rage he knew would eventually try to devour him, possess him. Rage toward whoever had taken from him all he was about to see. Rage toward whoever had substituted life as a test subject for a full, meaningful life as a firefighter. A life with friends who'd loved him. A woman—a beautiful, compassionate, intelligent woman—who'd loved him.

Q tore his eyes from the photo and looked behind him. Jessica was gone.

Sixteen

Q stared at a photo with a burned structure in the background, fire engines with bright red lights in the foreground, water spouting from hoses pointed at flames dancing from doors and windows. He swore he could feel those flames lick his gut with excitement. The same way the thought of being with Jessica again turned his blood to fire.

"You fucking fell down that ladder, dude, remember?" Kai laughed out the words.

When Alyssa realized there was no way she would be able to contain their language, she put the kids and their toys into a bedroom.

"Don't even start," Teague said, "or stories about you tripping over hose line will start coming out."

Teague clicked to the next picture, an image of two firefighters, their backs to the camera, but looking at each other, so their profiles were visible. A fire of some kind blazed in front of them, which created a dynamic, blurred background for the image. The firefighters were dressed in typical yellow gear, both with red helmets. The taller one wore the helmet, the shorter one held it under an arm.

His gaze paused on the shorter firefighter's hands. Twirling hair. It was a woman, and she was holding her helmet under her arm while she twisted her hair into a bun. Long, thick, copper hair. His heart thumped hard. He squinted at her face. Jessica. That was Jessica's profile. God, she looked so . . . young.

"How old was Jessica there?" Quaid asked.

"Would say . . ." Teague tilted his head. "Twenty-four-ish."

Really basic questions Q didn't know the answers to popped into his mind. "How old is she now?"

"Thirty-one," Kai said.

Q looked over at Kai. "How old am I?"

A stark look passed through Kai's eyes before he forced a smile. "You'll be thirty-three in a little over a week."

Thirty-three. Was that old? Was that young?

He turned back around and studied the picture. It spoke of comfort, camaraderie. Intimacy.

Teague continued clicking through pictures. Photo after photo after photo—in the fire station working, in the fire station messing around, outside training, at actual fires, working on the engines, playing basketball, sitting in lounge chairs with drinks. In every damn one Quaid was smiling. Even when soot or dirt covered his face, maybe even more so, Quaid smiled at the camera.

Q quickly lost track of anything the others were saying. He didn't need their commentary to know all he needed to know. The photos said everything that mattered to Q, at least everything that mattered right now.

He could see the relationships he'd had with the men around him, and with Keira and Jessica. They'd handed each other tools, let each other climb on their shoulders to reach something, teamed up together to accomplish a task, risked their own safety to save another in danger, taught each other, teased each other. They high-fived, punched arms, slapped shoulders. And they hugged. Guys to guys.

Girls to girls. Guys to girls. They all hugged. A lot. In nearly every photo someone had an arm around someone else.

And, God, they smiled. And laughed.

In every damned picture. Their happiness . . . no, their joy—pure, vivid, passionate joy—was palpable.

Then there were the photos of Jessica. Q watched the progression of the relationship between Quaid and Jessica. From interest to flirtation, flirtation to relationship, relationship to love. Yes, Quaid had definitely loved her. And he'd reveled in the way she'd clung to him. He'd leaned into her, held tight, kissed her head.

By the time they reached the last image, Q could see the man Jessica had fallen in love with. He could see why she'd fallen in love with him. And he could also see that man was not inside him anywhere.

While Q might have Quaid's feelings of loving Jessica, he didn't have the memories that supported those feelings and he knew without a doubt, what he felt for her now was *nothing* in comparison to what Quaid had felt for her.

Q focused on the screen, not sure if he could take any more. An arrow overlaid the image. "What's this?"

Teague and Kai shared a look. Teague said, "It's a video."

"Of what?"

"Uh . . . just your birthday one year. I don't think it will add anything to the pictures."

Q thought about seeing this Quaid in living, breathing color. Hearing his voice. Seeing his mannerisms. He was desperate to pick up *something,* some indication that he'd once been this man. "Play it."

The video began in an industrial kitchen, obviously in a firehouse judging by the men in navy blue uniforms, familiar to Q now after that barrage of photographs. He recognized the youthful faces of Kai, Teague, Luke and Seth. A few other men were there, too, people Q didn't know.

On the screen, Kai pulled bowls out of the refrigerator and piled them in his arms, while Teague and Luke held something that looked like a plastic pipe and Seth dug in a kitchen drawer. The other men stood around laughing and joking.

"Who's holding the camera?" Q asked.

"Keira," Teague said.

"Where's—"

Q didn't get Jessica's name out of his mouth before the door to the kitchen on screen opened and she flew in, her hair down and flowing over her shoulders with her forward movement. She held a brightly wrapped box under her arm and she wasn't in uniform. She was wearing faded jeans that fit nice tight hips and hung low on her waist. She dropped the package and her purse on a nearby counter, slid off her coat and unwrapped a knit scarf from her neck.

When Jessica looked toward the camera, her grin was so vivid, Q swore he could see all the way to her soul. Her eyes sparkled with joy and excitement. And, God, so much love. The stark difference between the woman on the screen and the woman crying after they'd had sex earlier made Q want to kill someone. Made him want to find the bastards who'd started this whole nightmare and rip their throats out.

Then, her gaze darted to the guys and her mouth opened into a surprised "O." Her hand flew there. She shook her head and, despite her obvious horror, started laughing. "Oh, my God. You know I'm going to get blamed for this. He'll *kill* me. Sending him flowers at work was already pushing his limits. Did they get here? Has he seen them?"

"They just came," Keira said. "He hasn't seen them yet."

Kai had the bowls on the counter. Teague and Luke had brought the tube over and Seth, his grin wide, spooned a thick frothy white substance into the tube.

Hands on both cheeks, she groaned, then looked up and around. "Where is he?"

"Your sister has him on the phone upstairs," Keira said. "We asked her to call and wish him happy birthday and keep him talking."

Q sent a look toward Kai. "What is that thing?"

"We affectionately refer to *that thing* as the Master Blaster Two Thousand," Kai said. "A handmade, state-of-the-art, whipped-cream-shooting weapon of lethal proportions. Observe the highly aerodynamic chamber of compressed air duct-taped onto the carefully salvaged PVC pipe."

The thump of footsteps sounded from the computer and Kai pointed at the screen. "Hey, man, this is the good part."

Q found the people on screen suddenly serious. "Here he comes," Kai said, his voice filled with urgency. "Seth, finish up."

They all went into another room, where recliners sat in a semicircle around a big screen of some kind. Behind those, the dining room table sprawled beneath a row of windows; balloons and flowers sat in the center of the table.

Kai, Teague and Luke whispered to each other as they took up their positions inside a doorway through which Q could see the stairwell beyond.

Kai glanced at Teague and Luke. "On three."

Q could see Quaid's lower legs as he came down the steps toward the living room. This was surreal. Bizarre. Watching himself . . . a man he couldn't remember being, relive an event . . . he couldn't remember living.

"One . . . two . . ."

The real Quaid turned the corner into the room, his head down. When he looked up, he slowed, eyes narrowed.

"Three!" Kai said.

Quaid stopped short, put his hands up, and turned his face away. "Oh, shit!"

Teague let the Master Blaster spray while Luke steadied the aim. Whipped cream spewed from the crude device, coating Quaid's perfect navy uniform. He cursed again and took a few stumbling steps back, laughing. In less than five seconds, the man was coated, head to toe, in snow-white foam.

How on earth could Q *not* remember that?

On the screen, everyone broke into boisterous laughter, catcalls and whistles. Laughter also erupted out around Q. The camera shook with Keira's amusement. Quaid stood frozen, arms held wide, mouth sputtering whipped cream. He slowly brought both hands to his face, wiping his eyes clear.

Q couldn't help it. He laughed, too. But, he ached with the absence of this memory.

Keira panned out with the camera and Q's gaze locked on Jessica. She was standing to the side, both hands covering her mouth and laughing so hard, tears streamed down her cheeks. The sight made Q's mouth curve, and made his eyes grow damp.

In the video, Quaid grinned and licked his lips. Shaking his head, he stared down at himself. When he looked up, he raised one white arm, dripping with froth, and pointed at Jessica. "You."

She gasped around laughter while shaking her head, barely able to speak. "N-no! It wasn't me."

He sauntered toward her, slowly, that dangerous grin in place beneath so much whipped cream it was ridiculously comical. Yet, Q was mesmerized by the cocky confidence of this Quaid. The swagger and humor and good nature. Q wasn't any of those things.

Jessica backed away, hands out, choking on the laughter still trying to bubble out of her. "I swear. It was Seth."

Keira panned the camera to Seth, who was doubled over with laughter. Everyone around Q laughed, too.

"I'm so nice," Quaid said, "I'm going to share." He laughed, low in his throat, grabbed Jessica's arms, circled her waist and pulled her fully against him.

"Oh, God!" she screeched and squirmed and laughed, gasping for air. "Quaid, you—"

Whatever she was going to say got cut off by Quaid's mouth—as he kissed her.

Q straightened. Eyes wide, lips parted, he watched his alter ego kiss Jessica. He heard her murmur, some mixture of surprise and pleasure that speared heat between his shoulder blades. He watched as both of them slowly closed their eyes in pleasure.

Their expressions were lost in what Q could only describe as . . . bliss. Quaid slid his hand behind her neck, tilted his head, and opened his mouth over hers. Another murmur sounded in her throat. This one softer, longer. And the way she kissed him back, with so much passion, want, need . . . Q's throat tightened, making it hard to breathe. Q had definitely not kissed her like that. In comparison, Q had been rough and crude. He thought of how he'd taken her in the bathroom, equally as rough and crude.

The terrible weight of disappointment and self-disgust made Q sink deeper into the sofa.

In the room around the lovers on screen, their coworkers hooted and howled and whistled. Quaid pulled back, wiping at the cream he'd left on Jessica's face and the way they looked at each other hollowed out Q's heart. Without even an inkling of doubt, he knew he didn't have the capacity to love like that. He was too damaged. Too scarred. And what he saw in their eyes had to have been only a fraction of what they'd felt.

Seth yelled, "Showers!" from the laptop and Q focused to see the man's huge grin in place, triumphant fist in the air. Followed by the rest of the group chanting, "Showers! Show-ers! Show-ers!"

Quaid grinned, leaned down and swept Jessica into his arms. Then he turned and started for the stairs. He kissed her until he reached the stairs and when he broke the kiss to see where he was going, Jessica's mouth slid to his neck, her hand clawed at his hair.

Quaid cut a quick glance over his shoulder. "Get the hell out of here, O'Shay."

"Not a chance, Legend," she said from behind the camera. "You do realize fraternizing on state property, and while on duty is grounds for—"

"Then you should be fired a few times over, sugar." He barked a laugh. "You don't think I know what you and Luke are doing in that engine bay? You may be working, but it ain't on fire apparatus."

Quaid lengthened his strides, got a head start off the stairs, turned into the bathroom and shut the door in Keira's face. The sound of a lock clicked. And Jessica's laugh penetrated the door, drifting out of the screen, traversing all those empty years, shivering over Q.

Whoever was behind this hadn't just taken five years from Q. They'd taken his whole goddamned past. And his whole goddamned future.

Gil Schaeffer held his pipe by the bowl and sucked a deep lungful of his newest tobacco. A rich, smooth blend of three different quality tobaccos, Cube's uniqueness came from a struggle for power between its sweet and fruity elements. Apropos to his situation he'd thought when he'd bought it.

He leaned back in the ancient leather chair and appreciated the sexual splendor of the dancer atop the bar in front of him. He'd chosen the back parlor of the Alibi Club tonight, hardly in the mood to mingle. Truthfully, he needed a place to relax so he could think. He couldn't say watching Courtney flatten her bare belly and double D's on the glossy mahogany less than a foot away *relaxed* him, exactly. But here he could shake off that uptight, senatorial layer he was finding more and more restrictive. Sometimes damn suffocating.

"Mmm," Courtney hummed, red-thong-clad ass in the air, knees bent, thighs spread wide, bare breasts rubbing the bar.

He found himself wondering what they coated the thing with to make the women's skin slide across it that way. Then wondered why this was the first time he'd ever noticed.

"I love that smell," she said, drawing Gil's gaze from the push and pull of her pale breasts against the dark wood to her black-rimmed green eyes. "The tobacco. Dark and edgy. It turns me on."

Gil's groin tightened, but his mind remained distracted. He offered his inane politician smile and nodded. Let his gaze slide up the curve of her back, and watched her smooth ass gyrate. The tension evaporated from his shoulders.

"What can I do for you tonight, senator?" Courtney crawled along the bar. Stretching out, she pressed up on her palms, threw her head back and bent her knees until the tips of her glittering scarlet boots touched her blond head. "My throat is achy. Could use a good rubdown."

Oh, this girl had his number, and played it expertly.

Giving him control. Hinting toward dominance. "You're lively tonight, Courtney."

"I'm lively every night, senator." She swung her legs around and pulled herself up by the pole at her back, then bent forward, her ass writhing along the big, round, brass shaft.

This one could offer him extreme stress relief. God knew he deserved it. He was pulling in a breath to accept her invitation, when someone slid into the seat beside him.

Courtney's gaze swung in that direction. Her eyes sparked. "Well, hello, major."

Gil didn't have to look to know the man's identity. The club only had fifty members, only three of those majors, and only one of which had reason to sit down beside him now.

"Good evening, Courtney," the newcomer returned in a smooth, confident tone.

Every ounce of Gil's tension returned, cramping his neck, clenching his teeth and fisting his hands. "Can't I get an hour of peace?"

"You could have if you'd returned my phone calls." Major Bruce Abernathy leaned forward, resting his forearms on the bar, his gaze appreciating the deep undulations of Courtney's hips. "But since you didn't, I have to interrupt your . . . peace. Courtney, beautiful," he said, "can you give us a minute?"

She bent to run a finger down the side of Abernathy's face, whispering, "I'll give you as long as you want." Her lips touched his. "You know where to find me."

The girl slithered farther down the bar, joining another dancer and treating Admiral Peck and Ambassador Manash to an erotic rubbing, touching, tongue-sucking girl-on-girl act. Gil was almost as furious with Courtney for forgetting he existed as soon as Abernathy plopped his womanizing ass in the next chair as he was for these damn problems at the Castle only months before his senate campaign kickoff.

"You sure choose the strangest times to chase pussy, Gil." Without taking his eyes off the women, Abernathy drank deeply from the amber beer in his hand.

"I'm relaxing," Gil said. "Or I was until you showed up, and I have everything under control."

"Yeah? Then you must have located O'Shay." He paused, still watching the girls. Courtney was rubbing something shiny over the other woman's breast while licking and sucking the opposite. "Must have the completed formula in your possession. Must have been just about to call me and let me know when Courtney distracted you."

Gil's blood pressure spurted into the two hundreds. He could feel the heat of tiny blood vessels bursting across the surface of his skin. "I've put Owen Young on O'Shay's trail. We'll have him within twenty-four hours. Probably less."

"Good start." Abernathy nodded absently, his attention honed now on Courtney's finger deep inside the other woman's mouth as she sucked until her cheeks caved in, pulling it out slowly, licking it up and down, then starting all over again. He took a drink of his beer, then rolled the chilled bottle against his forehead. "Getting hot in here."

After another greedy swallow, nearly downing the rest of the bottle, Abernathy said, "Q was due in Punjab two days ago. My troops can't just slum in Pakistan, Gil. If Q isn't going to follow through on gathering those weapons, the men and get the intelligence out of them, it's time for my men to move on." Abernathy pried his gaze away from the soft porn show atop the bar and used his glacial blue gaze to pin Gil in place. "You know our budget goes where we go, senator. And you know I'd like to keep the bulk of our budget with your project. But I have to admit,

I'm less than impressed with the way you've handled the development so far."

The top blew off Schaeffer's patience. "Who the hell do you think—?"

"You let extremist scientists dictate the speed of delivery. You let a few firefighters run circles around you. You let one damn lawyer hog tie you. You've got one job, Schaeffer. Only one that you've got to get right and that isn't your senatorial position, because we all know that's a given fuckup. You only need to wrap up this damn soldier of the future project. Not brain surgery, as they say."

A pop from the other end of the bar drew Abernathy's gaze again. One of the girls had pulled a can of instant whipped cream from behind the bar and was shaking it. Abernathy grinned and shoved his beer away. "Hold on there, ladies. I'll help you with that."

He stood and started in their direction, tossing Gil a dark look. "You've got two days to get Q to Punjab."

Abernathy snagged the can from Courtney's hand with the confidence of a man used to getting his way. He tipped his head back, squirted the cream into his mouth until it overflowed, then trailed the stream down his neck. With squeals of delight, one girl attacked Abernathy's mouth, the other latched onto his neck. While feasting on and being feasted upon, Abernathy wrapped one arm around each girl's waist and headed for the back stairway.

Jessica couldn't get comfortable. Couldn't find sleep. She kicked the covers off, but found her legs already bare and remembered she'd torn off the silk pajama pants Mitch's assistant had supplied early on in her attempts to sleep. Now she only wore panties and a tank top. But she was still hot. Restless. Dying for some fresh air. But Mitch had told everyone to sleep with their windows closed and locked.

She groaned in frustration and twisted onto her back, pulled the pillow from under her head and tossed it to the other side of the bed. She scraped both hands through her hair, then flung her arms out wide.

Quaid filled her mind. Quaid then. Quaid now. Where the hell was he? She'd thought he'd be sleeping with her tonight. Had expected him to come to her after he'd looked at the pictures.

And the pain that went away only when she slept, blossomed like a flower in her chest. She closed her eyes on the bittersweet memory of his confession of love. Sweet because of course he had strong feelings for her. Bitter because he didn't know why, didn't understand either the feelings or what they stood for. How much could words, or even feelings mean when the real moments in life that created those feelings were absent from his memories? Then he'd admitted he wasn't even sure he could live up to the commitment.

She really hadn't gotten her husband back.

She'd gotten the *possibility* of her husband back.

What the hell did she do with that?

Still, there were parts of this new Quaid she really enjoyed. His vulnerability. His openness. His almost-innocence, which was a strange way to see him after he'd nearly beaten that spy or assassin or whatever he was to death. But that was another thing she loved about this Quaid, his fierce protectiveness.

And if she had been prepared for that intense sexual version of Quaid, their sex earlier in the day might not have been so shocking and she might not have been too emotionally messed up to enjoy it. Because the passion ebbing from the man was toe-curling extreme.

Okay, this was not helping. She was going to fry in here. Rolling off the bed toward the window, she unlocked and slid it open. She inhaled deeply, letting the clean air cool her body, cleanse her mind, soothe her heart.

She could do this. She would rework her life to make it right for Quaid, too. They'd find a way.

Fear crawled out of a dark corner of her chest. He had no memory of having chosen her after dating many other women. Without any comparison, how would he know she was the right one? What if he wanted to date? What if wanting his freedom meant him wanting freedom from her, too?

God, these were never things she'd even imagined, let alone considered.

Her anxiety amped up her body heat again. She pulled at the fabric of her tank, fanning the air against her belly. Wasn't cement supposed to keep buildings cool, for God's sake? Oh, screw it. She crossed her arms, grabbed the hem and pulled the fabric toward her head.

"Don't."

A male voice.

Quaid's voice.

Jessica froze in place, her heart speeding from the kick of fear-laden adrenaline.

"Please." He softened his voice, the tone edged with a painful plea. "Please don't. I'm barely keeping my hands off you as it is."

SEVENTEEN

Jessica lowered her hands, swallowed and turned slowly. It took a moment to find him, sitting on the floor near the door in the deepest shadows, knees up, back pressed against the wall.

"What . . . ?" She felt stupid asking such a basic question, but it needed answering. "What are you doing?"

He didn't answer right away. The darkness, the silence, felt heavy and charged with emotion. "I just . . . needed to be near you."

With no other stimuli distracting her, his voice registered so clearly as Quaid's, it reached into her chest and squeezed her heart like a fist.

"I . . . didn't want to wake you," he said. "Why didn't you stay?"

She knew he meant for the pictures, but she didn't know how to put all the pain, failed hopes and dreams, misery, agony, and loss into words. "I . . . it just . . ."

"Hurt too much," he said, his voice a pained whisper, telling Jessica he felt the same pain.

Her heart cracked a little more. She twirled her fingers in the bottom of her tank. "Yes. I'm sorry. I should have been there for you. I didn't realize . . . I didn't think . . ." She gasped with a sudden realization, and that damn spark of hope that just wouldn't die flared again. "Did you . . . remember—?"

"No." He pulled an audible breath. "I'm—" His voice broke and with it, Jessica's heart fell into pieces. "I'm sorry, Jess."

She pressed her eyes shut. Nodded, because she didn't trust herself to speak.

"I want to. I want to remember so badly." The desire in his voice rasped low and needy and both Jessica's heart and body churned in response.

"It's not your fault."

He made a noise and Jessica lifted her gaze to him. All she could see was that he'd straightened his arms, braced them on his knees and hung his head between his biceps. His shoulders shook. And, oh, shit . . .

"Quaid?" Her voice trembled.

She crossed the room and knelt beside him. The industrial grade carpet bit into her knees. She could hear him now, suppressing his sobs. Her heart shattered.

"Oh, my God, Quaid. Baby, don't."

She put her hand around his ankle, slid it up bare skin to his shin. She realized he'd changed into shorts at some point. Scooting close, she put both hands on the leg closest to her and gave a comforting squeeze. The heat of his hip burned through the cotton of his shorts and into her thigh where she pressed against him.

The feel of his skin, the light brush of crisp hair against her hand, all that warmth, made her want to keep touching, caressing, exploring. She longed to move close, to feel him against her.

"Shh, baby," she whispered, pressing her cheek to his arm. "I'm sorry I wasn't there. I didn't realize . . ."

"Seeing everyone, seeing how happy we all were . . . especially y-you"— his voice caught— "only to see what my death has . . . done to you, how much pain you've . . . been through. . . . "

He heaved a breath and rested his head on his arm. His breathing remained choppy and Jessica ached for him. Her own tears wet her face. She reached up and scratched her fingers gently along his scalp, something that always used to soothe him. He let out a shaky sigh, fisted his hands and then released them.

"When I thought you were a dream, a fantasy, it kept me going, gave me something to look forward to. You kept me alive all those years. I've spent an hour looking at those pictures of us, then another three replaying them in my head. And I know I *had* you. You and me. We were . . . we were *us*." He shook his head, a sharp, angry movement. "And I don't remember a goddamned minute. It's killing me. Because, damn it, Jess, I want you. I want . . . *that*. I want . . . shit, I don't even know. Because I don't know what we had, because I can't fucking remember. But it's inside me and it's . . . God, it's so intense, so insane, I feel like I'm going to explode with it."

His ferocity seemed to roil inside her, kicking up a storm of hope and loss and love and anger.

"Jessica—" He lifted his head and looked at her. "I'm not that man."

"Quaid—"

"I'm not. And I never will be." His voice was cold and final. Bitter. "I know I look like him and sound like him, but inside, *I'm not him*. You just have to accept that. I have to accept it." He gestured toward the door. "They have to accept it."

"Baby, you've been through so much. Give yourself some time. Give *us* some time. You can't expect—"

"There is no part of him inside me."

His finality chilled her. But it also angered her. "You told me just hours ago that you love me."

"I do, Jess. I *do* love you."

"Then the man in those pictures *has* to be inside you somewhere, because there is no other possible way for you to love me. *None.*"

He breathed heavily and laid his forehead against his arms. "You've already gone through so much pain. I don't want to put you through any more when you realize I can't become him."

"I can accept that, if you can keep yourself open to memories that come, if they come." She spread her fingers over his head and pulled him toward her until their foreheads touched.

"Jessica." His eyes closed. "You are so stubborn."

"Persistent." She pushed his knees until his legs lay flat, then lifted one leg across his lap and sat on his thighs. "This is a one in a zillion opportunity, Quaid. How often do people get a second chance to find love with their once-in-a-lifetime? I believe in you as a person. I believe in your essence. No one, nothing can change that."

God, she hated using euphemisms for their marriage, but considering he was ready to bolt even after they'd had sex that he'd enjoyed, now would not be the time to tell him he was stuck with her.

She tilted her head and kissed him. Firmly, purposefully.

He met her kiss for the briefest moment, then pushed her back. "This didn't go so well last time. . . ."

"If you're referring to the bathroom, I think it went plenty fine for you. I wasn't expecting quite so much . . . passion, and had a few of my own head trips going on. You're not the only one with issues to get past, Quaid. We all have our demons. Besides, practice makes—"

"Perfect," he finished.

A small smile lifted her mouth as she thought of the baby they could have a second chance at making. "We're different people now. We'll have to learn how to make love to each other again. It's a tough job, but someone's got to do it." She leaned back and pulled her tank off over her head before he could protest. Then she tossed it across the room, to make a statement—she wasn't changing her mind and she wasn't letting him try to change it for her— and stroked his chest. "And I think we should start now. *Right* now."

Air shuddered into Q's lungs as he dragged his gaze over Jessica's full breasts, her strong, flat belly. All his focus seemed to collect, then center on her as if nothing else mattered.

And that was one of his biggest problems. He didn't just want her. He *craved* her. Had coveted her for years. Every part of him strained for the freedom she offered. The expression. The sensation. The connection. The release. Sonofabitch, how he needed it all. And she was the one and only place he could find everything he needed.

Yet, just like with the food, the more he wanted something, the more he resisted. And he wanted her a hundred times more now than he'd wanted her earlier when she'd come to him. Because now, he'd tasted her. Now, he knew exactly what she could give him. And he was ready and willing to beg. If he would only let himself.

"Jessie—"

A flash of impatience lit her dark eyes before she grabbed his wrists and drew his hands to her breasts. With her hands covering his, she cupped the mounds, caressed them.

Q's goal of staying in control vanished. His mind funneled to the utterly unique feel of her feminine body—her skin so soft he had nothing in his experience for comparison, her breasts pillowy, yet resilient. And her scent. God, her scent. Now she smelled like a combination of herbs and spice, flowers and sunshine. She smelled like pleasure, seduction, secrets and trouble. She smelled like sex. Like raw, wild, passionate sex—like their sex earlier.

She shimmied forward on his thighs, and pressed the heat between her legs against his erection. Sensation, so powerful it bordered on painful, surged through his entire pelvis. Jessica rubbed against him and her nipples tightened in his palms. All Q's banked lust broke loose.

He leaned in and kissed her. Instantly penetrated her lips with his tongue, seeking hers. Then circled in demanding, needy strokes, which made him think about tasting different parts of her. All of her. He wrapped her in his arms, suddenly ravenous. His mouth hungry to travel. His tongue restless to taste.

With her arms clutching his shoulders, thighs grabbing his hips, bare belly sliding along his, and those damn round, jiggly breasts rolling against his chest, it was a fucking feat he wasn't a comatose, drooling mess from the pleasure.

Her very essence rubbed the length of his cock with every rock of her hips. And each tilt began a slow, luscious wave that traveled up her body, sliding through them as if they were one, stomach to stomach, chest to breasts and right into their kiss, only to start again. With each move, everything in his body coiled tighter, grew larger, demanded more. Until that more made him grip a handful of her hair and pull back to break the kiss.

"More," was all he got out.

"Yes," she answered.

His body took action without a direct order from his brain. He pulled his legs under him, slid his arms around her waist and pushed to his feet. With her smooth, luscious thighs gripping his hips, he was holding Jessica just as he had earlier in the day. But tonight, it wouldn't end there. At least not the way it had before.

All Q could think about was getting Jessica horizontal, bringing his body in complete contact with hers, sinking his hands into her hair. . . .

When his legs hit the side of the bed, he leaned over, laid Jessica back with plans to follow her, press his body into hers and soak in the feeling of all that perfect flesh beneath him. But he took one sweeping gaze down that body and paused on the shape of a wing emerging from high on her inner thigh.

He slid his hands over her belly, pelvis, thighs, where he rolled her leg out. Her scent traveled on the heat of her body and wrapped around Q, making him dizzy with lust. He focused on the scar, just below the junction of her thigh and pelvis. Traced it with his fingers, while his mind struggled with flashes of memory or dreams or . . .

"Quaid?"

Jessica's voice pulled him back. "I've seen this. In my dreams."

He closed his eyes and pressed his lips to the purple flourish. Jessica sighed. He sucked at the tender flesh. She moaned and lifted her hips. Something about the sound made him open his eyes. He looked down at her phoenix. Alongside the bird, his hand spanned her thigh, big and rough and very male in comparison to her smooth flesh.

The sight, her sound, the combination, lit off thoughts he couldn't quite grab. But a cold trickle of discomfort traveled through his chest.

"Quaid?" Jessica said. "Are you okay?"

His hand tightened on her thigh. "Were . . . those dreams?"

Fear, clear and sharp, burst in her eyes. She propped herself up on an elbow and ran her hand over his head and across his shoulder. But she didn't speak. Didn't meet his eyes.

The cold river in his chest turned hot. Spread through his body. But no one memory fully emerged.

"Jessica." He waited until she lifted her gaze, her beautiful eyes a mix of regret, fear, plea and an edge of rebellion. "I have a strange feeling those weren't dreams. Did I imagine you with . . . ?"

God, why was it so hard to say? It had never bothered him before. He'd never felt this tightness in his chest. This need to grab her and shake her. This need to brand her as his. This need to choke any other man that ever touched her.

"Fuck." He ran a hand down his face. The intensity of his emotions made him push away.

Jessica grabbed his arm. "Quaid, wait."

"I don't understand. Nothing . . . makes sense." The combination of panic, fear and anger made a volatile emotion grow inside him, one he didn't like, one that felt too much like the desperation he'd felt at the Castle. "I thought . . . You said . . . Were they all *real*?"

"It wasn't . . ." Her hand tightened on his arm, her voice strong, insistent. "Quaid—"

His gaze sharpened. "Were they *real*?"

She hesitated, then said, "Quaid, I've never—"

"Don't you dare lie to me."

"—loved anyone but you. Ever."

The deepest place in his heart believed. But other dark places inside him needed security. He combed his fingers into her hair, pulled it back from her face. The motion tipped her head back so she looked directly into his eyes.

"You're. Mine." His voice shook and he took a breath. "That may not be right, but it's how I feel. It just . . . *is*."

Her eyes closed for a moment, then opened glistening with tears. "Yes."

"Say it, Jessie."

"I'm yours. I've always been yours. I'll always be yours."

His restraint snapped. His chest opened. Took her in. Wrapped around her. Closed. And locked.

He looked back at the phoenix and lowered his mouth to her skin. Pushing all other thoughts out of his mind, he kissed and licked and sucked at her flesh, determined to wipe out those memories.

Her quick breaths and moans told him she liked what he was doing, which was good, because he wanted to taste every part of her. But one part of her was pulling him harder than the rest. He slid his mouth toward her heat. Her panties caressed his lips. Jessica groaned and lifted toward his mouth. He licked the fabric, sucked silk and her flesh beneath into his mouth, rubbed it with his tongue.

When Jessica cried out his name, followed by, "Yes, God, yes," Q lost control. Her pleasure was so intoxicating, he suddenly couldn't get enough.

Starved. Starved. Starved. He didn't think the word as much as feel it at his core as he took her. His mouth was too hard, hands too rough. Somewhere, distantly, he feared losing control again. Hurting her again. But he couldn't control the frenzy. His fingers wrapped into the fabric at the hip of her silky underwear and jerked.

The fabric ripped. Jessica gasped. The combination of those sounds threw gasoline on a fire. Possessed. He was insane with the need to feel her on his tongue. To hear her call his name again. To own her. He didn't understand and pushed the thought away. Frustration joined need and lust and urgency and so many other turbulent emotions roiling to the surface.

When he covered her with his mouth, Jessica arched beneath him. Her pleasure electrified him. Her taste fueled his passion. He explored every delicate fold, suckled the soft center flesh that made her writhe and repeat his name over and over. He slid his arms underneath her and held her to his mouth when her pleasure peaked, stroking her with his tongue until her lunging ceased and her body went limp.

He kissed her stomach, her ribs, explored her breasts with his mouth, finally reached her lips and drowned in her kiss. She was liquid and wet and smooth and loose. And the way she moved her tongue in his mouth made his need to drive inside her too great to ignore.

He pushed up on his hands and looked down at the beauty beneath him. Her flushed face, heavy-lidded eyes, the smile curving her mouth, they all made his heart constrict. His need to be inside her intensified.

He leaned back, reached down and pushed at one leg. She smiled with a little mischievous edge that fueled his excitement, and opened to him. He knelt between her legs and pushed the head of his heavy cock into her wetness, glistening in the dim light.

Blood surged through his veins, rushing into his cock, through his pelvis, his thighs. And his body took over. The muscles of his ass contracted and he thrust forward, pushed himself deep, deep, deep until his entire length was buried in the most amazing encompassing sensation.

Jessica gasped. Arched. Dug her nails into his arms. And Q froze.

His body throbbed with excitement and lust, life and vitality. His heartbeat rushed in his ears.

"Jessie . . . baby . . . ?"

Jessica let out a breath, the sound a little shaky, and slowly bent her knees and flattened her feet on the bed. The shift tilted her pelvis and rubbed his cock. His breath hissed through his teeth.

"Ah . . . Christ, Jessie . . ."

She loosened her grip on his arms and lifted her hips, pushing him deeper. His mind twisted.

"Oh, yeah . . ." she breathed.

He slid easily, felt every ridge and indention inside her body. She pulled back. Repeated the motion. His own forward thrust came as natural, as automatic as breathing. And when his hips synced with Jessica's, a sound started in his chest, grew, coiled and rumbled toward his throat.

His hands gripped the comforter on either side of her head. His eyes rolled back before the lids closed in pleasure so extreme it wracked a shudder through him.

Sensation washed his body and emotion bloomed in its wake like a freshly watered field. He didn't understand, couldn't process, only knew that in this moment, he had never felt such perfection—of time, of space, of purpose, of existence. Without a doubt, he was right where he was meant to be. He was home.

For the first time in his memory, something felt completely, utterly, pristinely . . . right.

"This is . . ." *unbelievable* he was going to say, but didn't have the lung capacity as he labored for air. He finally ended up choking out, ". . . God, Jessie."

Then he opened his eyes and something he thought couldn't get better, became infinitely more erotic. Those fascinating breasts bounced with each powerful thrust. The muscles of Jessica's tight abdomen played in the shadows when her hips rose to take him deep. And that sight of him entering her again and again and again . . .

"Jessie . . ."

His pathetic rasp must have said everything because she said, "Let go, Quaid. I'm here. Let go."

Q couldn't believe how damn good it felt to hear those words—*I'm here.* How blessed it felt to have permission to let go and know he was safe.

And to let go, he needed more room, more leverage, more . . . just more.

He gripped her waist, slid toward the edge of the bed and found his feet. He drew her to him, the sight of her shapely, smooth thighs parting to wrap his hips a delicious pleasure. This time when he entered her, he was careful and in a position to stroke her as he pushed inside. This time when she cried out, it was definitely in pleasure, not pain. And this time, when he looked down on her as he let his body drive home the way it wanted, the way it needed, the electricity arcing through him sure as hell wasn't guilt.

His climax came swift and sharp and lightning intense, cracking through his body so hard his muscles jerked him into a rigid line. Only it didn't recede just as fast. Jessica kept thrusting and rocking on his cock for what felt like long minutes after his initial hit and each movement only floated the ecstasy out that much longer. Instead of the climax draining his body of stress and easing him into relaxation, Jessica pushed him back toward that peak of pleasure again.

When she came, her body arched, stretching long muscles, curving already gorgeous lines, and her face, God, her face—even hidden among the shadows—was the single most beautiful thing Q had ever seen. The only thing that had ever given him hope. And as her body squeezed his, he realized she still did that for him. She gave him hope.

When her body relaxed and her moans turned to sighs, Q eased her to the bed. He lay down beside her, wrapped an arm over her waist and dragged her toward the top until he could slide a pillow under her head.

She was slow to move. Slow to open her eyes. Limp and breathing hard. It made a foreign and frightening emotion expand in Q's chest.

Jessica rolled onto her side, away from him. His chest pinched for a millisecond. Then she reached back, curved her arm around his head and pulled him down for a kiss.

A slow, hot, sensual, tongue-tangling kiss. Already on his side, now as hard as he'd been a few minutes before, he pushed against the curve of her back, riding the shallow vertical indention rising from her bottom and fading into her spine. She pulled in a little gasp, sucking air from his mouth.

"Why are you . . . still hard?" she asked, lashes lifted enough for Q to see the confusion in her warm eyes.

The seriousness of her question made him curious about all those little nuances of sex he didn't remember, didn't understand. The ones he didn't want to talk about now, because his hips were nagging at him to move and his rigid cock was rubbing against her silky soft, sweat-dampened skin.

"Because . . ." he drew out the word, "you're a sexual goddess?"

"Quaid."

"Because . . ." He kissed her cheek, her jaw and whispered in her ear, "You're like nothing I've ever imagined. I'm ready to do it again. And hopefully again. And hopefully again after that. I mean . . . you know . . . if you want to."

She did that little breath-catching thing that threatened to pull a smile out of him. "How is that possible?"

"Whatever they did to my head at the Castle messed with me," he said softly at her ear. "Because for about the first year I was there, I never got hard. Then, I started dreaming about you, and I was hard all the time, dreaming or not. I couldn't live like that, so I took care of it myself. It wasn't like I had a choice. Then, after more experiments it stopped happening again. All the normal times a guy gets hard—thinking about sex, fantasizing, in the morning—I got nothing. Except when I dreamt of you. Whenever I dreamt of you, I was always hard. Then about a year ago, I stopped dreaming of you, and . . . the erections went away again.

"So, I know that I stay like this for, I don't know, three or four . . . you know."

"Orgasms?" she supplied.

He flattened his hand on her belly and smoothed it in a circle over her perfect skin, then let it glide lower, between her legs. With another scrape of inward air, Jessica's fingers wrapped around his wrist, but didn't pull him back. Her lids went heavy, her top teeth came down on her bottom lip.

Q explored the crisp, silky strip of hair over the swollen, secret folds "I think so. Let me bring you another one and you can let me know." He closed his teeth over the skin between her neck and shoulder. With his fingers sliding warm and slick along her opening, he rocked his hips into her.

"Oh, God . . ." she moaned.

"Jessie . . ." He sighed against her neck. "How long does this last? How does anyone get anything done?"

A soft bubble of laughter shook her chest. She reached behind her, gripped his butt and rolled to her stomach, pulling him with her. "They just fulfill the need until it's sated. . . ." On her stomach, she wiggled until her thighs were outside Q's. "Then they get back to work."

She reached up, grabbed the top metal bar of a plain steel headboard and pulled herself toward the head of the bed. Her body was sleek and strong and just looking at her rolled his temperature up the scale. Q's hips dropped between her legs, his cock rubbing her ass. Pleasure, sharp and sudden, stole his breath and broke his thoughts.

"And when the urge strikes again," she said softly, "they generally . . . make time, you know, to take a break from whatever they're doing and . . . fill the need." She looked over her shoulder and into his eyes as she lifted her hips until the warm, wet place he wanted rubbed along his cock.

Then she gave him that smile, the naughty one that promised delicious things and said, "I'm feeling needy."

EIGHTEEN

"Trent to Q. Come in, Q."

Q tuned into Trent's communication. "Here."

Trent's heavy whoosh of breath filled Q's head. "Shit, man, when you coming back?"

The uncharacteristic emotion in Trent's voice put Q on alert. "What do you mean?"

"You are scaring the shit out of me. If you jump ship, you'd better not leave me stranded, dude. You wouldn't do that to me, right? We've been through too much together, right?"

A growing unease made Q feel physically restricted, like when Gorin strapped him down.

"If I can't meet Abernathy with these guys and these weapons," Trent said, "I'm SOL. Schaeffer will abandon me here."

"Schaeffer . . . ?" Q's skin prickled. His muscles tensed. Electrical shocks ripped over his skin. His head exploded in pain as if Gorin were stabbing Q's brain with thousands of ice picks.

Q lunged upright, eyes wide, arms out in defense. And found himself alone.

In a room. A cement room. Dawn just hinted outside the single window. This was not his cell.

He looked down. Naked. Sheets half torn from the bed. He scanned the room. Pillows scattered on the floor. Comforter bunched at the foot of the bed. Not only was this not his cell, this was not like any cell they kept him in at any outside testing facility.

He rolled off the bed and landed on his feet. Then immediately reached for a wall to steady himself. His muscles ached. Strange muscles. His ass and thighs felt as if he'd done a thousand squats. His arms, shoulders, abs . . . shit, what the hell had they done to him this time?

With his hand on the cold cement, he looked down at his body, searching for injuries. He ran his other hand over a few red marks on the side of his lower abdomen. A deep, voracious sexual hunger erupted from nowhere, its force making him suck in a sharp breath.

His mind flashed to thick copper hair threaded in his hands. Her mouth moving over him. Lips and teeth closing over bite-sized areas of his flesh. The same thrill that had speared through him then cut through him again. His cock jerked. Rose. The sight brought a rush of thoughts so vivid his breath caught. He looked back at the bed. Swallowed.

Stupid. Just another dream.

Only . . . she'd never touched *him* in those dreams.

He looked at the door—solid metal. Looked at the knob—simple. At the deadbolt—absent.

No barred window. No keypad. No locks . . . at all.

Still looking at the doorknob, he touched his erection, throbbing with an unfamiliar discomfort. He winced. He was raw. And in that instant he knew—he was raw from being rubbed and ridden and then revived to succumb to some new sweet, sensual, erotic pleasure Jessica had to show him. Which always resulted in the rubbing and riding and reviving. Again. And again. And again.

He pushed off the wall, twisting toward the bed.

Gone. She was gone. *Why* was she gone?

He tried to keep the panic down. Tried to remember something that would ease the pain-laden fear squeezing his chest, but couldn't. Instead, his mind filled with Gorin. With all the times he'd discovered something Q loved—a favorite author, a new hobby, a developing interest—let him get hooked and then yanked it away, held it out there as incentive to do what Gorin wanted.

"Fuck, no." *Not Jessie. Please, not Jessie.* His head spun. He wanted to puke. He reached for the door and yanked at the knob. It opened so unexpectedly, Q fell back a few steps, then bolted out of the room.

Two steps into the hall, he came up against a hard body. "Hey, hey, relax."

Cash. He recognized the voice immediately. Knew where he was, why, remembered everything from the past five years of his life, but—again—no more.

"Jessica." Q fisted Cash's T-shirt with both hands. "Jessica's—"

"Fine. Jessica is fine." Cash's smooth, serious tone stopped Q's mind from tilting. He looked down at Q, pushed him backwards, and shoved a handful of fabric into Q's arms. "Get some clothes on, man. You're not alone in your cell anymore. Then, come out. I've got breakfast ready."

Cash left and closed the door behind him. Q turned toward the bed and picked up the T-shirt from the pile. He ran his hand over the fabric and breathed in relief at the soft brushed texture.

Q finished dressing and went to the kitchen, where a barrage of delicious scents made his stomach rumble. Cash looked up from washing dishes and lifted his chin toward the covered pans on the stove.

"There's eggs, bacon, potatoes, pancakes, hell, just about anything you could want," Cash said. "But go heavy on the eggs. You need protein for cell repair and brain function."

Q didn't answer right away. He'd spotted Jessica

through the sliding glass doors where she sat in a chair outside, feet curled up under her, pen to her lips, gaze distant toward the forest as if her mind were far away. She had her long hair in a loose braid that she'd pulled forward over her shoulder. She was bundled in a hooded sweatshirt, sweatpants and socks.

God, she looked . . . sweet and warm and so young, the way she had on the video the night before, which made his memories of last night seem that much more like nothing but another of Q's fantasies. Only the sting of the scratches on his skin told him this particular fantasy had become a reality.

"Leave her be for a minute, Q," Cash said. "Your body needs food."

He started for the door. "My body needs her."

A piece of plastic broke off in Jessica's mouth. She turned away from the blurred glaze of the colorful trees and pulled the pen from between her teeth. Sputtering, she spit out the casing chip. She was going to break her teeth if she didn't stop.

She turned her attention to the computer in her lap again. The Internet service on the property was painfully slow. Mitch had said it was a side effect of the security measures to block others from finding them by their usage. Whatever, it was damned inefficient. She waited for another video file from the stash of evidence she'd collected on Schaeffer over the years, but instead of watching the hourglass rotate on the screen, her eyes darted to the time in the bottom corner. Every minute that passed was one minute closer to facing Quaid. Her stomach did that tight fold and flop thing again.

She'd tried to do her yoga when she couldn't sleep, but her body was so sore, it had been an exercise in torture, not relaxation. Sure, Quaid was bound to have urgent needs after going so long without. And she hadn't experienced true pleasure since he'd died. So the two of them together . . . It stood to reason their lovemaking would be intense, when they finally reunited.

But the raw, lusty, blood-boiling sex that had resulted? No, that she hadn't expected. Excitement and need flooded her body without warning and Jessica closed her eyes to savor it.

She had to admit, after last night, she was beginning to believe he was right about his past self. Jessica had called him Quaid. And he'd looked like Quaid. But last night she had not shared her bed with the husband she'd known as Quaid.

Sex with Quaid had always been great. Fun, satisfying, fulfilling. He'd been creative, adventurous, loving, considerate, passionate—everything every woman wanted from a lover. Jessica couldn't have imagined wanting anything more or anything different. He'd been perfect, which was only one reason she'd had such a hard time moving on after his death. Sex with other men had been so unappealing, she'd had to do it high. And even then, she'd endured more than she'd enjoyed. But the sex had become part of her drug pattern. And the drug pattern revolved around the goal of forgetting, blocking the pain and filling the void.

That void had ended, along with all its extracurricular activities, the day she entered rehab, almost a year ago. Which also happened to be when Quaid's dreams of her had stopped. But Jessica knew they hadn't been dreams. Quaid hadn't said as much, but she guessed he knew as well. Yet, he'd still wanted her.

But that brought up a lot of fears. She wondered if he also knew about her drug abuse. If he even understood what that was and whether he'd want to be with someone with that baggage. She worried that while he was willing to accept his memories of the other men now, it wouldn't last. That there would come a time when he couldn't bear it. Which would bring up trust issues in their relationship later on.

This new Quaid was . . . unpredictable. In good ways as well as not so good. The man in her bed last night . . . Jessica blew out a breath. She still felt a little . . . overwhelmed. Q was . . . deep. He was raw and open like a wound. His anger and fear and regret were buried deep beneath his skin as if they were part of his genetic makeup. All that emotion came out in his sexual expression and . . . holy hell . . . had he expressed himself. In amazing ways.

The sex had been passionate, bordering on obsessive. Hard, edgy, dark, serious. Hot. God, just thinking about it made her wet. She squeezed her thighs together against the need that had been growing since the moment he'd last pulled out of her.

But he'd been right about who he was. Even if he regained his memory, or part of his memory, he'd never be the Quaid Jessica had lost. One part of her was painfully hollow with the realization. But another part zinged with the wild electricity this new Quaid brought to her life.

"Jessie?"

Her breath caught at the sound of his voice. He was questioning . . . and hurting. Apprehension tightened her muscles. She turned toward him. He stood in the doorway, wearing a chocolate acid washed tee and tan cargo shorts, and she went liquid. His body looked as delicious in clothes as it looked out of them. His frame filled out the style, his muscle stretched the fabric so it flowed and pulled just right. He was unshaven, his eyes dark and worried and . . . vulnerable.

"Hey." She smiled, genuinely glad to see him, while still not quite over her loss. "I was hoping you could get some sleep."

He stepped outside and closed the door behind him. He was barefoot again, his feet padding softly against the sandstone patio. He stopped next to her chair and she found herself anticipating his touch. But he dropped into a crouch, arms crossed over his knees and those deep, warm eyes burrowing into her with the kind of intimate intensity that made Jessica feel completely—dangerously—exposed.

"What's wrong? Why weren't you in bed with me when I woke up?" he asked, his voice the rough whisper she knew well from the night before, the one that had shivered through her as he'd driven her to orgasm after orgasm, wringing more pleasure from her body than she'd known existed.

"I was restless. Couldn't sleep." She lifted her fingers to his lips with a deep craving to taste them again. "You're the only person who ever calls me Jessie."

His eyes closed, long black lashes lying decadently against unshaven cheeks. His hand covered hers, guided her fingertips between his full, soft lips where he suckled and ran his tongue over them. A noise sounded in her throat. He pulled her fingers back, took her hand in both of his, holding her fingers gently, splaying them as if to inspect each tip.

"Well, damn." His voice, low and soft and still a little sleepy, rumbled over her, teasing her nipples tight. "I'm going to have to work on tiring you out a little better."

With those warm eyes locked on hers, he slowly licked the pad of each finger. The sight of his tongue against her flesh made her want so much more.

"Because," he lowered his voice and leaned close, "I slept better than I have for as long as I can remember."

He tilted his head, took Jessica's mouth with his and licked into it, catching her tongue in a sexy, slow sweep. She immediately curled her hand around his and leaned into his strength, kissing him back as if they hadn't just spent the last several hours having blistering, mind-rocking sex. And, God help her, she wanted to spend the next several hours doing it again.

"Now that is what I like to see."

Jessica startled at the male voice, breaking the kiss and pulling away from Quaid. Kai and Alyssa walked toward them from the direction of the supply room. They were both grinning—Kai's smile a mixture of relief and excitement; Alyssa's a gentler blend of happiness and hope.

"Did our prisoner talk?" Jessica asked Kai.

Quaid released Jessica's hand and stood, crossing his arms. Jessica's hands felt cold without his.

"Nope," Kai said. "Didn't think he would, but it was worth a try. I took a video of him so we can e-mail whoever he belongs to. Alyssa, the humanitarian that she is, checked his wounds."

"How are they?" Jessica asked.

She shrugged. The gentle smile transitioned into a matter-of-fact doctor mask. "Quaid can evidently do quite a bit of damage to a human being, no weapon necessary. It will take our prisoner some time to heal, but he'll live."

The reminder of Quaid's volatility sent a chill through Jessica's belly. She looked at Kai. "Any word from your boss?"

"He just texted me, asked me to call. I was coming to round up the posse for a conference call. Come inside?"

She nodded and reached up to close her laptop.

"What the . . . ?" Quaid said. "Who is that?"

Jessica followed Quaid's gaze to her laptop screen and stared at the still image of the video with the arrow in the center ready to be played. The hair on her neck prickled. "Senator Gil Schaeffer. Do you . . . recognize him?"

"Schaeffer . . ." Quaid's gaze went distant for a moment,

then he blinked. "Yeah. He came to the off-site testing facilities to talk to Gorin once in a while."

Jessica's heart thumped hard and picked up speed.

"Max Gorin?" Kai asked.

Quaid's eyes jumped to Kai. "I only knew him as Gorin. Never knew if that was his first or last name, but that Schaeffer guy never acted like anyone important. I mean, he never had security with him, not like that bitch from DoD, always had to have a fucking armed detail around her."

For Jessica, hearing Quaid say their names, knowing they knew he was alive all this time yet had hidden him . . . Her fury escalated. If she'd gotten him back sooner, maybe . . .

She shook the thought from her head. Too late for maybes. But the rage still burned.

"Dargan," Kai confirmed.

"That's what Cash said. I got all my information through Cash. No one was ever introduced to me. I wasn't a person, I was a thing. An instrument. A test rat."

"So, you saw this man"—Jessica pointed to Schaeffer in the video's still frame—"and this man"—she pointed to Gorin—"together in the last five years at one of the sites where they took you to . . . um . . . test—"

"Experiment." His eyes came back to hers with a hard, almost glassy quality. "They experimented on me, Jessica. I've been living with it for years, there's no point in softening the words. And the answer is yes. I've seen them together in the last *three months*. Why? Is that significant?"

Jessica stared at the image of Schaeffer and Gorin shaking hands. They were both much younger, both wearing suits, only Gorin wore a white lab coat as well.

She darted a look at Kai to find him already looking at her, his green eyes alight with excitement.

"Very." She redirected her attention to Quaid. "Schaeffer and Gorin own a company together called Millennium Manufacturing. Millennium is a contractor for the Department of Defense. They bid on manufacturing projects for the military. Because Schaeffer has a seat in the senate as well as on the Armed Forces Committee, his ownership of a company that handles military contracts is seen as a potential conflict of interest. As a condition of his positions, Schaeffer has to keep his assets with Millennium in trust for the term of his candidacy. He isn't supposed to have any dealings with the company—*at all*. Which means meetings with his business partner while a senator and a member of the Armed Forces Committee—"

"Can get him canned from both," Kai said, vengeful glee in his voice. "Without the power of his positions and contacts within the government agencies, Gil Schaeffer is nothing. He becomes a nonissue for us."

"It may be difficult to prove he visited the sites," Quaid said. "I don't know how you'd get access to their security tapes or logs."

Kai breathed heavily, shaking his head. "Pessimists, both of you. Play the video." He lifted his chin to the screen. "Maybe there's more on it."

Jessica hit the arrow and they watched the video play. Within the first ten seconds, she remembered what it was from—an attempt to raise public opinion of the senator during an election year. And she instantly recognized the significance for Quaid and the team—different from what she'd first thought. Her hope for the future shot skyward.

She stopped the video and grabbed Quaid's hand. Clutching the computer to her chest, she looked at Kai and pulled Quaid toward the door. "We have to show this to the others."

NINETEEN

Jessica's mind lifted in an upward spiral with all the implications of the video of Schaeffer she'd found as she
stepped into the main bunker. "I have something."

They all looked up from their work, Alyssa and Teague
in the living room, Mitch and Cash at one of the dining
tables. Even Kat and Mateo stopped coloring to peer up at
her.

Mitch took off his glasses and rubbed his eyes. "Yeah?"

"Yeah." She smiled, her hope rallying for the first time
since all this had started. "And it's really good."

Mitch and Cash rose from their seats and came into the
living area. Cash sat next to Jessica and Mitch stood behind the sofa, sipping his coffee. Kat and Mateo resumed
their chatter and their coloring.

"This video is from before the warehouse explosion,"
Jessica explained.

She pointed out Schaeffer on the video and then Gorin.

"We can't use that," Mitch started. "Schaeffer wasn't—"

"I'm not finished, Mr. Mouthy." She gave him a warning look. "This video isn't about Schaeffer and Gorin as-
sociating *before* his term in the Senate, it's about something
else. Quaid recognizes both of them from meetings
they've had *recently* at off-site test facilities where he's
been."

Mitch's eyes sharpened with interest and darted to Quaid, who was standing nearby, arms crossed. "Is there any way to prove that? Video surveillance we can steal? Witnesses we can blackmail? Log books? Anything?"

"Every site has tight security," Quaid said. "Good luck getting into it."

"Luck has nothing to do with it," Mitch said. "I'll talk to you about that in a minute. Tell us about the video, Jess."

"This is from Schaeffer's campaign during his bid for senate just before the warehouse explosion. He participated in a short-lived campaign while he was still with the DoD designed to increase his ratings by dolling up the use of taxes in defense-related research. This was one of the news interview spots. Just watch."

Jessica started the clip and knelt on the floor to give everyone a good view. A pristine lab filled the screen, complete with expensive-looking equipment decorating the counters in the background and workers in white jackets scurrying past in the distance, intent on their work. Schaeffer began the casual spot by introducing Gorin and discussing some totally bogus but politically acceptable and publically supported form of research to keep their nation safe from enemy forces.

"That's bullshit," Mitch said. "They never even planned on putting that project into action."

"They don't plan on putting two-thirds of their projects into action," Jessica said. "Most are just covers for the black projects."

Schaeffer called to someone off camera and another man stepped into view. Mid-fifties, gray hair, flat, dark eyes, placid smile.

Alyssa gasped. "That's Rostov. The scientist Keira shot at the ranch in Nevada."

"You're right, Jess," Mitch said. "This is interesting."

Jessica nodded.

Schaeffer introduced Rostov, spoke of more false projects. Then he called another person into the camera's view. A woman—young, wearing a white coat, and so stunningly beautiful she dominated the screen. She had an Eastern European look with high cheekbones, full lips, and exotic eyes. They weren't blue or green, but turquoise and against her pale skin and deep black hair, she was truly striking.

"And this is our youngest new addition to the scientific team—"

Crash.

Jessica jumped. Kat and Mateo screamed and ran to Alyssa. Teague and Cash jumped from the sofa, Kai at the door with his weapon drawn, all before Jessica had gotten to her feet.

Mitch was the only one who hadn't moved. His hands still curved in front of him as if he held the cup, but it had long since shattered on the cement floor. He had lost eighty percent of his sexy tan. His eyes were wide, mouth slack. He tilted forward and gripped the sofa with both hands.

"Mitch?" Alyssa extricated herself from the sofa and stood beside her brother, a hand on his arm. "Mitch."

When he didn't respond, she followed his gaze to the computer. Jessica did the same. Cash picked up a broom from the kitchen and worked on the glass shards, but his gaze stayed on the video.

"Dr. Dubrovsky," Schaefer was saying, "is a brilliant rising star in information systems security and will be creating an impenetrable barrier to our most valuable data."

"Oh, my God," Alyssa said. "Is that . . . ? I mean, she looks just like . . ." She turned wide, confused eyes back to her brother. "But Halina's last name wasn't Dubrovsky. Was it?"

Mitch's shock twisted into confusion and anger. "No. It was *Sin*trovsky," he said with clenched teeth. "And she didn't work for DoD. And she was a biological scientist, not a computer wizard." His fingers clenched in the soft sofa cushions, his handsome face tight with pain and fury. "What the fuck *is* this?"

"Kids in the room," Kai said out of the side of his mouth.

Mitch rubbed his face with both hands. "Sorry."

When he looked back at the now-frozen image of the three scientists where the video had ended, his brow was pulled into a tight V and his bright eyes had darkened to a complex hazel. His expression gave Jessica a completely foreign glimpse into a man she'd thought she'd known. This woman had meant a great deal to him. This woman had hurt him. And he was just discovering this woman had been involved with Schaeffer from the very beginning.

"You're right, Jess, that is good." Mitch managed a voice of power and optimism, but Jessica heard the stress beneath. He was as expert at hiding his injuries as she'd once been. "I'm going to take a quick shower and then we can make our call to Schaeffer."

Mitch walked out and Kai immediately turned to Alyssa. "What in the hell was that about?"

Alyssa's gaze returned to the last frame in the video, brow furrowed in distress. "The woman . . . she's Mitch's ex-girlfriend."

"So what?" Kai said. "He's got thousands of exes. For Christ's sake, the man is bedding three new women every week. I mean she's hot." He looked back at the screen. "Okay . . . she's kinda . . . out of the ballpark gorgeous, but so are all his others. Why is he so twisted over her?"

"She's the reason he seeks out all the others." Alyssa's

gaze met Kai's, her normally bright expression troubled. "She was *the One*. I never understood why he couldn't get past it. . . . Then I met Teague."

"Oh." Jessica's soft sound of pain echoed in the silence. She hadn't meant to verbalize her empathy, but she felt for Mitch. Knew exactly how that lifestyle could look so fun and carefree on the outside, yet could be the loneliest, emptiest existence on the planet. And she ached for him.

Quaid's big, warm arm slid around her shoulders and drew her to his side. A burst of confusing, complex tears sprung to her eyes. She burrowed close and looked up into his worried gaze. She'd lost her One. Now she had a second chance. She pulled his hand to her mouth and kissed his palm, soaking in the feel of his skin against her lips.

Before she turned back to the others, she gave his hand a squeeze and met his eyes. They were still confused, but stoked with a lot more heat.

"What I wanted to show everyone with the video," Jessica said, "was how Schaeffer linked himself to Rostov. It proves that Schaeffer and Gorin are linked directly to Rostov and that bullshit of a psychotic religious leader they tried to use to cover the incident in Nevada will be blown to hell. If this gets out, his campaign is dust. He can kiss the Senate good-bye."

Kai nodded. "That's powerful, Jess. I'm sure Mitch understands."

"I'm just going to check on him," Alyssa said. "I'll meet you in the supply room."

Quaid wrapped his other arm around Jessica and turned her into his chest, pulling her close. She was just about to close her eyes and sink into his support when Alyssa came to an abrupt stop, one hand on her belly, the other on the wall leading to the hallway toward the bathroom.

"Alyssa?" Jessica stiffened, pushed back from Quaid. "Teague . . . Alyssa—"

Teague twisted and sprinted toward his wife.

He'd just reached her when she turned to the group. "I'm fine. His son is just trying to give me kidney failure."

"Ryder, can you talk?" Kai's boss's voice was deep and commanding. Q would have pinned Waterbury as military or law enforcement, even without any information.

"I've got the team here," Kai said. "Can we stay on speaker?"

"Why the hell not? They already know enough to breach national security ten ways to Sunday. Your boy is Reginald Baker Alsadani," he said without pause. "An American-born Libyan. Semper Fi for twelve years, MARSOC for eight of those."

Kai turned his gaze on Alsadani, who was peering at the group from beneath a swollen left eyelid.

"What's MARSOC?" Jessica whispered over her shoulder to Q, who stood behind her.

He slid his hands around her waist and leaned close, breathing in her scent. She put her hands over his, the small gesture creating a warm spot in the middle of his chest. "Marine Corps Special Operations Command. Military special forces like Delta Force, SEALs or Rangers."

"How do you know that?"

"I don't know how I know half the shit in my brain."

"He's been out of the military for three years," Waterbury said. "Dishonorable discharge, but I can't see deep enough into the file to know why. The security clearance is too high."

"What the hell?" Kai muttered.

"We're not even at the fun part yet, Ryder. Shit, boy, you do know how to find trouble, don't you?"

Kai dropped into a chair, braced his elbows on his knees and scraped his fingers through his hair. "What do we have here, boss? A military contractor?"

"Nope, he washed out of that, too."

Kai's forehead creased in a frown. "How do you wash out of black ops after eight years in MARSOC?"

"How do you get dishonorably discharged from MAR-SOC in the first place?" Waterbury asked, adding weight to the growing suspicion.

Kai rubbed his temple. "If he's not active duty and he's not a legit contractor . . ."

"He's got to be working rogue," Waterbury said. "Unless, that is, one of you know him personally and this is all moot."

Kai's head came up. His gaze darted around the group. Paused on Cash. On Q. On Jessica. Cash and Jessica shook their heads. Kai's gaze darted back to Q.

All the strange visions Q'd had of the mysterious Trent and the Middle Eastern desert flooded his mind. The sick thought that he'd brought this guy to the team made him release Jessica and step over to Alsadani. He bent and gripped the man's face in one hand. Q studied his bruised features, thought back to what the man had looked like when Q had first spotted him scaling the ravine. But his memory was as blank as always.

Frustrated, angry with himself, with Gorin, with . . . so many unnamed assholes he didn't even know, Q pushed Alsadani's face aside as he let go. He turned to Kai, shook his head and lifted his hands as he shrugged. "He looks as familiar as all of you did yesterday."

"No," Kai said, his eyes sliding away from Q. "No one here knows him."

Q crossed his arms and paced, head down. A bad feeling grew in his gut.

"Then I'd say he was hired by an individual," Waterbury said, "not a government institution. We all know they use these guys for black ops. We all know they assassinate people. But anyone who sanctioned a burned asset as a contractor on a legitimate op is looking to end up in the unemployment line. That's serious business to eighty percent of us who are going for pensions."

"Why would someone hire a burned asset when they could hire a legit one?" Jessica asked.

"Generally for one of three reasons, my anonymous friend," Waterbury said with a hint of humor in his voice. "One, the job is too dirty for a legit contractor to take on—which would have to be a pretty damn dark job, something along the lines of kidnapping, torturing and mutilating a kindergarten class."

Q cringed as Jessica flinched and covered her eyes. He wished he could protect her from all this. Hoped like hell he hadn't brought even more pain and suffering to her life.

"Two," Waterbury continued, "the job had to be kept absolutely confidential. Burned assets are at the end of their rope. If they talk, they're SOL in the States. The only people who'll hire them after that would be Colombian drug cartels. That ensures their utter silence."

There was that Colombian drug cartel mention again. Q would have to look into that.

"Or three," Waterbury said, "the person hiring such a contractor is not lawfully employed by a legit government agency and therefore can't access or obtain acceptance from legit contractors."

Silence lingered in the room. Kai finally cleared his throat. "So, sir, if I told you that Reggie was hired by the DoD—"

"The *DoD*?" Waterbury said before Kai had even finished his sentence. "I'd tell you not to fly my damn plane again until you'd had a full psych eval. My insurance doesn't cover stupidity."

Q needed air. He turned out the supply room door and walked. And walked. And walked. He found himself on the edge of a ravine and stopped to look out over the hills on the other side. They rolled in gorgeous shades of golds, oranges and greens, but he couldn't appreciate the beauty, his mind too filled with turmoil.

He knew Jessica was behind him. Had heard her footsteps following him shortly after he'd left the bunker.

"Hey." Her soft voice floated over him and he closed his eyes to absorb the sound. "I'll leave you alone if you need time. I just want to make sure you're okay."

"If it turns out I brought this on, that all of you have suffered because of me, that all of you are in danger because of me . . ." He shook his head. "No, I won't be okay."

"We're all in this, Quaid." She came up behind him. "The rest of the team is in just as much trouble for breaking into that lab and rescuing Cash. Whoever's after us is after us all because of who we are, what we know."

"Not if Alsadani is from my past. Not if the reason someone is sending assassins after us is because of something I've done that I don't know about, that I can't remember." He turned toward her and even though he'd seen her every moment for the last thirty-some hours, just looking at her again still gave him the urge to sigh in pleasure. "There's so much I don't know about what they've had me doing the last five years, Jess. And if this is about one man wanting control, not a government entity trying to silence us, it's more likely he's after me, maybe Cash, but not everyone. I don't want to put you all at risk."

"We're all at risk all the time," she said. "We all have

shadows that follow us night and day. They always know where we are and what we're doing. And if we get too close to something they don't want us to know, like I do with Schaeffer, they threaten and throw their weight around. This could just as easily be Schaeffer pissed off at my intrusion into his life for years as it could be something you've done that you don't know about."

Q frowned. "Why would Schaeffer be pissed at you? What intrusion?"

She hesitated and wrapped her arms around her middle. "I've been harassing Schaeffer for years, collecting dirt on him."

"What kind of dirt? Why?"

"Anything and everything. To create whatever misery I can." A bitter anger crept into Jessica's voice. "Not only did he cover up what happened to us at the warehouse while he was still with DoD, but he dismissed your death as an *accident* and to push the heat in another direction, he insinuated your actions added to the safety hazards, because dead men don't talk."

Q's chest coiled tighter with every word.

"If you want to know the truth," Jessica said, her gaze distant over the ravine, her voice an angry rasp, "I stalk him. I've stalked him from the day I came to Washington. I photograph him whenever we're at a function together and I make sure he knows I'm taking pictures. If I know he's going to be at another event, and I'm not working, I show up, mingle, wait for him to engage in conversations with the right people and snap photos. I've even been known to set up accidental meetings just to get a photograph. I've placed trackers on his cars. I've dropped bugs in his pockets or pinned them to his blazer lapels when he's left his jacket on a chair."

She grew more animated, more forceful, more passionate and Q's stomach joined in the tension.

"He's coming up for office in a few months, and I'm going to do my damnedest to make sure he rates so poorly in the polls, even the garbage collectors union won't hire him."

Q took a moment to find his voice. "Did I . . . was it my fault?"

She opened her mouth and tipped her head, confusion sliding through her gaze, but then clearing in an instant. "The fire? No. Absolutely not. You did everything right. Which is another reason why it was so wrong for Schaeffer to cast doubt on your reputation. And, goddamnit, no one—*no one*—disgraces someone I love that way. *Ev-er*."

Now, his lungs had grown tight, too. She had sacrificed so much, and all after she'd believed he was dead. Even after he'd been gone, she continued to fight for his name, for his reputation. For his honor.

He stepped into her and pulled her close. "How did I get so damn lucky with you?"

"I was always the lucky one." She curled into him, her head fitting just under his chin. "They e-mailed the video of Reggie to Schaeffer. He's probably wigged out by now, which is when Mitch wants to call him. We should get back."

He released her, but instead of stepping away, she wrapped both arms around his neck, slid up against him and kissed him. God, she had a beautiful mouth. One that could ease his worries, make him forget immediate problems.

Which meant he should have been happy as they headed back to the bunker for the all-important phone call to Schaeffer. But when she took his hand and they walked through the trees with Jessica explaining her work as a lobbyist in Washington and how she'd been able to gain such access to Schaeffer, Q held on tighter than he had to, tighter than he should. And instead of relaxing into the buzz radiating through his body or savoring more happiness than he'd ever hoped to find, Q scanned the terrain for intruders, more fearful now that he had so much more to lose.

TWENTY

Q opened the supply room door and guided Jessica in with a hand low on her back. Before he followed, he made another sweep of the area, scanning as far as the trees allowed. No movement, no odd colors, no unusual landscape. He'd been listening closely during their walk and hadn't heard any indication of human movement. The guards at the borders of the property were out of range. Still . . .

"Quaid?" Jessica's voice brought his attention back and he closed and locked the door behind him.

Mitch was back, in fresh clothes, hair still wet from the shower, but he didn't look like his frame of mind had improved. His eyes and cheeks now appeared hollowed, his coloring still too pale, giving him an overall drawn quality. His jaw jumped with stress, his mouth pulled tight as he stared down at his phone and paced in a short line.

"Sure you don't want to talk?" Kai asked Alsadani. "This is your last chance. Then it'll be all about what we say you told us. You'll be toast, man."

The prisoner just stared from beneath that horrid bulbous purple eye.

Alyssa bent beside him, her fingers at his wrist. "He should be cuffed in a different way. He's losing a pulse in this wrist and his hand is swelling."

"So what?" The words were out of Q's mouth even while another part of him knew he should have held them back. Everyone looked at him. "He was going to kill us. Every one of us. He would have killed Kat and Mateo, too. Wouldn't have given any of us a second thought."

Everyone looked at each other. Except Mitch. He just scrolled on his phone and said, "I'm with you, Q."

Strange to have someone here call him Q. And while he still thought of himself as Q, he wasn't sure he liked anyone else thinking of him that way now. When he looked deep inside himself, fear burned like acid as he wondered if he knew how this Alsadani thought because he'd once been that kind of man. God, he hoped not. And if he had been, Q hoped he never remembered.

"Quaid's right," Kai said.

"And Alyssa's right," Teague said, and then looked at Quaid. "You and I both know how much it hurts to have our hands cuffed behind us that long."

He ground his teeth. "Fine. But I'll move him."

Across the room, Mitch pulled a Glock 9 from a holster on his hip, dug the keys from his pocket and tossed them to Teague. "If he breaks and I shoot one of you taking him out . . . not my fault. Just sayin'. I'm really in the mood to shoot someone. Creek, why don't you stay real close to him?"

Teague jingled the keys in his palm and crossed to Alyssa. "You're so lucky I was damn head over heels for you before I met that fucker."

A grin edged up her mouth. "Teague."

A heated smile lit Teague's blue eyes and eased his mouth into a lopsided smile. "I'll pay up for that curse tonight—personally."

"T-M-I, Creek," Mitch muttered.

Teague handed the keys to Q, wrapped an arm around Alyssa's shoulders and walked her back across the room.

Q moved behind the prisoner and bent to insert the key into the lock. At the guy's ear, he said, "I'm doing you a favor, here. If you cause any trouble, if you hurt anyone in this room . . ."—he lowered his voice to a scraping whisper—"I'll break your neck with my bare hands."

And, son of a bitch, he meant it. Deep down, he knew he'd do it. Couldn't imagine how, but was one hundred and ten percent positive he'd know how when it came time.

"Are we clear?"

Alsadani nodded once.

Q held the man's arm and clicked the lock open. He felt the guy start to push out of the cuff before the key had made a full turn. The next three seconds shifted into slow motion—Alsadani pushing out of the chair, twisting toward Q with his now free arm arching up. The sound of a Glock slide sounding to his left—Mitch, aiming. Q swiveled behind the man, swung a forearm around his neck, slapped his other hand to the opposite side of his head—

"No! Quaid, *stop!*"

Quaid froze an instant before pulling the man's head around and snapping his vertebra, Jessica's voice echoing in his head. Mitch held the blue-black barrel of his Glock an inch from Alsadani's head. Q could let go now. The guy wasn't going to do anything with a gun in his face. But he couldn't. Something inside urged him to kill.

To *kill.*

His breath came fast. Sweat ran down his face. His entire body shook with unshed adrenaline.

"Quaid," Jessica pleaded at his back, terror and tears in her voice. "Please, don't. Quaid, pl—please don't. This isn't you. *This isn't you.* This is who they created in a *lab.*"

The torment in her voice made him weak. There was no room for weakness here. No room for error. No room for miscalculations. No room for . . . *others.* . . .

"Quaid." Jessica's voice was closer now. She was an *other*. An other he wanted to make room for. "To make *us* work, you have to stop. If you want *me,* you have to let go of *him*."

Q dropped the man. Just completely let go of him so fast, Alsadani fell to the floor. If Jessica hadn't come up behind him and wrapped him in her arms, he might have— no, he *would have* kicked the man to death.

Mitch kept the gun trained on Alsadani's chest while Kai dragged the prisoner off the floor and slammed his back against the wall.

"That's the second time we've pulled him off you, fucking moron," Mitch said. "Third time's a charm and I, for one, am losing patience with you. Next time, nobody's going to get in his way."

Q turned away from the sight of Kai handcuffing one of Alsadani's hands to the metal bed frame bolted into the cement wall. Turned out of Jessica's hold and stalked to the opposite end of the supply room, where he felt like he'd been transported back in time to the day before, scraping his hands over his head, pacing the short length of the room, unable to get rid of his violent thoughts, unable to stem the fear of what he might have done to others already.

Then Jessica was there, holding him, running her hands over his shoulders, calling him back.

"It's over. Everything's okay. I'm here." She pulled at the hand covering his face. "Quaid," she whispered, her voice so soothing, so calm. "Quaid, look at me. You made the right choice. You proved you're stronger than their programming. You can beat this. We can beat this together."

"Why?" He rubbed his face one last time and dropped his hands. "Haven't I caused you enough pain? Why would you even want to try?"

He looked away, ashamed he couldn't be something

more, something better. But she took his face in both hands and turned it until he was looking into her eyes.

"Because I believe in you." She said it with such sincerity, such conviction. "I believe in you the way you've always believed in me."

Q shook his head in disbelief, humbled by her inner strength, and pulled her close in a fierce hug.

"Making the call," Mitch called from across the space. "And I'm recording, FYI. I know it's a lot to ask from this group, but don't say anything stupid."

"We're listening," Jessica said, still holding Q close.

Mitch dialed and put the phone on speaker. He cleared his throat, took a deep breath, and straightened his spine.

Q braced himself for the worst. Jessica slipped her hand into his and squeezed. How foreign and fabulous it was to have someone stand by him in a stressful moment. A group of someones standing by him. Cash was right—everything he'd ever wanted, ever dreamed of having in his life was right here.

"Schaeffer," the man snarled into the receiver on the other end of the line.

His voice was deep and gravelly, sounding far older than his reported sixty-two years. Q picked up the unmistakable wheeze of air battling in and out of damaged lungs even across the phone line. And he instantly attached the voice, the wheeze, to his face. When that clicked, he could also recall every time he'd seen Schaeffer and at which facilities. He leaned down and whispered to Jessica, "I need paper and pen."

She read the urgency in his eyes and immediately set out on a search, returning to him with heavy packaging torn from a bag of rice and a pencil Kai had been using to sketch surveillance routes for the guards.

"Senator," Mitch said, tone even, matter-of-fact, void of emotion. "Mitch Foster. I hope this is a good time to resolve our mutual issue. With the election only a few months away, I'd like to get this straightened out as soon as possible. I know how distractions during a campaign can damage a candidate."

Q jotted down the nicknames and general locations of the facilities where he'd seen Schaeffer, adding the type of security available at each location. He wrote *"Schaeffer met with Gorin at these locations"* at the top of the paper and handed it to Mitch.

"And I know how problems with the bar," Schaeffer said, voice now cool but clearly threatening, "can damage a lawyer's career."

"Better men—and women—have tried, senator. Let's just skip the threats and get right to the deal. We propose a live and let live scenario." He sounded so easy and unaffected. So ready for an afternoon stroll through those gorgeous woods outside. "We leave your assassin's confession off the airwaves and you leave us the hell alone."

"You have quite an imagination, but I don't have time for games, so we have nothing to talk about."

"Reggie would disagree." Mitch waited a beat. Silence filled the line and his mouth lifted at one corner. "Reginald Baker Alsadani is quite talkative with the right incentive. He's already told us all about his time with MARSOC. How you've got Owen Young running this little side black op now that Jocelyn is out of the picture. Strange to consider there are legit and non-legit sides of black ops. Your world fascinates me."

"You can say anything you want, Foster, but no one's going to believe a terrorist."

"Is that how you're going to spin this, Gil? Really?" Mitch asked with condescending humor in his voice. "You can see how this is going to go, can't you? You slander us, but with no evidence the issue falls away and I file a few more lawsuits against the government and you personally. You did hear how successful those were for Creek and my sister, didn't you?

"Then," he continued without pausing, "we slander you, and with the shitload of evidence we've collected, you've got big problems. As a gesture of early discovery, let me give you just a sample of the type of evidence we've collected against you.

"Campaign fund fraud, misuse of federal funds for uses including recreational drugs, political bribes, personal travel, and prostitutes—these photos will be sensational in the press, don't you think? We also have documents exposing kickbacks you've received from weapons, drug and chemical manufacturers for votes in the senate. Videos reminding the public of your very close link to Rostov—boy, wouldn't that look bad just weeks after the inferno that killed women and children?"

Mitch tsked as he studied the notes Q had scribbled.

"Well"—Schaeffer let out a heavy sigh—"that would all be problematic—*if* I was dead set on running for senate again, but as much as I'd like to serve another term, it's not my grandest goal in life, Foster. Unlike you, I have more than one reason for living. Besides, I could argue that exposing a homegrown terrorist cell will win me a lot of votes. Having to fight for my reputation when said terrorists create fraudulent accusations against me will only make me a more sympathetic victim. You know how the American people love to root for an underdog."

Every muscle in Q's body coiled and twisted. He couldn't see how they had more leverage than Schaeffer. Couldn't see how they would pull this off.

"Hmm." Mitch's hum sounded completely unconcerned. He was frowning at Q's notes. "What about Millennium Manufacturing?"

A beat of silence extended. Then Schaeffer's low, angry, "What about it?"

"Do you care about your business? Your multibillion-dollar business raking in the green from government military contracts?" Mitch waited, but got no answer. "Because Quaid can put you at several testing sites meeting with Gorin over the past few years. Years while you were in the senate. Years while you served on the Armed Forces Committee. Sites located all over the US—California, Nevada, Idaho, Arizona, Utah, Texas, Tennessee, Florida—"

"By the time we get through discrediting Q as a lunatic, no one's going to believe—"

"It's Quaid, Gil, not Q. *Quaid Legend*. He's a person. A man. Who had a w—" For the first time, Mitch faltered. His gaze flicked up and held on Q with unmistakable apprehension. Something tightened uncomfortably in Q's stomach. Whatever his misstep, it was obvious Mitch didn't make them often, because he sucked at covering. His gaze shifted to Jessica, the message in them clear apology before he started pacing again. "Who had friends and dreams and purpose. Remember his name, Gil. *Quaid Legend*. I promise it will haunt you to your grave."

Q pulled on Jessica's arm and whispered, " 'Who had a' . . . what? What was he going to say?"

Jessica shrugged without looking at him.

Anger burned in his throat. He gripped her arm harder. "Jessica, I told you I can't handle any more secrets."

She covered his hand with hers and looked into his eyes. "We have years of memories to revisit, Quaid. It takes time. We're not keeping anything from you."

"And you didn't let me finish, Gil." Mitch's even, overly patient tone had to be killing Schaeffer, because it was irritating the hell out of Q. "We can corroborate Quaid's statements with security camera footage we've already collected from the sites."

Kai held his arms out to the sides, palms up, with his

face crunched in a what-the-hell expression. Mitch returned a shrug, then made the motion of wings with his
hands.

"What does that mean?" Q whispered to Jessica.

"He's winging it," she whispered back. "Making it up."

Q clenched his teeth.

"When investigators uncover the connection between
your seat on the AFC," Mitch continued, "and the developments of Millennium followed by the million-dollar
military contracts? Well, Gil, even the government can
add one plus one plus one. Biiiiig no-no, Gil. And there
are huge penalties for employing insider information to
win government contracts. You won't just get your hand
slapped. You won't just lose your senate position or your
seat on the AFC. Millennium will be fined. The current
contracts it's fulfilling will be retracted. Those involved
will get prison sentences. The corporation will be pulled
from the list of approved government contractors. Then,
Millennium will be torn apart by a government investigation so deep and so long, neither you nor your business
will ever recover."

Mitch paused just long enough to let a heavy silence fall,
but not so long Schaeffer could develop a comeback.

"And let me ask you about your freedom, Gil," he drove
on. "Do you care about that? Because talking to the partner of your military manufacturing company when you're
consulting to the country's highest military committee and
having said company come out with just the right solution
to the military's latest problem, putting millions in that
company's pocket? That, sir, is called . . . espionage."

A deep laugh rolled over the line. "Espionage," Schaeffer said as if the idea were both humorous and ludicrous.
"I knew you were out of your mind, Foster. You just said
I was solving the military's latest problems. That is the *opposite* of espionage."

Mitch pulled in a breath and opened his mouth to reply, but words jumped out of Q's mouth first.

"Not when you sell your inventions to other countries." Everyone's gaze jerked toward Q. He ignored them, sidestepped Jessica and stalked toward the phone with so much insolent rage, he would have crawled through the cell connection and strangled Schaeffer until his eyes bulged if he'd been able. "Like the smart grenades you sold to the Hellenic Armed Forces in Greece? Or the antiaircraft laser to the Korean People's Army? Or the EyeBeam to the Free Syrian Army—"

"Who the fuck is this?" Schaeffer bellowed, his voice bouncing off the walls of the bunker.

Q was near the phone now where Mitch had set it on a table. He put his palms flat on either side of the phone and leaned close, speaking with a low, deliberately menacing voice when he said, "Quaid Legend, *Gil.* The man who gathered all the intelligence for every fucking weapon you created at Millennium and then sold overseas. Remember the name, Gil, because Foster is right." He lowered his voice to a rabid growl. "I'm going to haunt you to your grave."

"Don't bet on it, Legend." Schaeffer tried to maintain his superiority, but uncertainty wobbled in his voice. "You'll look like an asylum escapee as soon as my lawyer gets you on the stand."

Q laughed. True humor hit him at the center of his chest. "Bring it on, Gil. I'll make sure to shave my head for court that day so they can see every scar on my scalp from your experiments. I can't wait to tell people what a sick fuck you are."

"He's going to make an amazing witness," Mitch said to Q's right, where he stood, arms crossed over his chest. "Intelligent, well spoken, articulate. A jury will find Quaid highly sympathetic. And you know how the American people love to root for the underdog, Gil. I wouldn't want to be you when they hear the whole illegal imprisonment, heinous experimental testing story."

Mitch rolled back on his heels and chuckled then sighed. But when he spoke, his voice wasn't light, as his behavior implied. It was far closer to the dark tone Q had just used. "When I get done with you, Schaeffer, you will look like a rabid hyena. I will have the American people lighting your mansion up with Molotov cocktails and dragging you out to a hangman's noose."

Mitch paused, took a breath, and lightened his voice. "Now, back to my original reason for calling—our live and let live offer. Bet it sounds more appealing now. I'll even do you one better. I'll return your assassin, safe and, well, relatively sound. Where can we drop old Reggie off for you?"

Silence. Mitch stared at the phone. Waited.

Q straightened and cast a nervous glance at Mitch who met Q's gaze with steady confidence.

"Well," Schaeffer finally said, drawing out the word, heavy with resignation. "This is a problem I'd hoped we'd avoid."

A spark of hope ignited in Q's chest. He glanced at Jessica whose eyes had widened with surprise. Q imagined lots of time, no deadlines, no pressure. Just time to get to know Jessica. To learn everything he'd forgotten about this beautiful, generous woman. Nothing had ever sounded so amazingly blissful.

"Don't you worry about doing anything with Reggie, Foster." The icy edge in Schaeffer's voice cut into Q's fantasies and his attention shot back to the phone, then to Mitch. "I can take care of him from here."

Mitch frowned. Opened his mouth to speak. But Reggie jerked upright, the cuffs clanging against the metal bed frame. All attention turned to the prisoner, whose eyes were unnaturally wide and filled with panic. His mouth opened wide as if about to scream, but no sound emerged.

Reggie brought his free hand to his throat. Alyssa immediately stood and started toward him. Teague grabbed her back. They argued.

"What in the fuck . . . ?" Kai said, rushing toward him.

Reggie dropped back on the mattress and went into jagged convulsions, thrashing and grunting.

Kai grabbed Reggie's arms. "Get me something to hold his tongue down," he said to Cash. "It's blocking his air."

Cash turned and clawed through the storage shelves. Teague approached the foot of the bed and tried to grab the man's legs.

Q watched the activity in confusion. "What are they doing?"

"He's seizing," Jessica said, her hand so tight on his it stung. "They're going to clear his airway."

The prisoner jerked loose of Kai's grip and his uncuffed arm swung up, barely missing his head.

"Damn it." Kai clapped both hands on the man's head. "He's fucking strong."

Teague climbed on the bed and sat on the guy's legs, limiting his kicking.

Cash came back with a wooden mixing spoon. "It's all I could find."

"Great," Kai muttered, but grabbed the spoon.

He gripped the man's jaw and pried it open from the outside with pressure at the hinges. He squinted into the man's mouth, the thin end of the spoon's handle held ready to flatten the man's tongue.

Anger welled in Q's chest. "Why are they helping him?"

"What?" Jessica's gaze jumped to his. "He'll hurt himself if we just let him seize. He could die."

"Let him die." Q stalked toward the bed. "Don't save

the bastard. He'd kill us all given the chance. Get off him. Just let him die."

"Take it easy, Quaid." Cash got that worried warning look in his eye.

"Move back, Quaid." Jessica took his arm, her voice serious. "Let them work."

Kai finally pried Reggie's mouth open wide enough to insert the spoon's handle, but pulled back with a soft, "Holy shit." Then, "Everyone, get back."

Cash shot Kai a confused look just as Reggie coughed. Kai turned his face and raised his arm just before blood sprayed from the man's mouth.

"Fuck." Teague jumped off the man's legs and yanked at Cash's arm, pulling him back. "What the hell is this?"

Reggie continued to buck and jerk and cough blood. It splattered the cement wall, the floor, his clothes. With one last spasm, he went limp, eyes open and blank, blood still spilling from his mouth.

Jessica turned her back and put her hand over her mouth. Q didn't console her. This was exactly what the fucker deserved. Q had seen the carnage this kind of killer left behind. . . .

He dragged his mind back from that fork in the road. It would lead him nowhere. He'd followed too many detours to expect this one to lead him to any more information than the others. They always dead-ended in frustration.

By the time Kai laid his fingers on Reggie's neck, blood was leaking from the prisoner's ears and nose.

Kai pulled his hand away and shook his head at Mitch, who pushed more buttons on his phone.

Jessica made a sound in her throat and Q found she'd glanced over her shoulder. Now, she turned into Q, wrapped her arms around his waist and pressed her face to his chest. Q's entire focus changed. He enclosed her in his arms, held her tight and stroked her hair. The anger inside him ebbed. And he found it difficult to hold onto his hate when she filled him with so much love.

"Quiet down," Mitch said. "I have Schaeffer on mute. He doesn't need to know how rattled we are." Mitch took a few deep breaths, clawed a hand through his hair, then cleared his throat and pressed a button on his phone. "I knew you were a sick fuck, Schaeffer. The prison psychologists will enjoy picking your brain apart."

"All our subjects are injected with a high-tech material when they come to us," Schaeffer said. "It allows for remote control of those we send into the field. Reggie had obviously become a liability."

An ice-cold fist slammed into the center of Q's chest. His gaze darted to Cash's at the same time Cash's met his. And Cash wore the same look of shock Q felt on his own face. Q's breath wheezed out of his lungs. Terror tightened every muscle.

"I was really hoping to avoid this since we have so much invested in Q and Cash," Schaeffer said. "But I can see you'll make it a fight to the bitter end."

"Now hold on, Schaeffer—" Mitch started.

Something popped inside Q. Multiple snaps of pain burst all along his ribs and deep in his belly, knives stabbing his guts. He grunted and doubled over. Jessica reached for him.

"Quaid?" Her voice rose with panic. "Quaid!"

He couldn't breathe. Something hot leaked through his insides and seared like acid. Her face swam in his vision and he let go of her to grip his belly. His legs weakened. He stumbled backwards and hit the cement wall.

"Shit, Cash!"

Q heard Kai's voice, but his vision had gone dark.

"Teague," Jessica called, and the man was there in an instant, his hands patting Q down like a cop.

"Where do you hurt most?" he asked.

"St— st—" He couldn't draw air. His throat was on fire.

"Stomach?" Teague asked.

Q managed a nod and Teague's hands moved there. Q's legs went out and he slumped to the cement. Heat swallowed him. He couldn't tell if it was coming from Teague or if it was the burn in his stomach. But within seconds, the sear eased and Q draw a deep breath into his lungs.

As his vision returned, his first sight was Cash curled into a ball on the floor.

Q pushed Teague's hands away. "Cash. Help Cash."

Teague swiveled and moved to Cash.

"I've set these at a slower release rate," Schaeffer said. "That will give you time to consider a change of heart. If you do, I can administer a neutralizer for the compound now slowly killing them."

"You motherfucking —" Q started.

"Legend," Schaeffer said, "if you bring me the formula Cash created at the Castle within twenty-four hours I'll give both you and Cash the neutralizer. If not, well, American troops will be the ones who suffer, and I'll have two less witnesses to worry about, won't I?"

"Schaeffer—" Mitch started.

"Oh, and don't think about holding back anything or messing with the formula," Schaeffer said, "because if I discover you did, I'll simply reactivate the compound and let both of you die—just like Reggie. Only slower. Much slower."

TWENTY-ONE

J essica sat on the edge of a chair in a bedroom in the main bunker, hands between her knees, heart in her throat. Quaid paced as they waited for Alyssa.

"Baby," Jessica tried again. "You should sit down. You need to conserve your energy." She also hated the thought of him aiding the spread of whatever Schaeffer had released into his body, but she didn't think he needed to hear those stark words right now.

Quaid stopped and put a hand against the wall, the other against his forehead, wiping at the sweat. He was running a fever. He was pale. He occasionally suffered tremors. But he was faring far better than Cash, which the team attributed to Quaid's advanced healing abilities.

"Can I"—Jessica swallowed, feeling helpless and terrified—"do anything for you?"

Quaid didn't answer. He seemed to be in another world. She couldn't blame him. Hell, she swore she'd been caught in some bizarre low-budget sci-fi film and she wasn't the one injected with a lethal material who had an unknown amount of time left to live.

"Sorry." Alyssa swept into the room and closed the door behind her. "I had to fight Mitch for a legal pad." She took a chair beside Jessica. "Why does everyone think he's charming? On what planet?"

Jessica huffed a laugh at the unexpected humor.

Alyssa looked at Quaid, who still stood with his back toward them. "Are you sure you're feeling up to this, Quaid?"

He didn't answer right away. He swiped at his forehead again and wiped his palm on his jeans, then pushed off the wall and turned. His eyes clouded over. He thrust one hand out in front of him and swayed. Jessica jumped up and crossed the room before he fell off balance.

He leaned on her without arguing. "Let's do this before I can't."

She eased him onto the bed and sat beside him. Because Quaid had his forearm flung over his eyes, Alyssa divided her attention between him and Jessica as she outlined the hypnosis process.

"You'll be in control of yourself at all times. I will never be able to direct you or force you to do anything."

He peeked out from beneath his arm with a look that said: *And elephants fly.*

Alyssa sighed. "This is a very . . . sensitive . . . process. Many clients prefer not to have anyone in the room with—"

"No." Quaid grabbed Jessica's forearm. She startled, jerking back from his hold. Their eyes met and she knew he saw it—her fear. Hurt flashed in his eyes. Then sadness. "I want her with me," he said softly. "Stay? Please?"

Her heart melted. Damn it, this rollercoaster was making her nauseous. She looked at Alyssa, who shrugged. Jessica covered Quaid's hand with hers and squeezed. "Of course, I'll stay."

Alyssa led Quaid through a relaxation process first, then deeper into a hypnotic state. The grip of his hand had become so light, his breathing so even and deep, Jessica was sure he'd fallen asleep.

"Q." Alyssa's voice was smooth and soft. Utterly tranquil. Her switch to calling Quaid "Q" threw Jessica for a second, but it made sense to use the only name he'd known at the time he was remembering. "Go back to the last time you saw Gorin. Take your time. Nod when you're there."

A moment passed while Jessica just studied Quaid's handsome face. The strong bone structure. Full lips. The angle of his jaw. How could she have ever thought this man wasn't her husband? Amazing what the mind could do to block pain. Maybe, in time, after all this was over and the threat was gone, his mind would shift as hers had. Maybe, in time, he'd remember . . .

Something hitched in her chest. A sense of loss. Which was stupid. Of course, she wanted him to remember all they'd had. All they'd been. How deeply they'd loved each other. But she didn't want to lose what they'd newly discovered—a deeper, truer connection. A unique bond transcending time and memory. A raw, real, intensely satisfying sexual expression together.

His head bobbed slowly.

"Okay, good," Alyssa said in that smooth tone. "Can you tell me where you are?"

"Lab." His voice was languid, as if he were sleep-talking. "At the Castle."

"And what does he have you do there?"

Quaid licked his lips. "Mmm, guard straps me into the chair. Gorin shoots me up. I . . . I . . . Then I don't know."

"Gorin shoots you up with what?" Alyssa asked.

"Don't know. Makes me pass out."

Jessica's stomach sloshed as if she'd just stepped off that rollercoaster ride. She closed her eyes, trying like hell not to imagine Quaid's life like that day in and day out for five long years.

"Can you rest in that place for a moment, Q," Alyssa asked, "where you pass out? Then let yourself wake there.

Remember, you're safe. You can come out at any time. You are not strapped to that chair now."

Jessica raised her head and opened wet eyes.

Quaid nodded.

"And when you're ready, tell me what you see."

Quaid's hand immediately tightened on Jessica's. His breathing quickened. Jessica frowned at Alyssa, who put up a hand and mouthed *he's okay*.

"Q." Alyssa's voice slid into the space like an easy ocean wave. "Where are you? What do you see?"

"Shh." Quaid pushed the sound through his teeth in a sharp, demanding rasp. He held up his free hand. His face tightened in disapproval. "If you blow our cover, I'll blow your head off."

His continued expression of violence set Jessica on edge and clouded her hopes for his recovery.

"No one can hear me but you, Q," Alyssa insisted. "You're in no danger. I need to know where you are and what you're doing."

"This is a classified mission. No one—"

"I have clearance." Alyssa's voice strengthened while remaining nonthreatening. "From the highest level of the Pentagon and General George Ascott. He wants details on the op's progress and he wants them now."

Jessica looked at Alyssa and mouthed *who*? Alyssa shrugged. Jessica rolled her eyes and hid them behind her hand.

But Quaid's grip eased and he muttered, "Fucking brass." Then in a raspy rushed whisper said, "We've located the weapons factory and detained the Pakistanis running it. They have information on the raw material suppliers and technical designers, but they're not talking. We're waiting to rendezvous with Major Abernathy to turn over the weapons and prisoners."

Alyssa and Jessica stared at Quaid, absorbing the implications.

"Copy?" Quaid snapped in that rough whisper.

"Yes," Alyssa said, startled. "I mean, copy." She stared down at her legal pad, which remained blank, then asked, "Q, are you performing this operation remotely?"

"How in the hell would we do that?" The bite behind his words said that was the stupidest question he'd heard in months.

"So . . . you're at the site. You're . . . in Pakistan. On the ground. Physically."

A hesitation. "With all due respect, ma'am, you don't sound smart enough to be reporting to the Pentagon."

"Forgive me," she said dryly. "I'm new to this assignment. How did you get to Pakistan, Q?"

"The troops were already here. My partner and I teleport."

Alyssa's mouth opened and her eyes went wide at the same moment as Jessica's did. When Alyssa looked at Jessica, Jessica mouthed *oh, my God.* She pulled the pad from Alyssa, grabbed the pencil and started writing, all without ever letting go of Quaid's hand. She gave the pad back to Alyssa with her chest so tight she found it hard to breathe.

"Who's your partner?" Alyssa asked.

"Trent Dare."

Alyssa shot another look at Jessica. She shook her head and shrugged.

"Who is Trent Dare, Q?"

"Uh . . . my partner?" he said with that condescending *duh* tone. "I've got shit to do. Are we done here?"

"No." A funny little smile turned Alyssa's mouth. "Check the attitude. I'll tell you when we're done."

Quaid sighed, and wiped his hand down his face.

Alyssa read Jessica's note, then asked Quaid, "I just want

to clarify, Q, are you sure you're physically there? Not just there in mind?"

"I'm here in both."

"But remote viewing is done from a distance."

"I only view remotely while collecting intel." His tone indicated he was losing patience. "I have to travel to the site to execute the op. Why isn't Gorin answering these questions?"

Alyssa made an oh-shit face. "Gorin has . . . developed the flu. He's been puking for two days and isn't well enough to talk to us."

"Stupid motherfucker," Quaid muttered. "So obsessed he never sleeps. Knew it would catch up with him someday."

Jessica's stomach muscles ached from clenching. This horrible intimate glimpse into Quaid's life as Q turned her inside out.

"This information is very important to your superiors, Q," Alyssa said. "What you do is very special, very unusual. They won't understand unless it's all explained. There is a committee meeting later today where they're discussing your operations. Can you explain how you travel?"

"I swear to God," he rasped, voice still low as if he were hiding, "if you people stopped holding *meetings* and got off your asses, important things could happen. Explain to them that consciousness is the basis of all being. Matter is all possibility, allowing us to choose our own reality. I choose—in my reality—to travel as electrons do, by moving to parallel orbits without passing through interpreting space. Everything in the universe is simply a matter of choice."

"What in the hell . . . ?" Jessica whispered.

Alyssa's head turned sharply and she put a shushing finger to her lips. She grabbed the pad from Jessica and scribbled: *quantum physics.*

Jessica remembered the same headache-inducing phrase coming from Cash and rubbed her temple.

"And where else have you traveled for these ops, Q?" Alyssa asked.

He hesitated. "The Pentagon should have all this information."

"Q," Alyssa said, growing stern again, "this is information you will remember when you wake. This is information you need to bring back with you. To do that, you must recall it all now and have it fresh in your mind. Do you understand?"

Another hesitation. Then, "I understand."

"Think back. Start with the operation you're on now. Tell me all the information you have, then move backward in time, to the operation before that and so on."

Quaid had never been so exhausted. He felt like he was melting in the desert sun. His muscles felt like jelly, his bones like rubber as he leaned on Jessica as she helped him to their room.

Jessica eased him to the edge of the bed, then down the rest of the way to rest his head on the pillow. He sank into the softness beneath him with gratitude and relief. His eyelids were so very heavy and as much as he wanted to look at Jessica every moment he had left, he couldn't keep them open any longer.

He couldn't die. Not because he was afraid of death. Not because he didn't want to die. But because he couldn't leave Jessica again. He knew if he died now, it would break her.

Jessica sat beside him, stroking his head over and over. Her touch brought him heaven, and he relaxed into the mattress and absorbed the tingling comfort.

"You've been through so much," she whispered, her

voice thick with emotion. "I'm so sorry I wasn't there for you. I'm so sorry I didn't know."

She started to rise from the bed. Quaid caught her hand in his grasp, but she didn't startle. Maybe because now she knew he'd been trained to move fast. Now they both knew. Knew why he spoke so many languages—so he could manipulate people in many different countries. Knew why he hadn't known about his gift—because they'd drugged him while utilizing it.

"Don't leave me," he murmured.

She leaned down and pressed her forehead to his. "Didn't I already tell you I wouldn't?"

Yes, she had. Why didn't he believe her? Because there were still secrets between them. Between him and the group. There were things they weren't telling him. The same way Gorin kept secrets. Maybe the secrets Jessica and the group held weren't harmful to Q, but that wasn't the point. He needed honesty and he couldn't get it. If he couldn't trust the people who said they loved him most . . . whom could he trust?

Himself. Alone.

But he didn't want to be alone anymore. He wanted Jessica with him every moment of every day. He wanted to be part of this bigger team. He wanted to uncover his past, develop a purpose, move forward.

And he couldn't imagine that future without complete honesty in it. "Jessie—"

"I'm going to check on Cash," she said. "I'll be right back."

He was too exhausted to argue. He closed his eyes. "Tell him to stop screwing around." His words slurred. "Not going to get any more attention this way. I'll kick his ass if he doesn't get better."

Jessica laughed. A soft, sweet sound.

Before he released her hand, Quaid brought it to his

mouth, uncurled her fingers and kissed her palm, drifting into sleep even as he did. "Thank you."

"For what?"

For loving me. But the words didn't pass his lips before he floated into that place between consciousness and sleep.

Scenes from the forgotten half of the last five years stirred his mind—dark nights in sweltering jungles raiding guerilla paramilitary camps for intel and equipment. Long, filthy days scouting the streets of Vietnam for informants. Dark Greek nights lit up by flash fire and filled with tear gas during riots.

So many scenes played out in little clips. Clips pieced together to create a movie of shadows, deceit, surveillance. Secrets, lies and mysteries all leading toward violence, injury and death. Had he directly caused death? The twist in the pit of his stomach hinted that he had.

He saw blood. Heard gunshots. Screams. Pain clawed at him from the inside, like an animal trying to get out.

Q lunged upright and gasped for air. His gaze darted around the room, assessing, preparing . . . But it was empty. The room quiet. Voices drifted in from the living area. A surge of nausea caught him by surprise and he clenched his teeth and closed his eyes, willing it away. When it passed, he fell back on his elbows, turned and reached for the orange juice Jessica had left beside the bed and took a few slow sips.

Then he sank back into the bed, breathing hard, sweating. Utterly depleted. He tuned into the conversation in the living room through the partially open door.

"Teague's healing powers get sucked dry after only a minute or two working on Cash," Alyssa said. "He's not doing well at all."

Worry enveloped Quaid's chest, but he didn't have the strength to move, to speak.

"Has someone called Keira?" Jessica asked.

"He asked us not to," Alyssa said. "He asked us to wait."

"Quaid's healing abilities are obviously fighting whatever this is," Jessica said. "But not well and for how long?"

"If Quaid could repair himself after shattering every bone in his body, he can beat this." Kai was obviously wound tight again. The man definitely had anger control issues, though Q wasn't one to talk.

The room remained silent a moment and Q fought the pull of sleep.

"Look, it's clear we can't wait to go after the neutralizer," Jessica said, pulling Quaid back. "We're not giving up Quaid or Cash, and Cash doesn't have the formula finished. So Schaeffer's not going to give us the neutralizer.

"I know everything about Schaeffer, right down to when he brushes his teeth," Jessica said. "I have an in with his hairstylist, his new chauffer, one of his housekeepers. We socialize in all the same circles. I can get close to him. No one else here can."

"What are you saying?" Kai demanded more than asked.

"Thank you, Kai," Q muttered, resting his forearm over his eyes.

"I'm saying that I'm our best bet to get to Schaeffer and get that neutralizer." Jessica's voice had that determined tone that said they were in for a fight if they disagreed. "Kai, you need to fly me to Washington. I'll be ready to go in fifteen minutes."

Q's eyes opened and stared up at the gray ceiling. She couldn't be serious.

"I'm not flying you to Washington just to get your butt arrested," Kai said. "Or killed."

"I owe you, brother," Q murmured.

"Contrary to popular belief," Jessica said, "you guys aren't the only ones who can handle a gun. Schaeffer won't be calling the police with a couple of his fingers shot off.

If I have to spend a few years in jail to save Quaid and Cash, I'll do it."

"No, no, no . . ." Q tried to roll off the bed. Put his arm into it. Managed to get to a sitting position. He picked up the orange juice and took another big swallow. He needed the sugar rush.

"There's got to be a better way, Jess," Kai said. "You know a lot of powerful people in Washington. Don't you have an ally you can pull into your corner given all this evidence? Someone Schaeffer can't manipulate? His involvement is incredibly clear. Every op Quaid cited corresponds to a technical development within Millennium Manufacturing in the following six months, which then led to a military contract for Millennium within the six months after that."

A moment of silence followed before Mitch's voice cut in. "It's good, but it's not a slam dunk. We need corroboration if we want this all to stick. I need time to gather information on the weapons Quaid mentioned and records of the transactions."

"I'm not going to trial, and Schaeffer's no legal eagle. I'm a damn good bullshitter when I need to be. I work with these politicians all damn day, every day, I'd better be good. And if all else fails, I'll . . ." She paused, took a deep breath. "Damn it, I'll take all the information and your audio/video of Schaeffer's call to the Secretary of Defense."

Q's eyes opened in shock. The bold sureness in her statement came as if there would be no problem getting in front of such a powerful man. Which made a trickle of unease slide through his chest. An ugly unease. One he instinctively didn't want to look into.

"Will Dutch?" Mitch asked, surprise clear in his tone. "You know Will Dutch?"

"Yes. He's . . . a friend. He'll listen to what I have to

say. He'll look over the documents if I ask him to. He's smart. He'll see the connections. And he's not one of Schaeffer's biggest fans."

Q let his mind drift. He barely had the energy to remain sitting upright. He definitely didn't have the energy to make it go where it didn't want to go.

Jessica came in, nothing but a whisper of movement. Her simple presence eased his stress and lifted his energy.

She knelt in front of him on the floor, hands on his knees, worried eyes searching his. Good God, she was beautiful. She took his breath. Made him ache.

"Jessie . . ."

She scanned his body. "Is your fever up again? You took your shirt off."

He didn't remember taking it off. And he couldn't seem to formulate an answer, just shook his head.

"Why are you sitting up?" Frown lines crinkled her smooth brow. "Are you okay? Do you need something?"

"You." His eyes slid closed. "All I need is you."

"Well, you're in luck. I'm all yours. Lie down."

Grateful for the permission, he dropped back on the bed. Jessica wrung a cloth in the cold water on the nightstand and wiped down his face, his neck, chest, arms. It helped. Gave him a zing of energy.

"Don't go to Washington," he said, forcing his eyes to hers. "Wait until I get better. I'll go with you."

"We don't have time for that, Quaid. Cash isn't doing as well as you are. He may not even have twenty-four hours."

Quaid slid his hands up her arms and pulled her toward him. She came easily, willingly, and a rush of sweet gratitude filled him. He rolled to his side, taking her with him. He kissed her lips, gently, sweetly. Combed his fingers through her hair.

She kissed him back, and that already-familiar deep

bond they'd developed so quickly wrapped them in intimacy. And relief. And comfort. And joy.

His hand slipped under her top, caressed the soft skin of her back, fingers memorizing the sleek muscle there. He slid his thigh between hers and pressed it high to the core heat of her body.

Jessica hummed in pleasure, wrapped her arms around him and held him tight. "You have to get better, Quaid. I can't live without you again."

"Shh." His mouth slid to her cheek, her jaw, her neck. "We'll be okay."

He rolled her to her back, slid down her body, lifted her shirt and pressed his mouth to her belly.

She caressed his head and shoulders as he kissed his way up her belly, pushed her tank top over her breasts and groaned when he found them bare beneath.

He eased up on his elbows and looked down on her, staring at her breasts. This was the first time he'd seen her body in the light. They'd made love with most of her clothes on. They'd made love in the dark. Now, his hands caressed and shaped as his eyes watched. "So beautiful."

He lowered his mouth and treasured her with his lips and tongue, losing himself in the feel of her body, the softness and warmth of her skin, the sounds she made, the way she moved beneath him.

"Quaid," she murmured. "We'll have to finish this later, when you're well. I have to go get the neutralizer that's going to make you better."

What if she left and he never saw her again? He couldn't wait. Couldn't put off making love to her one more time. He pulled his mouth from her breast, pushed to his knees and brought his hands to the button of her shorts. His eyes wandered up her body as he flipped the button open, eased down the zipper.

And froze.

"Quaid?"

He didn't answer. His gaze was caught on a scar. A small, smooth scar beneath her left breast. He sat back on his heels and reached up, letting his fingers slide over the light flesh. Images flickered in his head. Extremely unpleasant images—Jessica and a man on a sofa in some big house. The images and sounds at this stage of his dreams . . . or visions . . . or whatever they'd been had always started out hazy, blurry, watery, distorted, sometimes so much so, he couldn't actually see or hear in detail what was happening, but enough to know . . . He hadn't seen—or experienced—her with another man in a long time. The memory slammed into him like a truck.

She touched his face. "Quaid."

Quaid took her hand, but didn't look away from the scar. "What's . . ." He swallowed, the memory coming back to him even as he asked the question. "Where'd you get this?"

She didn't even look at the scar, but pulled his hand away from it. "I . . . don't remember. Where were we?"

Secrets, lies and mysteries.

And memories.

Her avoidance created a weakness in his mind like a crack in a damn, and the memories poured in.

TWENTY-TWO

Q pulled his hands from Jessica's as he remembered the night she'd gotten that scar, the last night he'd seen her in his dreams.

Jessica had already been high when her flirtatious, *"What's a good looking secretary of defense like you doing at a party like this?"* had started a conversation with Will Dutch, one that had continued throughout the night.

She'd looked like a sparkling jewel in an elegant, deep emerald dress. He'd visualized the night fairly clearly up until the last hour. Until after Jessica had made her last trip into the room of the house designated for drug use. After that, everything had gone blurry.

The home where the party had been held was luxurious beyond Q's imagination. All the men dressed in tuxedos, the women in full-length gowns that sparkled and shimmered. But no one had been as beautiful as Jessica.

Q had watched the attraction grow between Dutch and Jessica, the building flirtation and Jessica's increasing but clandestine ingestion of cocaine and alcohol. Dutch had not taken part in the drugs, but had made his share of trips to the open bar and simply looked the other way when Jessica used.

When they'd escaped to a private room in the house to have sex—something Q had anticipated with pleasure at the time, something that made him want to kill the man now—Q had to admit, the man had been good to Jessica, at least in comparison to the others.

But the drugs had taken their toll and afterward, when Jessica stood, she passed out and hit the coffee table on the way to the floor. The sight of her torn dress and the vivid red blood on the carpet was bright and fresh in Q's mind, as if he'd dreamt it last night, not over a year ago.

"Quaid?"

Her voice pulled him out of the memory. Pain lingered in his chest, but he leaned down and kissed her belly button. "I heard you talking about the secretary of defense," he said, rubbing his lips across her soft, soft skin. "How do you know him?"

"Just work," she whispered, sitting up and kissing him.

Pain stabbed his heart. He pushed away, turned and sat on the edge of the bed, head in his hands. He couldn't think. His brain was so full. So confused.

She laid a hand on his back and he stood, needing distance.

He paced to the wall, then turned. She sat in the middle of the bed, tank top pulled back into place. "I told you, in the very beginning, I needed honesty. I *told* you."

Her face paled, and those brown eyes seemed to grow huge in the absence of color. She swallowed and nodded. "I . . . I got it . . . I fell and hit a table. Needed stitches."

He took one big step forward, hands clenched. "God *damn it,* Jessica."

She flinched and shrank from him. The gesture piled guilt on top of pain and he turned away again, rubbing his face with both hands. God, he was so tired. His legs felt like they would collapse under him.

"I was there that night, Jessica," he said, disillusioned by her continued need to keep secrets from him. "I know how you got the scar. I know how you know Will Dutch."

"Quaid." Her voice vibrated with tears and panic. He turned back and found her holding her locket, rubbing it like she expected a genie to pop out, though he didn't know what the hell a genie was. "Quaid, listen to me. If I could go back and live my life over, I'd do it all differently. If I'd known you were alive, if there had been even a *remote chance* that you were alive . . . I've never wanted anyone but you. I was crushed. I was trying to find a way to survive. It was the wrong way and I've suffered for it. But I thought you were *dead*."

He knew that. He understood all that. He could see that she'd obviously suffered. She didn't have to explain pain and hopelessness, or doing what you had to do to find a way to survive to him of all people. Yes, the memory of seeing her with other men hurt. But her lies, her secrets, hurt far more. And by the way she clung to that locket, he sensed there was another lurking nearby.

He closed the distance and when she dropped the locket, Q grabbed it. One solid pull and the chain snapped.

"Oh, my God, no." She lunged for the necklace. Quaid turned his back to her and opened it. She scraped at his back, pulled at his arm, stood on the bed and grabbed for it over his shoulder, begging, "Quaid, please . . . let me explain. . . ."

He fumbled with the small piece in his big fingers. Fending Jessica off didn't help. Finally, he caught the latch with his fingernail and pulled the locket open.

A gold band lay inside.

Quaid stared. He flashed hot. Then cold. His hands started to shake. Then his body. Jessica yelled at him. Pleaded with him, but all sound dimmed in the rush of blood in his head. He plucked the ring out of the locket and dropped the necklace. It bounced against the cement, but the sound never reached Q's ears.

He held the gold band up to the light and it gleamed. The ring was simple, elegant and polished, but marred with a heavy diagonal nick across one side. Inside the band, etched lettering caught the light. QUAID, ALL MY LOVE, FOREVER. Jessica. And a date. Six years earlier.

Jessica clung to his waist, face pressed to his spine, sobbing. Quaid held the ring at the end of his left ring finger, his chest so tight, he could barely draw air into his lungs.

He slid the ring on.

The gold band passed snugly over his knuckle, then lay loose around his finger above. He stared at it on his hand. An absolutely surreal sensation swirled in his head. Stunned at the way a simple gold band transformed his whole identity from a separate, lone man to the important half of something beautiful. Something vital.

Something he should have been told. *Immediately.*

"We're *married*?" He turned on her. "We were *married,* and you didn't tell me?"

The door to the bedroom pushed open and Kai, Teague and Alyssa came in, eyes wide with worry.

"What's going on?" Kai asked.

"We were *married* and none of you bothered to tell me?"

All eyes darted to Jessica, who held her face in her hands, then back to Q without a word.

"I told everyone not to tell you." Alyssa pushed to the front, her expression worried, but stern. "What you want and what you need are sometimes very different things, Quaid. As I told Jessica, pushing that information on you before you were ready could have sent you into shutdown. Your brain could have completely turned off and you could have been in a catatonic state for an indeterminable amount of time."

Fury and betrayal lit him on fire. He thought of Schaeffer, of Gorin, of all they'd taken from him for their own greedy purposes.

"Goddamned fucking scientists," Q growled, visualizing Gorin. "You all think you have the right to control other people's reality."

"Just stop there, Quaid." Teague stepped up next to his wife. "That's—"

Alyssa put a hand on his arm. "It's okay."

Now that Q had a choice—he chose his own reality.

And he teleported straight to Gorin.

"Quaid, don't do that . . ." The nervous tone in Alyssa's voice brought Jessica's head up. "Quaid . . ."

Jessica focused through blurry eyes, sure her traumatized mind had failed. Quaid held his arm out in front of him, looking down at his open palm. The sight of his hand faded and reappeared.

He dropped his arm, closed his eyes and, with a look of concentration, entirely faded from sight.

Jessica gasped. Alyssa swore. Everyone looked around as if Quaid would reappear somewhere in the room.

"Holy shit," Kai breathed, raking a hand through his hair.

Jessica jumped off the bed. "Quaid!" Fury struck through her like lightning. Outside, the sky responded with a flash of illumination. A roll of thunder echoed right behind it. "Quaid, goddamnit, get back here. Don't you dare leave me again."

Shaking with fear, with rage, with more emotions than she could name, Jessica clenched her hands and punched the air. "*Goddamn* you, Quaid. *Goddamn* you," she screamed at nothing. "You fucking coward."

Her insides caved. She curled in on herself and fell to the bed. No, she wasn't perfect. Yes, she'd made mistakes. But that didn't make her worthless. That didn't make her expendable. He hadn't been perfect either, and she'd stood by him. She'd mourned him for years. Now, she continued to stand by him even though he didn't even *remember* her.

"That . . . fucker . . ." she stammered through sobs.

"Has he always been able to do that?" Mitch's mildly annoyed voice entered the fray. "'Cause if he has, when I get my hands on that bastard, he's gonna wish he'd done it a hell of a lot sooner."

"What happened?" Cash's soft, rusty voice sounded in the doorway. "Where's . . . Q?"

Jessica scrambled to the corner of the room and rummaged in the pocket of the jeans she'd been wearing the day before. She pulled out Quaid's coin and sat back on her heels. Holding the coin out, she searched for light to reflect off the surface. But it was dull and flat.

Everyone was talking, but she ignored them, rushing to the single window and tilting the coin toward the sunlight until it sparkled in her eyes. She took a shaky breath and blurred her vision. *Come on. Come on.* Shadows began to swish and sway inside the reflection, then take shape. A figure, a man, moved through monochromatic, institutional hallways, throwing doors open.

"Need a doorway," she whispered, turning the coin to catch the light. "Come on, give me a—"

The sun peeked out from behind the clouds, hit, bounced and speared right into Jessica's eyes. White light blinded her. She squeezed her eyes shut and lifted her hand. The light grew brighter, bigger, and showered her entire body with heat. *Fizzle-pop,* the sound of a bubbling soda grew in her ears. Jessica's body went light, her head dizzy. Then she was moving, falling. A rush of air and pressure prickled over her skin. Adrenaline sizzled so hard her blood frothed in her veins.

Even knowing the process, panic rode high in her chest, choking her. The pressure made it hard to breathe. Then as suddenly as it had grown turbulent, the air calmed. The pressure eased. The turbulence in her skin calmed.

She focused on the cool cement beneath her hand. She shaded her eyes and squinted into the light. The intensity faded to reveal that monochromatic, institutional hallway where she'd seen Quaid.

She tuned into her senses and found the space eerily quiet. Down the length of the hallway, doors stood open, some still swaying. Which meant she'd just missed Quaid.

Using the wall and the floor for support, Jessica pushed to her feet, tested her surroundings for stability and started down the hall, following the path of open doorways. She peered into rooms only to find vacant offices, empty laboratories, as if the place had been abandoned. There was no sign of what institution this was or in what city, or state, or even what country. Hell, she could be on Mars.

This had to be a damn dream. It had all the crazy earmarks of a dream—the fuzzy-edged images, the distorted perspectives, the freaky sensation of total isolation and foreboding. Then again, maybe that all came with this bizarre state of consciousness.

A muffled *bang* sounded far off to her left. Jessica started down that hallway. Then another—*bang*. She envisioned more doors opening and slamming against walls and pushed into a jog.

Bang.

"Gorin!" Quaid's distant, furious bellow knifed through her. "Where the fuck are you?"

Bang.

Then she heard another voice. And an immediate argument.

Jessica ran. Her bare feet had good traction on the smooth linoleum and she sprinted down halls and around corners, moving toward the voices. Every hallway, every room, looked absolutely identical. If she ever had to find her way back to where she'd started, she'd be screwed. This was a house of mirrors, minus the mirrors.

She turned another corner and found Quaid—a splash of color inside an otherwise white rectangle. He had one hand wrapped around a doorknob, yanking at it, the other flat and pounding against the door as he peered through the one-foot-square window at eye level.

"Open this door, asshole," Quaid yelled. "If I have to teleport in there I'll be three times as pissed as I am now."

Jessica stopped twenty feet from him, breathing hard. "Quaid."

He jerked toward her, eyes wide. When he recognized her, his expression clouded with exhaustion. Sweat drenched his face, neck and chest. "Get out of here." He peered through the window again and slapped the door hard. "Open. This. Door. Gorin."

She dug her fingers into his arm and jerked him around to face her. "Newsflash, asshole, you're not the Lone Ranger anymore."

"The what?"

"It's a *who*. You have an entire team of people wrapped up in this with you. More than a dozen who have risked their futures, their lives, to see you safe. So, guess what? You can be as pissed at me as you want. You can hate me. You can fucking divorce me if that'll give you the vengeance you need." She drove a finger into his chest. "But you don't get to screw them, too."

"A team of people who lied to me."

"For fuck's sake, get the hell over it. You act like we tried to steal your DNA to create a serial killer. We wanted to keep you *safe*. We didn't want you to jump off a psychotic cliff. Excuse us for *caring*."

In a sudden show of exhaustion, Quaid slumped against the door, holding himself up by the handle. "Have you always had a mouth like that?"

"Shut the hell up. You're not one to talk."

"Newsflash, girl," he said "You're not persistent. You're just fucking bossy."

She crossed her arms, lifted her brows. "What are you going to do about it?"

Quaid's eyes slid closed and he let out a tired laugh. A laugh. He actually *laughed*. His mouth turned up in a real smile. A smile from the days when he used to be happy. Some of Jessica's anger evaporated.

She went to him and put her arms around his waist. "You're not in any condition to be doing this. You need to go back to the bunker."

Quaid ran a hand down her arm. "No, Jessie. *You* need to go back to the bunker."

He covered her hand, pried the coin from it and gave her one good push.

Jessica stumbled backwards, fell on her ass and slid on the linoleum. Her vision blurred. *Fizz-pop-sizzle* sounded in her ears. "Damn you, Quaid!"

Jessica kept a hand over her eyes as Teague's heat poured through her head, easing the pressure in her brain and soothing her stomach. She'd been back in the bunker at least twenty minutes and precious time ticked away.

"Cash," she called without opening her eyes.

"I'm here." His voice, weak and raspy, drew close from across the room.

"What Quaid does is different from what I do. He's really there, I'm not. He called it remote travel. What's the difference?"

"Hell if I know." Cash coughed, pulled in a breath that made it sound like he was drowning.

Once Cash and Quaid had been poisoned, Alyssa had kept Mateo and Kat down at the end of the long hall of

bedrooms with one of Brody's guys. Jessica was glad
Mateo didn't have to see his dad so sick.

She opened her eyes. Cash's face was pale and covered
with sweat. She pushed Teague's hands off her head. "Use
your energy on him."

"It's wasted on him." Teague sat back and wrapped his
arms around upturned knees. "Whatever is happening in
his body is too strong for my power."

"What Quaid was talking about," Alyssa said, "was the
theory of quantum physics. Or at least that's the theory he
was giving for how he traveled."

Jessica wiped both her hands down her face. She shook
her head. "I don't care what it's called. I don't care how it
works. I just want to know if one of you ridiculously intelligent people can teach me how to do it."

"I can . . ." Cash wheezed ". . . explain the concept . . .
of quantum physics. . . ."

Alyssa put a hand on Cash's arm and he stopped speaking, then she turned to Jess. "What makes you think—?"

"If I can get to D.C. from Utah without even trying, I
must be able to do what Quaid does with a little training.
Even a little understanding. He talked about traveling like
an electron. What does that mean?"

"Like an—" Cash frowned. "What the hell?"

They all fell quiet, but Jessica's mind was working, trying to fight the lingering pressure from her travels while
forcing her brain to wind around this bizarre concept.

"Quantum physics," Cash said, then dragged in a rough
breath, "is about how we . . . see our world. Quantum
physics says . . . we can view our world . . . through mate-
rialism, where . . . everything we know is a solid object.
Or through consciousness . . . where everything we know
is a possibility."

He paused, breathing as if he'd hiked an incline and had

to catch his breath. "In quantum physics, it is believed we . . . can find a state of consciousness where we take the possibilities . . . from each of our bodies—spirit, emotion and intuition—and convert them into actual events."

When Cash didn't go on, Jessica frowned. "I'm more confused than I was before."

"Quantum physics would say"—he wheezed in air—"that's because you're conditioned to . . . see the world from a materialist view. But, according to the theory, the reality is . . . everything is simply a matter of choice, and we choose our own reality."

Jessica was trying not to let her brain slide sideways. Quaid was a human being. If he could use this altered way of thinking to move his body through space, and she could move her spirit through space, she had to be able to make that leap in her thought process. She had to at least try.

"Kai," Teague said, "how long to get the plane ready?"

"An hour drive to the plane. Twenty minutes to get her in the air. Another two and a half hours flight time. Another thirty minutes to deplane—"

"We don't have that kind of time," she said. "So, how does quantum physics say one gets to this place where one can choose one's own reality?"

Mitch turned to Kai with one of those can-you-believe-this-shit? looks. "I'm thinking this would be a good time to rev up the plane."

Kai, looking equally dumbstruck, nodded. "Best idea you've had since I met you. I'll take care of that."

"On an altered level of consciousness," Cash rasped, his eyes falling closed. "We can't reach consciousness from a regular state of being . . . which is where we are now."

It clicked like a starburst in her brain. "Meditation."

"That's a staple of people who . . . practice quantum physics. They believe the ego holds such a tight rein on a person . . . the only way they can get past it . . . is through an altered state of consciousness—meditation, drugs, sleep, coma. . . . "

The excitement in Jessica's stomach turned to fire and burned. Quaid had dreamed of her with other men. But he hadn't been dreaming. He'd traveled and—"Oh, *God.* That's how Quaid reached me. He was asleep. I was . . . high."

Alyssa looked up from wiping Cash's face with a cool cloth. "Reached you? Where?"

Cash opened his eyes. Their blue depths were exhausted and regretful. "I'm sorry, Jess."

Loss overwhelmed her. It pushed emotions up her chest and created tears in her eyes. But she squeezed his hand and shook her head. "It just . . . is. He'll either accept it or he won't. But he won't have a choice if he's dead. So how do I do this?"

"I'd only be guessing," Cash said.

She heaved a breath and offered her own best guess. "Get into an altered state and then create my own reality?"

Cash coughed, then nodded. "That's what I'd do."

Jessica thought about where Quaid would go. If he'd gotten the neutralizer from the facility she'd just visited, he'd have been back already. So after Gorin, he'd have gone in search of . . . Schaeffer.

"Where would Schaeffer be?" She looked at the clock, thought of the day, the date. "Oh . . ." She looked at the clock again. "Shit."

"What now?" Alyssa asked.

"Schaeffer's probably headed to the speaker's dinner."

"The speaker *of the house*?" Mitch asked.

"Yes. Marc Jester. He throws a huge fall bash every year. Only the *who's who* are invited. Schaeffer was planning to attend and I was planning to stalk him."

"There's going to be a shitload of security." Mitch walked into the kitchen and pulled a beer from the refrigerator. "And, I swear, if that sonofabitch goes and gets himself taken again because he tries to walk right into that place—"

"He's smarter than that," Cash rasped.

"Good, because I'm not particularly in the mood to go pulling his ass out of the next hell hole they throw him into."

"Alyssa," Jessica said. "Can you help me? I'm going to try meditation first, but if I can't get deep enough with that, I might need you to try hypnotherapy. And you're going to have to teach me how to do it to myself because I'll have to make a stop before I can get into the party."

TWENTY-THREE

Q stared through the small glass square at Max Gorin. The man was crowded into a corner of a room barren but for a single metal bench, looking at Q as if he expected him to crash through the door and beat him to death.

"You *should* be scared, Gorin." Q slammed the door with his open palm again. Sweat slid down his face and chest. His heart beat fast and hard. His head felt light. "You created me. And if you don't tell me where that neutralizer is, I swear I'll find a way to get this door open or I'll gather enough energy to transport in there, and I'll show you just as much mercy as you've shown me over the years."

"I told Schaeffer to leave you alone." Gorin's voice came through the door high and tight. "I've been fighting to keep him from hurting you. That's why I'm in here. You should be grateful—"

Q hauled back and slammed the door with both hands. The metal rattled in its frame. "Grate-ful? *Grate. Ful?*" He had to forcibly unclench his teeth to talk. "I should be *grateful* that you stole my life? That you hurt the people I love? That you took everything that mattered away from me?"

Q looked up and down the hall. He needed something

substantial to break the glass on this door. Or something to work the hinges off.

"If you get me out—" Gorin's thin voice turned his gaze back. "If you get me out, Q, I'll help you find the neutralizer. I don't want you to die. We've come so far. We've done so much work together."

"It's Quaid," he said from behind clenched teeth, accepting Quaid's identity, even though he didn't have any idea what he was taking on. "My name is *Quaid*. I'm a person, Gorin, not a letter or a number or a fucking science project. And you'll tell me where the neutralizer is or you'll die a slow, lonely death in this room. If you think Schaeffer's coming back for you, you're wrong."

"If I tell you where it is, you'll leave me here to die anyway."

Quaid grinned. Wide and slow. "No. We have things to talk about. Lots of things to talk about. And you're staying alive until you've told me everything you've done to me over the last five years, you sick motherfucker."

Quaid's anger grew to an explosive level. He almost swore he could tear off the door with his hands. But he slammed the metal again and Gorin startled and cowered. "Where. Is. It?"

"Schaeffer has it."

"Where?"

"On him." Gorin slid his shoulder down the wall until he crouched in the corner. "It's on a key fob."

"A *what*?"

"A little gadget attached to his key ring." He turned his face toward Quaid, eyes wide with fear. "You're coming back for me."

"Tell me what you released inside us," Quaid said. "And your chances go way up."

"It wasn't me. I didn't know about it. I would never

have let them put that in you." He grew belligerent. "Who knows how that altered my tests—"

"*What* is it?"

"A bioengineered protein. I didn't create it, so I don't know the properties, but they can make it work almost any way they want. All I know is that you need to get the neutralizer to stop the chemical reaction that's been started in your body before it's done too much damage."

"Can he re-release it inside us or is it a one shot deal?"

Gorin went still. His brows fell, head tipped. "Re—? Is that what he told you?" He shook his head. "No. I hate it when he misrepresents—"

"Gorin," Quaid shouted and pounded on the door.

The man flinched and started babbling. "Once it's activated, it's activated. You either neutralize it or the subject dies. The neutralizer is simply another substance that bonds with the protein to form a different substance, one normally found in your body. When that happens, the effects of the engineered protein stop. It will take a few days for your body to recover, that's all."

Thank *God*. He was starting to believe there might be such an entity.

"When I get this fob, how do I release the neutralizer? And is there enough for both me and Cash?"

"There are two buttons—red for releasing the protein, blue for releasing the neutralizer. There are two fobs, one for you and one for Cash."

Quaid's fingers curled into his palms. "You do realize that Schaeffer's going to leave you in here to rot, right? That if you're lying to me, I'll die and no one will come back here for you. You'll starve to death. Ugly way to go."

"I'm *not lying,*" he implored.

"You'd better not be, or you'd better hope I die if you are." The thought of Cash dying made Quaid shaky with rage. "I swear to God, Gorin, if Cash dies . . ." No. He couldn't think about that. "Where is Schaeffer? Where is he? *Right. Now.*"

The sound of water in Quaid's ears grew louder; the adrenaline fizzed through his bloodstream faster. He was light. Powerful. Free.

Invincible.

He materialized, the scene coming into view as he took shape on the plane of existence he'd held in his mind as his purpose. Even before he'd fully transferred into reality, before he could move, he'd scanned the surroundings—quiet country road, rolling hills on either side, large estates dotting the tranquil terrain. And he was alone. Which was lucky, because as soon as he was one hundred percent there, Quaid dropped to his knees.

"Invincible, my ass," he rasped gripping the center of his abdomen with both hands. Pain squeezed and pulled and twisted his insides.

But it was always like that—the experience of transporting. A serious rush. He would do it even if he didn't need to go anywhere. Unfortunately, he needed to go somewhere now, but he couldn't even get up off his knees, let alone walk to the monstrous colonial estate atop a hill at least half a mile away.

In the distance, Quaid picked up the sound of an engine. A car. Luxury vehicle. No doubt headed to join the crowd already gathered at the house on the hill, where cars lined the drive and people milled on the porches and in the gardens.

Quaid took several deep breaths, forcing himself to his feet. And limped to the side of the road where he dropped on his ass beside a huge live oak. He looked up into the branches, breathing hard. And by the time the vehicle passed, Q had regained his breath and the pain in his stomach had mostly ebbed. But, shit, he was wasted. Completely wiped out. The trek to the house looked like forever instead of what should have normally been a sprint that would have barely winded him.

He thought of Cash. Wondered how badly his health had deteriorated. Quaid pressed his hands to his thighs, preparing to stand and his gaze held on his ring. His chest tightened with a myriad of conflicting emotions. His brain throbbed with even more conflicting thoughts. But the strange thing was—as angry, as hurt, as betrayed as he felt that she'd lied to him, knowing honesty was the one thing he'd needed most, the one thing he'd asked from her—he still didn't want to take the ring off. Couldn't imagine ever taking it off again.

He'd held onto that coin at the Castle because it had been the only thing in his possession that had been linked to his past, but it had never meant anything to him. This . . . He reached over and spun the band, the sensation familiar and comforting. This . . . meant everything.

Which meant he had to do what he'd come to do and then get back to her. Get back to Cash. Get back to his team. His family.

Q rose and inspected the estate on the hill. He focused on each face, searching for Schaeffer. He wasn't outside. Q peered through the windows, every detail as sharp from nearly a mile away as if he was standing in front of the house. Still, no sight of—

A man came into view at the edge of a window toward the front of the house. His height, his heavy build, the gray and black of his hair, caught Q's eye. A woman in a sparkling red dress approached from the opposite direction to shake his hand and he turned, his face coming into view—Schaeffer.

A slow smile came over Quaid's mouth. "Got you, sucker."

Only he eyed the terrain again, checked in with his body and decided that he was far too exhausted to make the hike—or would be too tired to deal with Schaeffer by the time he got there. And he needed to save his strength for the confrontation. He scouted out security and chose a location midway between two guards along the fence line among treelike shrubs.

He forced away the lingering unease and closed his eyes. His practiced mind went straight into a deep state of meditation. The sound of rushing water grew louder. The zing of adrenaline intensified until a sudden weightlessness, a tingling sense of power, came over him—that's when he knew he'd moved locations. The easing of those sensations indicated he'd landed at the site.

Quaid dropped to his knees amongst the shrubs. His belly cramped and a sweat broke out over his face, chest, and back.

"Shit," he bit out as his body cannibalized itself. "I'm going to . . . kill that fucker . . . when I get him."

By the time the pain subsided, Quaid was spent. He tried to sit up, but the muscles of his abdomen seemed to have frozen in a partial curl. The crowd of people had thickened, the sky had grown dusky with twilight and white string lights twinkled throughout the gardens. He was momentarily mesmerized by the beauty of it. The entire setting with women dressed in sparkling gowns and men in tuxedos. Couples held hands and strolled through the gardens, stealing kisses beneath the lights.

He didn't want to go through the rest of his life alone anymore. While that had been a foregone conclusion before Jessica had found him, now, looking ahead, his existence seemed barren without her.

Quaid's shoulders sagged. His head dropped and his gaze went straight to his ring again. He saw Jessica's face in his mind, eyes closed, lips slightly parted, expression angelic as she'd fallen asleep with her head on his naked belly after they'd made love the third, maybe the fourth, time. He wasn't sure; he'd been lost in such ecstasy.

He rolled onto his back and stared at the sky. Stars twinkled. If he died here, his last words to Jessica would have been angry words. His heart grew heavy, as if a rock had been set on his chest. A hollow sensation opened beneath his ribs. Followed by a dark streak of fear.

He couldn't lose her.

Motion five yards to his right startled him. Quaid scrambled back into the shrubs and stared as a vision of Jessica faded in and out of sight. That poison was either working its way to his brain or Jessica had found another element other than the coin that allowed her spirit to travel.

"Goddamnit." He closed his eyes and rested his face in his hands. He was sweating, shaking, breathing hard. He didn't have the energy or the time to fight with her again.

"Quaid." Her voice met his ears the same time something touched his shoulder.

He jerked his head up and glared at her. "Jessie, I don't need you—"

"You made that pretty clear when you vanished." She straightened and met his gaze with heat and anger. "Well, I don't need you either, Quaid. I used to think I needed you, but I was confusing want and need. Regardless, if you don't trust me, we don't belong together."

"That's not—"

Something was different about her. He narrowed his eyes, tipped his head. Then he realized what it was and his mouth dropped open.

"You . . . you're . . . *here*?"

"Yeah. I'm here. And teleporting is better than whatever that was I did in spirit, but they both still suck, and I may throw up all over you. But you can't get to Schaeffer alone. And I need this to be settled so I can figure out what I'm going to do with my life. Once I know you're healthy and safe, I can let you go to find the life you really want."

His mouth unhinged, his brain tangled. A familiar, uncomfortable craving developed low in his gut and he had to clench his hands against the desire to reach out and grab her. Because he'd come here to get the neutralizer and if he lost focus, everyone lost.

"So . . ." She squinted at the house. "You realize you can't get in there looking like that, right?" She turned her gaze on him. "Unless you have some power of invisibility that I don't know about." Then she smiled. Wry and smart-ass. And Quaid wanted to kiss it right off her mouth. "And it's by invitation only. So, unless you also have the power to create something out of nothing or can control minds—"

"As a matter of fact, I did use mind control to get my partner to turn over his beef jerky."

Her brows went up. "Oh. Well. I'll guard my jerky closely. Think you can bend minds to ignore duty? To put their own careers and lives at risk?"

He sighed heavily.

"I'll take that as a no," she said. "What do you expect to get from Schaeffer? The location of the neutralizer?"

"The neutralizer itself. Gorin told me he has it on him."

"And how do you know that's not Gorin leading you into a *trap*?"

He heard the bitterness in her voice and guilt leaked along his nerves. "Because Gorin won't get out of that cell until I have the neutralizer. It's in his best interest to tell me where it is. If going in isn't a possibility. I need a different plan."

She looked over at the house again. Quaid's gaze wandered over her beautiful profile, down the tantalizing slope of her neck. Want grew heavy in the pit of his stomach, spread down through his groin, and up into his chest.

"We can wait for him to come out," she said, "but we'd be wasting valuable time and I don't think Cash can afford it."

Quaid stiffened. "Why? He's bad?"

She looked back at Quaid, her face taut with tension, but hesitated. "You want honesty." Her eyes were serious. Matter of fact. "Yes, Quaid, he's bad. I don't know if he'll live long enough to receive the neutralizer."

Pain hit Quaid and stole his breath. He put his hands on his hips and glared at the house.

"Or, we can go in," Jessica continued, "find Schaeffer, hope your instincts on Gorin are correct and get the neutralizer."

"You just said I can't go in."

"I said you can't go in the way you're dressed."

He wiped sweat off his forehead, longing for the peace he'd experienced lying in her arms. Such ultimate peace. "That presents a problem, 'cause, yeah, I just haven't caught on to that invisibility thing yet."

"I know where we can get clothes." She considered him again. "I just don't know that you're up to it. You don't look so good and I'm not interested in getting nailed because you're off your game."

"Damn. You're harsh."

"Get used to it, Quaid—honesty is often harsh. People who care about someone sometimes spare them a truth that has the potential to cause big problems or pain but won't immediately change their life. I'll be back as soon as I can. I'm not great at this, so I need complete concentration and it takes me a while."

She walked away, shook out her arms and turned her face up to the sky.

Regret welled up and hovered like an impending wave

waiting to crash. "Jessica . . ." There was so much he wanted to say. "Where are you going?"

"To a brownstone one of my client organizations keeps for political parties and fund-raisers. We have a few extra changes of clothes there for unfortunate incidents of spills, tears, puking, etc. Wish me luck."

"Jessie . . ."

"Quaid. Please. Cash has very little time. You don't have much more. I need quiet."

Owen parked at the curb down the street from the bank. He reached across to the passenger's seat and pulled out the court order for access to Jason Vasser's safe-deposit box. Owen couldn't help but wonder if Jason had known Jocelyn was dirty. It stood to reason. Jason hadn't only been sleeping with her off and on for years, but had worked with her on many assignments.

Glancing over the document, Owen shook his head. "What a waste."

Of time. Of energy. Of focus.

Of love.

He folded the paper, slid it into the pocket of his suit jacket, and prayed this box contained something big he could hold over Schaeffer. Because Owen wanted out from under the bastard.

He pushed the door open and stood. A couple crossed the street a hundred yards away. Tall, blond male. Small, brunette female. In a split-second assessment, Owen recognized the pair: Ransom and O'Shay.

Adrenaline shot into his chest. He pulled his weapon. Rounded the back of his car while judging their trajectory toward the bank's front door. He'd go for O'Shay. Ransom was bulletproof. Literally.

Owen took one step with the intent to sprint, then froze. He was operating on automatic-damn-pilot. He wouldn't get away from the Schaeffers of the world by doing the same thing he'd always done. By doing things the way they'd told him they should be done. But he wouldn't get anywhere standing here with his gun hanging by his side either. He watched Ransom and O'Shay walk straight into the bank holding hands.

Then they were gone and it was too late to choose any plan of action—new or old.

He turned from the bank, stuffed his weapon into the holster at his hip and crossed his arms on the roof of his car. He let his eyes slide shut. Wiped sweat from his forehead.

"Nice, Owen." Well, he'd just have to do better when they came out.

He waited less than thirty minutes.

Owen balanced on the balls of his feet, muscles coiled. But he kept his body still, his mind quiet as he waited alongside a fence separating the bank's property from an alley behind a strip mall. He didn't know how O'Shay's powers worked and he didn't want her to hear him thinking or sense his agitation.

He remained cool and calm, so tranquil inside he'd forgotten how amazingly good it felt not to stress. As O'Shay and Ransom came out of the bank, Owen realized he needed to return to his Tae Kwon Do training. He needed this inner tranquility in his life.

Ransom carried a small cardboard box under his arm, his other hand holding O'Shay's. Both of them scanned the area, their steps brisk, their expressions tight.

They had something. They were nervous.

But Owen didn't get excited. Didn't let any emotion stir his insides. Only tracked the couple with his eyes as they neared him on their way to the car they'd exited. He heard the murmur of their voices as they came upon him, but not the words. He held his breath as they passed, waited half a second until O'Shay was in the perfect position and lunged.

He hadn't made a sound, but before his hand reached her arm, she turned. She had sensed him. Or heard him. Something. But, he'd expected it, and pushed his hand that extra distance to grab the collar of her jacket. He jerked her back and stabbed the gun into her neck at the same time. A sound of shock came from her throat, but she went completely still. Luke had whipped around and grabbed her arm, but it was all too late.

"Don't do it, Ransom," Owen said. Ransom's need to reach for his own weapon was written clearly in the man's expression. "Just come back here where we can talk."

With a heavy hand on O'Shay's arm, the gun digging into her skin, he dragged her backwards. Ransom followed with murder in his eyes.

"I'm fine." O'Shay's voice was rusty, her eyes on Luke. "He just wants information."

A shiver twitched beneath Owen's skin. The way she knew what was in his head was creepy as hell.

"Think about it from my perspective," she rasped. "It's pretty creepy *being* in your head. Can you ease up? I'd rather not have the tattoo of a nine-millimeter muzzle on my neck."

He stopped behind the fence and pulled back on the weapon.

"Thank you." O'Shay winced and raised a hand to rub at her neck. "Ransom, this is Owen Young. Colonel, you know Ransom."

"You're quite the little hostess," Owen said to O'Shay, but kept his gaze on Ransom.

"What the fuck do you want?" Ransom asked.

"To see what's in the box."

Ransom glanced at O'Shay. Her lips pressed tight.

"I guess I made that sound like a request," Owen said,

his voice darkening. "It wasn't. Show me what's in the box."

Ransom pulled back the cardboard top to reveal paper. They were reports or documents of some kind.

"You've obviously already gone through it. Took you forever and a damn day to come out of that bank. Don't you know I have other things to do? What's in there?"

Ransom's stance shifted into one of a hotshot cocky know-it-all. "As if you're not in on all this psychotic shit. Someone should put you bastards in one of these testing centers." He gestured with the box. "Let these psychos mess with you for a change. You are so goddamned twisted—"

A chill slid down Owen's spine. "What testing centers?"

Luke opened his mouth again, but O'Shay drew his attention with a soft, calming voice. "Ransom, wait." She paused, but Owen had no idea why. Then tilted her head toward Owen. "Show him."

Despite the incredulous look Ransom gave his lover, Owen braced for some escape routine they'd choreographed well in advance.

Ransom pulled a document bound in a black plastic report cover from the top of the box and held it out to him. "Hope you haven't eaten dinner yet."

Owen hesitated. He wasn't ready to let go of O'Shay, but he looked at the title on the cover, which read ESOPRE-VIR TRIALS, AFGHANISTAN. "What is it?"

"Drug trials," Ransom said, his disgusted tone confirming Owen's fears. "A new drug tested on a group of marines stationed in Afghanistan, colonel."

Ransom opened the report a third of the way, displaying images of men with horrendous open wounds on various areas of their bodies. Owen's stomach lurched.

"Drugs tested outside the U.S. so the manufacturer wouldn't have to deal with the expense or time restraints involved in volunteer safety." Ransom turned to another batch of images showing men with crew cuts, some in fatigues, displaying portions of a limb eaten off by disease. Owen recoiled and looked into Ransom's eyes. They burned with hatred. He hit the report pages, making the paper snap. "And look at the end result for this platoon, colonel."

He glanced down to images of a war zone—burned-out tanks, missile craters, dead bodies. "What . . . ?"

"They were disposed of," Ransom said. "Because they may have been infectious. Because the failure of this drug could not be known. So a raid was staged and the families of these men were told they died in battle."

"No." Owen shook his head, but somewhere deep inside, ice had formed. Visions of a village ravaged with oozing wounds exposing muscle and bone floated through his mind. Also the failure of a drug trial. He couldn't conceive of such things occurring regularly. Or maybe just couldn't let himself conceive of it. "This is bullshit."

"Is this bullshit, colonel?" Ransom turned to a report later in the bound volume and pointed at a signature.

Owen focused on the familiar script, which made his stomach roll and swing as if he were on a fishing boat at sea. Then he squinted to bring the name typed beneath into view: Dr. Gil Schaeffer with his title at the time of the report written below—Director, Defense Sciences Office, DARPA.

Everything inside Owen collapsed. He released O'Shay's arm and dropped his gun to his side. Taking a step back, he wiped a hand over his mouth, willing himself not to puke.

His gaze drifted to the box. "What else is in there?"

"More of these," Ransom said. "But you didn't let me tell you the best part."

Owen raised his eyes to Ransom, dread circling his belly like a vortex.

"The drugs these guys were taking?" Ransom tossed the report back into the box. "Supposedly going to amp their *psychic abilities.*" When Owen didn't respond, Ransom yelled again. "*Psychic abilities.* Schaeffer is a fucking lunatic, Young. Why hasn't anyone seen it before now? Why doesn't anyone see it *now?*"

Owen holstered his weapon. Conviction weighed like lead in his gut. He looked Ransom in the eye. "I see it." Then he turned his gaze on O'Shay. "Go. Take that shit and get the hell out of here so you can do something useful with it."

When O'Shay's mouth simply dropped open and she cast a what-the-fuck? look at Ransom, Owen yelled, "I said get the fuck out of here before I change my mind."

TWENTY-FOUR

Jessica's fingers curled into the fine fabric of the tuxedo as the sound of a crashing waterfall filled her ears. Her head went light and she had to force herself to concentrate on the spot where she'd left Quaid. No telling where she'd end up if she let her mind slip for even a millisecond. She wasn't in the mood for a side trip to Tangier or some equally remote corner of the earth just now. Maybe after this was over and she had to let Quaid go . . . again. The thought made her heart want to split open.

At least this time, she'd know he was safe. This time she'd know he had the potential to find happiness. And she'd . . . She'd just . . . Shit, she didn't know what she'd do. Maybe go back to rehab—preemptively. But she couldn't focus on that now or she wouldn't be able to put one foot in front of the other.

Finally, the sound dimmed and that sensation she'd often gotten at the first hit of any drug, started to wane. Thank God. It wasn't all that exciting now. Not now that she knew what came along with it. Not now when it brought back so many horrible memories.

She blinked as the rush faded. The night had darkened and she squinted, unable to pick Quaid out in the brush.

"Qua—" A strong hand came over her mouth, a hard

body behind hers. She stiffened, one hand reaching toward her mouth.

"Shh." He murmured at her ear, "It's me."

Relief and annoyance twined inside her. She grabbed his wrist and pulled it away. "Damn it—"

He put it back. "Security," he whispered, barely audible, "on both sides of us."

The hand over her mouth lowered, his fingers stroking her throat. His other arm circled her waist and his body fit against her backside. He was hard and his erection rode the curve of her lower spine. A mixture of sexual need and emotional craving to bond with him again on that primitive level brought tears to her eyes.

"You look beautiful," he murmured, his lips touching her ear, her neck, her shoulder.

Tortured, she pulled away, turned and held out the suit to him. "Just wait until you see the gorgeous women inside that house. I'll look like a field mouse in comparison. And I guarantee you will not go unnoticed." She forced a bright smile. "You'll have your pick. And as good as you are in bed, you won't be able to get rid of—"

His fingers dug into her bare bicep and she gasped at the streak of pain. He instantly relaxed his hold, but his eyes were fiery dark, face taut. "Jessica, I don't want anyone else," he rasped low, desperately. "Maybe I overreacted when I learned we were married. I'm sorry. I—"

He winced and bent forward, arm across his abdomen. "Fuck."

She grabbed his arms to support his weight. She wanted to believe he truly wanted only her. And she couldn't be angry with him. None of this was his fault. None of it was her fault either. She could only do what she could to make it right.

She pushed him deeper into the bushes. "Sit down."

He collapsed and Jessica crouched in front of him, a hand on his face. He was breathing fast, sweating, eyes closed. "There's no way you can do this, Quaid. You stay here, I can handle Schaeffer."

He grabbed her hand. "You can't go by yourself."

"I can't wait. If you're this bad, imagine Cash. We've all suffered enough. I'm ready to put an end to this. Rest. When I come out, you have to be ready to move again."

She took one last long look at his handsome face, her heart breaking. As she took her hand away, Quaid grabbed it. His eyes opened, exhausted, pained, and met hers.

"Jessie," he breathed. "I love you so much it scares the shit out of me. . . ." His eyes slid closed. He took a deep breath. Opened his eyes and started again. "But I never want to take this ring off. I never want another woman and I never want to be without you. Ever."

"Quaid." Her heart filled at the words she'd been waiting for, but terrified she'd never hear. "There's a lot about . . . before . . . that you still don't know. I've made a lot of mistakes. I'm not the same woman you married—"

He pulled back, dark eyes shining up at her. "Those men don't mean anything to me, Jessie. I know what we have is different. I've known from the first time you kissed me. Some part of me has always known. I think that's why it never bothered me to wait. Because some part of me knew you'd never find what we had with them."

The tears started. Her chest squeezed with both love and pain. She lifted her dress to clear her knees and knelt on the ground beside him. "It's not just that, Quaid . . ."

He laid his head back on the grass and closed his eyes in exhaustion, then forced them open again. He slid his hand down her arm to her hand and twined their fingers. "You mean the drugs?"

She bit the inside of her lip and looked away, shame pushing tears to her eyes.

"You forget, Jessie," he murmured, "I've been with you. I know about the drugs. I know about the men. And now, looking back, I know why. I know how hard you were trying to drown the pain. But even before I knew, I waited for you. Even before I knew, I never stopped wanting you. Never stopped loving you. You gave me the will to get through every day in that hell, Jess. I was even with you in the hospital that night you overdosed."

"Oh, God . . ." She covered her face with her hands. "I searched for you. When my heart stopped, I was so relieved. I was finally going to find you, be with you. I couldn't wait. But then . . ." She dropped her hands, but still couldn't bring herself to look at him. "You weren't there. I thought you'd be waiting for me, but you weren't there."

The memory of her utter devastation and hopelessness in that moment when she'd realized that she was absolutely alone came back and shot the same cold fear through her now.

"I was there," he said softly. "I just wasn't on the other side."

She looked up. "What?"

"I was standing by your hospital bed while they tried to restart your heart, calling you back. I knew if you died, I'd have lost you. And I couldn't lose you. I stayed there and willed you back to me." He squeezed her hand hard. "Some part of me was smart enough to marry you. You can bet I'm not letting you go now. You can fight it if you want, but I'm damned stubborn, Jessie. You can just forget about a divorce."

A fierce joy gripped her heart. She leaned down, took his face in both hands and kissed him. He drank her in with all the passion and love and hunger she'd come to expect from this new version of her husband.

He pushed her back by the shoulders, his eyes serious.

"And I want kids with you, Jessie. I want us to start trying for a baby. Life is too short to wait."

She laughed through her tears. Pressed her forehead to his. "We've already started."

Owen left the door of his Jeep Laredo open for the valet and jogged up the front steps of Speaker Jester's palatial mansion. A thick arm blocked him at the open double-door entrance.

"Sir," the security guard's deep voice vibrated in his wide chest, "your invitation?"

Owen stepped back and pulled his credentials from the inside of his blazer pocket while searching the milling crowd inside for his boss, Carter Cox. "I'm here to see DARPA Director—"

"I'm sorry, sir, but this is a private party," the security detail said. "If you don't have an invitation—"

"*Look* at my credentials, son. I have the authority to dispatch SEAL Team Six to nail your ass and never be questioned. Now, I'll say it one more time, and only one more time. Director Carter Cox. *Now.*"

The man swallowed. Glanced at his partner, then back at Owen. "Yes, sir. I'll go find him, sir."

This time when Owen stepped through the doorway, no one stopped him. He pocketed his creds and forced the tension from his shoulders. This was an elite group, one he knew included both Schaeffer and Cox, which was good. He could just get this over with now.

He took a glass of champagne offered by a passing waiter and drank it in one swallow. When he searched the crowd again, Cox was threading toward him with a frown on his face. "Owen. What's wrong? Do we have an emergency?"

"Not exactly, but something that couldn't wait." Owen put the glass on another passing tray. "I'm sorry to bother you off the clock, sir—"

"Ridiculous. You know there's no such thing in our work. What is it?"

"It's Senator Schaeffer, sir."

Cox glanced behind him. "I was just talking to him. . . ."

"I refuse to work for him. I'll give you more details during office hours, sir, but I just needed you to know immediately that he is asking me to conduct unethical, illegal and highly immoral acts, and I refuse."

Cox's mouth opened, his brow furrowing in confusion and disbelief. "I don't understand . . ." He collected himself. "This must be serious, Owen."

"It is, sir. I'll contact your secretary first thing when I get into the office tomorrow and make an appointment to meet with you."

Cox held out his hand and Owen shook it. "I can't wait to hear this."

"Where did you see the senator, sir? I'm going to talk to him right now."

"You are possessed when you get a bee up your ass, aren't you?" Cox chuckled and took an offered glass of champagne from another passing waiter. "He was headed toward the gardens, but was waylaid in the parlor. I doubt he made it outside yet."

Owen thanked Cox and turned toward the back of the house.

Jessica took a deep lungful of the country air and blew it out slowly. Standing at the edge of the patio in the shadows of the garden, she shook out her arms.

"I can do this." She whispered the reassurance to herself. "I can do this."

She had to do it. Quaid needed her. And she wouldn't let him down this time.

She smoothed the bodice of her dress over her abdomen, and checked the skirt one more time for dirt, grass or leaves. With the clutch holding her twenty-two clutched tight to her belly, she brought up that effervescent smile she'd used to hide the hole inside her and strolled into the crowd.

Lights twinkled in the trees. Jewels sparkled from every woman's ears, neck, hair. Dresses shimmered and glimmered. Smiles shone. She played the greeting game, so many familiar faces—some attached to good memories, some attached to ones she wished she could forget forever. But none of that mattered now, and she ignored her past, focused on her future and the one man standing in the way of that future.

After ten minutes of searching, Jessica's face was cramped from smiling. She ducked into a restroom, simply to give her facial muscles a break. Leaning on the sink, she closed her eyes. Good God, she was exhausted. The stress, the fear, the lack of sleep, the crying, they all combined and seemed to hit her when she needed stamina and strength and concentration the most.

She took a few deep breaths and stepped out of the restroom into the hall. She started toward the main part of the house and crossed another hallway, where someone collided with her.

"Oh, sorry." The man took her arms and their momentum turned her in a circle. "Hey, Jessica? Wow, you look amazing."

She stared into his face a moment, her stomach tight with apprehension. Then she recognized him and relaxed. "Sean. Hi, how are you?"

"Not nearly as good as you." His easy grin lit his face as he gave her a once-over. "Girl, that is quite a dress. Definitely your color."

"Thank you. How's Joel?" she asked of Sean's partner.

"He's fabulous. We were just talking about you the other day. Come say hello." Sean took her arm and started down the hallway.

"Oh, Sean, maybe later, I can't right now—"

"It's okay. He's right here. Just pop your head in. It will make him *so* happy."

Sean reached for a door, pushed it open and pulled Jessica inside. The room was stuffed with people. Music played in the background, and what seemed like fifty conversations filled the air. Jessica's shoulders tensed. This setting was too familiar. Her body recognized it, too. Her mouth went dry. Her nerves kicked up with anticipation. Her senses turned über-sensitive. Smell, touch, sight, hearing, taste—they all seemed tuned to their highest settings.

Sweat broke out on Jessica's neck and chest and she backed toward the door. "Sean, I can't stay. I'm sorry."

He held up a tiny bag of white powder. "A line for the road?"

Jessica froze. *Holy. Shit.* Her fingers gripped her purse until they'd gone numb. Her cottonmouth threatened to permanently meld her lips together.

She backed toward the door. "Uh, no, thanks. I . . . I . . . I . . . have to . . . to . . . meet—"

Sean put his arm around her shoulders and nudged her forward again, to where someone had already started lining out coke along a small mirror on a side table. No one around them paused to look. No one cared. They were all high, too.

Jessica stared at the pristine white powder. Couldn't tear her gaze away. Licked her lips.

It would feel so good to have energy. Energy would help her stay positive. Help her help Quaid. Help her stay strong for the days, weeks, months to come with all they still had to face. God, she was so tired.

"You look like you could use a little boost, girl." Sean pushed a rolled twenty into her hand.

Jessica found herself trapped. She couldn't use, but she couldn't walk away. She was stuck. Her feet were glued to the floor. Her gaze pinned to that perfect white line.

She didn't want this. She *didn't*. She was stronger than this. Wasn't she?

Nearby, a young woman broke from a small group, bent at the waist and vomited into a drink cup. Jessica's stomach clenched. Anxiety tightened her skin.

Sean sidestepped and blocked the sight of the retching woman. "Oh, those young ones," he said with a roll of his eyes. "Show her how a pro handles it, Jess."

She clenched her teeth, turned to Sean and pressed the twenty into his hand. Looking into his eyes, she smiled. "I'm not a pro anymore, Sean. Take care of yourself."

She turned and walked toward the door. One foot in front of the other. She expected the trek to be torturous. Instead, a sense of relief and victory rose inside her. When she reached the door and turned around for one last look, she had no desire to return to the drugs or that life. She had something far better waiting for her just beyond this house.

Back in the thick of the party, Jessica resumed her search for Schaeffer, but another ten minutes passed with no sign of him. The first tendrils of panic snaked up her chest with inevitable questions. Had he spotted her and slipped out? Was he coordinating security right now, strategizing an ambush that would render her useless to Quaid?

Then she caught sight of him on the opposite side of the room near the doors leading out to the opposite side of the gardens. Relief and renewed purpose fueled Jessica's struggle through the crowd.

Then she caught sight of Owen Young. Statuesque tall,

Tonka built, model handsome, the man was impossible to miss, even in a room as crowded as this. He stood half a head taller than most, his bright eyes intent on Schaeffer.

Jessica halted. Her fingers clutched her purse as her mind sought alternative plans. His had been the name in the assassin's head when Keira had read Alsadani's thoughts. He was working with or for Schaeffer—which didn't matter. He was involved.

"Shit," Jessica whispered. Now what? She hadn't planned on confronting *two* men. Young's name hadn't been on the attendees' list.

She started forward again, her mind circling for the information she'd learned of him over the years. So much buzz and flutter surrounded the man—from women. He was the object of many a fantasy among the women of Washington. Though, only a fantasy. He had been married for over a decade and, Jessica was pretty damn sure, faithful. If he hadn't been, she'd have heard about it. That kind of news spread through the female population of Washington like fire on gasoline.

Young worked his way through the thick crowd. He was in the midst of a divorce, she'd heard. Yet, still, no scandal. He was either stealthily discreet or . . . honorable? She couldn't help but think there had to be some level of honor in a man with his looks and his power who didn't use it as every other man in his position would. And had. But she couldn't risk Quaid's freedom on a gut feeling.

Young was farther away from Schaeffer than she was. But while she could probably reach Schaeffer first, he would be right behind her. He was stronger, far more skilled. Even holding a gun to Schaeffer's gut, she'd never escape. She'd be arrested. She'd go to jail. She couldn't care less about going to prison. She just couldn't go until *after* she'd gotten that neutralizer to Quaid.

She slid her hand into her purse, her finger into the trigger of her gun, and continued pushing through the crowd.

Halfway to Schaeffer, who stood laughing with Congressman Scott O'Reilly, Jessica glanced at Young again. He swept the crowd, and his gaze collided with hers. She felt the physical *snick* in her chest, like the chambering of a round.

He stopped. Stared. Shot a look toward Schaeffer, then darted narrowed eyes back at Jessica.

Desperation pumped adrenaline into her body. She could beat him there. She was smaller. She had more incentive.

Jessica turned sideways, put her head down and shouldered through the crowd. "Excuse me. I'm sorry. Excuse me."

With her heart ready to explode, every breath labored and quick, she reached Schaeffer quicker than she'd expected. She'd lost track of Young and didn't bother looking for him now. She stepped right into the middle of Schaeffer's conversation, positioned her purse against his rotund belly, and looked him directly in the eye.

Shock rounded his muddy brown gaze, followed by what she swore was a spark of fear. It gave Jessica a cocaine-worthy thrill. Screw the drugs, this was just as good. She put on her best smile, and this time she didn't have to work for it. This was a smile of vengeance.

Jessica sent the other man a sidelong glance, "Congressman O'Reilly, if you don't mind, the senator and I have an important matter to discuss."

"Of course, Jessica." The older man patted her shoulder. "You look beautiful, sweetheart. Dora is here tonight. She'd love to see you."

"And I'd love to see her. I'll find her as soon as I'm finished here."

Schaeffer's eyes seemed to plead with O'Reilly not to

go, but the congressman moved on, leaving Jessica and Schaeffer in a cocoon surrounded by people. She didn't waste any time, sure Young's hand would land on her shoulder any second.

She jammed the gun into his belly and received a satisfying grunt. The anger that shot through his eyes thrilled her. "It may feel small, Gil, but I promise fifteen hollow points into your belly will not leave you feeling pretty."

The anger on his face edged toward fear again. That gave her the confidence to reach out with her other hand and feel for his pants pockets. Nothing there but mounds of fat. She grabbed the right pocket of his blazer. Through the fine fabric, something small and hard met her fingers. She felt farther down the length and found keys.

"You may have just saved your life, Gil." Yanking it from his pocket, she held the fob up so she wouldn't have to take her eyes off him.

"If you choose the wrong button, Jessica"—Schaeffer's voice had that smooth-as-glass, cold-as-ice chill that made him famous on the Hill— "you'll give your long-lost husband an extra dose of bioengineered proteins that will kill him instantly."

A steel band squeezed Jessica's chest. Her hand shook when she raised her purse and the muzzle of the weapon beneath to the center of the abdomen and whispered, "Then you'd better tell me which button is the right one, Gil, because if Quaid dies—*again,* I have nothing left to lose, nothing left to live for, and no reason not to pump these fifteen bullets into your belly and watch your stomach acid fry your guts."

His condescending smile shivered, then fell. His clouded eyes searched frantically over Jessica's shoulder.

She jabbed the weapon into Schaffer's gut before Young or some other security guard grabbed her neck. "Which one is it, Gil?"

He licked his lips, his eyes studying hers. "Red," he bit out. "Red, goddamnit. Now take that gun off me."

Gorin told me the blue button was the neutralizer, Quaid had said. *I'm nothing but a witness to Schaeffer.*

Jessica put her thumb over the blue button and turned it toward Schaeffer. His eyes went wide with panic. Even as his mouth formed the word *no,* Jessica had all the confirmation she needed, and jammed down the button on the remote control.

With relief and triumph and hope pulsing through Jessica's body, she punched the gun into his stomach and cut off the snarl forming on his lips. "Shut up, Gil."

She searched his other pocket, found another fob, and pressed the blue button. Holding both tight, she used the weapon still hidden inside her clutch to push Gil toward the back door. "Outside."

"Why?" Gil's eyes burned with rage. "You got what you wanted."

"Oh, no, Gil. This is just the beginning. And you're not leaving my sight until I know the neutralizer worked."

With the weapon pointed at his side, her other hand wrapped around his arm as if she were accompanying him out to the gardens, Jessica smiled at guests and acquaintances as they made their way through the room.

They stepped through the doors without incident and continued past the guests enjoying the warm evening. Storm clouds hovered half a mile off like a warning to Jessica of her unstable emotional state. As if she needed a reminder.

Her tension increased with each step closer to the edge of the patio and that space that lay between the security of the crowd and Quaid. She wasn't a warrior like the other members of the team had become over the years. She was just Jessica. As soon as she knew Quaid was feeling the effects of the neutralizer, she could relax. She could give him the gun and call the others to find out how close they were. Mitch and Kai would show up first. Hopefully soon.

"Where are we going?" Schaeffer demanded.

"As soon as I see that Quaid's all right, we can go our separate ways," she lied. The crowd thinned and her hand tightened on the weapon. "Remember, Gil, Keira taught me to shoot. Don't test me if you want to keep your balls."

"Your career is over, Fury," he growled. "I will bury you."

"You should be more concerned about your life at the moment." They were finally alone, standing at the border of the patio, the party noise and lights dim behind them. She stepped away from him and nudged his side. "Go. Straight ahead. And the name's Legend. Mrs. Legend, you asshole."

"I can't see anything out there," Gil said, incensed as if this was all one big inconvenience. "It's all *dirt*."

"Put one Ferragamo in front of the other, Gil." She clenched her teeth. *"Go."*

He gave an irritated huff, looked down at his feet where the patio ended and the darkness began and stepped off the edge. He grunted and went down on one knee. His black suit disappeared against the black dirt. Jessica gripped her weapon tighter and tried to track him.

A hand darted out of the dark and grabbed her ankle. Jerked. Jessica went down hard. She rolled to her side, scrambled to her hands and knees and kicked off his grasp. She lunged and she clutched the purse still holding her gun.

A shoe came down and crushed her wrist. Jessica cried out. Another hand gripped her chin and jerked her head up, cutting off her scream. She opened her eyes to a different face, one she didn't recognize, but which terrified her.

"Hello, *Mrs. Legend.*" His voice, cold and pleased, raised the hair on her neck. "You don't know me, but I'm a friend of your husband's. The name's Green. Your husband likes to call me Ice Man."

TWENTY-FIVE

Without warning, a cool wash of relief spread through Quaid's body. It loosened all his muscles. Wiped out every ache, every pain. The reprieve was so unexpected, so sudden and so absolute, Quaid thought he'd died. That his body had given up and let go, but his mind just hadn't figured it out yet. He'd read somewhere that there was a seven-minute lag time for the brain to recognize the body had died.

He opened his eyes. Clouds, lighter than the sky, drifted in, covering the sparkling stars. He wouldn't see that if he was dead, would he? Quaid lifted his head. Looked at his hands. At his legs. Then he tried to move, pressing his hands to his thighs and pushing to his feet. No pain. But one hell of a lot of fatigue. His muscles felt as soft as butter.

"Sir."

The authoritative voice put a dead stop to Quaid's growing relief.

"Sir," the voice said again, closer now. "This is a restricted area. You need to return to the house."

Quaid dropped into character, a manipulation technique he'd been taught by one of the best ex-CIA operatives. Or so Gorin had told him at the time. The man had taught Quaid how to fool anyone into believing anything he wanted them to believe.

There was so much still to unlock within his mind, but even after the short hypnosis session with Alyssa, Quaid had a hell of a lot more tools at his disposal than he'd had before.

He let his weak muscles work for him as he turned to look at the security guard approaching. "Oh, hey, dude." He wiped a hand over his face and struggled to get to his feet. "Sorry, man. Sorry. I just, you know, drank too much and it was so hot in there. I just came out to get some air . . . and . . . Where am I again?"

"The speaker's dinner." The guard's tone held reproach. "Speaker of the House—"

"Ah, yeah." Quaid snorted out a drunken laugh. "Jester. Now I remember."

The guard stopped five feet away and watched him struggle. "You can't be out here."

"Yeah, sure, I got it. But I'm pretty damn sure I can't get to where I'm supposed to be by myself."

The guard put his hands on his hips, sighed and looked in both directions. "I'll help you to your feet, but you're on your own after that."

"Sure, sure. Hey, thank you, man, thank you."

The guy put his hand out, but Quaid needed him a lot closer. He reached for the guy's hand and purposely missed. The impatient guard grabbed Quaid's arm and dragged him up. Staying loose brought Quaid's body up against the guard. In three seconds, Quaid had his weapon. He gripped the man's jacket, shoved him back and delivered a hard chop to the side of his neck.

The man's eyes rolled back in his head and his body went limp. Quaid wasn't strong enough to catch him, so he broke his fall, then dragged him up beside the house. The guy would have one hell of a headache when he woke, but it was better than the alternative Q could have used.

He pushed aside the roiling unease surfacing with the memories and looked through the nearest window. Jessica was gone. Schaeffer was gone.

"Shit."

He forced his feet into a jog along the edge of the house. By the time he turned the first corner toward the patio, he had to put his hand against the siding to keep his balance. When he'd found his footing, he looked up and directly into Jessica's face.

He'd assessed the entire situation within two seconds— four men, all armed. Jessica, unarmed. Held hostage with a gun at her head. By Green. Ice Man Green. And that's where his mind slid off the rails.

"Jess, transport," was all he got out before his lungs seized up.

"I tried," she said, struggling against Green's hold.

"We meet again, Q." Green's arm was tight around Jessica's waist, pulling her back and up against his body. He tilted his chin, staring down at her from his nearly four-teen-inch height advantage. "And now I've met your *very lovely* wife." His big hand opened wide over her abdomen and slowly slid lower. "No wonder Q was so juiced to escape. I'd want to get back to a hot little thing like you, too."

A feral mewl came from Jessica's throat.

"Quiet now," he whispered, his gentle tone so twisted in opposition to his violence.

"Don't," Quaid ordered.

Jessica grabbed Green's wrist and tried to shove it away. Green chuckled, as if he were indulging a child, and smacked Jessica's temple with his weapon. Her head snapped sideways. She muffled a cry in her throat.

"Good girl," Green said in a low growl near Jessica's ear.

Quaid wasn't sure how he moved so fast, but in the next moment, he was within two feet of Green, the gun he'd stolen from the security guard point blank at Green's forehead. And the first look of shock Quaid had ever seen rounding Green's icy blue eyes.

"Let. Her. Go."

"Or what? If you shoot me, I shoot her. Lose, lose, Q."

He took a step closer. "It's *Quaid*."

A car approached from behind. Quaid's blood boiled. "Tell them, Green," he said. "If they shoot me, you're dead."

"Enough," Schaeffer barked. "In the car."

No one but Schaeffer moved, opening the passenger's side door. "If you want your wife safe, Q, drop the gun and get in the car."

Jessica sucked in an audible breath. Her eyes rounded and pinned on Quaid's face. He couldn't look at her. He'd already been contemplating the trade in the back of his mind, hoping there would be some moment of opportunity when he could get the upper hand. With Green involved, he should have known better.

Green tightened his arm around Jessica's waist, pulling her backside into his hips. "I'm kinda hoping you make the wrong choice here, Q. I'd much rather have her than you."

"Let her go *now*." Quaid took a shaky breath and his chest closed in on him. "And . . . I'll . . . go."

"No—" Jessica didn't get the scream out before Green slapped a hand over her mouth. The sound of flesh on flesh stung and knotted Quaid's stomach. Beneath Green's hand, Jessica continued to plead with Quaid.

"Put down your weapon, Q," Schaeffer said. "Don't give me trouble here. That will only lead to a whole lot of trouble for every member of your team—Cash, Jessica, you. Green will let Jessica go. Then you get in the car. That's fair."

Fair. Quaid caught a bitter retort in his throat. He couldn't stand to see Jessica tortured or threatened another minute. He gritted his teeth, turned the gun sideways and crouched to lay it on the ground.

With Jessica's pleas filling his head, thoughts of the past five years floating in the background, it took everything Quaid had to let go of that gun. As Q, he would have taken death. As Q he would have killed as many of these fuckers as he could on his way out. As Quaid, he couldn't endanger Jessica that way. He couldn't let that be her last memory of him.

As soon as the gun left Quaid's hand, Green shoved Jessica aside. He strode directly to Quaid and planted a fist into his gut so hard Quaid's spine rippled with the shock. He was still coughing, gagging and wheezing for air when Green pushed him into the car.

"No!" When Jessica finally had the ability to scream, she couldn't draw in enough air to make it worthwhile. All the car doors closed. The engine revved. And the same fiery panic that had terrorized her in the warehouse looking into Quaid's eyes as he lay broken on the cement floor blazed through her body now.

"No, no, no, no, *no!*" She rooted on the ground for her purse. Sank her fingers into the beaded fabric and ripped the gun out, aimed and fired at the retreating taillights. And fired. And fired.

When a hand covered hers, she looked up at Mitch and realized she was still sitting on the ground. Wallowing in the dirt like a pig. And didn't give a goddamn.

"Quaid," she panted. "They . . . they took him. Mitch, *they took him!*"

Mitch looked to his right, to someone Jessica hadn't noticed—Owen Young. "Are you going to take care of this or am I?"

"I got it." Owen turned and walked away.

Rage ignited inside Jessica. Propelled her to her feet.

Kai grabbed her arm. "Hold it together, Jess. We'll get him back."

She pushed him away and twisted toward Young. He'd stopped near the house and spoke on his phone. Beyond him a crowd had gathered. People stared in horror out the windows and into the darkness.

"What is he doing?" Panic clawed at her. She felt like she was drowning. She turned to the man that pulled miracles out of his ass. Mitch threw a set of keys to Kai, who was already running toward the front of the house. He caught them like a pro receiver and disappeared into a sea of cars.

"Mitch!" Jessica put her hands to her head. She was still holding the gun. "What the fuck?"

Mitch took her by the arms and bent to look directly into her eyes. "Kai's going after them. Young's on our side for the moment. Hold it together, Jess."

He released her as if he had the utmost confidence she was going to do just that. But she couldn't even breathe. Couldn't breathe. Rain pelted her face. Hard and cold.

She turned and sought out the car's taillights. Futility and confusion and despair instantly turned to white-hot rage. Goddamned sonofabitch. That fucker would not take Quaid from her again. He would *not*.

Lightning streaked the sky. Thunder clapped so loudly her ears nearly exploded. Her body quaked. The ground shook. The air quivered. And that's when she knew—she didn't need stillness and inner quiet to harness the weather the way she did to transport. Just the opposite.

She let go—let all her fears rise to the surface, let all her anguish overwhelm her, let all her fury roil and rage.

Her focus narrowed until all she could see was the dwindling sight of the car with her husband inside. Overhead, lightning streaked through clouds even darker than the night sky. Jessica pushed them with her mind toward the vehicle. She tried to control the car with the power of the wind. The car slowed, but didn't stop.

Fear whipped inside her. "Why doesn't he transport?"

"They drugged him." Mitch's voice penetrated her focus. She looked at him, as if he'd appeared out of nowhere. She'd forgotten everything and everyone around her. He was soaked. Water streaked down his face. "He can't transport, Jess. Not unless they tell him to. You know they drugged him the second they had him. He's too powerful for them to control otherwise."

"*What* can I do that will stop *them* but won't hurt *him*?"

Owen stepped up next to Mitch, his light eyes bright in the darkness. "I've dispatched Black Hawks from Bolling Air Force Base. They'll be on them in ten minutes."

"Brilliant." Mitch cut Owen an angry glare. "And Quaid will be dead in eleven."

Jessica twisted toward the road, stomach tight. She had to do what she could. Hurt was better than dead. She refocused on the heat of the storm and the electric currents flashing bright in the dark clouds. She focused her energy on redirecting the current downward. And added fear. Added pain. Added anger.

Lighting cut and cracked throughout the sky. Thunder roared like a beast. Jessica brought the storm down on the car like an avenger.

A series of bolts nailed the car. Huge sprays of sparks arced off the metal. The car swerved, slowed, but picked up speed again in a frantic pattern. They had a good lead on Kai, as he raced behind them.

"The lightning won't produce the damage you want," Mitch said from beside her. "The car is too protective."

"It's all I have."

"If you can angle it through the windshield the metal

won't protect them." Mitch gave her a serious sidelong glance. "And maybe you could turn Green and Schaeffer into French fries."

"What about Quaid?"

"He's in the back. Probably passed out on the seat or the floor."

Jessica growled through her teeth. She wanted to dig her teeth into something, claw at something. She wanted to draw blood.

The image of Quaid attacking Alsadani flashed in her head. She remembered the sight of him slamming Alsadani up against that ravine wall over and over. Like a rabid animal. Because, she could see in hindsight, he'd feared for the team's safety. For her safety.

Now she was living that rabid sensation. The need to do whatever it took to protect Quaid.

The rightness of it fused all the loose ends inside her. Quelled all her uncertainties. Calmed all her fears of wrong versus right. And solidified her will to fight for Quaid to the very end.

She reset her feet in the mud. Locked her elbows and knees. Fisted her hands. And focused.

Quaid floated in that place again—the one somewhere between waking and sleep. But this was different. Here he didn't drift on serene waves, but got tossed on dark, angry seas. Anxiety surrounded him like a bubble, filling him with fear and desperation. As if he was needed somewhere and couldn't get there. As if his very sanity depended on getting out of this chaos but was trapped.

Light burst behind his closed eyelids—one blinding flash, followed by a waterfall of tiny lights. A hard clack and roar rolled over Quaid before fading, an invisible dragon drawing near. He was thrown one way. Jerked another. Pain crushed his shoulders, stabbed his ribs, rammed his skull. But the ache that threatened to kill him was the one ripping at him from deep within.

A startling crackle filled Quaid's ears, followed by a cacophony of voices, all shouting yet muted, blended, as if he were listening underwater. And something was burning. Then he was spinning. And spinning. And spin—

Smash. Crash. Bounce. *Smash. Crash.* Rock.

Everything went still. Everything went quiet.

Quaid drifted back into that sea of anxiety. He wanted out. He wanted to go back to where he'd been, but he couldn't remember where that was.

He put all his focus into opening his eyes. Nothing happened. He worked to move his hand. No go.

Fumes drifted into the car. Gasses from whatever was burning. Something toxic that made Quaid's stomach roll. A groan met his ears. His groan. That was a good sign. Right? And so was the fresh, wet air whisking in from somewhere nearby. And the sweet, soothing sound of rain pinging against metal. So beautiful. It reminded him of something, but he couldn't remember what. Still, he smiled internally.

A revving car engine drifted to his ears. He tried his eyes again. Concentrated all his energy on sliding his eyelids up. They fluttered, but didn't move. He drifted. Came back to the distant sound of helicopters. Apaches . . . no. Black Hawks. Three.

Light drifted in from somewhere. Faint. Gentle. Then distant voices.

The car came up fast and skidded to a stop. There came the click of a door and footsteps so crisp, so loud in the silent night.

Footsteps ceased. Heavy breathing filled the space. The crush of glass. Pressure on Quaid's neck.

"Fucking A, Legend." A man's voice—a familiar voice— hit his ears. "You are the biggest pain in the ass."

Quaid didn't know why that struck him as funny, but he wanted to laugh. He couldn't remember the last time he'd wanted to laugh. Yes, he could. It had been with Cash. Or no, maybe Jessica.

Cash. Jessica.

A fist gripped his heart. He sucked in air, the sound loud to his own ears.

"Hold on, buddy. You're okay."

Kai. It was Kai.

"Let me drag some of this dead weight out of the way . . . no pun intended . . ." But he gave a dark chuckle that linked to something in Quaid's memory. Something he didn't like. "And I'll get you out. But don't fucking move, moron. Foster borrowed this car and it doesn't have shit in the way of emergency gear. Last thing I need is you tweaking your neck, freaking paralyzing yourself and having to listen to Jess bitch at me for the rest of her life about all the *amazing* sex I cheated her out of."

Jessica. The image of Green, with his hands on her, that dark chuckle—

His muscles flexed and he sat upright on a wheezing indrawn breath. His head floated off his shoulders. He gripped a seat back to steady himself.

Kai dropped a body to the pavement, turned back to the car and froze. "Fuck me," he muttered. "Legend, what in the hell did I just tell you? What part of *don't fucking move* didn't you understand? *Lie down*."

"Sorry, chief." The words scraped out of Quaid's throat. They felt awkward. Foreign. Kai must have found them odd, too, because he looked up from assessing Quaid's legs and abdomen for injuries with an almost haunted look in his eyes. But Quaid pushed forward with what he needed to know. "Jessie. Where's Jessie?"

"I'm right here."

Her voice sounded behind Kai, and he jumped clear

out of the car's open doorway. Stumbling backwards, he swore in combinations Quaid had never heard.

"Where the *fuck* did you come from?" Kai finally said from somewhere behind the car.

And there in the doorway, silhouetted in the lights from the other car, Jessica stood soaked to the bone. Smeared with mud. His body softened with relief. He clenched the seat tighter to stay upright.

"I transported," she said, tucking her dripping hair behind her ears. "Once I got my shit together, I mean."

"Are you . . . ?" Quaid took a breath, growing light-headed again. "Are you okay?"

Those big, worried brown eyes warmed with her slow smile. "I'm supposed to be asking you that."

His muscles gave in to relief and he slid back to the floor with a groan. "Jessie, come here. I need to touch you."

She crawled onto the backseat and looked down on him where he lay on the floor of the car with the uncomfortable hump in the foot well jabbing his back. Her face was mottled with mud, her hair dripping wet, her smile the brightest he'd ever seen.

And she'd never looked more beautiful.

The *whap* of the Black Hawks' blades came close. It was a nice sound. The sound of safety. The sound of brotherhood. The same kind of brotherhood he'd found here with his team.

He'd never felt luckier.

More cars. More lights. More people.

Mitch crossed his arms on the roof of the car and peered in at Quaid. "Kai wants off my shit list. After this stunt, I might just let you take his place."

"Yes," Kai hissed, a fist in the air.

Beside Mitch, another man appeared. A man Quaid didn't know, which made him instantly tense. Jessica murmured reassurances.

Quaid's gaze found hers. "Gorin. You have to get to Gorin. I have to know about all those years—"

"Gorin's dead." The stranger offered this information with a stern face, but curious eyes. "I'm Owen Young. I had to take a look at the man that's caused such a stir. Officially unimpressed. Gorin died the same way Alsadani died. Get your ass out of here." He turned to Mitch. "I'll clean this up. You all clear out and stay low profile. And when I say low, Foster—"

"I hear you. I hear you."

"Until I contact you." Owen put a finger to Mitch's chest. "Stay available."

"Yes, sir. And you'll let me know about Dubrovsky," Mitch said. "And Schaeffer."

Owen grinned. "Yes, sir."

When Mitch stuck his head into the car again, Quaid asked, "What about Schaeffer?"

Mitch glanced toward the front passenger's seat where Schaeffer had been sitting. "He survived the crash. The other three are dead. I'm hoping he makes it so I can clip electrodes to his balls and get some questions answered." His gaze rested on Jessica and he tilted his head toward Quaid. "Is there anything wrong with him?"

Her eyes danced to his as she sputtered, "That's a loaded question."

Quaid used the last bit of his strength to yank on the arm he still held and pulled her off the seat and on top of him, where he found her mouth and kissed her quiet.

"I guess that answers my question," Mitch said. "Get your filthy, soaked asses in my car before the cops get here."

Mitch disappeared and they were alone. Quaid pulled back from the kiss, laid his head on the floor and gazed at the dented roof.

"Gorin's dead." Disappointment and anger slipped into Quaid's relief. "There's still so much I don't know."

Jessica took his face in her hands. "We'll find your answers, Quaid. Gorin isn't the only person who knows what happened to you. And there's Trent. Alyssa can help you find him. Help him."

Despair slipped away and hope filled the space. He kissed her. "I want to know about my past, and I will find Trent. But what really matters to me is everything from this day forward. I want to start making memories, Jessie. New memories. *Our* memories."

Her smile grew, her eyes filled with joy and she nodded, pressing her forehead to his.

"One more question." His warm breath brushed her cheek. "Why is your last name Fury and not Legend?"

She pulled back to look in his eyes. "Because we wanted to stay on the hazmat team together and the department had a policy that spouses couldn't be stationed at the same firehouse or serve on the same team. We had a small, quiet wedding and were keeping it secret for as long as it lasted."

His mouth twisted up at one corner and he cupped her face in his hand. "I love your name. Maybe we can use it to name our first baby girl. But . . . I want you to have my last name. Marry me, Jessie. Again," he whispered, his heart beating in his throat. "I want to carry that day with me. Always."

She pulled back, caressed his face with her gaze. "I will absolutely marry you—again. And we'll make all new memories."

He kissed her, slowly and sweetly. When she looked down on him again, her eyes glistened a warm, rich cinnamon brown. Eyes he recognized deep in his soul.

And Quaid knew exactly where he would always belong.

Read on for a sneak preview of the next in the Phoenix Rising series, *Shatter,* coming in January.

Heather Raiden sat on the floor of her darkened home, sandwiched between the arm of her sofa and the wall of windows looking out over the western most portion of Lake Washington, Seattle. She rested her arms on her upturned knees and watched the stalker where he huddled in the metal dingy he'd rented from a local sport's outfitter under the name Dane Zimerelli. The black BMW he was driving had been rented under the same name at the airport with an unspecified return date.

She lowered the glasses and stared out at the one a.m. blackness. "I hope you're freezing his balls off out there, asshole."

Three nights. He'd been out there watching her house for three nights. Had dropped anchor in the perfect location to view Heather's living room, kitchen and bedroom, all on the lake-side of the property. He probably had a glimpse the driveway as well and had been watching her comings and goings.

"Maybe I got lucky and he's a run of the mill rapist or serial killer."

At her elbow, Dexter whined. She ran her hand along the Sheppard's silky-soft fur. "You're right, Dex. I'm not that lucky."

Resting her hand on the dog's shoulders, she looked

into his golden brown eyes and sighed heavily in resignation. His brows moved with his darting gaze, making him look truly worried. He was an incredibly sensitive animal, frighteningly intelligent.

"This is obviously a problem," she told him, her mind winding around and around solutions she'd already considered. Cops would brush her off. Private investigator would take time. Ignoring the Zimerelli dude had potentially lethal consequences. She'd trained seven long years to prevent lethal consequences. Training she had, admittedly, hoped never to use. But deep down, she'd known they'd come for her some day. "I can't let it go on."

She hurried through the darkness to her bedroom with Dex's nails clicking behind her on the hardwood. When she stepped through the door, he pushed past her, jumped on the bed and lay in that alert pose, head up and watching her every move. "I can't just sit here and wait until it's too late," she told Dex. "Let him plan. Let him call in reinforcements. The last seven years will have been wasted if I don't *act* now. All my sacrifices wasted."

She dropped her hands to the sink and closed her eyes, absorbing the weight of loss that always came with the thought. So many sacrifices. But only one she regretted. Only one that haunted her.

Already dressed in black, Heather slipped on the black, lightweight sport shoes and tightened the laces. In the bathroom, Heather wrapped her long hair into a bun.

Resigned, focused, Heather headed for the door leading to the garage and pulled her slim black jacket from the peg. She slipped it on, crouched in front of Dex standing faithfully at her feet and hugged him tight.

"*Yalyublyutebya,*" she said in Russian, then repeated it in English with more emphasis because once just didn't feel like enough. "I love you so much, sweet boy."

With a kiss to the side of his face, she stood, met his eyes

and firmed her voice when she commanded him to protect the property. *"Zashchita."*

In the garage, Heather located her black canvass duffle
at the base of the stairs. A fine adrenalin buzz sang through
her blood and made her breath come faster. The duffle's
zipper sounded like ripping fabric and tension pulled at
Heather's skin. Crouching with a flashlight held between
her teeth, she pulled the Sig Saur forty-five semi-auto from
the bottom of the bag and check the remaining contents—
lock hacker, silencer, extra ammo magazines, rags, bleach-
laden wet wipes, latex gloves. With a jerk of the zipper and
a tug on the car door handle, she was ready to launch.

As she turned the key in the engine of her BMW.
Heather experienced a tangle of deep, complex emotions—
fear, resignation, and the dark thrill of power. Of taking
control over her life.

The door rumbled open and Heather backed from the
garage. Raindrops tattered against her roof, splashed her
windshield. "He's gonna be so cold by the time he reaches
the dock his dick is going to snap like an icicle."

She left her sleepy Laurelhurst neighborhood for the
streets bordering the University of Washington, still dotted with cars and pedestrians. After locating his rental, she
parked a block down and turned off her car to wait.

Fear drummed its fingers on the back of her neck.
What-if's teased her mind into tangles. Her schooled
neighbors would take care of Dex if anything happened to
her. She'd set up charitable trusts to receive her assets. But
having her death in order didn't help her face the possibility.

Zimmerelli finally emerged from the dark lake's surface.
He jogged to his car wearing a dark parka, the hood pulled
over his head and carried only a backpack over one shoulder. The lights of his car blazed on and Heather's heart
surged with adrenaline. Dual jolts of excitement and fear

shot through her belly. She waited until he'd driven a block before following. Waited another block before turning on her headlights.

Her first step was to identify him. Then identify his purpose for stalking her. If she got beyond that without a deadly confrontation, she would consider digging into his role in her exposure. But if Zimerelli had been sent by whom she was almost certain he'd been sent by, they'd never get past the confrontation.

His BMW turned toward a business district with shops and restaurants and bars.

"Probably needs a few drinks to warm himself up." Better for her. He'd be off his game if he was drunk. Slower. Sloppier.

But he bypassed all the watering holes and made another turn into The Summit Hotel's parking lot. Heather pulled to the curb until he'd parked, then backed into a spot fifty yards away beside a large commercial van.

"Nice place for a stalker," she murmured, shutting down the car and taking hold of her Sig.

A newer hotel, the rooms here were all high-end suites, clustered half a dozen to each small. Lucky for her, she knew the rough layout of the suites. Lucky for her, the rooms were large, the buildings insulated from each other by the ample landscaping and surrounding forest. Lucky for her, the grounds were deserted, the other units dark.

The rain had stopped and parking lights cast oval pools of warm light at scarce intervals. When the man stood from his car, his hood was down and his hair looked as black as the wet asphalt. But that's all she could see of him as he set a purposeful stride toward the buildings. His height and the fluid, strong way he moved suggested he was youthful and fit and wouldn't be an easy take down.

She reached across the console and found the silencer inside her duffle without taking her eyes off Zimerelli.

When he'd disappeared inside, she pulled her lock-picking kit from the bottom of her bag and slipped it into one pocket, latex gloves in the other, still watching the room. Lights filled the windows. Blinds lowered.

Heather knew exactly where he was headed. She'd spent enough time on the lake in those frigid conditions know how he'd warm himself up—the shower. He'd turn it on hot and he'd let the water pound him until he stopped shivering.

To calm her growing jitters, she closed her eyes and visualized every step of her plan. Get in, look around, grab information, shoot him—if necessary—and get out.

Before she let her mind sabotage her, Heather climbed from the car, scouting the parking lot for witnesses. She was alone. No security cameras. She pushed the Sig into the waistband of her leggings, then followed Zimerelli's path.

At the hotel room door, Heather tilted her ear close and concentrated on the sounds within. A running shower eased a sliver of tension in her shoulders and made her breath hitch with relief.

She crouched and unrolled her lock picking kit on the welcome mat, praying this hotel lock was one of the millions worldwide that would break under her hacking device. She thought of Dex and her heart pinched. She thought of how she'd lose her job if she were arrested.

"Stop thinking." She shut out all the what-if's and fears and focused on the thin, palm-sized electronic device. A quick connect to the door handle and she held her breath as she connected the second cord to the unit.

A green light appeared above the door handle. Her heart jumped. *Yes.*

She turned the handle slowly, silently, easing the door open a crack and found the security slide in place. Her stomach dropped. She traded the device for a flexible piece of plastic from the kit, slid it into the open space and finessed the slide's arm over the metal ball.

When the door pushed free, a painful wash of relief slid through her body. She slipped inside the room and the relief instantly faded, replaced by the kind of fear that came when she was in way over her head.

Okay, skip the shooting part. Just find out who he is and get out. Deal with the rest after you're gone.

Yes, far more realistic. It was one thing to be trained, another to have experience. She had none of the later.

Heather darted directly to the backpack sitting on a side table, flipped the pack over and dumped the contents on the bed. Extra clothes, bottle of water, notebook, pen, flashlight, power bars, instant warming packs. No ID.

Shit.

She opened closets and drawers—nightstand, dressers, desk. Nothing. No wallet, no luggage tags, no receipts. Time for plan C. Unfortunately, she didn't have one.

"Shit," she whispered, her gaze locked on the bathroom door.

Just do it. Don't think.

Heather held her Sig ready and turned the bathroom knob with the other. As she inched the door open, steam poured out. She slipped into the humid, clouded room and closed the door.

Everything was bright white—white marble floor, white granite counters, white sinks with chrome fixtures, white toilet, white spa-type tube with an arched chrome shower curtain rod and a pristine white shower curtain, and a full wall of mirrors.

In stark contrast a pile of black clothes sat in a rumpled pile at the base of the shower. And a black 9mm Beretta lay on top. The weapon would have blended right in with the fabrics if it weren't for the shine of moisture on metal. And the gun was just a quick reach beyond the curtain.

With her own weapon pointed at the shower and her heart knocking hard against her chest, she crossed the marble tile and grabbed the gun.

Mitch Foster stood under the shower's hot spray long after he'd cleaned off, trying to raise his body temperature. His fingers and toes were ready to fall off from hypothermia.

He turned the shower's massage setting to *hammer* and steamy water thumped his neck, shoulders and back, all the areas where most of his tension gathered. There and at the center of his chest, beneath his ribs.

Tomorrow, first thing, he'd confront her. He couldn't wait for this Dexter dude to show up any longer. The guy had to be away on business. Or maybe he and Halina were on the outs. Mitch would just have to take the chance of confronting both her and her boyfriend.

A sound tugged at his ear. A sound outside the shower. His thoughts evaporated and the hair on his neck prickled into tiny needles. The skin across his shoulders rippled with gooseflesh. He eyed his clothes pile through the inch gap between the curtain and the wall. Mitch eased his hand through the space and felt for the gun.

He realized it was gone at the same moment the shower curtain whipped aside. Shock blazed over his spine in a hot wave. He straightened with his hands half way up in a partial surrender.

"Fucking sonofabitch," he said, letting his frustration out in his voice. "You don't even have the decency to wait until a guy is dressed?"

The threat was hidden among the steam filling the room. The water dripping in his eyes, didn't help. But whoever it was had dressed in black head to toe, and he was small.

"You afraid I'm too much of a threat under normal circumstances?" he asked. "Pretty chicken shit, dude. If you walk away now, I won't tell your boss how badly you handled this."

Mitch shook his head like a wet dog, flinging water across the bathroom. A surprised sound came from the intruder's direction. A sound that spiked shock and a whole different kind of fear through his body. A high-pitched, *female* sound.

He wiped the water out of his face and push his hair back. Mitch's mind snagged on that information, and he looked at the situation with a different perspective. There *were* a handful of women who'd like to shoot his balls off after the number of dates he'd broken and phone calls he hadn't returned over the last two months—all thanks to this damn quagmire—but this . . . ? He didn't date women this extreme. At least that he knew about.

The woman backed toward the door, no more than a fuzzy black shape in the steam. But her arm remained outstretched, with a powerful semi-auto in her hand.

"I'm just going to turn off the—" Mitch started.

"No. You're not." She finally spoke, her voice rough. "You're not going to do anything. Don't move."

The sting of needles traveled from his neck straight down his spine. That voice . . .

She opened the door several inches and the steam rushed out like mist returning to a genie's lamp, clearing the air.

And he stood there facing Halina.

Halina.

His stomach sprouted wings and darted wildly around his abdomen. His mind turned to oatmeal. He hadn't been prepared for this. Of all the people to ambush him—she was the very last person on the face of the earth he'd expected. In the very last place he'd expected.

His anger reheated—fast and furious. "What the *fuck*?"

Her eyes were wide with shock and she shifted her weight, uneasy. "Exactly what I was thinking."

Indignation joined the fury. Then hurt spiraled around it all making him volatile. He slapped off the water. Jerked the towel from where it had fallen on the floor and pulled it around his hips. "How the hell did you get in here?"

"Don't. Move."

Her low, dark tone tensed Mitch's fingers where they struggled with the knot in his towel. He lifted his head and looked at her again. Studied her expression while trying to ignore how incredibly beautiful she'd become over the years, as if she'd grown into her stunning features and striking bone structure.

Really damn beautiful.

"Why are you still pointing that at me? It's pretty clear you can put your gun down, Halina."

"Heather," she said through clenched teeth. "It's Heather now. It's been Heather for a long damn time."

Mitch jammed one end of the towel beneath the other edge so it stayed then put his hands on his hips. "I am *never* calling you Heather. Fuck that. And *fuck you* while I'm at it. What the hell happened to going back to Russia with your *husband*?"